THE PERFECT 10

Louise Kean was born in 1974 and works as a campaign producer for the film industry in Soho. A graduate of UEA, this is her third book. She lives in Richmond, and is 'taken', for now at least . . .

To receive regular updates on Louise Kean, visit HarperCollins.co.uk and register for AuthorTracker.

By the same author:

Toasting Eros
Boyfriend in a Dress

LOUISE KEAN

The Perfect 10

HarperCollins*Publishers*

HarperCollins*Publishers*
77–85 Fulham Palace Road,
Hammersmith, London W6 8JB

www.harpercollins.co.uk

A Paperback Original 2005
1 3 5 7 9 8 6 4 2

A catalogue record for this book
is available from the British Library

ISBN 0 00 719892 2

Set in Sabon by
Palimpsest Book Production Limited,
Polmont, Stirlingshire

Printed in Great Britain by
Clays Ltd, St Ives plc

*For my sister Amy, with
love . . . remembering Larry
Mize, and his quiet village.*

'No one can make you feel inferior
without your consent.'

Eleanor Roosevelt

Magic numbers

The colour of my eyes is dependent on how much I weigh today. They are either the silver grey of a morning mist across a Canadian lake as the sun rises and catches the cold gleaming water. Or they are the colour of dishwater, greasy and thick with grime, dirty with all of the family's Sunday roasting pans, and forks and knives, and casserole dishes and baking trays – murky and grimy and ugly.

Depending on what I weigh, my hair might be the browns and caramels of a thick chocolate bar that melts and shines and drips promise by the fire. Or the flat brown of a library carpet, laid in 1972, and trampled on by cheap shoes and schoolchildren every day since – tired and thin and lifeless . . .

Depending on how much I weigh today, my breasts may be round and full, reminiscent of a Russ Meyer vixen, ready to be grasped, voluminous and juicy. Or they are veiny and sagging, the skin at the top indented and ravaged by stretched tears, sitting lazily on my ribcage, flattened and blotchy, and dry.

I will love or hate myself, depending on how much I weigh today.

ONE

Proud

Here's what they don't tell you when you lose seven stones in weight.

They don't mention the loose skin. They forget to tell you that you'll end up with a rice cake-grey stomach that wrinkles and crumples beneath pinched fingers like tissue paper. They don't divulge that on the upper inside of freshly toned thighs two flabby folds of stretched skin will stand guard over your pelvis, like a pair of spitefully unskinned chicken breasts, with a Stalinist determination not to budge. They don't let on about the pubic pouch that they guard so angrily, that refuses to deflate in line with the rest of you, lending your naked profile a hermaphrodite edge.

They make believe your life will be a series of ketchup-red headlines yelling, 'Now Sunny Can Wear a Swimsuit and Feel Fabulous!' or, 'Sunny Buzzes With So Much New-Found Energy She Could Burst!'

The truth is that the energy reserves alone can be spiteful. Some days I'm woken at dawn by the sun streaming in through the cracks in my curtains, and I'll roll over in bed, hug my pillow, and determine to drift in and out of sleep until it's too hot to stay under the duvet any longer. My new

3

'healthy lifestyle' denies me this simple pleasure. As soon as I open my eyes I am buzzing. I can no longer spend an entire Sunday in front of the television with the papers strewn out before me, carelessly picking at the foreign news, munching on Maltesers. My metabolism is so wired I wake up feeling like I've been drip-fed crack in my sleep. My body wants to run everywhere: to the train station, down supermarket aisles, from my bed to my wardrobe in the morning. It disconcerts people. They assume I am running from something, and maybe I am. They don't tell you that some days you will fall so violently off the diet wagon that you will consume a family-sized tub of salted peanuts in twenty-five minutes – your hand dipping rhythmically in and out, passing nuts to lips without thought or care, and that it won't matter an ounce if you run to the gym the next day. The perception is that anybody who loses a lot of weight has an iron will, and this is simply not true: you are mostly good, and occasionally bad. Detoxing is for monks, or freaks. A rogue band of particularly freakish monks actually invented the concept. They had remarkably clear skin, but they were still mad.

They won't tell you that your nearest and dearest will inhale sharply if you eat a Quality Street in front of them, secure in the knowledge that the second you digest its seventy nutrition-free calories, you will regain every pound of weight you have previously lost. All seven stones of flesh will instantly bubble and gurgle under your skin – not gone, just hiding – until you suddenly and violently explode like a puffer fish into your old fat self. Despite the effort and determination and willpower you alone have mustered, people will still believe that you need to be protected from yourself. Thus the phrases, 'But you've done so well so far!' and, 'Move the chocolates over here out of temptation's way.' Cue a kindly smile in your direction. Try not to speak with your fists when this happens.

4

They don't tell you that you won't find anything you actually want to wear in any of the clothes shops you were too humiliated to enter pre fat busting. The kind of shops where skin-and-bones teenage assistants used to eye you suspiciously if you so much as glanced at their carrier bags.

They don't tell you how vain you will become. They won't alert you to the fact, in advance, that you won't know how to cope with looking in the mirror and seeing something you actually like, without succumbing to self-obsession, and fixating on the bits that refuse to become perfect, no matter how many miles you run, or how little dairy you eat. They don't tell you that you will replace an addiction to food with an addiction to losing weight.

And they won't tell you that you won't be in love with Adrian any more.

Adrian, who couldn't see past your belly, and who shouldered the burden of your unrequited love for so long.

Adrian, who was responsible for so many tears in front of the TV on lonely Saturday nights.

Adrian who inadvertently squished your soul daily for three years.

You just won't love him any more, and it will really confuse you.

Because you'll sleep with him anyway.

The sun is up, omelette yellow by 6 a.m. I am lucky enough to live in a suburb where the leaves are swept away by anonymous brooms before I leave my house in the morning. On holiday in Jamaica three years ago, my body clock refused to adjust to the time difference, and I woke every morning at 5.30. Stepping out on to my balcony to another postcard day, I witnessed an old muscled Rastafarian who called himself 'The Original', trawling our private beach for fish with handmade nets, before the tourists stumbled out of bed with cloudy heads full of last night's rum, and the aftereffects of a 'cigarette' bought from a kitchen hand. Nature wasn't allowed to hamper my holiday, didn't mar my swimming and splashing fun, and living here is the same. You spend your money, you get your return. Nature – in this case excessive leaf droppage – doesn't tamper with my walk to Starbucks in the morning.

I blow on a Grande Black Coffee-of-the-Day, put aside twenty-seven Two-Fingered Fondler orders that came in yesterday, comfortably cross my legs, and sit back.

At the outside table next to me is a guy, twenty-eight, thirty maybe. He wears jeans, and a T-shirt that demands in screaming yellow on grey 'Who's the Daddy?' It tells me everything. There is no need to go to the effort of talking to anybody new any more. Just lower your eyes, and read the logo on their chest. It will say more about who they want to be than a month of conversation. My favourite T-shirt is pink, and says 'Prom Queen'. Now you know everything you need to know about me: if you have to state it like a sandwich board hanging around your neck, it probably isn't obvious.

His hair is spiky, and has been styled with care, if not expertise. He has ill-advised highlights that a cute gay boy-band member might get away with, but not your Average Joe. He fondles a Frappuccino and has just sat down, pulling up his chair with a confidence that suggests it has been reserved for him, for life. He has the look of a man waiting for somebody to arrive. But he is neither anxious nor nervous; he doesn't glance around himself with apprehension, or casually pretend to read the discarded money pages left behind on his table. He waits with pleasure. His whole manner suggests that these are a few perfect moments to be snatched before whoever he is waiting for turns up, and ruins the image he has of himself, sitting at a coffee shop in a wealthy London suburb, on a perfect autumn morning, ruling the world.

And I know he'll do it before he does. I see an almost natural blonde exit the newsagent's and swing her hips past my table before she strays carelessly into his eye line; like a clay pigeon sprung from its contraption, I can hear a voice scream 'PULL' in this guy's head. She carries the Sunday papers – one serious offering whose ten other sections will be discarded as soon as she finds the enclosed fashion magazine, and the obligatory news of the screws, which will be devoured first. She wears a pair of dirty low-slung jeans over a small pert peach of an arse. She has the messed-up dirty-blonde hair and clean clear skin of an early morning angel who has been forced out of bed to get Sunday's essentials and is now, half dreaming, making her way back to her bed, and the man in it. She wears her genetic luck comfortably. She is the woman every man would like to wake up to. The Daddy inhales as he watches the Peach amble across the quiet road in front of us. And he watches her lightly jump to the kerb and the soft bounce in her peach of an arse as she does it. I hear his stomach grumble with hunger. There is nothing apologetic in his leer. As she moves round a corner, almost out of sight, his eyes remain fixed on those low-slung jeans, and his stare emits a residue that leaves a filthy film on my fresh coffee.

For a while I thought it was love that made the world go round, in my younger foolish days. Now I know it all comes down to sex in the end. It's the constant screwing in every continent that makes the world turn. Every sexual spark that fizzes inside all of us sends out a peculiar energy into the stratosphere that spins us, like the men who ride the back of the waltzers at the fair – scream if you wanna go faster! – and the sun and the moon, gravity and all of that other stuff has nothing to do with it. It's all about sexual sparkles. If everybody stopped thinking about sex, all at once, our little star would fall out of the sky like a yo-yo snapping off its string. Working on this theory I realise that I am actually placing mankind in jeopardy, not doing my fair share. But feeling defensive only hardens my heart.

The Peach disappears, and the Daddy sits back, crossing his legs, glazed and freshly raised, like his morning muffin. Moments later a reasonably attractive brunette with wide hips and a foundation line that skims her jaw appears behind him, and taps him on the shoulder. I see all the faults first these days, passing instant judgements. I'm not proud of it, but it happens automatically, and is almost impossible to stop. My therapist finds it 'concerning'. I tell him I find his collection of snow globes concerning, but he ignores that.

The Daddy turns towards Wide Hips Foundation Line, and though the glint in his eye disappears, he shamelessly kisses her with a lust she didn't earn. When I see his tongue flick into her mouth I look away embarrassed. She smiles, pleased and flattered by this unusual passion, then hurries inside to buy a coffee to avert any embarrassment when he makes no offer to buy it for her. She obviously doesn't like confrontations. She doesn't have the confidence to say, 'Couldn't have bought my coffee while you were buying yours? Couldn't think that far ahead? Couldn't be bothered? Or am I just not special enough to warrant a bagel?' The Daddy and I wouldn't last five minutes. He turns back and stares at the corner where the Peach disappeared moments earlier. Wide hips returns, juggling change, a cheese-covered bagel and a cappuccino, and pulls up a chair. I silently do the calorie sums. That's too many for breakfast. She is comfort eating. I blame him, in my head. She begins to chat, and I notice that she has a habit of flicking her ring finger as she talks, stroking a band of gold with an embedded diamond, and I know what she will never know. She will never realise that in those brief moments before she arrived, her fiancé just traded up for the Peach. I can't watch them any more.

I sip my coffee, which is still so hot that it burns my tongue. I take it strong and black, like my dustbin liners – that's the only comparison I can truthfully make. There is no room for calorific drinks in my diet, I just need the caffeine. I look up at still trees, and yellow-brown leaves that cling to their branches, knowing their days are numbered. I glance around at a litter-free street; even the teenagers consider it rude to drop their wrappers here. A rare saloon car passes noiselessly as I wait for something important to occur to me in the way that it should when you are just watching the world go by. I have always felt that time spent on my own, in a public place like this, should be full of magnificent thoughts. It makes sitting on my own less self-conscious. But mostly it's just shopping lists, credit card bills, errant vibrator orders, and late birthday cards. Then I generally read *Vogue*. But today a thought does occur to me: there may be nothing at the end of this long hungry road, and I'd be a fool to disregard it. There may be no emotional pot of gold, I may still be alone, and I'd be imma-ture – no naïve, no breathtakingly stupid – to ignore it.

But I still ignore it.

It will be a lighter kind of lonely at least. I close my eyes and quickly dream a little dream of being emotionally dependent on somebody else, somebody bigger than me. I could maybe be a little weak, possibly a trifle pointless, just for a while. I could let somebody else make the decisions, just for once. I also decide to ignore the fact that, tradi-tionally, arm's length has always seemed like the perfect length to me. It's what I'm used to, at least.

As a child, while my sister and the other girls on my street were playing kiss chase with the boys down the road, I was searching my parents' newspapers and scouring pre-watershed television for a fat role model: a woman who was big and really beautiful. But I grew up in the eighties, when aerobics grabbed the attention of the Western world, and Olivia Newton-John sang about getting physical, and leg warmers even became fashionable outside the swing doors of the local gym. My favourite film as a child was *Grease*, and I would spring out of bed early on Saturday mornings and watch it on our video player before my parents woke up. 'You're the One that I Want' was their weekend alarm clock for many years. I must have seen it hundreds of times, maybe even thousands, and I can still recite every character's dialogue when it comes on at Christmas, or over Easter weekend. At the end of *Grease* Sandy, in hooker mode to snag her man, wore black satin trousers that were so tight they had to sew her into them.

Try as I might, I couldn't find my fat *femme fatale*. In magazines or on TV fat women existed only as the big old butt of the joke, and in films fat women never made the romantic lead. But instead of just biting the bullet instead of the cake and going on a diet, I decided to be my own role model, to be big and beautiful myself. Then maybe as I grew older, little fat girls might pass me in the street and know that everything might turn out OK in the end, in the same way that I desperately scoured streets with my eight-year-old eyes to find a reason to be hopeful, even then.

But I didn't even manage to convince myself. I didn't think that you could be both big and beautiful in anything other than an advertising slogan, and yet I tried to live it, clung to it as a philosophy that justified my choice not to diet. As I got older, as long as I'd take in front of the mirror meticulously applying make-up each morning, concentrating solely on the face and hair and never looking down at the body beneath, I knew the body was there, bulging and bruised, and I hated it. I just wouldn't admit it to myself.

I brush the crumbs of my Skinny Blueberry Muffin from my running trousers and note childish screams and the noisy padding of developing feet running somewhere behind me. I turn to face the commotion: three children, one barely out of nappies, one roughly three years old with a shock of red hair completely dissimilar to his brothers, one older, maybe six, and precocious. Their mother is mousy but elegant, tall and exhausted, and has wild tired eyes that dart from the pavement to the shop to the road, her long slim fingers desperately hanging on to little hands that don't want to be held.

I turn back to my coffee and take an apprehensive gulp, but this time it doesn't burn my tongue. I sit under the umbrella that shields me from the early Sunday morning sun, and try to regain some semblance of peace. I hear chairs being pushed back and open one eye to see the Daddy and his ignorance-is-bliss girlfriend hastily moving off down the road, away from the fresh childish din. I daydream that I might spring to my feet and shout, 'Don't be a fool, Wide Hips Foundation Line! He can't be trusted!' But of course I don't. I don't draw attention to myself like that.

It's becoming harder, being seen. I notice people looking, men looking, and although these should be tiny triumphs, glances that spell sexual desire from the opposite sex, they unnerve me. I don't want men looking at me uninvited, thinking things about me that I can't control. I don't want them picturing me late at night with one hand on the remote and the other in their pants, the way that men do with women they've seen during the day. And yet here I am drinking my low-calorie drink, about to go to the gym, to burn and bruise off this week's two pounds of fat, on a quest ultimately to prove to the man that didn't want me that he was wrong, that he should have had some imagination, should have guessed what I could be.

It is frightening to go unnoticed for so long and then suddenly pop into everybody's sight with a magician's puff of smoke and screaming 'Ta-da!'. Some women have dealt with it all of their lives and either enjoy it or ignore it or have at least learnt to live with it. I was invisible before, which is ironic considering I took up twice the space. Nothing suddenly gets simple, no matter what the WeightWatchers Slimmer of the Year might tell the *Sunday Mirror*. When you win a bit, you always lose a bit too.

The three brothers grim descend on to the table next to me, landing themselves on metal chairs that scrape the pavement, squabbling. The red-haired horror shrieks as his older brother snatches away the piece of wood he has been playing with, and begins banging it on his legs and the table. And this is no musical child prodigy; I can't even make out a rhythm, never mind a tune.

'Charlie, give it back to Dougal,' their tall and exhausted mother demands.

I smirk at the name Dougal, although I don't know why. You hear much worse these days. I can't think of a soap star called Dougal at least. Strangers sometimes smirk at my name when they hear it for the first time, but I am proud of it. I think that anybody who fails to see something positive in Sunny must have their own issues to deal with.

'Sit there and be quiet. No, actually, come with me.'

All the children shriek in unison, and the youngest tugs at his mother's hand to drag her into Starbucks. I pray she will usher them inside, but she accosts a stray waitress who has, in a moment of craziness, decided to come and clean tables. The mother asks for three fruit juices and a Skinny Mocha, and tries to settle the boys at the table again. I stare off into the distance until the oldest brother begins to run round and round my table, and little shrieking Dougal follows his lead. Short stumpy slightly unsure legs make a

12

dash for a tree ten yards away. I glance over my shoulder to see what their mother is doing while they run amok – she is negotiating a straw into the youngest one's mouth while furtively glancing towards her other two sons. I don't know what I expect parents to do with their children, I just don't think they should be allowed to shriek. If I ever have children of my own they will be impeccably behaved in public. They will have character, and be witty and charming, but they will not bang things, and they will not scream. They will only be allowed to do those things at home.

'Dougal, come back here! Charlie, for God's sake put it away!' Their mother's voice raises at her eldest son, who has decided to urinate up against the tree. Both children momentarily freeze, and Charlie pops his little penis back into his shorts. They start running round my table again – children burn off so many calories without even realising it. The older boy, Charlie, nudges my chair every time he passes, and I hastily put my coffee cup back down on the table rather than risk a stain on my white Lycra vest top with built-in cooling something or other. I check my watch – the gym will be open in twenty minutes. It is an 8 a.m. start on a Sunday, as if God won't allow exercise before morning has truly broken on his day. Only ten more minutes of the shrieking before I can go.

Even this early, even for a Sunday, the road is peculiarly quiet. It's getting late in the year for the tourists, despite the heat. Because of it nobody managed a good night's sleep last night. Maybe now they are tossing and turning and kicking off sheets, trying to rescue another hour's rest.

Charlie stops running, and stands in front of me, staring.

'Yes?' I ask him flatly, unimpressed.

'Who is going to look after your dog when you die?' He motions his little head towards an old sleeping Labrador chained to a railing five feet in front of me.

'It's not my dog,' I say, and Charlie shakes his head at me and 'tut's.

I 'tut' back. Charlie raises his six-year-old eyes at me and starts running towards the tree again.

I guess the dog belongs to either an old man, practically knocking on heaven's door at the Garden Café a little further down the street, or an elderly lady at one of the other Starbucks tables, resting from the heat. The weathermen have predicted that today will be one of the hottest days of the year, despite it being 27 September, and yet she wears a heavy charcoal-grey overcoat that looks as if it was standard issue in 1940, and a claret woolly hat with a fraying bobble. I look away quickly, gulping back tears. Her vulnerability is almost poetic. If she tried to sell me a poppy I'd be hysterical. Of course, now, as she wipes some lazy dribble from the side of her eighty-year-old collapsing mouth with a handkerchief, I am repulsed. It's old people with all their facilities intact that I appreciate the most.

The kids are still running and screaming, and I thank merciful God that I have never had enough sex to get pregnant. Obesity was a great contraceptive at least.

A man walks past my table. He is average, forty-ish. I see his back, his jacket, his jogging bottoms, a balding head covered by thinning hair that is too long.

Before us all, an audience paying little attention, he walks calmly towards the tree ten yards in front of our tables, and with one jerky movement scoops up Dougal, and carries on walking south, away from us. I don't see his face. Admittedly I am appreciative of the drop in noise levels, but I am also confused, and I straighten my back, turning to face his mother, to somehow check that this is OK, that he must be the child's father, or uncle, or a family friend. Because things like this just don't happen right in front of you. She isn't looking up, but instead tries to wipe fruit juice from the edges of her youngest son's mouth.

I say, 'Excuse me,' nervously but loudly, and she glances at me and then automatically in the direction of her elder sons. Her naturally concerned expression falls, as if all the muscles have just been sucked out of her face by a Dyson, and her eyes widen. She pushes herself to her feet as she sees Dougal's red hair over the shoulder of the man quickly walking away. Her mouth opens and a scream leaps out as if it's been waiting in her throat for the last ten years.

She darts forward two paces, but she hasn't let go of her toddler's arm and he screams. I jump up. She tries to move forwards, hoisting her youngest child in the air by his little arm as he cries out in pain, and Charlie, who has resumed urinating against the tree, turns around in confusion as he hears his mother's cry.

'He's got my child! He's got my child!'

I can't quite believe this is happening, but I kick back my chair and start to run.

Ahead of me I can see the Stranger has his hand clamped over Dougal's mouth, and as they turn the corner at the end of the street he breaks into a jog. They were always called Strangers when I was a child, and they were a constant threat. There were washed-out adverts tinted a dirty orange or a grubby yellow, warning us not to get into their brown Datsuns, or go and look at their puppies, or accept their sweets. Now they have longer medical-sounding names that I'm sure children don't understand. The idea of a Stranger still scares me, and I am nearly thirty. These new words just can't put the same fear of God into a child.

My trainers bounce off the pavement and the sudden rush of adrenalin through my muscles is sickening. My calves and thighs expand and contract as I round the corner and see the Stranger holding a struggling Dougal, but he is sprinting

15

now towards the alleyway across the road. I have only been down that alleyway once and it scared the hell out of me: I kept expecting to see a corpse. It is full of gates to gardens and nooks and hiding places.

Feeling sick, I run faster. The man is by the road and he almost runs into a car, dodging it only at the last moment, but he isn't as fast as I am. I push myself on, not aware of my breathing, not looking at anything but Dougal's shock of ginger hair, which was so unfortunate five minutes ago, but is now vital. I can run five kilometres in twenty-seven minutes now. This time last year I couldn't run to the bus stop without throwing up. Thankfully for me, for Dougal, I've streamlined since then. Far behind me, back by the Garden Café, I can hear his mother screaming his name, but I just run.

I hear the Stranger breathing now, wheezing and coughing hard, ten feet in front of me, making for the alleyway. My strides are long and elegant, I run on my toes, my arms pumping at my sides, my chest open, and I feel sick as my biceps and quadriceps push me on. There are no rolls of flab bouncing or ripping at my stomach now.

Three feet from the entrance to the alleyway I am almost within touching distance of the Stranger but he stops sharply and spins around to face me: he looks scared and sick as well. I see a bead of sweat streak down the centre of his nose. I slam on my own brakes as he removes the hand that is covering Dougal's mouth, and swings it, arm outstretched, clenched fist towards my face. Uncorked, Dougal starts to scream, his face as red as his hair, his eyes wide and watery and desperate. We are all scared. I try to lurch out of the way, but the man's punch strikes the side of my head. I stumble like a speeding car hitting a boulder in the road. I have never been punched before. I am on the pavement and cry out at an awful evil feeling that shoots behind my eyes,

16

and I am momentarily blinded. I blink back tears, but my calves and my thighs spring me up off the floor.

I turn into the alley twenty steps behind the Stranger, who has shifted Dougal and jammed his tiny head into his shoulder to muffle his screams.

Overgrown bushes swipe at my face as I run along the dirt track alley. All of our actions seem loud, louder than usual. Every twig that snaps, my breathing, the Stranger's breathing, the pounding of our feet hitting the dirt track. He keeps running, but he's slowing down and tripping, and I'm getting faster, but wincing at the aching knife of pain that has been forced through my temples where his dirty hand smashed at my forehead. I open my mouth to shout at him to stop, but a feeling of dread silences me, a need not to call attention to the fact that I am a woman, chasing a man down a lonely passage.

The alley is three hundred metres long and narrow like a bicycle lane. The bushes are overgrown and make it dark, but the morning sun is so hot and bright that I can see him ahead of me. He hasn't ducked out of sight into any openings in the shrubs, and he can hear me closing in on him in my trainers and running trousers, as if I got up this morning and chose my best 'chasing a child snatcher' outfit. Sweat is pouring off us all and I focus on the damp patches spreading across the back of his dirty beige polyester jacket. He is wearing his best 'child snatcher' outfit himself. The air is filled with flies, and smells rotten, and even though it cannot possibly be this man who smells so bad, I can't help but believe that it is.

I am almost at his side, and I throw a hopeful arm out for Dougal as I launch myself into the Stranger's back, terrified.

We fall messily.

Dougal is on to all fours in front of us, scraping his little hands and knees on dirt and leaves. The Stranger slams face-first into the wall and I stumble down behind him, onto him, and the dirt. Instantly we are both scrambling to get up. I hear him mutter 'shit' as he crawls forward to get to his feet, and I am surprised that he speaks English. He looks English, but still I am shocked.

I can hear my heart and my head pounding, and another man's voice maybe fifty feet behind us, shouting, but I can't tell what. The Stranger lurches to his feet, as I am on all fours, and I scream, 'Dougal, get behind me!'

The terrified mop of red hair and tears and bloody knees, and a bruised face with the Stranger's fingerprints embedded in his cheeks, runs as fast as his ridiculous small legs will allow, behind me, before the Stranger is fully upright.

I can hear the cries of a man getting closer behind us, shouting, 'You sick bastard, you sick bastard . . .' and the pounding of his feet on the dirt. I look up and notice that the Stranger's glasses have smashed, and his face, an average forty-five-year-old face, is red and stained with dirt and sweat. He looks down at me, with either confusion or fear or disgust, and then his eyes dart upwards and behind me at the menacing sound of larger feet than mine running towards us all, and I can clearly hear the chasing man's voice now, shouting, 'You sick fuck! You sick bastard!'

I raise myself onto my knees as the Stranger lunges forward. His dirty old badminton trainer makes sharp hard contact with my stomach, and seems to sink further in than it physically should. I scream in pain, folding forwards. He calls me a 'bitch', but in a tone that lacks conviction.

Dougal screams as I hear a blurred and breathless voice behind me yelling, 'You sick fuck! I'll fucking kill you!'

The Stranger turns and runs down the alley, towards the sunlight at the other end. I lie on my side and clutch my stomach, and moan at a pain I have never felt before. I have never been kicked in the stomach before. Dougal is behind me crying and pawing at my back. I push myself up onto knees that nearly buckle, and my stomach yells with pain, and my head thuds noisily with pumping blood and bruising. I turn and accept a screaming, crying red-faced child into my arms. He holds on to me tightly, then pushes me away, then holds on again.

The pounding of large feet slows, but passes us, and the chasing man shouts as he speeds up again, 'Go back the other way,' and then coughs so hard I am positive he won't catch him.

I pull little Dougal's head away from my chest, and hold it between my hands, and ask him if he is hurt. He nods his head, and continues to cry. I push myself to my feet, and holding Dougal in my arms, ignoring the thrashing pain in my stomach, and the thumping in my head, and the aching in my legs, and the tightening in my chest, I struggle back down the pathway, back the way we came.

Dougal quietens down slightly as we walk the long walk – we were two-thirds of the way down the alley. Where was the man planning to go? Did he even have a plan? Or was it just an impulse, a shocking unexplainable moment of opportunity?

Eventually I say into Dougal's ear, 'There's your mummy,' as we reach the sunlight. His face whips around to see his hysterical tall mousy mother clutching at her other two children. Dougal starts to kick and scream and struggle with me to be set free, and I lower him to the ground. He runs into his mother's arms, and falls instantly silent, as she cries loudly for the both of them.

I lean against the wall, wiping stinging beads of sweat out of my eyes, clutching at my stomach, trying to control my breathing. It only takes a couple of seconds for me to start to cry as well.

I hear the wail of police sirens coming close, and see a small gathering of people across the street staring at this strange soap opera by the opening of the alley. A police car screeches up, and I shield my eyes from its electric-blue lights, which remind me of the flashing neon signs outside strip clubs in Soho.

The doors burst open as the wailing siren stops, and a radio full of static says, 'We've got him this end.'

I wipe my eyes, and want my mum to hug me too. I want to tell her that a Stranger with broken glasses and a rotten smell hit me, and he kicked me, and I'm finding it all suddenly very personal. He wanted to hurt me. I cry because I am scared by what I did. I am scared at the thought of chasing a child snatcher, a Stranger, down that alley. I cover my eyes with my hands and feel sick, as a nauseous sliver of pride turns my stomach and a voice in my head whispers what I know before I can silence it. I ran fast.

I throw up a cup of black coffee and half a Skinny Blueberry Muffin on the street. That's all there is.

Staring down at the pavement, I feel proud.

Cagney has the sick little fuck up against a wall, and the sick little fuck has the audacity to tremble. Cagney can't punch him, but not because he doesn't want to. Cagney wants to obliterate him, wants to bring the wall down upon him, wants to see his nose battered and black and pouring with blood, and to hear him moan as the life and the evil seeps out of him. But a policeman has a firm hold of Cagney's arm at the elbow, and is forcefully prising him away. They should let him smash the sick little bastard apart with the fury of God; they can't do it themselves, at least not in public, without being accused of police brutality, and sparking a peaceful protest of civil rights banners waved by bored housewives and fools. Cagney, on the other hand, has never been a policeman, so he can punch whomever he wants, if he is willing to take the consequences. And in this instance, the end very surely justifies the means. Still a constable pulls his arm away forcefully.

'Let go of him. We'll take it from here – let him go.'

'You sick fucker, you want to mess with kids? They should let me kill you now!'

'I'm sorry. I didn't mean to do it,' the man whispers as tears stream down his face.

The rage inside Cagney surges up like a twenty-foot Atlantic wave, but a second policeman grabs his other arm, and pulls him off, throwing him to one side. They spin the man around and slam the side of his face up against the wall, slapping a pair of handcuffs on him.

'Whatever you do, it'll be too good for him! There's no justice any more.' Cagney bends over with his hands on his hips, and coughs loudly. Speaking has pushed his body over the edge. His chest feels magnificently precarious; it may collapse at any moment. He feels bile rise in his throat, and throws up a little, at the end of the alley. He wipes his mouth with the back of his hand, stands up and leans back against the wall, clutching his sides.

He knows better than to run. A man in his condition shouldn't run. There is no official medical term for his condition. He just knows it by the affectionate term 'Jack Daniel's'. He has a minor case of 'Marlboro Reds' as well, but he doesn't think that one is terminal. Neither of his conditions need be life-threatening, as long as he remembers not to run.

One police car pulls off, carrying the man, and Cagney glares after it, trying to catch his breath. A policeman from a second squad car approaches him with his hands on his hips like a sheriff of a small town, about to quick-draw.

'Are you ready to go, sir?'

Cagney looks up at Constable Cary Grant, and shakes

his head, aware that nothing may come out when he tries to speak, that his trachea may have combusted from the heat and the fury in the back of his throat.

'What?' It is all Cagney can manage, with any clarity.

'Sir, we'll need you to come down to the station with us.'

'Why?'

'To file a report.'

'Why?'

'So we can prosecute that bastard for snatching kids.'

Cagney is repulsed at the constable's efforts to appeal to some shared sense of old-fashioned ethics while nobody else is listening. He knows that in a court of law the policeman wouldn't be calling that bastard a bastard – he'd be too busy looking over his shoulder at all the do-gooders and politically correct morons.

'I can tell you everything I know here.' Cagney inhales as deeply as he can, and concentrates on not falling to the ground. He steadies himself against the wall as casually as he can. 'Some woman starts shouting outside my office . . .' take a breath, '"He's got my child," et cetera . . .' Breath. 'I get downstairs, and some girl has already gone haring after him, but the mother is beside herself . . .' huge breath, redness of the face, lung collapsing, 'and what else can I do?' Pause for emphasis, and oxygen. 'But it's the girl you want to talk to. She'd already got the kid back by the time I caught up with him.' And relax. And fuck it, breathe hard.

Cagney looks down at his feet, wheezing, suddenly aware that he is impressed, which is rare these days. The girl was stupid, she was doubled up when he ran past, probably badly hurt, but it was impressive none the less. Stupidly impressive. Cagney nods his head once, in approval. And then shakes it. She got lucky. She couldn't have fought him off if he'd gone for her instead. Some things are still meant for men to deal with.

22

'You need to come and file the report, in the proper way.'

The constable looks at Cagney with confusion; Cagney shrugs it off. Why isn't he grasping his hero moment? – that's what this fool is thinking. But he doesn't know Cagney, and it's going to take a lot more than a bit of a jog and a man half his size to make him want to wear a medal.

'I'm not involved, just speak to the girl.'

'If you didn't want to be involved you should have stayed in your office. Now we have to go.'

The policeman grabs Cagney's arm, and Cagney gives up, allowing himself to be guided towards the police car. He has used up his energy store for the month. Cagney hasn't been in a police car for ten years, but it smells the same – of fear and disinfectant – and he feels just as caged. He looks down at his lap as they stop at traffic lights, and passengers in passing cars stare in.

'You did well today, mate,' the officer remarks from behind the wheel.

Cagney ignores him.

The police radio crackles, and Officer Charm chats away for a minute, letting out a brief snort of laughter.

The radio lazes into a stream of static, and the officer turns round to face Cagney as the car sits at a pedestrian crossing, allowing an elderly couple with a black Lab to idle across like they own the road.

'I don't know what they're putting in the coffee in Kew, but the girl didn't want to come down the station either. She wanted to go to the gym! The pair of you have probably saved that kid's life today, and we've nearly had to cuff you both to get you to make a report!' The policeman laughs again, but Cagney looks at him with disdain. The officer turns back to the wheel, shaking his head, and muttering, loudly enough for Cagney to hear, 'Rude bastard.'

Cagney concentrates on the view, appalled.

She wanted to go to the gym? She saves a boy's life, and she wants to go and lift weights?

'What was that?' The officer partially turns his head towards Cagney in the back of the panda car.

Cagney repeats himself, loudly.

'The world's gone to hell.'

I fidget outside of the police station, waiting for a taxi to arrive. I said they shouldn't waste a squad car on dropping me back home; I don't pay taxes for them to ferry me around. In truth I didn't enjoy the experience of sitting behind the thick smeared glass in the back seat. It reflected me badly. I'm going to go to the gym, but it's not as if exercise is the only thing I can think about, especially after this morning's incident. I just need to clear my head. They kept calling it 'an incident' in the station. There was an 'incident report', and it makes it sound less threatening if I think of it that way. I just need to run it out of my thoughts. I don't want to go home and sit around and dwell on what could have been.

I was in the station for a couple of hours. It was quiet, not frenetic the way it is on the television. I didn't see gruesome pictures hanging on the walls of dismembered prostitutes. A couple of people came and went, I had another cup of coffee, eventually, and the policemen seemed to crack a lot of jokes, appearing to enjoy their crime fighting.

It took an hour for the medical. It was all conducted in a small green room with a neon strip light, behind a battered white screen on wheels, on a tired old hospital bed that looked like it was playing host to the biggest germ party ever thrown. I was rigid with discomfort for the entire examination, afraid that I'd catch something itchy from the foam in the bed, embarrassed at the skin crêpes around my stomach when they made me lift up my top. And then, of

24

course, I kept crying. They said it was shock – a young policewoman with stern hair and thick eyebrows held my hand a couple of times and called me brave, which made me cry even more. I'm not great with compliments, any kind. My hand would involuntarily dart up to shield my eyes, as the tears started to swell anew, but she kept yanking it down, to test my blood pressure, or witness my shame – I'm not sure which.

The result of one dirty fist to my head, and one badminton-trainer kick to my stomach is nothing more than some nasty bruising. I was surprised. I felt sure something must have been broken or ruptured, a vein popped or a bone cracked. At the time of being kicked, being punched, the pain had been obscene. It wasn't just the force of the blows, it was the shock.

I tried my best not to forget anything. I told them about the smell in the alleyway, which seems to have smeared itself permanently on my skin like Satan's own brand of moisturiser, but I don't think they wrote that down. They said that the assault charges against me will actually be vital in prosecuting the Stranger, as 'kidnapping' for such a short period of time could be hard to prove. It seems so odd to me that the man's intention was clear – to take the child – and yet now they have to prove it to people that weren't even there, and the events of the morning will be painted differently by his lawyer in court. He may be able to plead temporary insanity or something similar. I told them that I thought he was scared by himself, not insane, but they didn't write that down either. The policeman said they'd be in contact, with the details of what happens next. There is, of course, the prospect of a trial, as well as some kind of trauma counselling that I can go for, as the victim of a violent crime. When they said this I explained that he hadn't used a gun, and they looked at me strangely again. They gave me their phone number and said I could call them if I remembered anything else, and that the counsellor would be in touch shortly, so I said fair enough, as nonchalantly as I could muster.

I didn't tell them that I already have a therapist. It feels indulgent. I started seeing him about eight months ago, when I first realised that I might need to talk as well as run. I like to discuss abstract theories, and he likes to make me find some relevance to them in my life. Given a heavier case load, I don't think he'd still be seeing me, but I pay my money and he listens. I find it interesting, although I've learnt that he doesn't deal in answers. He doesn't think we are talking about the right things. He thinks I am avoiding my own issues, that I need to focus on the real. He nudges me in the same direction every week, and I dodge it. But as I say, I pay my money . . .

I already know that I don't want to talk about the incident, relive it or even think about it. Even with only a few hours' hindsight it seems strangely unimportant, because I did it, I suppose. I can't say that to my therapist; he'll have a field day. But to retell it will make it terrifying, will give me nightmares that I am sure won't creep up on my dreams unless I am forced to rehash it all. It almost never happened, and in fact it was over in a matter of minutes, and hopefully Dougal is young enough not to be scarred and scared for life. I have come out of it with nothing more than a black eye and a bruised midriff.

I jump up and down on the spot a few times, then lean against a railing, and check my watch. Taxi drivers always claim to be no more than ten minutes away. They are liars. The only time a taxi will ever arrive on time, or early for that matter, is on an evening when you are going out and you haven't decided which shoes to wear. In these instances they will be tooting their horn angrily outside of your flat before you've even hung up the phone to taxi control.

I hear a lung-disturbing cough behind me. I turn round and shield my eyes from the sun, and make out a figure standing rigidly about fifteen feet away under an old Judas tree. I recognise him as the man who chased the Stranger this morning. He is close enough to lean against the tree trunk, but he doesn't. He is wearing a thick, black roll-neck jumper, and black trousers – doesn't anybody listen to the weather forecasts except me? It must be thirty degrees, and it's not even midday yet. His arms are folded in front of him.

He is tall, over six feet. I approximate that he is late thirties, but it's hard to tell because his face is scrunched up, squinting at the sun, so that his expression makes him seem older than he actually is. He could be thirty, or fifty, but the negativity pinching at his eyes suggests he is one hundred. He is still very red in the face, and I'm not sure if it is the heat or the run that has caused it. He looks like a man who has had the life knocked out of him, who has just lost a custody battle to a promiscuous and alcoholic wife, or finally had his sentence quashed after fifteen years in jail for a pub bombing he did not commit. I wonder what could make a man look so drained. Maybe the Stranger attacked him, and there was some kind of fight . . .

His face is broad and pale, and he could do with stepping out from that shade and into the sun for a while. His hair is dark and short but slightly bushy on top – he must have to tame it every morning – and I can tell he finds this irritating. I'm sure he hates his hair. It is peppered with grey around his temples, and he has distinguishable sideburns, also dusted with grey. His features are strong but cold, his eyes are deep-set and his nose is positively Roman. He reminds me, standing there staring off into the distance, of those old sepia photographs of ageing Hollywood leading men you see in documentaries, who were a harshly flawed attractive that seems inexplicable these days. He looks like a closed book that wants to stay closed, and the dust is already starting to settle on his hair. It is hard to see what is muscle and what is fat beneath his black jumper, but I only realise that I am staring when his eyes dart upwards and catch mine. Our gazes lock for a frame – not even a second – but it is enough for my cheeks to flush pink with humiliation. I spin round, and walk two paces forwards to check for my cab, but the road is completely empty, and I feel like a fool.

I hear him cough again, but not to attract my attention. His cough is out of his control – this is clearly not a man who runs regularly. My breathing had regulated itself minutes after the incident, moments even, whereas his lungs sound as if they may still collapse. I glance back over my shoulder to approximate how much he weighs and his eyes dart up and catch mine again.

I touch my toes, for no reason other than to do something quickly, and I feel ridiculous. It must actually look like I am trying to impress him with my arse, or worse, my flexibility. I am giving him the impression that I actively seek out children to rescue on Sunday mornings in an effort to meet men. But can I walk over there and explain that I was merely working out his body-fat-to-lean-matter ratio? I'm not sure, given the circumstance, which version will sound less appalling.

I am going to have to speak to him. If I see him at the trial I will die of shame. I need to clear up this awkwardness, and make it plain that I don't find him attractive. It's an old habit that is refusing to die, the need to reject first.

I push myself up from the railing I am leaning on, and inspect my running trousers for specks of my morning vomit, summoning up the courage to small talk. I cross my arms, and walk determinedly towards him with my head down. I

28

hear him cough again, uncomfortably. I glance up only when I sense that I am a few feet away, feeling the temporary coolness of the shade of the tree above me.

He stands very straight and looks at me, and then away furtively for somebody that might rescue him this time, but we are the only heroes in town today. I'm going to clear this mess up as quickly and as cleanly as possible, and walk away.

'Hi.'

He just stares at me.

I feel my throat contract, but continue, 'I'm Batman, you must be Robin . . .'

I laugh; he stares at me blankly.

'We both ran after the same man this morning . . . the man who took the child . . .' I can't bring myself to say the word 'snatched'.

Even though I am now blocking him from the sun, the scrunched-up expression on his face doesn't budge.

'This morning, literally,' I check my watch, 'a couple of hours ago? We ran down that alley . . . I was on the floor, you ran past and told me to go back the other way . . .' I am speaking too quickly, I know. And my cheeks are flushed, I know this too. 'You know, this morning? Surely you can't have forgotten already?'

'I haven't forgotten. Yes.'

'Yes?'

'Yes I am that man.'

'Oh. I thought you meant "yes?" as in "what do you want?".'

I laugh sharply. He looks away. And maybe even shrugs his shoulders in agreement, but I might be dreaming that. Finding me unattractive is not a reason to be this rude, although most men I've met think it is reason enough to cut me dead.

'I thought I recognised you, but I wasn't sure because, you know, I was on the ground when I saw you the first time, which is why I was looking at you just then to make sure it was you . . . Anyway, I'm just waiting for a cab, to take me home.' I try to finish brightly, but it just sounds needy.

He stands in silence.

I could walk away, of course. I may never meet this man again, we may be on different days of the trial – who cares if he thinks me rude? I could just walk off as if I hadn't said a word . . .

'I can't believe how long it took, in there,' I say. I gesture towards the police station with my head. 'But some of that was the medical. I'm a little bruised.' I point to my stomach.

I get nothing, no reaction whatsoever. I should just walk away.

'But of course it's nothing really, considering what happened. I guess you caught him then? Good for you.' I give him a thumbs-up gesture, and actually recoil at myself.

Silence. Why can't I stop talking?

'I don't really know what I was thinking, but I guess in those situations you don't really think, do you? You just do . . . I mean you just act . . . or you don't know how you'll act . . . you can't plan for it . . . why would you?' My voice trails off pathetically into a whisper, 'Or whatever . . .'

I think I might cry again, from the effort. My eyes start to sting. A lump grows in my throat.

He is properly older than me; a grown-up. I only ever feel like an adult if I am holding a baby. Twenty-eight doesn't feel as mature as I dreamt it would when I was a child, and it seemed that my life would be sorted and settled by twenty-five at the latest. He looks around, and I look around, and he smiles weakly at me, unimpressed. I thought he might be different from the rest, given his efforts this morning, which makes me feel stupid. It was a rare moment of heroism that you rarely witness these days, but it doesn't really say anything about *him*. I never feel that I am meeting anybody new. We are all trying to be the same person, the same ideal, and the result is that we blend into a big ugly gloop of unexceptionality. The same hair, the same clothes, the same trainers, the same opinions, the same jokes, the same lives. Why would I expect this man to be any different? I am not interesting to him, not blonde enough, not bubbly enough, or whatever his criteria, and that is all that matters in his head.

But then he juts out a hand, to be shaken. 'Cagney, Cagney James.'

My eyes widen involuntarily. That's not a name, it's a 1950s detective show, complete with black-and-white opening credits, and old-fashioned sirens under the theme music, and bad edits and childish graphics.

I remember my manners and offer my hand to be shaken. 'I'm Sunny. Sunny Weston. Just Sunny.'

I see his eyes widen too. He has trained his face into deadpan but this time his reaction was too quick to suppress. I wonder if he is ever caught so off guard that he smiles.

'Your name is Sunny?'

'Yes.'

'Sunny?'

'Yes . . .'

'Like Perky, or Happy, or any of the other dwarfs?' He looks at me with incredulity.

'And who was Cagney?' I ask. 'The dwarf who liked to drink and sleep with hookers?'

We are still shaking hands, our fingers clenched in a mutual rage. Given the chance I believe we would break each other's bones. Simultaneously we pull away, equally alarmed.

I wriggle my hand to cast him off me, and pray my cab will arrive and toot its horn and that will be that. I glance up at his face but he is staring at his fist. I won't call it electricity. It was just . . . funny. Weird funny, not ha ha funny. Not good funny.

I step backwards when he speaks.

'That was a stupid thing you did this morning, Smiley.'

'I'm sorry, Caustic, I don't understand.'

'No surprise there. This morning, running after that bastard. You shouldn't have done it. I was only a few feet behind you; you should have waited. You could have been hurt. Or can't bad things happen in fairyland?'

'I was hurt, as it happens, but my ego survived, getting the child back and all, and not losing a lung in the process.'

I stare at him, shocked at my own tone, shocked at his. I need to make this normal. I don't know why I am behaving this way.

'Anyway . . . he looked really scared, actually. I don't think he quite knew what he was doing . . .'

'And that justifies it, does it?'

He straightens his back. I cock my head. I feel angry, and I can't explain why.

'Of course not. But it's not black and white, is it?'

'Not black and white? Snatching a child is not black and white? Is it the colour of ice cream and butterflies, Sunny? Is it a magical adventure on a unicorn?'

'No, but it's not black like your lungs or white like your hair . . .'

'Well, Miss . . .'

I stare at him expectantly until I realise he has forgotten my name, and is waiting for me to fill in the blank. 'Weston,' I say irritably.

'Well, Miss Weston, what is it exactly? I'm dying for the insight.'

'Look, *Cagney*,' I enunciate his name with sarcasm, and instantly regret it, feeling ridiculous.

He looks at me with disdain.

'I obviously didn't mean that it was OK to do what he did.'

'How else could you mean it?'

'I meant that, although not making it right or justifying it in any way, there must be a reason why he did it.'

'He is a sick bastard. That's all the reason there is.'

'Well, yes, he probably is sick, in some way. But he wasn't just made that way. As a baby, he wasn't born wanting to hurt people or . . . snatch children . . . or whatever.'

'Of course he was! Some people are born sick.'

'You don't really believe that?'

'Utterly. What do you believe, that he wasn't breast-fed until he was eighteen and his daddy was a drunk, and it's all his parents' fault?'

A line of sweat trickles down the back of my neck. I hate him.

'Is that your excuse, Mr James?'

'I think, given who we are comparing me too, I turned out OK.'

'Yes, ignorant and angry is very healthy.'

'I might not be hugging this tree but I'm not hurting anybody.'

'Maybe not hurting, but boring. I pity your wife.'

The skin around his eyes tightens and his jaw locks. My hands are shaking with rage.

'Do I look stupid enough to be married?' he fires back at me.

'You look stupid enough to do most things.'

Two policemen walking into the station glance at us suspiciously as I raise my voice, and I smile at them as sweetly as I can. I wait for them to go through the swing doors, and turn to Cagney, half expecting him to be gone. But he is standing in exactly the same position, staring at me with what can only be contempt.

'I wouldn't be stupid enough to do you,' he says flatly, and I flinch.

'I, like most women, wouldn't be stupid enough to let you try,' I say, my voice as controlled as I can manage.

'Well, women today are too busy burning their bras, and lifting weights,' he motions with his eyes, just in case I didn't realise he was talking about me, 'to know a good man when they see one.'

'Burning their bras? Are you still trying to pay in shillings? News flash: it's the twenty-first century. If you see a *good man* do point him out to me because I'm not sure they still exist. I've missed them all so far!'

'Maybe they saw you first.'

Cagney glares at me, and I glare back. If I wasn't outside a police station I'd slap him.

'Hello?'

We both spin violently towards the voice and see a tall, elegant but gaunt woman approaching us. It takes me a heartbeat to recognise her as Dougal's mother. Her eyes are swollen from crying. None of the children are with her, thank goodness. Cagney and I stare at her in disbelief. This is a strange day.

'I really, really have to say thank you, to you both.' Dougal's mother puts her long arms on her hips, then removes them and clasps her hands nervously, then flicks hair from her eyes, then wrings her hands in front of her. An awful thing has happened to her this morning. I feel some of the rage ebb in my stomach like sweet relief, and I am over-whelmed with gratitude to this woman for shattering what-ever it was that had gripped Cagney James and me just moments ago. I wasn't myself – that is my only excuse.

'Please, there is no need to thank us . . . me.' I glare at Cagney. 'Anybody would have done the same thing. I'm just glad it's . . . you know . . . as OK as it can be.'

She smiles a weary smile at us both, and flicks the hair at her eyes again.

I take a step towards her, away from Cagney.

'The boys are with their father. Dougal is terrible – shaken and upset and . . . anyway, Terence, that's my husband, Dougal's father, when I explained, well, he can't thank you both enough, of course. And he suggested that you both come to dinner, next week – we live locally, in Kew – and that we might say thank you that way, although of course it will never be enough to say thank you, but he suggested it, so I thought I might still catch you here . . .'

I am horrified. I gag with disbelief. This poor woman has been through an unspeakable horror only hours ago, the kind of hell that a mother can only dare imagine, and she is offering to make us dinner? It is the most inappropriate thing I have ever heard.

'Oh, I really don't think that's necessary. I think we probably just want to forget all about it . . .'

'Oh, my goodness, no, you must come. Terry wants to thank you himself, and it's the least I can do. It won't be anything elaborate. Probably duck, or whatever the butcher has in fresh . . .' Her voice trails off and her eyes become a matt version of their previously glossy selves. I have a feeling they will be permanently matt soon: any joy she has is being slowly replaced by fear . . .

But her reaction is as if she has dropped a plate from my chinaware, or spilt red wine on my trousers. It is so horribly embarrassing I don't know what to say. I stand open-mouthed, completely aghast. So she carries on talking.

'Of course, you must bring your partners, or somebody, of course you must, but do please say you'll come. Next Friday?'

I turn to face Cagney, who at least looks equally as appalled.

'I just . . . I don't . . .'

'Please do say you can make it.'

'Well then, I guess, I suppose . . . I can make it.' I shudder as I accept.

'That's fantastic. Thank you. And you?'

'Cagney James. I can make it on Friday.'

'I'm sorry I didn't catch your name. I'm Deidre Turnball.' She offers her hand for me to shake and, as anticipated, she just rests her fingers in my palm for a few moments before offering it to Cagney as well.

'Sunny Weston.'

Deidre scrambles for a pen and paper in her bag, and scrawls down 'The Moorhouse, 12 Wildview Avenue' for us both, and offers us separate scraps of paper. She has written '7 o'clock' as well. I stare at it with disbelief.

'See you then,' Deidre says, flicking her hair from her eyes, turning quickly and striding elegantly away.

I look down at the paper, and hear a car toot its horn, and an old man leans out of a minicab and shouts my name.

'She hasn't left her phone number,' I say numbly.

'Probably ex-directory as well,' Cagney replies, reminding me he is there.

I look up at him, and he looks baffled, and embarrassed as well. And then I remember that the last thing he had said to me, before Deidre appeared, was some kind of insult. I try to speak, but when nothing comes out, I exhale loudly in his direction, and walk away.

I sit in the back of the cab, close my eyes, and go over what has happened.

I can't believe the morning I have had.

I can't believe I have to have dinner with Deidre, and

Dougal, and the whole Turnball family, next Friday, at 7 p.m.

I can't believe I have to see Dougal again so soon. I can't imagine what it will do to him to see me again so soon.

I cannot believe I have to sit at a table and play polite with a man as offensively archaic as Cagney James.

And I bet it won't be low fat.

TWO

An inspired puff of air

I meet Lisa for Box-a-fit at midday. It will clear my head before this afternoon. Unless there is a natural disaster I always see my therapist on a Monday at three. I have known my two closest friends, Lisa and Anna, for over twenty years – we practised Bucks Fizz dance routines in the playground together at eight, and attended Duke of Edinburgh sessions as a teenage triumvirate, if only to go to the discos, and not the hikes.

Lisa is married now, of course, as is Anna. They both settled down aged twenty-five with university boyfriends, who had quickly replaced sixth form boyfriends in the girls' freshman year. Anna isn't a member of this gym, or any gym now, as far as I am aware. She is still trying to breast-feed her first child, Jacob, who is eleven weeks old. Both Anna and Lisa have failed to recognise me on a number of occasions when we have agreed to meet outside tube stations or cinemas. They are used to seeing the old me.

Anna says, 'You don't even look like you any more, Sunny. Even your smile isn't as wide . . .'

Lisa strides towards me confidently as I wait outside the gym, her long blonde curls swinging naturally down her back, pulled off her face with two clips at the sides. She has a slight fluffy hair halo, because she doesn't use any product on her hair. She never has. Natural is Lisa's defining characteristic. Her broad face is clean and shiny. I can see a couple of tiny red veins on otherwise smooth cheeks, and she has the finest of lines playing with the corners of her eyes. She does, however, have a large angry swollen spot on her chin that glares at me menacingly as she gets closer. Lisa has never worn make-up during the day, and even on a big night out she will apply one lick of mascara to each set of eyelashes, and a hastily slicked streak of lipstick to each lip. I always admired how she looked so healthy and clean, but now I wonder whether a dab of Touche Éclat here and there would be such a sin.

Lisa ran everything, from the 100 metres to cross country when we were at school, and she is still super fit, of course – naturally fitter than I am. But that would only show in a half-marathon, not in a class like today's, with just over an hour's worth of fitness needed. You wouldn't be able to tell, if you glanced through the window to the fitness studio on a tour of the gym, that she had been in training her whole life, and I had been in training for just over a year. Lisa's husband, Gregory Nathan, is a very slim man who was the 5,000 metre steeplechase champion at her university. When he laughs I think he looks like a dog. He works in the City now. He is some kind of underwriter, big in insurance, apparently. Big enough that Lisa was able to give up her job in publishing eight months ago, to really think about what she wanted to do, and hasn't decided yet. She keeps threatening to open a boutique of 'lovely knick-knacks, candles, and linen, and cushions, and beautiful glass vases', but hasn't quite managed to bother just yet. Thankfully for the lovely knick-knack market, one hundred other shops selling exactly that have opened in that time in and around West London.

Lisa and Gregory live in Richmond, and they run by the river, together, every Saturday and Sunday morning.

Lisa was the first person to realise I was losing weight, when I had officially shed one stone and four pounds, and she was the first person to notice that I had changed my eating habits. We met for brunch one Saturday, to have a girls' catch-up, and I ordered a tuna salad with red onions and walnuts, instead of a burger and chips with coleslaw. Anna hadn't realised, but Lisa came right out with it.

'Are you having salad, Sunny?'

'I just fancied something green,' I said with an innocent smile. I wasn't ready to get into it with them, and at that point was unsure whether I would even be able to see it through. One stone down but eight more to go didn't feel like something to shout about. Plus the first stone had fallen off, but now the reduction was slowing up. I realised that I was going to have to do something drastic, and join a gym, and the thought scared me. Not because I wasn't any good at sport, but because I thought I would look like the worst kind of deluded fool, in my billowing T-shirt and tracksuit trousers, walking on a running machine, red-faced and out of puff. Now, if I see anybody even close to my old size in the gym I try and give them a big smile, if they will meet my eye, but invariably they don't.

'But you look like you've lost weight, in your face.' Lisa eyed me with a smile, trying to get me to admit it.

'Diet?' Anna asked, picking up a piece of bread and soaking it in olive oil.

'Kind of,' I said with a small grin, admitting that maybe I was a little pleased with myself. 'But more of a health kick, than a diet. I'm just trying to think about what I'm eating,' I said, adjusting the napkin in my lap.

'God, who can be bothered? I never thought it worried you!' Anna said, staring at me intently, trying to get me to admit a lifetime's worth of bad feeling to her soberly and over a casual lunch.

'Of course it bothers me, a little bit. I just want to be healthy,' I said, and then I was embarrassed.

'Are you doing any exercise?' Lisa asked with a smile, interested.

'I've been walking a lot, but I think I might need to join a gym,' I grimaced, as excitement swept Lisa's face.

'Join mine! Then I can help. It'll be fun!'

'OK, maybe, but I'm not ready for anything too major. It's been a long time since I have done any real exercise. I have to work my way up to it . . .'

Lisa mouthed, 'It'll be great' across the table, and toasted her glass of lime and soda in my direction.

'Do you remember that cabbage diet you went on in sixth form, Sunny, the one that made you fart constantly?' Anna burst out laughing, and turned to Lisa. 'Do you remember, Lisa, when we got into your dad's car that time he picked us up from the cinema, we'd just seen *Ghost*, and just as Sunny sat down there was that really long farting noise! And then the car smelt so bad your dad had to wind the window down, and nobody said anything, because nobody knew what to say!' Anna laughed so hard she knocked over her drink.

'And do you remember the Slimfast?' Lisa said, with a broad smile. 'How much weight did you put on that week, Sunny? It was nearly ten pounds, wasn't it?' Lisa snuffled with laughter, little snorts escaping from her nose.

'I read the instructions wrong,' I said, trying to smile convincingly.

'Didn't you think you had to drink a shake *with* each meal?' Lisa said, collapsing into laughter. 'Poor Sunny, you know I don't mean it like that,' she said, wiping the tears from her eyes.

I nodded but I couldn't say anything.

'And that time . . . that time . . .' Anna could barely get the words out she was laughing so much, 'that you decided you were going to wear ankle weights everywhere,' giggle giggle, 'to tone up your legs,' laughing harder, 'and you wore them to college, and by the end of the day you couldn't even lift your feet up, and you had to take them off . . .' Anna lost control and laughed for twenty seconds, as she held her sides and tried to breathe, 'but you still couldn't lift your legs, and you couldn't even step up onto the bus, and you had to shuffle . . . had to shuffle . . .' Anna started losing it again, 'shuffle all the way home! Not lifting your feet off the ground!'

Both Anna and Lisa were wiping their eyes, caught in the middle of a laughter downpour, drenched in it, and exhausted. Ten minutes after that they were able to order lunch.

Lisa was so enthusiastic about the gym I almost didn't join. Her obsession with fitness had always been so alien to me. I just could not understand what pleasure she could derive from running at 6 a.m. in the rain, as opposed to, say, eating fish and chips in front of *EastEnders* every Tuesday. Part of me, although envying the way she looked in jeans, was pleased not to be her – it looked so joyless, and seemed so obsessive. But now, somewhere down a sweaty road, I have joined her sisterhood.

We kiss hello and chitter-chatter down to the changing rooms, where Lisa strips off to get changed without a second thought. I manoeuvre myself so that my back is facing her as I unhook my bra, so she can't see how deflated my breasts have become. The talk almost immediately falls to Anna.

'She has put on over . . . five stone.' Lisa whispers it with shame.

'God, did she tell you it's that much?' I ask, so sad for her already.

'And that is with the baby . . . out.' Lisa pauses before the last word to give the sentence added impact and dramatic effect, and it makes her sound a little ridiculous. As if she is one of those narrow-minded, middle-aged, middle-class women who wear too much hairspray and who have honed their sensibilities to be easily shocked just so they can wallow gloriously in the outrage. I glance around the changing room to see if anybody else is listening, but thankfully they aren't.

'But, Lisa, a lot of that will come off with the breast-feeding. It burns up a huge amount of calories – over one and a half thousand a day,' I say.

Lisa shrugs a hopeful 'maybe', but I see a delighted glint in her eye as she wonders how anybody could let themselves go so badly, indulge themselves so much. I wonder if she has forgotten who she is talking to, as we both snap on Lycra training shorts.

'I just mean, Sunny . . . she ate everything!'

'Yes, I know, but she was on that crazy diet just before she got pregnant,' I say.

'It was only Atkins,' Lisa retorts.

'Yes but she's a vegetarian,' I say, still baffled. I gave up all the weird and wonderful diets when I was a teenager. If the cabbage soup diet does work for somebody, it is a short-term goal, a quick fix for half a stone, not a recipe for life. Admittedly I didn't diet much during my early twenties, I mostly just ate, but I could tell even then that counting points or drinking shakes or not eating fruit was not going to keep me occupied for the time it would take to lose half my body weight. I needed to change the way that I ate, not just cut back for a while.

'Well, anyway,' Lisa pulls her hair into a ponytail in front of the mirror – her jaw line is so smooth, not a wrinkle in sight, 'she'll have to join the gym now . . . I mean, how much have you lost, Sunny?'

'About seven stone so far,' I say quietly, and hope that nobody hears.

'Right, and you've got like a stone to go or something?'

'Kind of, maybe two . . .' I say.

'Right. Well, that isn't that much more than Anna, and she put that all on in nine months! You took a lifetime to get that big!'

'Uh-huh,' I say, and nod once, turning to leave the changing room. I make a mental note to go to see Anna soon, and take her some unroasted nuts and a small bar of dark chocolate as a treat.

Lisa is, of course, oblivious to the way she sounds, so there is no point saying anything. I just never want to think like her. Of course, in the class, I become her. I am zoned and focused. I can picture my muscles flexing and stretching, I monitor my breathing, I know exactly how many calories I am burning as we roundhouse kick to the left and right, and bruise the boxing bags with our jabs and undercuts, and skip like boxers for ten minutes until my cheeks fizz with saliva. Then we hit the floor and do twenty minutes of sit-ups. Lisa and I smile at each other occasionally in the mirror, sharing the high. It's not just chemical, it's the knowledge that we are effectively airbrushing ourselves, refining and toning and perfecting.

Barry, our instructor, is a hard squat ex-squaddie. Lisa and I shake out our muscles after an hour and twenty minutes, and only then do I notice that we are surrounded by red-faced exhaustion. The other class members are fighting for breath, and somewhere to go to sit down.

'Good effort, girls. Ten out of ten.' Barry puts a hand on each of our arms, anointing us with a fitness blessing. We give him a suitably reverent smile, stopping just short of genuflection.

We head to the bar upstairs with wet hair after long hot

showers. Lisa's spot has grown bigger with the heat, swelling to a dangerous level: if it were a volcano I'd be evacuating about now.

Two guys stand in suits by the bar, with fresh pints of lager, and squash rackets poking out of their gym bags. One of them smiles at us as we squeeze past, and apologises for his bag, which barely sticks out at all.

Lisa sighs and says, Thank you!' in an exasperated tone.

He looks confused and a little insulted, and I mouth 'It's fine, thanks' at him and smile a little weakly as we walk past.

We order two black coffees and the girl behind the bar says that they will take a few minutes and she will call us when they are ready. We settle ourselves in a corner away from the plasma screen showing men's tennis on clay courts somewhere hot.

'Have you thought about yoga, Sunny? It would help with your definition,' Lisa says as she reads the back of a gym pamphlet, eyeing up the new classes on offer.

'I could do. I guess I am still concentrating on the fat burning at the moment, the high impact cardio stuff, but I know that yoga is supposed to be good.'

'I mean, it doesn't appeal to me as much, but I've been working my muscles for longer, so they are in better shape. And you never know, it might help with your loose skin.'

'Maybe,' I say, and look over to the bar to see if the drinks are ready. They are just being poured, so I grab my purse, saying, 'I'll get these,' beating a hasty retreat before I actually start to cry.

I pay, but the cups are a strange shape and they burn my fingers, so I carry Lisa's coffee over to her, and pop it down on the table as she thanks me. I turn to go back and grab the other cup, but the guy with the squash racket from earlier has followed me over, carrying the second cup.

'That's what I like to see, black coffee, not undoing all your hard work, not like us boozers. Where do you want it?' he asks with a smile.

'Oh, you didn't have to do that, thank you. I can take it from here,' I say, thinking, how lovely! How chivalrous! How unusual!

'No worries. I'll pop it on the table,' he says with a cheerful grin. He has an Australian accent and thinning hair. He is equal parts muscle and fat, and I think his chest looks welcoming, and I decide he must give good hugs.

'I'm sure she could have managed,' Lisa mumbles under her breath, but both the Australian and I hear it and I give her a strange look.

'That was my pleasure,' he says to me pointedly, smiling, and walks back to the bar.

'Lisa, that was a bit rude. Do you know him or something?' I ask.

'No, thank God! I mean, could he have been any more obvious? Jesus! And look at him – he's all fat! Like you want some huge fat guy hitting on you.'

'He was just being nice, I think,' I say, blowing on my coffee, embarrassed.

'Well, if you flirt with guys like that, Sunny, you only have yourself to blame,' she says, and flicks her hair, picking up the leaflet again, not making eye contact with me.

'I wasn't flirting . . . I was just . . . being polite . . .'

'OK, if you say so.' She throws the pamphlet down and smiles at me with quite apparent disbelief.

'What's wrong?' I say, confused.

'Just don't be so naïve, Sunny. I could have every guy in here hitting on me if that's what I wanted, but it's just about respecting yourself. I know you aren't married yet, so it's different, but . . . don't be too obvious.'

I am sure my mouth falls open.

'Are we still running on Thursday? I know the weather report is bad, but it would be such a shame to miss it. I love that we can jog together now. It's so much nicer having somebody to run with in the week. I'm so happy for you, Sunny – and for me too, of course, because I get you to run with!' She lifts her coffee cup and toasts it in my direction. It's her way of apologising but still I feel hurt.

I check my watch. 'I'm really sorry, Lisa. I have to dash. I have a delivery at three.'

I grab my bag, and peck her goodbye. She looks slightly baffled as I run off, and I'm completely unable to make eye contact with the big Australian as I dash past.

'It might help if you talked about the incident in a bit more detail – the emotional impact you feel it may have had on you.'

'No.'

'Not yet?'

'Never.'

'But you understand that it will need to be confronted, at some point?'

'Not really. It's over. It's done. I've told you what happened. I don't want to think about it. You could do with some new rugs.'

'All you've told me is that a child was snatched and you helped get him back – there must be more to it than that.'

'It wouldn't kill you to co-ordinate in here. It would make it easier.'

'Make what easier?'

'Focusing. Your books aren't even in height order. I can see one shoe poking out from under that chair. That's off-putting.'

'Try and cut off from that. What do you want to talk about today, if not the incident?'

'Where's the other shoe?'

'What do you want to talk about today?'

'My life is too spotless. I want romance!'

'Do you feel we may have covered that already?'

'No.'

'We have gone over it in most of your sessions.'

'It's not resolved. In my head.'

'Which parts?'

'All of it. I'm still having the daydream.'

'Which is perfectly healthy. Daydreams aren't necessarily harmful. They can simply be a manifestation of our hopes, harmless wish fulfilment. It is only when we find them disturbing that –'

'Maybe if I told you again?'

'Is it the same one as before?'

'No, it's different.'

'Has Adrian made a reappearance?'

He sees me bristle like some old hen at the sound of the name.

'Why would you ask that?'

'I'm just trying to work out how is it different, Sunny.'

'Let me just tell you. I'm having an argument with my tall, handsome husband – who doesn't exist – and we are bickering about unimportant things, but he can't be mad at me for long. It's a fight about who will drive to the dinner party we are going to. He is wearing a chunky-knit sweater. It doesn't descend into any real kind of nastiness. It's not one of those kinds of arguments, the way that people can be to each other, spitting out unforgivable venomous spite . . . You know. We don't do that. Because my husband – my imaginary husband – loves me too much, and I him. I know he will never leave me, with a coward's note about his lust for his secretary. And he knows that I will never get drunk and perform a sexual indiscretion on his brother –

he has a younger brother, reckless and attractive, possibly bisexual, always off trekking in the Himalayas, or skydiving. The point is this: we just can't be unfaithful to each other, in my mind, because unfaithful is for other people with weak relationships, common relationships, relationships that stream past me daily. We don't score points, I don't demean his manhood – he is average in length but has great girth – and he doesn't take food out of my hands for my waistline's good. We don't want to trade up or trade down or trade each other in. We are in love.'

'I see. How exactly is that different to the previous daydream?'

'We never fought about who would drive before. Because in my daydream I hadn't passed my test. But I passed it last week in my dream. Really, I've been driving for years.'

'Congratulations anyway.'

'Thank you. Parallel parked.'

'Why do you think you still want to talk about this? Why do you think this daydream is in any way unhealthy?'

'Because I don't think I understand love! And, seriously, it's becoming more pressing! I think I have a picture of it in my head that isn't real, and that is going to stop me ever actually falling in love, or even recognising it! I thought I was in love with Adrian, and that was five years of my life . . . but now . . .'

'Do you think that you might know love when you find it, and that it will replace the daydreams?'

'No! I think that while my perception of love stays the same I won't be able to see it in reality. I think I am emotionally unhealthy in that respect.'

'And what would you say your perception of love is?'

'Love is the thing that keeps you safe at night. Love doesn't hurt.'

My therapist adjusts his glasses. He looks as if he is in

his late fifties, but he is sixty-two, with dark brown hair smeared in grey. He wears a jumper and jeans. The jeans are old man jeans – they don't really fit, in any acceptable way. His jumper is navy and cream and claret, diagonals and squares and lines. It doesn't really fit either. His clothes just sit on him. He doesn't write things down often, although he has a pad and a pen on the desk behind him in case of emergencies. He doesn't have a deep or soothing voice. It's quite bland. Some days I find it annoying. He sounds like a bank clerk, or a travel agent, or any of those faceless voices at the end of a phone line who just want to put you on hold. He crosses his legs. He always sits in the same position, and rubs his left elbow with his right hand every few minutes. He is divorced, but has a long-term girlfriend now, although they don't live together. I have been seeing him for eight months. It costs me eighty pounds a session, and I come once a week, on a Monday afternoon, for an hour and a half. The 'incident', as I am now referring to it, was yesterday, but I'm feeling fine about it already.

I talk with my hands. I grab my knees and pull them up close to my chest. I do that a lot now that I can. I always sit in the big low chair, although there is a sofa. I scrape my fingers from the front to the back of my head when I am really thinking. Not hard, just to feel my hair. Today I am wearing jeans that fit, with a feint line that runs vertically down the middle of each leg, which is slimming. My black shirt is soft but has a large stiff collar that sits slightly away from my neck, avoiding foundation smears. I wear clear lip-gloss. I apply my mascara heavily at the roots of my eyelashes to give a lengthening effect without clogging the tips. When I see photos of myself I never look the way I think I might. My nose is slightly longer than I imagine it to be, my cheekbones slightly higher. I think of myself with a big round face, but it is actually quite angular now. I have

50

the 'first signs of grey' in dark brown hair, but I colour them out so you wouldn't know, but then the world is turning grey these days. I look anywhere between twenty-six and thirty-two, depending on who you ask. I am actually twenty-eight. Everybody says I look younger now I've lost the weight, but in my head at least, I look exactly the same.

I don't think I have ever been in love, which is the reason I started seeing my therapist. He doesn't seem to think it's a problem, but at twenty-eight I beg to differ. Of course, previously, when I hadn't taken control of the fat situation, I couldn't have seen him, for fear of the criticism. But now that I can say, no matter what he throws at me, I'm not hiding any more, I'm working hard, I'm being a good girl and I'm on a diet, we can talk about the possibility of fat being the problem. Now I am winning this battle I can consider dropping those walls of defence. He thinks I have bigger issues to confront, but he won't tell me what they are exactly. We have to 'find them' together. I enjoy our time, though. It's nice just to blurt it all out – things that you can't say to the people in your life, who would be upset, or concerned, by the rubbish in your head.

'Do you feel under pressure to fall in love, Sunny?'

My therapist is trying a new tack today, it would seem. Good for him. He must be so bored with me by now.

'No. It's completely the opposite. I have never had any pressure, from anybody, to date or to marry. Nobody. Which is a relief, of course. I think they are all just too embarrassed to say anything. My mother doesn't even meddle – how are you, still single? Why aren't you seeing anybody? Your standards are too high! None of that. No pressure at all.'

'Do you see her often?'

'My mother? She comes to visit every couple of weeks, and vents about my father, and his obsession with the car parking spaces in Sainsbury's, Tesco, Waitrose . . . I think all men of that generation eventually become obsessed with supermarket car parks. Are you?'

'No.'

'Well, you've got a couple of years yet.'

'We were talking about your mother.'

'Yes. She comes to see me, on the train because my dad doesn't like her driving the car – she mounts kerbs like a crazy woman – and she asks me to make her a cup of milky tea and then we chat about other people's lives really. With a feigned interest, at best. We don't mention mine.'

'Do you feel that she is interested in your life?'

'Well, sometimes she'll ask about work, but only how I am getting on financially, whether it makes me happy working for myself. She doesn't like to talk about the nature of my business – not that she officially disapproves of sex toys: she watches Channel Four.'

'Do you think she might not want to intrude? Do you think she might be waiting for you to offer some information?'

'I really don't know what she thinks . . . about the lack of men in my life . . . I don't think I want to know. Maybe she believes I am happier on my own, or assumes things go on that I don't choose to share with her. She talks about the inadequacies of my sister's latest flings as if they are all the same man, and all a disappointment at that.'

'Do you feel inadequate compared to your sister? Do you feel that your mother doesn't see you as enough, on your own?'

'No, there has never been any suggestion from anybody that I am not enough on my own. I think they consider me more than enough on my own. Nobody seems to think that I might like to be taken care of. I just take care of myself. I always have.'

'How does that make you feel?'

'Strong.' I run my fingers through my hair. 'And sad.'

Some would say it was a strange sequence of events that led me to establish shewantsshegets.com. But rather, it was one rather pedestrian happening, coupled with a slightly crazier occurrence, in addition to my deep-rooted wish to quit my then job. In the first instance I just happened to catch a TV programme that I wouldn't normally have watched. I fell upon it late one night as I lay in bed cracking my way through a family-sized bar of Galaxy and a mug of hot chocolate, after a vanilla-scented bath. There was European Championship football on BBC1, *Young Musician of the Year* on BBC2, a crime reconstruction show that terrified me on ITV, and a party political broadcast for the Liberal Democrats on Channel Four. So I flicked to Channel Five, and settled down with a documentary about an ex-porn star in the US who claimed to be called Elixir Lake. She had huge blonde hair that looked as if it must have been set in rollers every half an hour. She also had swollen, precarious-looking breasts, on the brink of explosion: the nipple of her left breast was constantly erect and pointing diagonally down towards the floor in rock-hard shame.

Elixir Lake had, after a particularly unpleasant attack of herpes, decided to get out of porn, but porn was all she had known since she was a girl – a common problem. It was then that Elixir had her brainwave. She decided to cherry-pick pornography that she believed would appeal to an underexploited sector of the market – women – and sell it via this strange new phenomenon called the World Wide Web. Elixir's porn stream exploded, so much so that within eighteen months she was selling warehouse loads of soft-core videos. Elixir herself had only ever done soft core; 'No shit, no anal, those were my rules,' she said seriously through plumped-up frosted-pink lips and a deep red lip line. But as well as the videos she was also being asked for dildos and vibrators and all manner of toys by her female clientele. So Elixir seized upon the demand, and now she was living in a six-bedroom house with a pool shaped like a vast pair of bosoms, and a tennis court shaped like a tennis court, in the hills above Los Angeles. Selling rather than swallowing proved more profitable for Ms Lake. But then maybe if she'd done shit or anal . . .

A week later Mrs Browning died. Mrs Browning lived three houses along from me. But whereas I lived on the top floor of a converted house, Mrs Browning lived in a four-bedroom house alone in the heart of wealthy Kew. Her husband had died eight years ago, and she had been on her own ever since. She had nieces and nephews who she was close to, because she and Rudolph had never had children of their own. They were German Jews, who had been fortunate enough to make it out of Germany in 1934, as teenagers. Rudolph had found a job as an apprentice on Savile Row, working his way up until finally he was running the business for the last twenty years of his life. Elsa dedicated a bench in Kew Gardens to her husband after his stroke. The plaque read, 'He loved this place, and its peace.' It made me cry every time I saw it, when I would sit with Mrs Browning after a walk around the Gardens on alternate Thursday mornings. Rudolph's bench was on top of a small hill, overlooking the Thames at the bottom of the gardens, and shaded by an oak tree.

Mrs Browning was the first person I spoke to when I moved to Kew three years ago. She watched me from her window for fifteen minutes, before walking slowly but precisely to my front wall, leaning on it patiently as I unpacked a large box full of books from my car, then introduced herself, and asked why my husband was letting me lift all the heavy boxes.

I liked her from the start. She had some mischief in her.

For the past two years she had received a gentleman caller every Tuesday afternoon for tea. I called him her boyfriend, and she would laugh and shake her head and say that boyfriends were for beautiful young women like me, and she was merely the only person left in Kew as ancient as Wilbur Hardy, who was ninety-two and walked with a cane, but walked none the less. She would smile and refer to him as a harmless rogue. And I don't know if it was because of those words, but I always thought that he grinned like an old-time crook. His suits were either mustard yellow, or apple green, or plum purple, and all had matching waistcoats. If I happened to be there when Wilbur rapped on the door on a Tuesday afternoon, Elsa would wink and say, 'Don't trust them, Sunny. Only one in one thousand will be worth the wait.' Wilbur would always kiss my hand as I squeezed past him on the doorstep, and I would get embarrassed, even by such a mannerly show of affection from a ninety-two-year-old man. Elsa would wink again and mouth, 'Don't trust them,' one more time, before she let him in.

Wilbur Hardy had died on New Year's Day. His son had paid Elsa a visit to tell her and she had smiled sadly and said merely, 'He was ancient. It was bound to happen sooner or later.' His son had then informed her that Mr Hardy had managed many businesses and bought many licences, working from his study, right up until that New Year's Day. Some of these businesses were highly profitable, and had been for many years, and were administered by his sons, and nephews, and nieces. Some of these businesses were dormant, however, acquired often just for fun and what Wilbur Hardy regarded as pocket change. Wilbur had left Elsa a number of these dormant concerns in his will. He had not left her property or money, but merely things that might make her smile. He had left her the exclusive UK licence to distribute Female Belly-Dancing Garden Gnomes for the next twelve years. He had left her the exclusive licence to distribute fingerless gloves in Ethiopia for the next seven months. And he left her a newly acquired licence, bought only two months previously, to distribute two new sex toys for women, known as 'Three-Fingered and Two-Fingered Fondlers'. They had just started to be distributed in the US, and Wilbur had read about them as a funny fanciful 'and finally' story in the *Sunday Telegraph*, and enquired about the licence. Finding that it was up for sale, and this time predicting a healthy profit margin, he had snapped it up for a little more than eight years, and a little more than fifty thousand dollars. He had changed his will yearly, his son told Elsa, on the thirty-first of December. And so Elsa got the licence for the Two-Fingered Fondler and, following Wilbur's lead, had changed her will the following week.

Mrs Browning simply fell asleep on a Sunday night, and didn't wake up on Monday morning. When her nephew paid her a visit on the Monday lunchtime as arranged and received no answer from repeated rings of the doorbell, he let himself in and found her comfortably in bed, peacefully passed away. Her nephew, having met me on a couple of occasions, kindly let me know that evening.

I cried for an hour, and then remembered what Elsa had said about Wilbur. She was ancient, it was bound to happen sooner or later. And with that I resolved to stop crying but make sure I put a bench next to Rudolph's in Kew Gardens, and think of something suitably appropriate to say on its plaque that wouldn't be too sentimental for her. A week later her nephew called me again, one evening as I sat with macaroni cheese and a jacket potato for dinner, watching *Dirty Dancing* on video. Elsa had left me fifteen thousand pounds and the licence to distribute something called a 'Two-Fingered Fondler' in the UK for the next eight years . . .

* * *

'Do you think, given the nature of your business, that people around you might assume that you have a healthy attitude towards sex, and that you just aren't telling them about your sex life?'

'No. There were definitely raised eyebrows when I started the business, because it was sex-related and because it was me. But I suppose nobody actually said anything disparaging. My Uncle Humphrey laughed a little too long for my liking.'

'How did that make you feel?'

'It bothered me at the time, but I have never liked him anyway. He's an aggressive man, and his skin flakes so badly that my Aunt Lucy makes jokes about the snowstorm that is changing their bedding. It makes me retch.'

My therapist turns in his chair and writes something down on his pad. I know what it will be. Something to do with physical imperfections. He tries to steer me on to that a lot. We've discussed it. I roll my eyes, but he isn't looking. There are no photos in this room, hanging on the walls. The wallpaper is a cappuccino colour, with a brown flower swirl pattern, quite modern in comparison to everything else. Maybe they had to redecorate the walls recently. Maybe some nut job slashed an artery and graffitied the walls with his blood. The windows are big, and the curtains are well made but a depressing rust colour like dried ketchup on a cracked plate. He turns back to face me.

'Do you think you might think about love and sex a disproportionate amount, given the nature of your business? And the fact that you work alone and from home? Did you dwell on these things when you worked at the office, for instance?'

'Not as much, no. But working from home is a positive thing, I am sure of that. It has changed my life dramatically, for the better. Office work didn't suit me; I was too sensitive to the politics. I'm much happier now. I can't bitch at myself – not consciously, anyway – and I can't stab myself in the back. I don't berate myself for being ten minutes late to my computer in the morning and then ignore the extra hour and a half I put in every night. The office environment almost made me lose my faith in mankind. The petty bitterness at the core of so many people, men and women, depressed me to the point of tears, daily. My business is – ironically – much more wholesome than that.'

'Tell me again, how long have you been working from home?'

'I resigned a year and three months ago today.'

'You told me that was because of Adrian.'

'Yes. About that – I feel like I may have painted him in a harsh light, to you. I was thinking about it yesterday. He is perfectly nice, you know. He just subscribed to a female aesthetic that wasn't me. All he really did was show a complete disinterest in me, sexually. He wasn't cruel or unusual, in finding me unattractive. I just wasn't his kind of eye candy . . . then.'

'And you resent him for that?'

'Not at all. It's the way of the world.'

'Did you ever think that he might change his mind, that he might fall in love with you anyway?'

'When I was still fat? I imagined it, a couple of times. But when does that ever happen? The preference for personality only exists in the movies, or soap operas, where ugly ducklings manage to bewitch the heart of some local stud, but then suddenly transform, courtesy of some decent hair straighteners and daily contact lenses, into models. Personality is only important when differentiating among the beautiful women. Beautiful and boring is so less appealing than beautiful and interesting. But interesting on its own, without the arse to go with it, wasn't ringing Adrian's bells.'

My therapist turns to write something down, but then changes his mind.

'Do you think you might be harbouring a subconscious grudge against him for this? Do you think you might subconsciously believe that men are only interested in sex?'

'There is nothing subconscious about it. I do believe it. Men *are* only interested in sex.'

'And yet your business, which is based on sex, is mostly funded by women?'

'It's true, ninety per cent of my sales are to women. Where are you going with this?'

'So do you think everybody is obsessed with sex?'

'No, not everybody. Maybe most people. Most people are obsessed with sex, yes. But not all. Most.'

'Where does the belief come from? Because your business is doing well?'

'Maybe, but I think my business is doing well because women in particular find it easier to buy sex-related items over the internet, because it reduces their embarrassment. It means they can avoid the humiliation of eye contact with an Ann Summers sales assistant in a too-tight T-shirt knotted under her breasts and a mouth full of sexually liberated attitude and chewing gum. You can't walk into a sex shop, peruse the vibrator wall, pretend not to look shocked at the gimp masks, pick the least intimidating-looking vibrator – to prove you aren't taking it too seriously – carry it to the counter, pay for it, walk out of the shop without making eye contact with any passers-by, and get all the way home on the District line with a "discreet" bag that everybody knows came from a sex shop, without confronting certain truths. That is a torturous amount of time to be carrying a mechanical penis in public. And do you know that the traditional vibrator – penis shaped, I mean – isn't even my biggest seller, in any shape or size? A vibrating hand is my biggest seller – the two-fingered version with a pulsing thumb. There is a three-fingered version, but the words "vulvic bruising" are used twice in the small print, and it puts people off. The Two-Fingered Fondler has a "hot breath" function as well: if you hit a certain button a puff of air emits from the knuckle of the second finger, which should be positioned as per diagram G on the box for maximum impact on the necessary biology.'

'Am I missing a point?'

'My point being that women don't even want a penis. They just want a hand and a puff of air. I think that means something.'

'What do you think it means?'

'I don't know. But it means something. Do you know what I always wonder? I always wonder who draws those diagrams on the boxes, the Fondler boxes, and whether somebody had to "sit" for them? But I suppose it wasn't an easel and beret moment, some old French artist, holding his thumb up in front of him. Plus the diagrams aren't in oil or watercolour or even charcoal – it's a 2B pencil at best. Some expense was obviously spared. Did you know that the knuckles can rotate? If the fingers are in rotate position themselves, and not "thrust" or "tickle"? But it's the puff of air that does it, apparently. I get a lot of positive feedback about it, via the website, as if I am in some way responsible. Apparently it's inspired.'

'Is it?'

'Is it what?'

'Is it inspired? The puff of air . . . ?'

'I don't know. The customers seem to think so.'

'Haven't you tried it yourself?'

'No.'

'Why not?'

'I don't know,' I say a little too defensively. 'There was

this one time, I did get one out of its box, and not just, you know, "inspecting it for delivery damage".'

'And?'

'And I got distracted . . .'

'Distracted?'

'I tried to make it play chopsticks on my keyboard.'

My therapist gives me a strange look. He doesn't usually register any kind of emotion, or surprise, or anything. But that was definitely a 'look'.

'Sunny.' He says my name as if he has reached some kind of conclusion, and my back straightens for a life-changing insight that has so far, in eight months of therapy, eluded me. 'Do you think you might put too much emphasis on sex?'

I've heard that one before. This is nothing new.

'You feel relatively sexually inexperienced and instead of seeing sex as merely just one of any number of natural human instincts, you are building it up into something that it is not? You are putting it, and in fact your lack of it, at the core of your life, when it deserves no more importance than say talking, or laughing, or eating?'

'Eating?'

'Not just eating. Talking, or laughing, or any number of human instincts.'

'But you said eating last. With emphasis.'

'There was no emphasis, Sunny.'

'Are you suggesting that I've replaced one obsession with another? I still eat, you know.'

'Of course you eat.'

'I've had a coffee, and a yoghurt drink, and a Skinny Blueberry Muffin already today. I'm not starving myself. I was in Starbucks for an hour before I came here.'

'Starbucks? Are you going there now? You were so against it when it first opened! It wasn't local, or atmospheric enough for Kew – weren't those your words?'

'I know. But then I tried it. Now I'm addicted to their Skinny Blueberry Muffins. It is a tasty yet low-fat snack.'

'How does that make you feel?'

'Well, it doesn't exactly fill me up, but it's breakfast.'

'No, I mean how does it feel to sacrifice your principles for your diet?'

'Look, I have a healthy relationship with food now. My diet is not the enemy, and food is not the enemy, necessarily. I know that you think that there is something unhealthy, emotionally, with the diet thing, but truly I am just focused. I had a lot of weight to lose. You could never understand.'

'Why not?'

'Because you've never been fat.' I state it with force, like a dare. I challenge him to disagree, because I have a thousand arguments up my old fat sleeve on this one and he will never win.

It still feels strange to say the 'f' word out loud, and not cringe, or whisper. Just the word still manages to hurt me a little.

'We all want to lose a few pounds at some point,' he says, and it's like a starting pistol in my head.

'But a few pounds is not fat! Not properly self-conscious afraid-to-go-swimming-for-being-laughed-at unloved fat!'

'But, Sunny, it is this perception – that you were unlovable because you were overweight – that interests me. Many overweight people are very much in love, and are loved in return. A person's weight is by no means their defining characteristic.'

'Maybe before it wasn't, in "the olden days", but not today. Nobody loves fat any more. That's the last century speaking. I know, I live it. Complete strangers whispered "fat bitch" to me as I walked past them in the street. They didn't know me, but they wanted to hurt me, because of it. Tell me that is not a defining characteristic – a person you've never even seen before hates you, and that's not "unlovable"?'

'But is it possible you lost the weight without addressing your own issues, not those of the strangers in the street, but your own?'

'No, I just woke up. I was unhappy and I confronted that. That was healthy, I think.'

'Not if the only answer you have found is losing another pound. When will you stop? If you still feel unloved in two months' time, or whenever it is that you hit your "target weight", will losing more weight be the only answer? This is what concerns me, Sunny. There are bigger issues than just "fat" involved.'

'OK, now I want to talk about the emotional impact of the incident.'

'Anything other than the diet, right?' my therapist smiles. He has the measure of me now.

Adrian joined the Feel Good Company, specialists in vitamins, minerals and homeopathic painkillers, seven months after I did. I was the office manager, and spent most of my days hanging around the reception area, listening to Seema from accounts complaining about the photocopier. Our offices were furnished like a bad living room, with large vases of deteriorating dried flowers and burnt-amber sofas that had seen better days. Posters advertising Calcium and Fibre hung on the walls with a pride of place usually reserved for photos of grandchildren. The carpet was thinning in front of the reception desk, and the daily papers were spread across a glass coffee table, alongside *Pharmaceuticals Monthly* and *Scientific Nutrition Quarterly*, which nobody ever read. I dished out the better parking spaces to my favourites. Jean from distribution was a lovely lady, the same age as my mother, and prone to wonderful endearing ridiculous statements. As the year 2000 approached, she asked me seriously if the Millennium Bug might affect her Carmen rollers.

My boss was the head of human resources, a terribly serious Canadian woman who could only laugh at pain. Her assistant, Mariella, was a jumped-up brunette in secretary's spectacles, who wore short skirts and tight T-shirts, and who hung the phone up on me daily. She had a way of walking that accentuated both her breasts and her arse, and all the men agreed that she was vacuous and pompous and a fool, but they still wanted to sleep with her. It took me a while to get my head around that, and it can still confuse me on my less lucid days. A man doesn't have to like a woman, or respect a woman, or enjoy her company, to want to have sex with her. She just needs big breasts or long legs. Her face really isn't important either, as long as she's not buck-toothed or cross-eyed. I suppose what confuses me is that I am attracted to potential husbands, whereas Greg from Royalties, a tall handsome boy with blond hair and blue eyes that Hitler would have endorsed, was enticed by the possibility of a quick vigorous shag. He had plenty of time to find a wife, or she would find him, and for now at least he just wanted to have fun. I didn't have that luxury. I was looking for somebody to see past my big old trousers and my big old belly and take me on wholesale, for life. I was sure time was running out for me, at twenty-four. Young and fat had to be more attractive than old and fat I chided myself; snag somebody quick!

Adrian came for his first interview on a Wednesday, and he was eight minutes late, because of the trains. He ran in, adjusting his suit jacket nervously.

His second interview was on a Friday, which I took to be a good sign. He was twenty minutes early, and sat in reception nursing a strong tea made for him by our post boy, Simon, at my suggestion. I didn't speak to Adrian that

64

day because I was too busy. Mariella arrived, breasts high and out, and bobbed hair swinging, and greeted him with a smile as big as Julia Roberts', and a wriggle of her arse. Adrian didn't seem to notice. That was the day I fell for him.

Adrian started working for the Feel Good Company five weeks later, in IT support. His predecessor had been sacked after returning to the office one night drunk to phone for a cab home from his desk, logging on to a porn site, and then promptly falling asleep. Six hours and five hundred pounds later, he woke up.

Adrian was twenty-six, and didn't like IT at all. It paid the bills, he said. Simon who wore his jeans so low I was familiar with every pair of underpants he owned, observed that I 'flustered' when Adrian was around. I would make excuses about having to be somewhere else, or pretend to be busy with building contracts, or reprimand Simon for some minor misdemeanour. Anything to avoid looking Adrian in the eye. Because when I did, I laughed. My attraction for him overwhelmed me so much it actually made me laugh out loud.

He was tall, six foot one. He had longish shaggy dark brown hair that hung around his ears and in his eyes. He had a large nose, and a complexion that suggested he could get away with factor ten in mid-summer Rhodes, although he was prone to the odd freckle. For his first week he wore pale shirts, blues and greys, with his suits. When he realised that he could get away with wearing jeans he switched to dark denim – not baggy like Simon's, but not tight and high like an old man's. They fitted him well. He wore a battered old leather belt, and sweatshirts with small logos, in bottle green, and navy, and claret, and grey. He wore expensive fashionable trainers. He carried a record bag, in which he kept his Walkman and a copy of the *Sun*. He supported

Liverpool, although he had never been to Anfield. I knew all of this without ever having spoken to him for more than thirty seconds. A minute was the absolute limit for me, and then I'd make my excuses and walk off, to laugh elsewhere, rather than laugh in front of him like a crazy woman. He made my hands shake. He made me bite my lower lip. He didn't have a girlfriend.

He would rove the building, retrieving lost files and restarting crashed computers, and when he wasn't busy he would come down to reception and chat to Simon, and flick through the paper. He started taking sugar in his tea, and put on half a stone, so he began running in the mornings before work, and lost it. I heard him talking to Simon one day, about a year after he had joined, gossiping about who had shagged who in the office, who they hated, whose computer he would deliberately take an age to fix. I was using the franking machine in the post room when I heard him refer to me as a 'lovely girl'; I thought I was going to throw up.

I made an effort after that. He could have been one of those men who just disliked fat women, made jokes about them behind their backs, easy fodder. But I was a 'lovely girl'. There was no mention of 'but you wouldn't, would you,' or, 'shame about her arse'.

After that I cracked jokes in his presence, and made him tea.

It was a dark day when he told me he thought he was falling in love. With somebody else, of course. She was a trainee PE teacher, and he had met her in his local pub. I thought I hated her. I didn't know her, hadn't even seen her face, but I hated her. Of course, when I pictured her she was effortlessly slim. Her hair and her eyes and her clothes changed in my mind daily, but she remained a size ten. I was morbidly jealous. I was sure that she didn't even have an issue with food, that she could eat two biscuits and leave the rest, that she could have a couple of spoonfuls of ice cream and proclaim herself 'stuffed' and return the carton to the freezer for another day. She could buy a bag of chips and feel sick after eating a third of them. She wouldn't have to force herself to stop eating them, she just could, without thinking, throw them away. She felt 'full'. I never felt full. If you tried to take a chip from my bag you'd get my teeth in your finger. And that was the only difference between Adrian's girlfriend and me, in my head. But she got lucky, because she got Adrian. Eleanor Roosevelt said that nobody can make you feel inferior without your consent, and it is absolutely true. I didn't really hate Adrian's girlfriend for being thin. I didn't hate Adrian for not picking me. I hated myself for being fat. And what did I do when I felt bad? I comfort-ate. During the years I worked with Adrian I was a size twenty-four. On the outside I was big and jolly and made-up and polished and laughing. Everybody passed comment that I was, of course, 'happy with myself, didn't have a problem with my size' and they loved me for it, in a Platonic sense, at least. Of course, while I thumped around the office being big and happy and proud I still went home at night alone. Everybody else, the ones who did 'care' about their appearance, started getting engaged, and married, and pregnant. I just got their compliments, about how 'great' I was, what a wonderful role model, to be fat and happy. 'Sunny by name, Sunny by nature,' they'd say . . .

It was a happy day that Adrian announced he had split up with the now qualified PE teacher, two years later. She just wasn't the one, he told me. He wasn't in love with her. Then he put his arm around my shoulders and said we should run off together. I said, 'I don't run anywhere,' and laughed, and he squeezed my shoulder, and answered his phone.

A Monday was the blackest day of my life. Adrian was still single, a year after breaking up with the teacher. We had worked together for three years. I trundled into work in high-heeled boots that I convinced myself were comfortable. I bought them from the plus size shop, where the heels are wider and therefore give your legs more support. Plus the legs themselves are wider, so you can actually zip them up. It was a small victory when I was finally able, three months ago, to buy my boots from 'normal' shoe shops, without the zips jamming around the ankle. My legs are toned now, and those boots fit comfortably, but of course I still look down and see fat that shouldn't be there. My legs don't look any different to me, but they must be thinner. I wear size twelve jeans now, that magical Perfect Ten still eluding me. Logic dictates that my legs have changed, but my eyes refuse to see it.

On that Monday, in my fat girl boots, and a pair of long grey trousers and a black shirt, with my hair freshly straightened and my make-up impeccable, I walked into the post room to chat with Peter, our new assistant. Simon had left to join the police force six months earlier. Peter was just as amiable, and just as young, but a little more forthcoming with office gossip.

'Morning, Peter,' I announced in my usual 'bubbly' tone.

'I have gossip,' he declared with a sly smile on his face.

I looked at him through narrowed eyes. 'Is it any good?'

'It's top drawer.' The look on his face told me he wasn't lying.

'Tell me then!' I clapped my hands together excitedly.

'Adrian went home with Mariella on Friday night.'

My world fell apart. The smile stayed fixed on my face, but the lump in my throat kicked at my words, so they barely came out. A sumo wrestler had landed on my chest, and smashed the air out of my lungs.

'Oh my God! I didn't know something was going on between them.' My voice broke on 'them', but Peter didn't notice.

'I don't think it is. But I bet he shagged her.'

'No doubt!' I smiled, and turned and walked to my desk opposite the kitchen. I checked my emails and mentally pleaded with myself not to cry. Peter had no idea. Of course Jean did. She came to find me later, while I ate a double helping of cheesy pasta for lunch at my desk.

'Have you heard?'

'About Adrian and Mariella?' I asked without looking up from my lunch.

'Oh, Sunny, you'll find somebody lovely.'

'Sorry?'

'And I'm sure Adrian and Mariella won't turn into anything.'

'Jean, you know I'm not bothered about Adrian, don't you?'

'Oh. OK. I just thought you liked him.'

'Why would you think that?' I said, still not looking up.

'Sunny, you're a lovely girl, really pretty, lovely hair, you always dress nicely – why don't you ask him to go for a drink?'

'Are you crazy?' I looked up then, and the tears in my eyes were obvious.

'He could do a lot worse than you, you know.'

'I know. But I'm not interested, Jean.' One tear spilt onto my cheek. Jean looked as if it were her heart that were breaking but said, 'OK, I have to get back.' She smiled at me, and brushed down her cardigan.

Of course, I couldn't ask him out for a drink. The squirming embarrassment, the silence just after I blurted it out, the dawning realisation that he was going to have to let me down gently, because I was a 'lovely girl'. A tiny part of me did scream, 'If you don't ask, you don't get! Men aren't that bright; they just don't see it unless, like Mariella, you make it screamingly obvious.' But then the voice of reason told me what we all know is true. If a man wants to ask a woman out, he will, especially a fat woman who isn't exactly fending off admirers. I was there, primed and basted and ready to be plucked off the shelf, I wasn't 'intimidating'. If Adrian had any feelings for me he would have asked me already. But asking him, hearing the rejection out loud, was too much for me to bear. That was the day I realised I had to leave the Feel Good Company, before the irony killed me.

It took me another six months to pluck up the courage to hand in my notice. In that time Adrian slept with Mariella again twice. She was interested, but he wasn't, and it fizzled out, but the threat of it always loomed the morning after a heavy night before, because it is, of course, so much easier to sleep with somebody a second or third time. My leaving drinks were held in the office itself, with four hundred pounds' worth of drink consumed in reception by eighty-five people. We had a buffet, and I can never walk away from a buffet; they are my nemesis – even now, when I can tell you the calorie and fat content of every plateful of sausages on sticks and mini quiches and peanuts and mozzarella sandwiches and mini pizzas. All that food laid out in front of me is still hard to resist. Buffets for the serious dieter are to be avoided like wine tastings for an alcoholic.

Adrian with his big northern laugh was one of the last ones standing at my farewell do. I had masochistic daydreams that he wouldn't even attend, or stay for a few beers, then head off for more fun elsewhere with his mates, or even worse, slide off with Mariella at about half-past nine. But at 11.30 he was opening one of the last bottles of red wine, with a cigarette hanging out of his mouth, laughing with one of the guys from systems support. He poured out a couple of glasses and brought one over to me, as I stood teary-faced, waving goodbye to Jean whose husband, Jeremy, was waiting downstairs in the car and who was already angry because she was drunk and an hour late.

'Here you go, love. Have another one of those!' Adrian thrust a glass of wine at me.

I took it, but put it down behind me on the reception desk saying, 'I've had too many already, I'm starting to feel a bit sick.'

'Come on, it's your leaving do! You can't back out on me now! Where are we going afterwards?' Adrian did a little dance and drops of red wine threatened to fly out of his glass.

'Well I don't know where you're going, Adrian, but I'm going home.'

'No! We have to go clubbing or something, give you a proper send-off.' He flicked ash on the carpet. My mouth opened to reprimand him, before I realised that the carpets weren't my responsibility any more.

'I don't go clubbing.'

'Why not?'

'I'm too old.'

'You're only twenty-seven. What are you talking about – you're younger than me! And I'm not too old! Come on, let's go on the pull, pick ourselves up a couple of teenagers!'

'I don't think that's going to happen.'

'Come on, Sunny, why not?' He was pulling at one of my hands, grinning, trying to get me to dance, certain I would be persuaded, because life was simple for Adrian.

'Because . . . I'm dressed for work.'

'You look lovely!' He winked.

'It'll be all hot and sweaty!'

'That's a good thing!' He winked again, but this time it was accompanied by a dirty laugh.

'I'll be twice the size of everybody else in there!' I blurted it out because of the wine, and because I felt like I was being backed into a corner, and because it was the truth. He only looked embarrassed for a moment.

'Shut up! What difference does that make? Come on, let's go and have a dance.' But he wasn't dancing any more.

'No, you go. I'm going to go home in a minute.'

'Fair enough. Where's Peter?' Adrian smiled, but his bubble had been burst and he stumbled off.

He wasn't hitting on me, although that's what my nicer friends would have said, to raise my hopes. But in these instances I firmly believe in being cruel to be kind. It hadn't even occurred to him that we could go home together, and I never would have let it happen: couldn't have been naked with Adrian without feeling violently exposed and vulnerable. The sex would have lasted for minutes, if he could manage a sloppy erection after that many drinks, and the excuses would have lasted an hour. I'm sorry about my sagging stomach, my bulbous arse, my huge thighs, everything! Everything! Besides, I had never pictured Adrian and I just having sex, fucking. We would have to be making love, because he liked me, and I liked him. I didn't have that animal instinct in me that craved thrashing violent passionate orgasms. I wanted somebody to love me, and to make love to me, softly, and without apologies, to look into my eyes, and only my eyes, and not even think about the body beneath them. I wanted the body to become completely unimportant, just machinery, and I wanted all the fireworks to be in our heads. I wanted mental and emotional orgasms. I wanted his eyes to stare into mine, and a moment of realisation to hit us both like a volcano erupting, convincing us both that it was the best, most intimate, most overwhelming orgasm either of us had ever had. And it would have nothing to do with how we looked, and everything to do with who we were.

But Adrian fucks with his eyes closed. I know, because they are closed now. The first time I had sex with Adrian I just wanted to prove I was good at it. He initiated the kiss, and I didn't want him to regret his decision. And so it was a twisted sexual theatre of shivers and breaths and acrobatics on my part. I tried desperately to be energetic and adventurous and slightly filthy, while steering him away from my body parts that I still deemed unacceptable. My stomach still hung out hungrily like a deflated dart player's belly, the skin refusing to tighten and just accommodate the muscles that were left. It was my restricted zone, to which I tried to deny him access, twisted and turning and planting him flat on his back any time his hands, or worse, his mouth, crept near it. But he managed to kiss my belly anyway, and didn't seem to hate it with the vitriol that I did. I scratched and sucked and made vigorous, to prove a point. It was the ultimate vindication, after years of rejection. Now I was good enough to sleep with.

It was a bland encounter. Of course, I faked a couple of orgasms for his ego, while my own ego shrivelled inside of me, occasionally knocking on my conscience to ask, 'What are you doing?' I ignored it and kept on rocking. And in the thick of it I did feel good, if not satisfied. He kissed me with passion, not love, but it was a passion that hadn't existed a year ago. Somehow, and I wasn't even sure exactly how, I had made Adrian want me, and that was enough for that night, at least. To expect the sex to be good as well would have been plain greedy.

The second time I had sex with Adrian I tried to concentrate on enjoying myself. I spent far less time giving him oral sex, and focused all my attentions on having an orgasm proper. No such luck. Sex with Adrian was a pretty pedestrian affair. It was fine, if fine is not too damning a word. What man wants to be described as 'fine' in bed? In fairness, he had a lovely penis, long and pale and smooth and clean, and thick as well. It was so pleasing to look at, it was almost sanitised. It just didn't seem to hit the spot. I reprimanded myself mentally, while faking my second orgasm that night, for not relaxing enough to let it happen naturally. Maybe it was my own fault. Maybe I had, in my head, built this man into a sexual demi-god, able to dish out thrills with one thrust of his wand. The sexual explosions I had imagined were almost impossible to match in reality. Plus he was a little quick with his thrust, and not quite as deep as I'd hoped. I tried to make him go slower, and harder, but he had his rhythm and he was sticking to it, like UB40. It's reggae or nothing. I imagine slow and hard is the thing that will really do it for me. I don't know for sure. I've never had an orgasm with somebody else around. If that sounds tragic I console myself that at least I have had an orgasm, and if some sexual bright spark manages to get me there I will at least recognise it for what it is.

This is the third time I have had sex with Adrian, and doing anything more than twice makes it a habit. But this time we are approximately two bottles of red wine and eight minutes into the encounter, and Adrian has already begun his thrust for home. His erection is precarious; neither one of us expects it to last much longer. I'm a little bored. I look up at his eyes, squeezed tightly shut, and I imagine that he might open them, and slow down, and kiss me tenderly, and stir something in me that hasn't been reached yet. I wonder if he has his eyes closed so that he can picture somebody else, but now they spring open, and he smiles, and says my name, and then carries on pumping, which sounds like a Sid James special set in a petrol station.

My feelings for him are old, and forgotten. I am having sex with him simply because I can. We are not in love, and never will be. He is a sweet man, but he doesn't know how to hold my hand or stroke my hair in a way that will move me. It is all mechanical, insertion and lubrication and squeezing and pulling. We make random impersonal sex noises, both of us lost in our own worlds, trying to please ourselves. We are not a couple, having sex. We are two individuals using each other to get off. I think this should be the last time we have sex, but I doubt it will be.

The first time, three weeks and four days ago, we met for a drink on a Thursday to catch up, and he had been astounded at how different I looked. Men often dish out 'compliments' lazily, and Adrian is no exception. His words were, 'You look about two hundred per cent more attractive than the last time I saw you!' I could have cried. Men don't seem to realise that I have just lost weight, and not become a whole new person, and thus an insulting remark about my appearance last year is still an insulting remark about me, even if they are cushioning it with some current nicety. 'You look good' or, 'You look great' would have done nicely, but Adrian messed it up. I had to ignore it, if I was going to stay in my seat. Even the smallest reprimand for his choice of words would have made things uncomfortable. Plus Adrian isn't the kind of man who thinks about things like that. He is 'easy-going'. Intellectual effort is a fun time wasted.

He didn't see the need to be subtle in his advances, because that would require thought. It didn't occur to him to tread softly, or try to mask the fact that he now found me attractive, simply because my body shape had changed. My face was and is still the same, just thinner. My eyes are still my own. I haven't had surgery. Yet. The words coming out of my mouth are exactly the same, the only difference being that Adrian seems to find them more interesting now, or is going to the effort of pretending to, at least. We had a few drinks and got a cab to go home, and he kissed me. Despite the two hours leading up to it, and how obvious it would have been to any onlooker, I was still surprised when he did it. He had rejected me, albeit unknowingly, for four years, but his kiss wasn't hard to earn. I just had to be thin enough. This confused me. Now, instead of being 'Sunny' I was 'Sunny who he would like to have sex with'. Nothing groundbreaking had been said during the evening, no pivotal conversation had. It's a depressing thought. I had been good enough all along, just not thin enough. We had both exited at my house, and we had the first night of sex. At the time it didn't feel as rushed as it sounds – I didn't feel like a slut – I'd been waiting for four years, after all.

We had sex twice that night, but not in the morning. He had promised to call me when he left for work the next day, and sure enough he did . . . two weeks later, last Friday, drunk in a cab and en route to my house but he couldn't remember the number.

Foolishly I reminded him.

This evening, Monday, thirty-five hours after the 'incident' – I've almost forgotten all about it – we at least arranged to meet when we were both sober. We went for a coffee, but that turned into wine, and we ended up back at mine, and now we are having sex again. I am afraid that we have become fuck buddies, but I don't want to confront him because I have nothing to say. Adrian is a nice but average thirty-year-old bloke, with a big laugh and good hair and trendy trainers. He works in IT. I know what I am getting, I know that his favourite film is *Rocky IV*, I know he prefers Indian to Chinese, I know he reads his horoscope, and is mildly left wing.

Adrian is still somebody's dream man, if such a thing exists, but I am starting to wonder whether he is still mine, now that I am learning to differentiate between liking somebody and being attracted to somebody. I realise that I have to feel something deeper: he can't just be funny, or bright, or look right. There has to be something that makes him right for me, even though I admit that I don't know what that something is. Maybe it will be something small. Maybe we will both like film quizzes, and sit late into the night on his battered old leather sofa making our way through two bottles of wine and a bar of dark chocolate, and quizzing each other, until we decide to go to bed . . . It could be that small, I think, but it will matter, of course.

Adrian rolls off me onto the bed. This time I made the necessary pleasurable noises without going to the effort of actually faking an orgasm in its entirety. I don't have the energy or the inclination. He doesn't seem bothered.

Adrian mumbles something into the pillow.

'Sorry?' I ask.

He raises himself up on to his elbows and looks at me seriously. 'Who would have thought it, eh?'

'Thought what?' I stroke the hair out of his eyes.

'You and me.' He smiles at me, and kisses my forehead.

'It's not the strangest thing that's ever happened.'

'No, I know. Not now. It just shows . . .'

'Shows what?' I ask.

'You know,' he closes his eyes and hugs me, drifting into sleep, 'what a difference a year can make.'

'Well, people's feelings change all the time,' I say, nervously trying to stop him before he goes too far.

'Hmmm?' His eyes are still closed, and he presses his face into my neck. 'You've done so well . . .' And he falls asleep.

Three hours later I am still awake, while Adrian snores loudly on the other side of the bed. Yep, I've done so well.

THREE

The monkey nut miracle marvel man

Cagney B. James cracks a nut in his right hand. His father, Tudor B. James, is the only other person alive who knows what the 'B' stands for. His mother knew as well, but she died twenty years ago, so Cagney isn't as worried about her letting it slip. The sign on his door neglects the 'B', and merely reads,

The Agency
C. James Proprietor

Tarnished silver lettering on heavy oak, and a window. It could be the door to a funeral parlour, or a gambling den, or any number of things, and that's the point. The shell crumbles in his palm. Like a hooker giving a hand job, it's a well-practised technique, just without the constant AIDS testing. Maybe the odd splinter, but hell, that won't shut down his immune system. He kicks the pieces towards the bin.

Leaning back in his chair, Cagney places both feet up on the desk in front of him, and listens to the noises outside his window, with eyes closed. The bottle bank swallows ten green Merlots, fed by a ruddy old major in wellingtons and a tweed jacket with elbow patches as red as the veins in his cheeks. You can't sleep in Kew for the sound of recycling. 'Luxury' family saloons purr up, and uniform beige court shoes and black city loafers dive out of passenger seats and hit the ground running, as a tube lazes graciously into the station.

The butchers fire up the rotisserie chicken at 9 o'clock every morning, and the smell drifts through Cagney's window with the warm air, mixed with the plastic croissant and coffee smells seeping out of Starbucks. Just the thought of hot food before midday makes him retch. He forces himself to stomach it for five seconds, before spinning round and slamming the window shut with a force that makes the flower seller across the road drop his bucket of tulips and exclaim, 'Prick!'

Cagney hears it.

The flower seller used to be big-boned, voluptuous, heavy on the eye: a fat, fat man. He was reassuringly huge, pleasantly swollen, with a stomach that children could bounce on, and flesh concertinas where his neck should have been. Cagney hasn't spoken to him in the ten years he's sold his flowers opposite the office. The flower seller had obviously stopped eating sometime last year, and Cagney noted the slow but steady loosening of his shirt buttons, and his neck suddenly appeared one day, unexpectedly, like a highland fling from an old set of bagpipes that you thought were broken. It was then that he lost Cagney's respect, and just when Cagney had been working up to saying 'good morning'. If he liked his food – and he obviously had liked Ethiopia's share of food and never mind about the famine – why deny it? He had been sturdy before, big and fat and happy – and that made him worth something, in the Cagney James pamphlet on life. A kindred spirit that almost got a hello. The fat flower seller of Kew, as much a part of the village as the gardens themselves, and the ever-increasing quota of camera jockeys from April to October. American tourists felt they knew him on sight, from the slide shows back home entitled 'Our Trip to Europe'. Now the man's friends have trouble recognising him from three feet. Cagney is pretty sure it has hurt his pocket as well. Japs don't feel the need to stop and chat to him, his new slimmer frame and loose skin so much less charming, or snapshot friendly. He is threatening now; he looks so average that you have to wonder what nastiness is on his mind instead of sausage and chips. It suggests to Cagney that although the body may now be 'healthy', he has lost another friend to the new century. Yes, he *was* a friend. If Cagney had ever actually needed to buy flowers, that's where he would have got them, but not now. And all for what? For a woman, probably.

'Poor bastard.' He swears loudly, alone in his office.

Cagney indulges his demons. He gives them their head, and lets them breathe. He smokes Marlboro Reds, but without passion. They are a habit, not a crutch. He drinks whiskey, mostly Jack Daniel's, but he doesn't mind which brand if it's on sale. Straight, no ice. There is no desire he feels the need to suppress. He doesn't feel lust any more, trickling its fingers down his spine.

He's not hurting anybody but himself. And that used to be allowed.

He read in the paper that you shouldn't skip breakfast, and loath as he is to ignore the sound advice of a 'celebrity doctor', he now takes a shot of whiskey each morning, sharp and decent, harsh but so honest it borders on the poetic. What great advice it had been.

Of course, he'd absolutely love a muesli bar instead, or a carrot juice, or a live yoghurt, or a vitamin garlic essential fucking fatty acid pill, or better still a month in a glorified country prison with nothing but rice cakes and fizzy water on the menu, or another lecture from another expert who knows better.

He just hasn't found the time.

As much as he really wants to pay some overpriced, long-haired, four-eyed Freudian Jungian Cantian freak to tell him he really wanted to screw his mother and kill his father at the age of two but if he looked away they wouldn't actually exist, his income just won't stretch to that and the whiskey, and what a goddamn tragedy it is. Everybody's life had become everybody's business, and what a loss to society that Cagney refuses to play along.

Want Nothing – that is the title of Cagney's Pamphlet on Life. Subtitle: Live with your lot.

There are so many headlines, every day so many new headlines that litter what used to be 'news' papers, saying exactly what they said yesterday: some new way of preaching 'open up'. Somebody has redefined 'emotionally healthy' for the nation, but Cagney's in-built dictionary doesn't agree.

A man, a MAN, should have basic needs that can be paid for with a twenty. Only then will they always be met. A MAN should never let his weaknesses wear him, or expose himself to the ridiculous banality of 'self-improvement'. A MAN is a MAN at birth, and that should be good enough. Most importantly, a MAN should know when to shut up.

Cagney's only weakness is monkey nuts. He likes the routine, the crack between his fingers, the bits that fall away. Everywhere he goes he leaves a trail of shells. It drives people crazy, and although he thinks about giving them up, that's as good a reason not to as any.

He searches the internet occasionally for the nutritional value of the monkey nut, hasn't found it yet thank God, but is afraid he might stop ageing at forty, live to one hundred, and become the Monkey Nut Miracle Marvel Man.

The sound of footsteps on the solitary flight of stairs that lead to his office signal the arrival of somebody with size twelve feet. Hopefully his secretary will stop them coming into his office. He'll have to hire a secretary first, of course.

'For fuck's sake . . .' he swears, under his breath this time. He just can't find a man to take on the job, and a woman would end up crying if he didn't bring her muffins on a Friday, or throw a party every time she had her roots done.

The door swings open and a human Labrador bursts in. 'Boss!'

Cagney stares blankly at the smile that greets him, and says nothing. The new arrival continues to smile. He is wearing communist khakis and a polo shirt, a jumper is tied around his shoulders in a Fabulous Five idiotic let's-grab-a-dog-and-a-picnic-and-find-ourselves-a-dead-body way, and he stands, arms outstretched in greeting, as if years have passed since last they met. His name is Howard. They spend far too much time together for Cagney's liking.

'You call, I come running!'

'You'd think I'd learn not to call.'

'I got your nuts!' Howard winks, and slings a bag on the desk.

'Does that explain your erection?' Cagney brushes the bag straight into his desk drawer, as Howard looks down at his crotch to double-check Cagney is joking. Satisfied that he is not actually sporting wood, he grins and props himself, full of beans and life and marrow, on the edge of Cagney's desk.

'Did I ask for a lap dance?'

'Invading your space, boss, duly noted.' But Howard doesn't move.

'I won't pay you for it, even if you strip. Especially if you strip.'

'If you'd get another buggering chair in here, Cag, I

wouldn't have to sit on the desk! Nope, that came out wrong – I don't want a buggering chair, just a chair would be great – preferably one without straps to hold me down or a hole in the back for anal penetration.'

Howard slaps the desk and laughs loudly, but stands up as Cagney winces at the air of stupidity that fills the room like cheap heavy aftershave so much it gives him a headache. He almost manages to ignore his name's abbreviation.

'So, what's up, Mo' Fo'?' Howard crosses his arms, hugging himself, and leans back slightly, chin in the air.

'Howard, you're from Fulham. It's not the hood.'

'I'm still trying it out, seeing how it hangs on me . . . my nizza.'

'Will you be singing "Mammy" later?' Cagney mumbles, but Howard doesn't hear, as he raps quietly to himself. Cagney catches the odd 'fuck', the odd 'whore', and something about being 'straight out of Compton'. Cagney thinks hard to remember how old Howard is, and when he realises it is twenty-four, he closes his eyes. Was he this foolish fifteen years ago, this blind, stupid, idiotic and pointless? This impressionable, dull, random, inane? This vulnerable? Cagney can't remember a time when he felt differently from the way he feels now, and although he is the last person to claim his life has any kind of point, he has surely never been as disposable as Howard. He remembers the days of polite conversation, of small talk, of respect and integrity. He has never tried to 'rap'. Making swear words rhyme has apparently become an art form. He racks his brain, searching for something, anything pure. He finds the Indian Ocean lapping at a secluded beach, and he clutches on . . . the swell of rage subsides. Cagney opens his eyes half a minute later: a grinning Howard stares back at him.

'Finding your happy place again, boss?' Howard winks for the second time in five minutes.

'Fetching as it is, Howard, I think you might like to know that you have a brush sticking out of the back of your head.'

'I couldn't get a comb to stay.'

Cagney stares at him, incredulous. He actually pays this boy, pays him to live, to eat, to house himself. He employs him when what he should really do is have him put down. But work is work, and Cagney can't do the younger ones himself; he is old enough to be their father. He glances at his calendar, a subconscious habit that has crept up on him over the last year. September 28 – three months to go. To death or freedom, he doesn't care which. To forty. Countdown officially commenced nine months ago, but he's had one eye on that calendar for ten years.

Cagney visualises the half-empty bottle of Jack in his drawer, and the beaker he stole from a hotel in Brighton ten years ago that has never known water. He controls the urge to lunge for it.

What he knows is this: in the thirties, in the forties, a guy like him was permitted his idiosyncrasies, with no pressure to air dirty laundry or bandage over neurosis, or cure it somehow. The world deserved – no, it needed – its share of alcoholics and depressives, not that Cagney sees himself as either. But if he were a member of one of these underground clubs, he wouldn't feel ashamed. He lives in a dirty world, full of vicious tricks, and at some point you accept it. He doesn't greet the mornings with a smile any more. And so what? He's no daddy to a doting toddler, no strong husband to a soft sweet-smelling feminine bundle. He's nobody's hero.

Howard fidgets, and Cagney looks up to see him adjusting the brush that sticks out precariously from his short bushy blond hair, admiring himself and using Cagney's frame as a mirror. It is one of the only things that sits permanently on his desk, propped against an old coffee cup that has stuck itself spitefully to the wood. A roughly framed quote from a newspaper he'd read on a train nearly ten years ago, as the clock struck midnight, and he had turned thirty: 'Love is the delusion that one woman differs from another.'

'Put that down, and lose the brush, Basil.'

'It's Howard. Oh, Basil, Basil Brush! Boom boom! You're unusually sunny today, boss, and I think I know why! Stop me if I'm wrong, but could it have something to do with a new hero in town? Eh?'

'Oh, for Christ's sake, how have you heard about that already?'

'The waitress I shagged in Starbucks told me.'

'Is she a waitress in Starbucks, or did you shag her in Starbucks?'

'Both. Anyway, boss! I knew you had it in you! I wish I'd been with you, we could have caught him quicker. Now tell me everything that happened. Julie . . . Jenny said you went running off after this guy, and –'

'I don't want to talk about it.'

'Modesty, Cagney, that's what makes you the man that you are. But fuck that, tell me what happened.'

'Nothing happened. I heard some woman screaming, and that's that.'

'Fine. Don't tell me. Iuan will tell it better anyway.'

'Iuan knows?'

'Everybody knows! It's the talk of the village!'

'But how? It only happened twenty-four hours ago! And on a Sunday, for Christ's sake!'

'Come on, boss, don't be shy. Did you hit him?'

Cagney sighs. This is just what he knew would happen. He shouldn't have done anything, should have just sat at his desk and ignored it all. Now he's in for at least a week of people trying to talk to him, perfect strangers accosting him in the street to discuss it, the entire nosy-busy-body-caring-sharing-smile-on-its-face-village falling over itself to ask him how he feels and offer a thousand shoulders to cry on when he needs them. Then they'll congratulate each other for Cagney's heroics, believing they've finally turned him with their sweet sensitive carnival of Champagne liberalism. They got him in the end, that sour old hack always dressed in black, their village Grinch, not painting or singing or living the life glorious with the rest of them. They got him with their cheerful persistence, and forced him to care by trailing their lives for him to see and share, like multi-coloured ribbons flying from the backs of their push bikes. They got him, while shaking sad heads at their knowledge of life's problems, courtesy of that morning's *Guardian* newspaper. Yes, they'll think they got their man in the end, as Cagney got his, but theirs were rugby tackles of love. Cagney winces at the thought, and looks down at his desk, at the piece of paper with a hastily scrawled address and Friday's date written in big black letters. It will be awful. It will be the kind of dreadful appreciative small-talk-filled evening that could actually kill him. But how can he not go?

Plus that ridiculous girl will be there. Sunny Weston. What the hell was that? Something inexplicable had happened between them. In any other situation, with any other woman, he would have ignored her, or walked away. Ignored her *and* walked away. But something had made him argue with that girl. Her ridiculous perky face with a big black eye, her smiley 'wasn't it all a big adventure and there is no evil in the world that can't be fixed with a hug' demeanour. Her name, for Christ's sake! She hadn't seemed familiar, she didn't remind him of any of the women who had ruined his life. She had just stood there, babbling. Having done some-thing brave and admirable and positively manly she had undermined it all with some gibbering and blushing and turned everything sour. Yet when he shook her hand he had felt a wave of something unfamiliar, and he had felt truly uncomfortable.

Whatever it was, it is not worth thinking about. Other than that he is going to have to see her again, on Friday, and no doubt with some big dopey boyfriend propping her up, laughing at him. Cagney can't bear it. He will have to take somebody . . .

The brush falls out of Howard's hair and on to the floor with a bang.

'Bugger. Ah well, for the best.'

Cagney shakes his head to clear the notion. Howard is not a dinner date option.

'Now, as charming as I find this moment we're sharing, Howard, we have a job to do.'

'Great!' Howard claps his hands together with enthusiasm, but Cagney ignores it and carries on.

'Jessica Fellows, nineteen, blonde, looks like a spender and a screamer, probably just the one hit needed, SW6, ten thirty.' Cagney checks his watch. 'I'll have to tell you the rest in the car.'

'Photo?'

'Here.' Cagney throws it across the desk and Howard whistles.

'Hello, Foxy!'

Cagney is already at the door. 'No time for masturbation, Howard. We have to go.'

Cagney takes the stairs two at a time, as Howard scuttles behind him.

'So this Jemima . . .'

'Jessica.'

'That's what I said. What's she been up to, the dirty rabbit?'

Cagney doesn't answer, as he swings the street door open

and just stops himself crashing into the side of a lorry at the last second, parked so closely to the door he is unable to get out.

'Jesus H. Christ!'

'I meant to tell you about that.' Howard slams into the back of him.

'How the hell did you get in?'

'Christian very kindly let me come through the shop.'

'How sweet of him. It's probably Christian's fucking truck!'

'A fucking truck, bloody good idea! Mobile.'

Cagney pivots and Howard jumps out of his way, following him to a door at the end of the corridor.

Snatching it open, he is orally bitch-slapped by a shrieking Barbra Streisand. Videos lie in piles on the floor and against the walls, in no discernible order. Signs hang from the ceiling, pinned to the walls, screaming in orange and purple 'Tom Hanks: Don't even ask!' and 'Rewind/don't rewind. Life's too short!' It is a video carnival. The garlands that hang down from the ceiling are straight off a Notting Hill float. It looks like Liberace's funeral. Cagney steps gingerly over huge plastic Buddhas that lie drunk and comatose, passed out across the floor, and marches towards a figure high-kicking in the middle of all of it, in a cropped yellow T-shirt and leather trousers, singing with his eyes closed. Somehow his split kicks and step ball changes manage to miss every paper rose and fuchsia peacock feather surrounding him.

Cagney stops suddenly, two feet from the chorus line, scared by the speed of the flying limbs. The dance doesn't stop, and eventually Cagney coughs, as gruffly as his surroundings allow.

'Don't rain on my parade, Cagney.' Christian, eyes still closed, performs a jazz jump that causes Cagney to flail backwards into a life-size Dolly Parton cardboard cut-out. Christian stops moving, stands perfectly still, and slowly opens his eyes.

'Have you bent Dolly?'

'She's fine.' Cagney brushes himself down quickly, and suspiciously eyes the two-dimensional wig and breasts behind him.

'Doesn't everything have to be bent in here, Chris?'

Howard bounds forward to check out Dolly's cardboard breasts, and Christian raises his eyes to heaven, and whispers to Cagney, 'Stupid as a stick.'

Cagney nods twice.

'Cagney, can I just enquire, why the interruption? You can see it's display day, and I've already had that dog without a leash bounding through here this morning.' Christian gestures with his eyes towards Howard, who is pretending to squeeze Dolly's assets.

'Sorry, the sedatives aren't working, but I'm trying him on arsenic. You only have yourself to blame, anyway – there's a bloody great van parked outside my entrance.'

Christian grabs at a remote control and Barbra stops shrieking. Cagney exhales with relief.

'Well, Cagney, a real man can always find a way in or out, but that's by the by.' Christian winks at him, and in reply Cagney sighs, and checks his watch. 'Look, I'm sorry, I know it's a big sodding nuisance, but I thought it would be gone by now. It's the Buddhas – they had to come by special delivery from Bulgaria, and now the driver has scuttled off for a lard sandwich. But it'll be gone by the time you get back, I swear.'

'Swear on the cardboard.' Cagney gestures with his head towards the life-size cut-out.

Christian gasps in mock shock. 'Don't call her that – she'll hear you!'

Cagney raises his eyes to heaven in exasperation.

Christian smiles. 'I swear. I swear on Dolly and Barbra and Sandra Bullock! The truck will be gone in half an hour.'

'Thank you.' Cagney nods his head, and looks around. 'So what's this week?'

Christian claps his hands and jumps once. 'Bolly Dollywood! I thought of it in the bath! I've got *Nine to Five* next to *The Guru*, next to *Lagaan*. Honestly, I know I'm wasted here – I mean if I didn't own it, that is. But what can we do but juggle life's balls?' Christian smiles, but stops talking, staring at Cagney intently. 'How are you, Cagney?'

'Peachy.' Cagney doesn't smile.

'Really? Because I heard . . . you know, about your uncharacteristic act of bravery yesterday morning – although what you were doing in the office at eight a.m. on a Sunday I don't know. It must have affected you, and if you haven't cried yet, you will. It's the shock, it can be delayed.'

'If it helps I can tell you I'm welling up right now.'

'Stop it, Cagney. Stupid little jokes instead of conversation, not giving a straight answer to anything – there are a thousand self-help books with your name on, and you're not buying any of them!'

'If I talked about my feelings you'd know I had some.'

'Don't be a fool, Cagney. The world's moved on, and you must too. This hard-man act you're projecting isn't convincing anyone. It's so 1987.'

'I'll have you know I'm up for Best Male in a Non-supportive Role. And I intend to win.'

'You need to talk. It's good to talk. Like in the advert! You used to go out, Cagney! Occasionally, to the pub – I mean albeit on your damn own, but at least it was slightly social. I don't think I've seen you with anybody but stupid, stupid Howard or Iuan for months, years even. And that's no way to live! You need to get out, let your hair down. Maybe the odd femalia?'

'Is that one of these new sexual diseases?'

'Women, Cagney. I mean Women!'

'Christian, I meet women every day, and you're right, they are all odd.'

'Well, I know that but then breasts don't hoist my mast. But, Cagney, you are emotionally harboured in lonely straits: if you insist on giving boys the thumbs-down, then you are going to have to learn to be nicer to the opposite sex! This angry young man act only works for the young – you just look surly, and the bags under your eyes are as black as your mood. A quip here and there won't convince anybody that really cares that you're happy, Cagney.'

'I'm scared of laughter lines.'

'You're scared full stop, and that's the truth without a card or a bow.'

Cagney bristles, and checks his watch again. 'Look, I've just been busy. How about you? Any special . . . someone round at the moment?'

'No, no lucky boy right now, just some interesting possibilities, but bless you for risking the hernia and asking, Cagney. You know me: footloose, commitment free. You should try it . . . you might like it.'

'I don't have your gaydar.'

'I'm not talking about men, Cagney. No self-respecting homosexual would have you with your moods. But women, Cagney – girls, if you like. Speaking of which, I hear there was a Supergirl in your Superman scenario yesterday.'

'Sunny Weston.'

'Yes! I knew I knew her! She comes in here, rents some lovely films. I call her desperately shrinking Susan – you know she must have lost stones and stones in the last year. She's practically disappeared. Not that she didn't have it to lose, but you have to admire that kind of commitment.'

'What do you mean, she was fat?'

'Huge! Big as a bus!'

'She didn't seem . . . I mean she didn't look fat.'

'Well, no, not now, Cagney, that's what I'm telling you. That girl has obviously been on some kick-arse Nazi regime diet, and we're not talking Rosemary Conley and prancing about with a tin of baked beans in your hands. I mean in a year, Cagney, she is half the woman she was. Impressive, no?' Christian mocks an Italian accent, and Cagney finds himself hugely irritated.

'Diets are for fools.'

'Now, Cagney, that is unfair. I personally am always on a diet, as you well know, and you are just lucky that that whiskey hasn't hit your hips . . . yet. So she was the one who got the kiddie back?'

'Yes, well, she was on the floor when I saw her, but the kid was with her, and . . . you know her then? She's local?'

'Yes, lives by the Gardens. Very smiley; I like her. She has eyes like Judy Garland. I think she has hidden pain, Cagney, and that's the best thing about a woman in my book. Like Oprah. Or any of the alcoholics – Marilyn . . . Sue-Ellen . . .'

'Women are all the same. There is no best or worst.'

'Glass of bitter for one, Cagney?'

'A lifetime of reality, Christian.'

'Well, I like her. She looks like she needs cuddling.'

'Cuddling? Gagging, more like – she was screaming at me outside the police station for a good ten minutes. If she was soft before she sure as hell isn't now.'

'You're being unkind, Cagney, I know it. I'm sure you must have provoked her, or been mean. And in which case, good on her, I like them feisty!'

'You don't like them at all!'

'No, now that's the irony – I love women, I just don't

92

want to manhandle them. And you loathe them, for all their fluffy loveliness, but they are the only ones that get your juices going. Life's a bitch, ain't it? Anyway, if she made your blood boil, Cagney, it's probably only because your penis was refusing it entry, you've been celibate for so long. There is a fine line between love and hate, Cagney – maybe you've met your match.'

'There was no match, just a lot of hot air. She did nothing more than irritate me.'

Christian raises his eyes and tuts.

'Look, Christian, when you've finished your psycho-analysis, I have a favour to ask.'

Christian mock gasps and throws a hand over his mouth. Cagney stares at him dully until he stops.

'Fine. What do you need?'

'I've been invited to . . . I mean I have to go to this thing. And I have to take somebody with me . . . and I was wondering if you could, you know, come along. It's going to be hell. I need the support.'

'Cagney, are you asking me out on a date?' Christian eyes Cagney seriously, before a smile breaks across his face.

'Don't be so fucking ridiculous, and if you're going to make a big bloody song and dance about it let's forget I said anything.'

'No! No way, you are not getting out of it that easily. I will come with you, to . . . what is it exactly?'

'It's a dinner thing. A dinner *party*, I suppose.'

'Wonderful! I love them! Where, who, why? Is there a theme – tell me it's fancy dress! I have a fabulous Carmen Miranda . . .'

'Christ, no. No, it's just a dinner, at the kid's house.'

'What kid? I don't understand.'

'The kid, the parents of the kid, the one that got . . . you know . . . snatched.'

Christian's face drops, and he suddenly looks his age, which is only a year older than Cagney. He is so animated all of the time, it gives him a youthful air that Cagney just doesn't have – not that he cares; he's not about to start wearing sailor shirts and tight jeans to grab hold of thirty-five again.

'Oh, Cagney, that's fucking awful. Tell me you are joking.'

'No, I'm afraid not.'

'Don't go.'

'I said I would.'

'Why? What in God's name possessed you to say you would go to something so terrible? The first invitation you accept in years is this? Do you just love the pain, Cagney?'

'I don't know, but that Sunny Weston was there, and she said she would go first, and then I would have just looked rude . . .'

'You always look rude! Rude is what you do best! Why change now?'

'I don't bloody know, alright? But before I knew it I had said I would. And I was scared the kid's mother would start crying again.'

'Cagney, in all seriousness, it's plainly an obscene idea. Talk about post-traumatic syndrome – you'll be suicidal by the end of it.'

'I've said yes now, I have to. And she'll be there, probably with some stupid rugby-playing thug of a boyfriend . . .'

'Oh no, no boyfriend.'

'How do you know that?'

'Because I know, Cagney. She never comes in here with a man. Plus she was big as a house before. No, she's a single girl. And a thought occurs . . .'

'No.'

'If she is going to be on her own . . .'

'No.'

'And you are going to be on your own . . .'

'No.'

Christian crosses his arms and takes a step back, eyeing Cagney slyly. 'I don't think I should come. I think you have feelings for this girl.'

'Are you insane? She's practically half my age!'

'Oh, Cagney, she must be thirty, and you're not even forty yet, although I know we are officially counting down. That's a good gap. I was dating a thirty-year-old recently – Brian, he was still young enough to be fun. I love that generation. They're just so . . . carefree and pretty.'

'I'm not interested, in her, or the goddamn dinner, or any of it, but I have to go, and you have to come with me, to stop me gassing myself in their Aga.'

'Let me think about it.'

'Fine. Time's up. Friday at six forty-five. I'll meet you here. We have to go. Howard!'

They both turn to face Howard, who is cautiously licking a flower garland. They mutter an incredulous 'Jesus' simultaneously.

'Come on, Howard, for Christ's sake.'

'Nice T-shirt – can I get one of those?' Howard stops by Christian, appraising his yellow chest that reads 'Be Gentle Yentl'.

'You concern me.' Christian shakes his head at Howard, and turns, disappearing under a sea of paper flowers.

Cagney is already in the car, revving the engine, when Howard jumps in, wanting to chat.

'Christian's great, isn't he?'

'He speaks very highly of you.'

'He's old, and gay, and yet really funny.'

'Strange, isn't it?'

'I'm just saying, not often you find a sausage jockey who doesn't want to, you know, get in your boxers.'

95

'You're a very attractive man, Howard – who can blame them?'

'Have you ever tried it?' Howard looks at Cagney curiously, actually expecting an answer.

'Have I ever tried what?'

'Up hill gardening. Seriously, Cagney, it's a valid question. I haven't myself.'

'Howard, you went to public school.'

'No, now you see, that's a myth. Didn't see anything when I was there – no soggy biscuits, nothing. And my brothers swear the same thing. Could have done with the excitement, to be honest. So is that a no, then?'

'Yes.'

'Yes, it's a no? Or yes, you have tried it? I mean, I've never seen you with a woman who's not business and you don't even enjoy those. It would explain things . . . and you're in good shape, for an old bloke. And Christian, he's like your only mate, apart from me and Iuan.'

'Howard, you work for me, as does Iuan. You are not my friends.'

'OK then, just Christian. I mean, you guys have known each other for years. Ever been any lingering looks, you know, a little bit of Boy's Own sexual chemistry over a banana daiquiri? You can tell me. I won't like leave my job or anything. I'm very PC.'

'Permanently challenged?'

Howard body-pops with his arms and grins, and Cagney sighs for the twentieth time in an hour. They sit in silence as Cagney manoeuvres the BMW with understated speed around women drivers in Land Rovers, before putting his foot down.

'It's an eighty-pound fine for driving in the bus lane, Cag. You might want to pull over.'

'You should have told me that before I changed lanes. I'll take it out of your wages.'

'Not again!'

After five minutes of blissful silence, Howard remembers the conversation they were having.

'So?'

'So you're thinking of not talking for the rest of the journey?'

'Good one, but no. So have you tried the man thing?'

Cagney exhales deeply, and stares out of the window as they sit in traffic. Finally he turns to Howard, who pants expectantly for a juicy answer.

'No.' And then, as Cagney thinks aloud, 'But I bet it's a lot easier.'

'I very much doubt that!' Howard grimaces, and then is momentarily diverted by a couple of teenage girls leaning on railings. Before Cagney can stop him, Howard winds down his window, and is shouting, 'Is there grass on the wicket? Are you ready for cricket?'

'Tosser!' The girls make hand gestures at the car as the lights turn amber and Cagney steps on the accelerator.

Howard laughs heartily, as Cagney shakes his head.

'What were we saying?' Howard looks perplexed.

'You were explaining the rules of metaphysics.' Cagney reaches into the glove compartment with one hand, to pull out a file.

'Come on, Cag, we're bonding! You were saying you weren't gay, but it must be easier if you are. More painful, though! Jesus! Can you imagine, I mean, up the shitter! My God, my eyes are actually watering!'

'Howard, we have a job in ten minutes and it's a fair bet that you don't know what you're doing. Take the file.' Cagney thrusts it into Howard's lap.

'OK, one last thing and I'll shut up. You don't like boys, you don't like girls – what do you like? Jesus, should I keep Jenson out of the office from now on?'

Jenson, Howard's dog, is the smelliest, most overly affectionate, loudest animal Cagney has ever encountered. And it is the size of a Shetland pony.

'Am I sexually attracted to women? Yes. Do I like them? No. Do I trust them? No. Do they possess any logic or reason? No. Do they cause anything but pain with their vanity and self-centred conceit? No. Do they just want to fuck with men's minds and ruin our lives? Yes.' Cagney turns to face Howard, who is grinning at him stupidly. 'Have you been eating M&Ms again?'

'This is so exciting.' Cagney can barely make out Howard's whisper.

'Driving still gets you worked up, eh? You can stick your head out of the window if you want. Do it now, there's a truck coming.'

'No! You, and the fat-girl-gone-thin – at the dinner party. You are completely going to fall in love!'

'Have you lost your mind?'

'On the contrary, dear Cagney, it's perfect. The bitter and cynical old private eye, the ugly duckling that's become a swan – it's all going to turn out brilliantly.'

'I am not a private eye.'

'In the movies you would be.'

'Your daydreams are even more special when you keep them to yourself.'

'Cag, honestly, mate, it always happens that way. It's destiny. Just remember me when you need a godfather for your first son.'

'Howard, read the file, look at the photo, remember her name . . .'

'Fine, fight fate if you want to, but it's going to happen. Some sweet misunderstood young thing, some soft lovely vision of innocence and purity, and you saved a child's life together! She's going to melt your heart, Cagney, just remember where you heard it first, and then give me a pay rise.'

'What's her name?'

Howard opens his mouth to speak, but nothing comes out.

'The job – what's her name?'

'Bugger!' Howard starts skim-reading the file, and Cagney smiles slightly to himself.

He knows what life has in store for him. He's been around the block and back again, parked, and put money in the meter. No young girl is going to turn his eye these days, no soft something with breasts that bounce as if conducted by his own personal baton. The fight has gone out of him.

Cagney sits in the BMW, eyes fixed on his rear-view mirror. She is due to show any time. A red door opens in a two-million-pound house ten feet behind his bumper, and a twentysomething wire frame of designer labels and sunglasses emerges, swinging a bag full of credit cards paid for by a husband who is a little more suspicious than he used to be, a little less of a fool.

She is a blonde, a blonde to distract a Catholic priest from his altar boys. Cagney sighs, tired, focused, bored. As she struts towards her convertible, her skinny hips swing so hard he listens out for the sound of bones slapping. Cagney spots a twentysomething guy walking towards her reading his newspaper too high, not paying attention to where he is going. Cagney punches a number quickly into his phone, and the collision comes as the blonde, Jessica, reaches into her bag for her mobile. Cagney punches his phone again, and the ringing stops. They are smiling now, laughing, the guy is on the pavement picking up the contents of Jessica's bag. Cagney watches in his mirror as she dusts herself off. The guy dabs at the coffee he has been carrying, which drenches his polo shirt – you can see his chest through it. Jessica points towards her door, and the guy follows her up the steps. The door closes behind them both, and Cagney moves. Howard's not one for subtlety.

The BMW bleeps locked as he walks towards the red door, camera tucked in his pocket. The wind whistles past him as he pulls the collar of his charcoal wool overcoat up around his ears, a man walking fast from A to B on one of the last days of September, nothing to see here. The temperature has dropped fifteen degrees overnight. He ducks down the side of the house and nobody notices.

Twenty minutes later Cagney sits back in the driving seat, watching the red door in his rear-view mirror. Howard emerges, and jogs down the steps of the house, turning to wave goodbye to the hand, arm, naked shoulder at the closing door. He saunters down the road and slips into Cagney's blind spot, before the passenger door rips open and the wind stabs into the car.

'Wow!'

'I don't want to know.'

'She was like, really professional. I'd say that girl's got some kind of paid experience, if you know what I'm saying. My sweet Lord.'

Howard whistles, impressed, in the passenger seat, as Cagney pulls the car out.

'Can I put the radio on?'

'Have I ever said yes before?'

'No, but –'

'There's your answer.'

'But I need to relax, Cagney. I've got the afterglow! Have you got a cigarette?'

'Yes.'

'Can I have one?'

'Have I ever said yes before?'

'Honestly, Cag, been taking those social pills again?'

Cagney waits at the crossroads for a people carrier packed with kids to pull out in front of him.

'That was a good one, though, Cagney. I'll give you that one for free. I mean obviously not, Cagney – I still need to get paid – but figuratively speaking, I'd give you that one for free. If I could afford it.'

Howard gives up with a look of frustration as Cagney ignores him, concentrating on the road. They sit in silence, but for the steady hum of suburban London as they pass at fifty miles an hour. The sun shines unexpectedly as Cagney steers the BMW west along Chiswick High Road. Old leaves on the trees swing delicately above their heads, like twenty-pound notes as they flutter in the breeze.

'Are we driving straight back to the office, Cag?'

'You can walk if you like.'

'No, I meant can we stop off at the supermarket first, if I'm quick?'

'Have I ever stopped for you before?'

'No'

'Do you just really like hearing me say it?'

Howard sighs, and starts to rap quietly, as Cagney winces almost imperceptibly. But the rapping needs to be stopped, and Cagney has something on his mind.

'You're not supposed to have sex with them, Howard, you know that. I could lose my licence.'

'Cagney, I'm shocked. I did no such thing!'

'I was taking the photos! Do you think I just point the camera in the general direction, then cover my eyes in case I see anything bad? I have to look, Howard. Believe me, it doesn't fill me with fun, but I have to. And I saw you.'

'What you saw, boss, was nothing more than a little harmless fellatio. The little fella was out before I could stop her, and I was scared to interrupt her flow. I have what I think is a very reasonable fear of teeth, in that area. Did you get any good ones?'

'What?'

'Photos.'

'I got enough.'

'Can you get a second set? I'd like one for my wallet.'

'No more sex, no more blow jobs. A kiss is all we need. Stop pissing about. I'm not your pimp.'

Cagney swings the car off the South Circular past the Gardens' wall.

'Is Iuan in today?'

'If he's not he's sacked. And that truck better have moved as well.'

Cagney indicates left towards the station. The truck has indeed gone.

Christian stands outside Screen Queen admiring his handiwork. The life-size Dolly is front and centre, surrounded by the Buddhas and garlands. It looks as if a gay bomb has exploded in the window. Cagney swings the car down an alley, parks, and turns off the engine.

'Come on, Cagney, you have to at least admit that it was a good one – the coffee, the paper – it was seamless!' Howard jumps out of the car. Cagney walks back up the alley towards the late morning bustle of Kew village, and Howard strolls behind him.

'It was heavy-handed, and obvious, and you've used it six times in the last month. Every time you ask me what I think, and every time I tell you the same thing. If she had half a brain she would have seen it for the set-up that it was. Luckily for us, Jessica is as stupid as she looks.' Cagney doesn't glance back, but talks into the wind, as Howard strains to hear.

'I use it because it works. It's bloody perfect, you miserable old bugger. Besides, you only ever give me the stupid ones, anyway.'

'Like attracts like. I don't fight that golden rule.'

'You wouldn't have liked her, Cagney – too modern for your blackened old heart. She was quite worldly, for a nineteen-year-old, if you know what I'm saying. It's going to take a real angel to get to your soft centre.'

'As I said, like attracts like.'

Cagney doesn't follow Howard through the agency door but heads instead towards the front of the video shop, where Christian is standing with two very old Kew men in 1940s suits, who are smiling at the window with him. Cagney stops and listens a few feet away, as Christian effervesces.

'You see, it's the juxtaposition of East and West. It's the Buddha, the Eastern idol, and Dolly, the Western idol. Plus you get your second rental for half price – it's art meet commercialism. It's the Zeitgeist, don't you think?' Christian turns towards the two octogenarians, with their tweed jackets and moustaches, for a response.

'I flew a Zeitgeist in '43, I think . . . You know it costs me over forty pounds to fill up the Daimler at Sainsbury's now? Shocking. The world's gone to hell.'

The three of them stand and nod, before one of the old men starts coughing furiously. The other ignores him, common as it is to see his sidekick fighting for breath, expecting him to drop dead any day.

'Are you married?' the non-cougher enquires of Christian.

'No.' Christian is bewitched by the window, and answers absent-mindedly, slowly shaking his head.

'Any plans?'

Christian turns to face him, and registers the question. 'I'm homosexual.' Christian pronounces every syllable in the word slowly.

'Ah yes, you did tell me that. Mind like a sieve these days. I remember now.'

The coughing old man has stopped, and addresses his friend. 'Albert, this is the queer fellow. God, man, your mind has gone.'

'I know, I know.'

'It must be hard.' Christian smiles and nods sympathetically. 'Well, lovely chatting but I have to get on, Albert, William.' Christian nods sweetly at them both.

'Absolutely. Cheerio.' The old pair turn in slow motion and inch away, as Albert barks loudly, 'Damn shame.'

'Did I buy bread?' William replies.

Cagney walks towards Christian, trying to think of a positive thing to say about the window. Howard was right about something for the first time in years: Christian is Cagney's only friend, and much as he'd like to, he shouldn't alienate everybody. He needs a plus one.

'It's . . . colourful.'

'It's one of my best.'

'Don't they bother you?' Cagney gestures towards the old boys, slowly moving away at snail's pace, still shouting at each other.

'Goodness no, they're thoroughly harmless, and bloody charming. I'm not a fool, Cagney. They are eighty; you went to prison in their day.'

'If you say so.'

Christian carries on staring at his window, and addresses Cagney without looking at him. 'Cagney, I'd be spending my time at Her Majesty's pleasure if we'd stopped moving on fifty years ago, and you just have to put up with people asking how you are, and telling you that you drink too much, which you do. So fair's fair, Cagney. I think you can handle it.'

'Whatever you say.'

'The truck's gone.' Christian nods in the direction of Cagney's door.

'Right.' Cagney straightens up and walks away.

'Cagney,' Christian calls out to him, and Cagney shouts, 'Yes?' without turning round. 'You are allowed to stop and talk. I wasn't hurrying you along.'

'Right,' Cagney shouts again over his shoulder, as he pushes the door open, and flies up the stairs two at a time.

Kew is where Cagney has chosen to hide for all these years. Tucked away from the bustle of London life, yet still close enough for the work the city brings. It is a sanctuary. It was his saviour, in a way. Living in the centre of the city had driven him down and into himself, behind a locked door and a bottle. He doesn't know what it is that keeps him in the village, but it is safe, it is home, for the next three months at least; for the last ten years. And the blossom on the trees lifts his heart a little, and he can stride through the Gardens and be alone in a matter of minutes, and relax without prying eyes. Something about Kew and its implied intimacy, without actually having to be intimate, has kept him going.

Upstairs in the office Howard is doubled up with laughter, supported by a solitary filing cabinet to stop him from falling, while Iuan, dressed in a fluorescent orange track-suit, pretends to choke in Cagney's chair.

'Is that seat taken?' Cagney strides around the desk and stands expectantly by the side of Iuan, who eventually moves, grudgingly. When he stands up you can see that Iuan is six feet three, with short, spiked auburn hair, and a long face that draws horse jokes from his friends. His nose and ears are a little too large, his mouth a little too wide. He looks like a caricature of a better-looking self, his features stretched just out of attractiveness.

'What was the funny?' Cagney asks as he sits down and

instinctively reaches for his drink drawer, hand on the knob, before he remembers he has company, reaching instead for his ever-ready nuts.

Howard explains. 'Iuan just saw a man choking on a piece of garlic bread in the pub – show Cagney the impression, it's classic.'

Iuan resumes the faux choking, clutching at his throat in mock alarm, but is cut short.

'That's charming. Is that why the ambulance is parked outside?'

'It is. I was on my way out when it happened. I didn't catch the ending.' Iuan's accent is soft, and still clearly rings of the Valleys. The tone of his voice can confuse the unpractised listener, who may concentrate on the lyrical sounds he makes, and not the words he utters. It is widely accepted as the reason that he manages to have sex with as many women as he does. By the time they actually register what he is saying, it is invariably too late.

'So you don't know if he died or not?' Cagney asks, flicking through a file.

'No, I had to get back here. Knew you were on your way back, didn't I.'

'Ah, the integrity.' Cagney slams the file shut and looks up at them both. 'Someone needs to get this morning's photos developed, Howard, and somebody else needs to phone in this week's ads, Iuan.'

'Shall I do the photos?' Howard offers.

'That would seem to be the plan.'

Scooping up the camera from the desk, he bounces out of the door.

Iuan reaches inside the filing cabinet for a sheet of paper containing a list of phone numbers. 'The same as last week, is it?' Iuan runs his eye over the list.

'No, ditch *The Times* – women callers. Go with the men's,

the cars, the computers, and the *Telegraph* and *FT*. That's enough.'

'Same as usual?'

'Yep.'

Cagney tears open the plastic bag carefully, and grabs a handful. He sits back in his chair, closes his eyes and cracks a nut in his palm, as Iuan pulls the phone towards his side of the desk, places the piece of paper firmly down, sucks on the pen between his teeth, and dials the first number.

'Hello, yes, I'd like to extend my advert in the miscellaneous section. Name C. James. One hundred and twenty-six characters with punctuation again . . . Yes. Same again, exactly . . . I can, if you want me to, my lovely.' Iuan begins to read aloud, slowly and painstakingly enunciating each word in his lilting Welsh accent, sounding like a local comic reading a sexist joke as the woman on the end of the line waits for the punchline.

SUSPICIOUS OF YOUR WIFE/GIRLFRIEND? CHEAP RATES FOR 100% RELIABLE INFORMATION. WE'LL SHOW YOU WHAT SHE'S DOING. MALE CLIENTS ONLY. PHONE 8AM–10PM. And he adds the telephone number.

Cagney recites the ad in his head as Iuan reads. It has been the same wording for nearly ten years. The phone number has changed a couple of times, he dropped in the word 'girlfriend' after a year when he realised that long-term lovers were just as worthy of suspicion as wives. 'Male clients only' was added after the first week, when sixty per cent of his calls came from women. He still receives the odd female call, but he has his reply memorised as well: 'We only work on behalf of men, and we don't deal in same-sex relationships either. It's not prejudice, I just don't have any females on my staff . . . No, unfortunately I don't know of an agency that does deal on behalf of women. Maybe you should try a private investigator. I can give you a number, or you can check in the Yellow Pages.' Hang up.

Occasionally some hormonal type on a tirade would shout at him about sexism in this day and age, and he would bite his tongue, and not point out that 'this day and age' was the problem. But it only served to prove his point, and ultimately reconvince him that it was more trouble than the cash it was worth to work for women. That was the deal. He has been accused of misogyny many times over the years, mostly by women who come looking for him after some weak-willed dollop of a husband has admitted the set-up and pointed the finger in Cagney's direction. And every time he explains that the word 'misogynist' is bandied about far too recklessly.

Cagney doesn't hate women. He just doesn't like them. Some less than others . . .

Iuan makes half a dozen more calls, and finally hangs up the receiver.

Cagney opens his eyes.

'Are we having our staff meeting today, Cagney, because if so, is it possible to do it soonish? I've got my Dynamic Yoga class in an hour.'

'I still can't believe they let you in.'

'The yoga is the dynamic bit.'

'So you said. Tell me again, how exactly can touching your toes be considered dynamic?'

'Boss, it's much more than that. It's about tapping into your chakra; it's about finding inner peace. But yes, it's true, it does make me remarkably supple. I can get both my legs behind my head now, Cagney. Do you want to see?' Iuan drops to the floor, and grabs both of his ankles.

Cagney starts reading the file in front of him, ignoring the painful grunts coming from the front of his desk. Two minutes later Iuan is swearing under his breath, and Cagney looks up to see a foot pinned behind Iuan's increasingly red neck.

'Shit it, I'm stuck. I should have warmed up. This has never happened before, Cagney. I'm generally very limber. CHRIST!' Iuan cries out, and starts to breathe heavily on the floor, unable to move. 'Cagney, could you possibly give me a hand?'

Cagney looks up again as Howard bursts into the office.

Howard halts, and beams at the scene before him. 'Oi oi! Want me to step outside again, boys?'

Cagney is looking back down at his file, unimpressed, when he hears Iuan's left ankle snap.

'Howard, see if that ambulance is still outside.'

FOUR

Addicted

My therapist has made us coffee, which is unusual. Normally his assistant, Penny, brings in the drinks. She has put full-fat milk in my coffee on five separate occasions, and each time I have been forced to ask her to remake it. I wonder whether she does it under my therapist's instruction, to chart my reaction, or to see if I will drink it at least, but every time I send it back. Of course, she just might not be that bright.

'Where's Penny?'

'She has the day off today.'

'Not sacked then?'

'No. She doesn't work on Thursdays.'

'Why not?'

'She's part time.'

'Why can't you see me next Monday?'

'I'm going on holiday.'

'Anywhere nice?'

'Marrakesh.'

'Lovely. This seems a bit much, though, two sessions in one week. I feel like I was only here five minutes ago.'

'I thought you might like to talk about the incident before I went away.'

'But I'm seeing you on Tuesday, right? I'm only missing a day . . .'

'Nonetheless . . .'

'Ignore that for a second because I have some news . . . about Adrian . . . We are kind of a couple . . .'

My therapist stares at me to go on.

'I've seen him a few times recently. Seen a lot more of him than I expected, to be honest. I didn't tell you . . . well, I don't know why. Because I thought it would just be temporary, and that he was drunk, and then we'd have to talk about that as well, and it would just make me feel bad. Anyway, on Monday night he said "you and me", like we are a couple . . . What do you think of that?'

'What do you think of that?'

'I asked you first.'

'I don't have an opinion.'

'Oh.'

'So what do you think of that, Sunny?'

'I don't know.'

He has taken the wind out of my sails. I thought he might be excited for me. I thought I might borrow some of that excitement for myself. He doesn't seem that interested.

'How have you been, apart from that? Do you feel ready to talk about the incident yet? On Monday you said you felt ready, but we ran out of time.'

'No, I've forgotten all about that.'

'You haven't thought about it at all?'

'Not really. Only that . . . Jesus . . . I have to go to this hateful bloody dinner party tomorrow night.'

'Dinner party?'

'I thought I told you. The child's mother asked me round to dinner, to say thank you. Isn't that awful?'

My therapist looks momentarily alarmed, but regains his

composure. 'It's a strange decision, although I am still not sure exactly what happened.'

I pull my legs up in front of my chest, and yawn from exhaustion. I am not used to my sleeping pattern being broken by a wandering hand in the middle of the night. My body clock is still adjusting.

'OK, I feel like you are going to go on about this until I tell you, so this is it: I'm having a coffee and this woman turns up with her three kids, all boys, and they are playing about outside Starbucks, and she is distracted by the youngest one, and this man comes along . . .' I pause. 'And this man comes along and picks one of them up, the one called Dougal.' I gulp. 'And he starts walking away with him. But the mother, who is beside herself, of course, has to look after the other two kids, so I run after him.' I stop and take a deep breath.

My therapist is looking at me blankly, waiting for me to continue.

'I don't really know why I did it, other than I couldn't just sit back and watch while a child got abducted, so I ran after him. And I caught him, but then he kicked me.'

'He kicked you in the face?' My therapist looks appalled.

'What? No! Christ, how awful! Why would you think that?'

'The black eye?'

'Oh, right. God, I thought you were just getting carried away! No. I forgot – he punched me first.'

'He assaulted you, twice?'

I grimace. 'I don't like the word "assault". It sounds evil, or sexual, like "sexual assault". But anyway, I managed to get Dougal off him, and that was that.'

'How did you do that?'

'I just kind of launched myself at his back . . . Jesus, that was stupid . . . I didn't really think it through at the time.' I gulp again.

'But they caught him?'

'Yes, well, there was this other guy who caught him.'

I picture Cagney James in my head, and I know that I have been blocking him out until now. I will see him tomorrow night, and it makes me feel . . . uncomfortable. It's a feeling that I can't quite put my finger on. If there was a gun at my head I'd call it nervous excitement, although that's not quite right either. It's like a life-changing exam that I can't wait to sit because I've studied and I think I might ace it, but simultaneously I know that I might choke on the night, and all of my studies will have been in vain. I feel that seeing him again is important, although I don't know why, given that he was abrasive and confrontational. I shouldn't be excited. No good can come of this dinner.

'He was strange.'

'The man who snatched the child?'

'No, well, yes, of course him, but I was talking about the man who caught him. I had a conversation with him afterwards, and it was just . . . peculiar, that's all.'

'Peculiar how?'

'I don't know.' I rake my fingers through my hair. 'It was like he knew me somehow, or I knew him, but he just made me angry. He started shouting at me. I don't think he likes women very much. I guess he must have fallen for a rotten apple somewhere along the line. Actually, he might be gay. I didn't think of that, but he was wearing a polo-neck sweater . . .'

'He made you feel angry?'

'Do straight men wear polo-necks? Not big chunky knit roll-necks, but polo-necks . . .'

'Angry how?'

'Do you own a polo-neck?'

'Angry how?'

'What? Oh, yes, we were shouting at each other, having

113

an argument about . . . God, I can't even remember what about. I just remember being so mad with him, when Dougal's mother turned up.'

'Was he angry as well?'

'He was horrible! Really insulting, for no reason.'

'Well, that might not be so strange: you might both have displaced your anger at the child snatcher on to each other, as you were both so involved.'

'Oh . . . maybe. Could be . . . I suppose. I was really angry . . . but . . . I don't know. Maybe that's it. I know I felt like I could kill him or something. I felt really passionately violent towards him!'

I laugh a short, sharp laugh, surprised at my own words. I haven't thought about it until now. That's a lie. I haven't let myself think about it. It has occurred to me, like a thought bubble popping in my head, a few times.

'Violent?'

'No, that's the wrong word. No, that's the right word! I felt violent in that I wanted to make him understand something, or just grab him and . . . just make him listen . . . I don't know . . . he seemed so determined that I was wrong, about something. I'm not sure what exactly. But I was wrong and he was right, that was the gist of it.'

My therapist turns and begins to write something on his pad. I take a sip of my coffee. Five minutes later I realise that my therapist is still writing and my coffee cup is empty.

'Working on your novel?'

My therapist smiles. 'Just some notes, for myself, for when I get back.'

'This is my time, though, right? I mean, I am paying for this time . . .'

'The notes are about you.'

'What do they say?'

'Just reminders of what you've said.'

'Oh, OK. Shall we talk about Adrian now?'

'Do you want to?'

'Not really, no. I don't know why I brought it up. Other than I don't know what to do. I've asked him to come to this dinner party with me tomorrow night. I think I should at least try and make it work.'

'You don't sound very enthused, Sunny, given the time we've spent discussing him in your sessions.'

'I know. It's typical. You pray for something so much, and then you stop praying, because you realise you don't really want it any more, and then it happens, and it's confusing. I don't know what I feel. It could be nothing more than vindication. It could still be love. I told you we need to go over that some more! If we'd had that sorted by now I wouldn't be so bloody mixed up.'

'I can't explain love to you, Sunny. It happens. You will know when you feel it.'

'I think you're wrong, but OK.'

'What about this other man?'

'Cagney. Cagney James. Isn't that the most ridiculous name you've ever heard?'

My therapist raises his eyes at me, suggesting that I can't possibly expect him to answer that question. I don't see why not. It's not as if I'll report him for unprofessional conduct for a little harmless bitching.

'What about Cagney James, Sunny?'

My therapist smiles when he says my name, and I feel fondly towards him. I know my name is atypical as well, but I'm used to it.

'There isn't anything to say. He was just this very rude, confrontational man, who made me rude in return.'

'Do you think what you have classified as rage might

115

have been some kind of electricity between the two of you?'

'Sorry?'

'Sexual electricity?'

I sit up very straight and cross my legs, and my arms. He raises his eyes at me.

'Have you lost your mind? Are you on Morrocan time already? He was horrible.'

'Horrible how?'

'He was dressed completely in black, for a start.'

My therapist eyes me up and down. I am dressed completely in black today.

'Yes, but it's fine for a girl. A man just looks like he wants to be Robert Palmer, or Jack Kerouac. Both bad looks.'

'I agree. You look nice today, by the way.'

'Sorry?' I have uncrossed my arms, but I cross them again. My therapist has never said anything like that before. I think he is strange on Thursdays. I am only ever coming on a Monday again.

'I said you look nice. How does that make you feel?'

'Oh, I get it. Can I take a compliment, et cetera, et cetera . . . Can we talk about Adrian again? I need to know what to do while you are away.'

'I can't tell you what to do with Adrian. Can you take a compliment?'

'Yes.' I whisper it.

'OK, you look nice today.'

'Stop saying that! I heard it the first time. You're being weird.'

'You can't just thank me for the compliment?'

'No, it's weird.'

'You think it has to mean something sexual? You think it must mean I am sexually attracted to you, and you aren't comfortable with sexual attraction, and therefore you can't take the compliment.'

'I've had sex with Adrian, three or four times, if you must know. I must be getting more comfortable with the sex thing. Four times.'

'And how did it feel when he told you that you looked nice?'

'He didn't.'

'How did it feel when he said "you and me", that you were a couple?'

'Like he should have asked me first.'

My therapist grabs for his pen, and I pull my legs up to my chest.

He stops writing and looks at me squarely. 'You begrudge Adrian for assuming you would want to be his girlfriend, and yet you've asked him to come to dinner with you tomorrow. Why have you done that?'

'I guess I thought I should . . . you know . . . they said I could bring somebody . . . I've never really had anybody to ask before. I thought I'd take advantage of it. That bit feels nice, at least – having somebody to take somewhere. Besides, I can't just have a whole truckload of feelings for somebody, and then they just drive off, and I don't have them any more. And Cagney will have somebody with him. I don't want to look like the only single girl at a swingers' night. I want to take somebody for a change.'

'Sunny . . .'

I always get hopeful when my therapist says my name like this, waiting for him to tell me what to do. And I always forget that he never does.

'Sunny, I think you might need to consider that your feelings for Adrian have passed. It may have been love, it may have been an elongated crush. It doesn't belittle what you felt at the time, it just means you don't feel that way now. And you might even find that you have feelings for Cagney

117

James, or they might be transferred feelings of protection, and gratitude, because of the incident, and the role that he played in it. But I would advise you to think about all of it while I am away.'

'Jesus! You'd better extend your ticket because that'll take me months!'

My therapist smiles at me.

'Fine, I'll think about it.'

'Good, now,' he checks his desk clock, 'we have another half an hour.' He looks surprised. It does feel like we have covered a lot. 'Well, we can talk about some of that now, unless there is anything else you'd like to go over?'

I run my hands through my hair, and inspect my manicure. Am I feeling as brave as I thought I might, when I decided this morning that I would bring this up?

'I thought we might talk about my diet,' I whisper.

'OK. What would you like to talk about specifically?'

'Well, first I'd like you to agree not to say at any point, "How does that make you feel?".

'Why?'

'Because! It's annoying. And exhausting. I'll make you a deal – if I know I feel something about whatever I'm saying, I'll just say it. How's that?'

My therapist smiles again. 'OK. Let's talk about your diet. And, for the record, I think this is a positive sign, you bringing it up, and I promise, for the next half an hour at least, not to ask you how you feel.'

'Good. Thank you.'

'So, why did you decide to diet?'

'I don't know really. It just started one day. I was bigger than I'd ever been, and bordering on depressed. And I just decided.'

'Why do you think you stuck to it, this time?'

'I ask myself the same thing. I'd tried before, but it never worked. I think I just found my willpower. It became like a cause or something. My cause. And my cause wasn't, you know . . . overseas work in Africa, or . . . helping the homeless – any of the good causes. It was to be thin. How's that for shallow?'

'"Cause" is an interesting word: why would you put it like that?'

'Because it suggests . . . a painful process. What's that quote: a cause is like champagne and high heels – one must be prepared to suffer for it?'

'And how did it take shape? How did you manage to keep focused? Remind me again how much you decided to lose?'

'Nine stones. I don't like saying that bit. It makes me feel like a freak.'

'And do you mind me asking how much further you have to go?'

'A little under two stones now.'

'Still that much?'

'I know it seems like a lot. But you haven't seen me naked.'

'Right.' My therapist gives a little cough. I have embarrassed him. It's the kind of reaction my dad would have to a young woman saying that to him. It makes me like him a little more.

'So how do you stay focused?'

'Well, to begin with, in the first couple of months, I don't know, it was hard. I just stopped myself from eating, somehow. I mean I didn't stop completely, I just changed what I ate. And the weight started to come off. Then I joined the gym. Nobody really noticed at first. I guess it was when people started to notice that I got really focused. I felt like I was winning.'

'What did people say?'

'It's not even what they said, it's how they'd look at me.

119

As I got thinner, well, it's like silent applause as you walk down the street, or run at the gym. These are things we are told to be proud of. And so I started to feel proud of myself, I suppose.'

'But what about your relationship with food – how did that change?'

'It didn't really. I was still thinking about food all the time. I am now, as we sit here. I'm thinking about what I'll eat for lunch, what I ate for breakfast, how long I spent at the gym this morning, which muscles I worked, how many calories I burnt, when I'll next go to the gym, what I'll weigh this week, what I weighed last week, what I'll weigh in a month's time, what I'll be able to wear then that I can't wear now . . .' My words trail off in embarrassment. It's the first time I've admitted this to anyone. 'So I am still obsessed with food. Just in a different way.'

'It sounds as if you find this shaming.'

I sit up straight. 'I do. It is, isn't it? So many people don't even think about what they eat. Why do I have to be constantly preoccupied with it? Do you know what is horrible – I mean this made me feel like . . . the lowest of the low. On Sunday, after the "incident" – ten minutes after it had happened, sitting in a police car going down to the station, to make a report on a big thing, a big, big deal that I had been involved in, do you know what was going on in my head? I was calculating the calories I had burnt chasing the Stranger down the alley.'

'How does that – sorry.'

'How does that make me feel? No, it's fine.' I can feel the tears in my eyes. I take a deep breath to try to stop myself from crying, but my voice still breaks when I say, 'It makes me feel like a bad person. Losing weight is all I care about now. I don't care any more about people, about things. I don't care about Adrian. I don't care that he says "you and me", about me and him, and that is huge! That is what I've actually prayed for! I'm not even considering his feelings. Is that all in the past now? Have I become that shallow in a year? I don't care that I saved that baby . . .'

I can't stop myself crying, and I look down and away from my therapist, anywhere but at his eyes. If I see any kind of sympathy, I'll lose it.

'Are you scared, Sunny?'

'Yes. I can't make myself stop now. I'm scared that I am addicted. That it's taken over me. That it's out of my control now. I have to have my weekly weigh-in; I have to hear encouraging remarks from near-strangers – the woman who serves me at the tube station, the man in the newsagent's where I buy my magazines: you've lost weight, yes? Lots of weight? It was intentional, yes? I've never known approval like it and . . . what if it goes away?'

'Do you think that other people, other women, might feel like this? Have you considered that it might not be so scary if you realise you are not the only one?'

'But surely this isn't how everybody else lives, all the thin people, obsessed with themselves?' My voice raises.

'They might. How do you know?'

'It just doesn't seem right, to be this self-involved!'

'What if you found out that they all were this self-involved, and that is what life will be like for you from now on? Would that make you stop dieting?'

'No.' I can barely hear my own voice and my therapist is straining to listen to me. 'All I can think now is that I want to be thin. I've spent my whole life being "less", being invisible to some men, horribly nastily visible to others, and their snide remarks, and their jeers. And I've faced it all on my own. I want somebody to look after me. When I was fat, nobody wanted to look after me.'

My therapist turns round and reaches on to his desk for a box of tissues that I have never seen before. I am crying so hard that I need to mop my eyes and my cheeks and my nose.

'Sunny, do you feel like you have to be perfect before somebody will love you?'

'I don't know. I hope not. I know that getting healthy has fucked me up.'

'You're not fucked up.' My therapist doesn't sound strange saying 'fuck', which surprises me. Things don't faze him. Words certainly don't faze him. My dad would sound bizarre saying that word, or uncomfortable.

'You could stop dieting tomorrow, Sunny. I am sure you are a very healthy weight now. I'm positive that you don't need to lose another two stone. You could just decide to be healthy, and not to be thin. Anything is possible. It's all within your control.' My therapist hands me another tissue, and I blow my nose loudly.

I look him in the eye, and with some composure say, 'It won't end tomorrow. I don't know where it will end. I am addicted.'

My therapist's watch makes its familiar little bleeping noise.

'We can carry on, Sunny, if you want to. I don't have another session for half an hour. I feel like we've had something of a breakthrough. And I feel like we need to talk about this seriously. There are things I can tell you about, when you start feeling out of control, ways of monitoring your own behaviour . . . It's called Cognitive Behavioural Therapy. Breaking cycles of behaviour . . .'

I sit up and wipe the last tears away from my eyes. 'No, I'm fine. I'll still be here when you get back. I won't have wasted away by then! I think that's enough for now.'

'One last thing, to go with all those other things you have to think about. I want you to consider that maybe it's not that you won't find anybody who will love you until you are "perfect" in your own eyes. Maybe it's that you won't allow yourself to be loved until then.'

'OK, well, I don't even understand that, but I'll try.'

I walk home past Kew Gardens' wall, looking at the branches of the trees that hang over the sides. They don't seem to want to break out, they are just curious, wondering what's going on outside of their little vegetative paradise. They seem to have realised that in their case at least, the grass is always going to be greener on their own side. Cars stream past me, heading towards Richmond, and I remember that I have two dozen boxes of crystal whips waiting to be posted when I get home. It's mild, and I tie my jumper around my waist. A white van stuffed with builders sweeps past me and toots its horn, and one of the men – somebody's husband or father, no doubt – leans out and shouts, 'Nice tits.'

I look away. I want to shout 'Stop it!' after them. I want to scream, 'Leave me alone, stop looking!' I used to be self-conscious when they didn't toot their horns at me, but at some girl further down the road. Now I get the toots, and the shouts, and I hate it. I don't need to know that they find me acceptable now. What does it matter? It's just sex.

I'm glad my therapist is going away. I don't think I am ready to go where he wants to take me. The thing is, I already know that nine extra stones must be about more than just flesh – must represent something else, some deeper issue. It is inexplicable that fat cells, just excess body matter, can define a person. But that one word – fat – made me feel so worthless, my entire life.

But I feel disloyal somehow for making my own life easier, for complying and seemingly agreeing with rules that I still judge to be unfair. And I've done it all just to be accepted, just to be let into the clubhouse, instead of standing outside in the cold, yearning for the warmth within, and the glass of brandy, and the cigar, and the slapped backs, and the love, and the respect.

Sometime last year I chose not only to conform, but to try to be top of the class – not being fat isn't enough, because thin, and beautiful, is the best! Beautiful wins the big money every time, especially for women. Now I know that soon I'll have the right body, and I'll need the right hair, the right tan, the right make-up, the right clothes to go with it. It's like being offered a trip to the Maldives, when the only place I thought I'd ever get to was Margate. The possibilities are intoxicating. I'm drunk on the promise of being beautiful, and I don't want to sober up, because I'm tired of fighting. I choose to fit in now, but believe me when I say I hate myself, just a little, for doing it.

When Anna answers the door the first thing that I notice is that the right side of her hair is dry, and the left side is wet. Her eyes look tired, with creased black bags underneath spitefully dragging the rest of her face down. She looks like the Anna I have known since I was a child, but bloated, her belly and cheeks and thighs pumped full of seawater, as if she drowned in childbirth, but also survived. Her face looks like a balloon that needs some air siphoned out before it pops.

She wears a maroon tracksuit that she has worn the last three times I have called round. It is simultaneously snug and loose over her newly bulked-up frame. I am wearing skinny jeans, high black boots and a raspberry Fred Perry polo shirt, and a thick black belt with an antique buckle.

'Hi, Sunny, look at you!' she says with half a tired smile. I hear the baby crying behind her and follow her in. He quietens down as I lean over his cot and widen my eyes. He looks like Anna, with dark hair and dark eyes, beautiful lips.

'He is going to break a thousand hearts,' I say with a smile.

'I know,' she says wearily, as if she is already dealing with the fallout of crying teenage girls on the phone and at her front door. She dumps herself on the sofa, resting her head on the cushion, closing her eyes.

'Is Martin still at work?' I ask, seeing that the clock reads half-past six.

'No, he's playing football. Lucky for some,' she says, monotone, with her eyes still closed. She pushes her hands through her hair and feels the wetness on one side. 'I got halfway through my first attempted blow dry in six weeks, and he woke up,' she says, to herself more than me.

I fish into my bag. 'I brought you some walnuts, and some Green and Black's Dark – it's good chocolate, apparently!' I pass it to her with a conspiratorial grin.

'Great . . . thanks,' she says, taking it and tossing it on to the sofa next to her. 'Not that I should be eating for the next year.' Anna opens her eyes, and glances down at her belly.

'Oh, Anna, that will all fall off once the breast-feeding kicks in!' I say it as if it were the most obvious thing in the world, and she shouldn't give it a second thought.

'The breast-feeding doesn't work,' she says flatly. 'I can't do it. We've given up. We're on formula.'

'Oh, well, wait until he's crawling. You'll be running around after him, and going to water babies, and pushing the chair down to the park – you'll be back in your jeans in no time!' I say.

'Whatever, Sunny,' and it is cold, as if it were my fault, as if had I had the consideration still to be fat, she wouldn't

125

feel so bad about herself right now. I see her eyes glaze over with tears, but it is Jacob who starts to cry. I reach into his cot and lift him out, rocking him to and fro as I watch my step amongst the soft toys and play mats and wipes and muslin and nappies on the floor. He stops crying, and I can hear him breathing quietly in my ear. His head smells wonderful, his little fingers curling and uncurling by my cheek.

'But look at what you got,' I whisper, and stroke Jacob's head.

Anna pulls herself together suddenly. 'I know, of course, it's true. I can't imagine even wanting to make time for a manicure or a pedicure now – those things seem so shallow. My life didn't have any point before. I really couldn't care less about any of it – shopping, the gym – none of it matters, Sunny, once you've had a baby.'

I smile at her but say nothing, turning my attention instead back to little Jacob, who is trying desperately to support his own neck. He is quiet, looking over my shoulder, around the room.

'Jesus, that's the first time he's stopped whimpering all day.' She pauses. 'He must fancy you, Sunny.'

Anna reaches over to the end of the sofa and retrieves a half-empty packet of chocolate Hobnobs. Through a mouthful of biscuit, she offers me the packet. 'Want one?' Some crumbs scatter from her lips.

'No, thanks. I'm stuffed; I've just eaten,' I say, and puff out my cheeks.

'What, last month?' she says, as more biscuit sprays out of her mouth. I look hurt, and she looks embarrassed. 'I'm sorry, Sunny, you know I don't mean it. I just don't want you to get obsessed. You can have a biscuit, for Christ's sake. One Hobnob won't kill you.'

'I just don't fancy one,' I say, and pull my head back to

check on little Jacob as his head rests on my shoulder. His eyes are closed.

'I think he's asleep,' I whisper, and Anna heaves herself up from the sofa, taking the baby from me with expertise, and laying him gently in his cot.

We both move over to the sofa so as not to wake him.

'So, any men on the go?' she asks, picking out another Hobnob.

'Kind of.' I nod and shrug.

'Good for you,' Anna says as she notices a stain on her trouser leg that looks like tomato and starts to scratch it off. 'You look great, Sunny, you really do, but don't lose any more.' She stops scratching and looks up at me.

'Not much more,' I say with a smile, trying to sidestep it.

'You're not meant to be skinny. Hell, I barely even recognise you now!'

'That doesn't mean it's not me. It just means I used to eat differently. I just want to be healthy, that's all.'

'Well, obsessed isn't healthy. Don't just be all about the diet. It will get really boring really quickly, and men hate it when women talk about food all the time.'

Maybe she means to be kind, but she is tired, and her words tumble out clumsily. Or maybe Anna is having trouble not being the most attractive woman in the room right now. Maybe being gorgeous is what has always defined her, in the same way that I let being fat define me. Maybe now we are both scrambling, a little desperately, for some other definition of ourselves, because we aren't sure who we are if we don't look a certain way. Maybe now we have to dig a little deeper.

'How about the park next week? We could walk down to the common if the weather's nice?' I say, as I pick up my handbag and move into the corridor.

'Lovely,' she says, and I think I see tears in her eyes again, as she tugs open the front door, just as Martin pulls up in his company Audi.

He waves, I wave, Anna looks away.

'Wow, Sunny! You look great! Still going to the gym, I see. Look at your arms, fantastic tone!'

'Thanks, Martin. Nice to see you,' I say as I kiss an embarrassed hello. 'Jacob is looking wonderful, so handsome!' I speak before he can, I don't want him to say anything else.

'I know! Just like his father!' Martin says with a smile and a wink.

'Whoever he is,' Anna says evenly, with a sarcastic smile in Martin's direction. But he ignores it.

'I know, isn't he great, so big and strong. Between them they are eating me out of house and home!' He gestures towards Anna and laughs, and I don't say anything. 'Seriously, Sunny, can't you drag my wife along to a few of your classes, give her some of what you're having?' He laughs heartily again, but then the baby starts to cry, and he waves a quick goodbye before moving past Anna and darting inside to see his son and heir.

'He doesn't mean it,' I say as I give Anna a hug goodbye.

'Of course he bloody does,' she says quietly in my ear.

I don't want to be a tool for Martin to hit Anna with. I don't want to be the thing that makes somebody else feel bad. I just want to be slim, for me. I would never wish the way I used to feel about myself on to somebody else.

But I see that we need a shared definition of 'desirable' that isn't based on looks, for me and Anna – and Martin, for that matter. Couldn't it be that a ten out of ten for effort is the new Perfect Ten that we all aspire to? Being perfect shouldn't have to be a dress size. What size was Mother Teresa? Although that's a bad example because she was tiny.

What about the Virgin Mary? Supposing that she was a size ten before she had Jesus, what are the chances that she didn't put on some baby weight around her stomach during pregnancy, and that she wasn't carrying a few extra pounds when the Three Wise Men turned up?

And isn't it interesting that a clothing size ten only relates to women's sizes, and not men's. Can a man ever be a Perfect Ten? Or are the deciding criteria just different?

Women at the least need an image of the Perfect Ten, for the soul. We need something to aspire to that, in striving to achieve it, and possibly even succeeding, benefits us all, and not just plastic surgeons, Giorgio Armani and Calvin Klein.

Cagney stares at a photo of a twenty-year-old Grace Kelly lookalike, perched on the side of a boat in the Caribbean. The breeze plays with her hair, as she shields the sun from her eyes. The beach sits behind her in the distance, deserted and remote. He is hypnotised. It's the beach and the boat that he longs for, the isolation, and the peace, not the woman. NOT the woman. But his eyes are drawn to her slim freckled legs, and the shirt she has knotted at her midriff. Her feet point elegantly towards the cameraman, which reminds him why he holds the photo in his hand, and he tosses it away as if it's burnt his fingers.

A punter stands in front of him. His name is Sheldon Young. The Grace Kelly type is Sophia Young, his wife. His much younger wife. Sheldon is a fool – Cagney knew it by his weak-as-water handshake and apologetic grin. Cagney sits in his chair while Sheldon looks around for a second seat that isn't there, finally positioning himself uncomfortably in front of Cagney's desk like a rookie private who doesn't know how to salute a captain, and relates his life story to Cagney, without being asked. They always feel the need to explain.

'Sophia and I were married two years ago, Mr James, on her eighteenth birthday. I was forty-five.'

Sheldon is in reasonable shape, but with thinning hair and small hands. Cagney pitied him on sight, for believing himself capable of keeping any woman happy.

'I was in investment banking, and I'd made my millions, but I'd never found a reason to stop working, Mr James, until she walked in. As luck would have it, my assistant, Margaret, had just broken both her legs in a horrific skiing accident, and the temping agency . . . well, they sent me an angel.'

Sheldon beams at the recollection. Cagney shudders.

'I believe we fell in love at first sight, Mr James. Sophia had only been out of college for three months, she was unsure what to do with her life, thinking about travelling, but of course she was too young and too innocent to have any idea of where to go. I took her to lunch that very first day. She was from poor stock – her parents were both simple, working class, but somehow they made this beautiful fragile fawn. Our engagement was announced in *The Times* four weeks later.'

'It's good not to rush into these things.' Cagney nods his head at Sheldon, who smiles back in agreement. 'Do go on, Mr Young. It's edge-of-the-seat stuff.'

'I know it sounds like a fairy tale, Mr James, but any man who's been in love will know what I mean when I say that I had never felt true happiness until I saw her face.'

'It sounds dreamy.'

'It was like a dream, Mr James, a beautiful intoxicating dream. We made plans straight away, and we had every intention of spending the rest of our lives bobbing about on unfamiliar oceans, sipping champagne, and tasting paradise. But now that paradise is lost.'

'Good God.'

The smile that plays on Sheldon's face falls, but he is too self-involved to clock the horror on Cagney's face.

'She thinks she's in love with somebody else, Mr James. She wants children, you see, and I don't, I never have. Too selfish, I suppose, to surrender my freedom, and to share her with somebody else. But in the last six months she's grown restless. She is a beautiful person, Mr James, as beautiful on the inside as out, like a tender lamb. But we want different things. Recently she's been distant, she doesn't like to be touched, and yet in her eyes I can see that it hurts her to be hurting me, and I believe it's killing her. She's just such a warm and loving girl, like a wide-eyed young rabbit.'

Cagney can't take any more. Apparently this girl is the whole farm!

'If she's such a saint, Mr Young, why is the bunny screwing somebody else?'

Sheldon visibly flinches at the word. 'She wants to be a mother, and I won't give her that. It's my fault! I should have told her before we were married. She deserves to have children, and to share her love with them. I just can't be the man to give them to her.'

Cagney is confused. 'I'm sorry but I don't understand. If you love your wife that much, if you believe she deserves this supposed happiness that you can't give her, why are you here? Just tell her you want a divorce, and let her get on with it.'

Sheldon looks embarrassed, looks down, around, anywhere but at Cagney when he answers, quietly, 'I can't let her have the money. There's no pre-nuptial agreement, you see, and I'm afraid the man she's picked is not a wise choice. It's our handyman . . . you understand? And I believe she thinks she's in love with him. But he's a rogue, through

131

and through. She doesn't want me any more, and I won't stand in her way, but I can't let him squander my money, Mr James. I worked hard for it, it's the key to my life, it lets me do what I want to do.'

'But, Mr Young, by the looks of it you have enough money to share. You could still take all the boat trips you want, and pay her hairdresser's bills.'

'Mr James, I resent the implication that Sophia is a drain. She has cost me barely a penny since the day we were married. She is not a gold digger. But this rogue is. And besides, I've made some bad investments. There's not as much as there was. There isn't enough left to support us both, separately.'

Sheldon looks down at his feet, embarrassed. That's not strictly true, is it? Cagney thinks, clocking the Rolex, and the cufflinks, and the manicure.

'Let's cut to the chase, Sheldon. You love your wife, but she doesn't get the cash without getting you as well.'

Sheldon coughs nervously. 'Mr James, I just need some evidence. It'll be easy enough to get. I've nearly caught them myself a couple of times – she's too lovely to be discreet. Just a few photos and then this whole sorry matter can come to an end. I want her to be happy. I just can't afford to pay for it.'

'Well, Sheldon, I'd love to help but my business is not catching people who are already having affairs. The lovely Mrs Young and Bob-a-job might actually be in love, and who am I to sully that?' Cagney always marvels at the fact that he is able to say that part with a straight face. But it's an excuse they swallow like a scoop of vanilla. 'My agency acts only in cases where there is suspicion of promiscuity, and I use trusted members of staff to initiate meetings, and secure any evidence we need. I am not a private investigator and it sounds like that's what you want. They are more expensive, but I can give you some numbers if you like.'

Sheldon interrupts Cagney as he reaches for the number of Richard Hill, a private investigator with the proper licence. Over the years they have batted work to each other, and although Cagney knows that Mr Hill makes more out of their unofficial deal than he does, it isn't enough to worry him.

'No, Mr James, you misunderstand me. I don't want you to catch her with him. I want you, or a member of your staff to initiate a "honey trap", which I believe *is* your business. And then, you see, Sophia will realise that this lout isn't for her, and that there are plenty of other men who can give her what she wants. She'll come to her senses, break it off with this nasty piece of work, but I'll still get my divorce. Finances . . . intact, so to speak.'

'Sheldon, you must really love your wife to do this for her.'

'I do.'

'OK, here's what I need to know: where she goes during the day, whom she meets, her hobbies, what she likes, where she drinks her coffee, where she has her hair done, things like that. It can take as little as a week; the longest it's ever taken is three months. Depending on the time and the man hours the cost will vary, but you are looking at a minimum of one hundred pounds, and a maximum of ten thousand.'

'Money's no object.'

Tell that to your wife!

'When will you start?'

'You leave me the details, we'll start straight away.'

When Sheldon finally leaves, having disclosed all the necessary information, Cagney sits back in his chair, cracks a nut in one hand, and holds Sophia Young's photo in the other. She certainly is a looker, but he's seen better. There is something about her, though, an unusual innocence around the eyes. But what difference does it make? She's screwing around on her old man and, by the sound of it, she'd planned to take him for everything he was worth and hook up with some younger model from the start. Hell, her and the handyman were probably sweethearts since school, cooking up this scam together. Poor stupid Sheldon, he'd walked right into it. He's come to his senses late, but just in time.

Cagney stares at the photo again: there would be worse things than having her on a boat like that, in a place like that. He had been startled when Sheldon first passed him the photo, because she looked just like Gracie, and the boat and the vista – that was his dream. In three months' time Cagney was headed for an ocean just like the one in the picture, and a yacht like the one the lovely Mrs Young was using to rest what looked like a great arse upon. He probably won't be able to afford anything quite that special, but a one-berth is all he really needs. The sounds of the city will fade away, and finally he'll know peace, with only the ocean lapping below him for a soundtrack. He would never be alone with the waves for company, friendly locals in every port who'd come to know him as the eccentric loner, the sole captain and crew of his tiny boat, who'd drink with them in their makeshift pubs, and toast the stars on seemingly limitless beaches. Cagney looks back down at the photo again – would it be so terrible to have somebody along for the ride? She has a touch of Alice around the eyes as well . . .

The phone rings and breaks his daydream. Cagney snatches at the receiver.

'Cagney James.'

'Boss, it's Howard.'

'How many bones did he break?'

'Just the three.'

'What did you guess?'

'Five. I owe you a tenner.'

'Wonderful.'

'They're putting on the cast now.'

Cagney rubs his eyes and thinks. Iuan finished his only current job yesterday, but Cagney planned to start him on another one tomorrow morning. It is a youngish girl admittedly, and he can feasibly give it to Howard instead, but when Iuan had shown Howard the photo yesterday he had screamed, and it made Cagney doubt his ability to 'finish the job'. That was the way it worked – Howard took the young ones; Iuan took the ugly ones and without complaint, knowing as he did that all results had to be deemed objective by the agency's punters: offering a handsome man to some of Iuan's women would be like giving a peasant the keys to a palace, and then acting surprised when they tried to move in. Cagney took anyone over thirty. It had never failed them before, but then they had never been a man down before, and it is sensitive business. There is always the risk of trouble, and a fine line kept his licence most days – Howard and Iuan both know to play dumb in the right situations. Cagney can't very well just put an advert in the Jobcentre. Both Iuan and Howard had come to him by chance, and it had worked out well.

Iuan arrived in Kew as a traffic warden nearly a year after Cagney moved in, promptly issuing Cagney with a parking ticket at least once a week for the following four months. Iuan had quickly become his nemesis, although Cagney was forced begrudgingly to admire how little Iuan seemed affected, or even cared, when Cagney got the white rage at another parking violation ticketed. The Welshman was cheerful whatever the conditions, and he was funny-looking, both of which occurred to Cagney on the day that one of his clients refused to settle up, complaining that Cagney was too attractive for his wife, who was bound to be all over him like a cheap suit given the opportunity, invalidating Cagney's results. Cagney promised Iuan the same money he got as a warden, plus the opportunity to kiss women for a living. Iuan didn't finish writing his last parking ticket.

Similarly Howard was employed out of necessity six years later. Cagney had been nursing a whiskey and mulling over a conundrum one night, whilst waiting for a pizza to arrive. He had been working for a week on a job for Paul Taylor, a seventeen-year-old boy, suspicious that his seventeen-year-old girlfriend, Janine, might actually be the slapper everybody told him she was. Despite having completed all of the necessary observations, Cagney was reluctant to move in on Janine, and he knew why. Cagney was nearly thirty-seven, more than twice her age. Not only did he have no idea how to casually bump into Janine in her local Ritzy's nightclub, he was scared of what people might think if he did. Then Cagney heard the doorbell ring, opening it to a large Hawaiian and a good-looking idiot. Cagney offered Howard more money and the chance to kiss women for a living. Howard delivered his three remaining pizzas to Cagney that night, and went to work for him the next day.

Cagney sighs: now, of course, there is his newest target, Sophia Young. Typically she should go to Howard, but if he is going to have to take Iuan's quota, it throws the workload up in the air. Cagney will unfortunately have to do Sophia himself. He feels a rush of something down his spine, but ignores it.

'Howard, make sure Iuan takes the crutches, even if they

won't go with what he's wearing, and tell him he's going to have to recuperate in the office for however long it takes. We can be a man down in the field, but we'll cope if we've got extra support at HQ.'

'Love it, boss! Love the military talk, love it all! I'll tell Iuan. We'll be back in an hour.'

Cagney checks his watch – it is already half-past four.

'Don't bother, Howard. I'll see you BOTH tomorrow morning at eight a.m.'

'Great! You're my dawg.' Howard hangs up before Cagney changes his mind.

Cagney cradles the receiver in his hand for a while until an angry tone bleeps at him to hang up.

He sits in the shadows of early evening as the streetlights fire up outside. He doesn't flick on the light, but instead reaches for his top drawer, and pulls out the bottle and the beaker.

Pouring himself a large measure, Cagney spins round and stares at the village as it darkens, as the commuters begin to spill out of the station, and shop lights come on. He turns and reaches for the photo from beneath a pile of papers where he has stuffed it. His feet rest on the windowsill, as two gulps demolish his whiskey. Pouring himself another one, Cagney looks out of the window with the photo in his hand, and acknowledges the thoughts that have been creeping up on him recently, the thoughts he has banished as best he can.

I can feel my libido again. Something has sparked it back in to life.

My bed is lonely. The pillows are a substitute, not a comfort.

I wake, at 3 a.m., every night, wide awake and with nothing to do and nothing to hold.

Something is missing . . .

He glances back down at the picture of Sophia Young. She resembles all the women he has loved: Gracie, and Lydia . . . but most obviously Alice. It is in the paleness of her eyes, and the fullness of her lower lip, and her youth.

Cagney was three months from twenty-five when he met an eighteen-year-old Alice, clinging to a life buoy in Lindos Bay. He had spent the year on his own, travelling Europe, contemplating mountains and oceans, guessing at his destiny. His first marriage had collapsed in swift disaster the previous year, and the naivety of his decision-making had shaken him to his core. While utterly blaming himself, he feared for his fate. Some crazy idealism had mismatched the notion of beauty with goodness in his young and foolish head. He had been hoodwinked, conned, led a merry dance, but by his own eyes. When he had married Gracie he had fallen for the curve of her back, a strand of her golden hair, and no more. He determined that when he married again, as he was sure that he would, his eyes would be wide open, and he would know without doubt that his new wife was beautiful on the inside as well as out.

Cagney swam out from the long beach, heading for the smaller beach on the other side of the bay, testing his youthful lung capacity, enjoying the heat of the beaming Greek sun as it shone on his back, and the clear blue water around him. He was two-thirds of the way across when a wedding boat set sail from the short pier, and circled the bay, so that the wedding party might wave to the tourists. And the tourists waved back smiling, thankful that they sat in shorts and bikinis, and were not sweating in suits and dresses on a wedding boat in the afternoon haze. Cagney waved his arms vigorously too, shouting 'congratulations' and 'hurrah' at the passengers, and they raised their champagne glasses in acknowledgement.

After treading water for ten minutes, and watching the boat disappear around the other side of the rocks, Cagney spotted a buoy fifty metres away, and front crawled at speed to hang on for a while, and give his legs a rest before swimming into shore. As he raised his head ten feet from the buoy he saw an arm clinging to one side, and he pushed on, pleased at the prospect of company. He hadn't spoken to anybody that day, other than the lady who sold him bread and fruit at the supermarket on the way to the beach, and the idea of conversation appealed to him. He had felt a little lonely all week.

'I know the captain,' were her first words, popping her head round the buoy so that Cagney could see her. 'He drinks ouzo with breakfast. I thought it wise to hold on to something large until he passed.'

Her eyes were two pale blue saucers, brighter than the sun above them and clearer than the water they swam in.

'I'm Cagney,' he said. 'It's beautiful here.'

'Yes it is, you're quite right. I'm Alice. I'd shake your hand but I fear I'd fall.'

'You'll have to let go at some point, unless you plan on staying out here all night.'

'Oh, no, I'll go back eventually, when one of my friends pedals out from the beach to get me.'

'What if nobody comes?'

'Somebody always comes. They know I only have the strength to get out here, and not back. I'm not that strong a swimmer.'

'Then why not swim half the distance, and back safely to shore?' Cagney asked.

'Because it's nicer out here.' Alice had smiled at him with her wide mouth, her impossibly full bottom lip rolling out across her face.

'I suppose you know that you are very beautiful,' he said.

'Yes. I may cut my hair at Christmas, it's all getting a little obvious.'

'Are you still at school?' Cagney approximated she was anywhere between sixteen and twenty, but with a wet face and hair it was truly hard to tell.

'I'm eighteen. I have just finished secretarial college, although I don't plan to work.'

'What do you plan to do?' Cagney had asked with a laugh.

'Just not work really . . .' Alice had replied with an honest shrug, and Cagney had laughed louder.

'What do you do, Cagney?'

'Not much at the moment. I was in the army, and I've been thinking about joining the police when I go home.'

'How awful,' she said, with a scolding look of concern.

'Why?' Cagney asked, afraid that he had upset her, that she was of better stock, and he had just ruined his chances.

'The helmet wouldn't suit your head at all!' she had stated matter-of-factly, and Cagney had laughed again.

In spite of his worthiest intentions, he had fallen in love for a second time, and it had happened in minutes.

'It doesn't look like your friends are coming today,' Cagney said, with his hand shading his eyes, looking towards the beach.

'Maybe they have forgotten me,' she said with a frown.

'I'm sure that's not true, but perhaps there aren't any pedalos free. Shall I take you?'

'I thought you might offer. Should I climb on your back? I am only light, thank goodness, or we should both drown. Although I doubt whether you would have been quite so kind if I were significantly bigger.'

'What did you think of the wedding?' Cagney asked, as he surged powerfully forwards through the water towards the beach.

'I thought it was lovely. Of course it was. The beach is beautiful. It is perfect.'

'So you'd like to marry that way?'

'Absolutely, if only because my parents wouldn't attend.'

'Why don't you want your parents at your wedding? I wish my mum was still alive to see me get married.'

'When did she die?'

'Six years ago.'

'Were you close?'

'Very.'

'What a shame. I don't like them, or rather, they don't like each other. They keep threatening to disinherit me, and in a way I wish they would, because at least then I would have to focus on something, make a living. But I don't believe they will ever really cut me off, they couldn't fight over and about me if I was self-sufficient. They use me as a pawn. But then, I suppose I use them . . .'

'Are they very wealthy?' Cagney asked.

'Very.'

'And you don't want their money any more?'

'Of course I want it, it just makes life a little aimless, that's all. I'm sure I'll never settle on anyone or anything until I am forced to look after myself.'

'It's not all it's cracked up to be,' Cagney said, lowering his feet down to touch the ocean floor, standing waist-high in water, sliding Alice off his back.

She stood three feet away from him, in a white bikini, shielding her eyes from the sun, biting her lower lip, her long blonde hair tickling the water that lapped at her ribcage.

'Shall we meet this evening?' she asked, as Cagney's heart leapt in his chest, causing tidal waves on a beach a thousand miles away.

'I'd love to.'

'How long were you planning to stay in Lindos?' she asked him that evening, as they sat on the beach with a bottle of red wine that Cagney had bought from the woman in the supermarket, eating green grapes and feta cheese for dinner.

'I had been planning to leave tomorrow.'

'And how long will you stay now?' she asked.

'I'll stay until you want me to go.'

A week later Cagney proposed, by the life buoy in the bay. Alice said yes as they reached the shore and Cagney lowered her off his back and on to the beach.

Two days after that they were married on the wedding boat, and the Greek captain threw rice as they sank ouzo shots, arms entwined, poured from a bottle kept below decks, reserved for special occasions. As predicted, Alice's parents did not attend the ceremony, although she had invited them that morning when she had called to tell them they were gaining a son.

Cagney would have bet his life that he slept with a smile that first night, naked and without sheets, on a Lindion bed, with his beautiful new bride curled tightly in his arms.

It was the following morning that Alice's parents did arrive, storming into the villa they were renting for Alice and three of her friends for the summer, banging on the bedroom door, demanding to know what was going on. Alice had wrapped herself in a discarded sheet and sloped off to confront them, telling Cagney to stay in bed for now, that she would come and get him when she felt they were ready to meet him.

Cagney waited all morning. Eventually, at 1 p.m., he ventured out of the bedroom, to find the villa deserted. So sure was he of his new bride, he chose not to question it, but instead to tug out the copy of Pushkin he was reading before he met Alice, propping himself on the terrace, feet up on the wall, overlooking the bay, waiting for his new family to return.

At 8 p.m. they arrived back, with Alice dressed in her mother's clothes. Alice's parents chose not to introduce themselves, but sat either side of Alice as she placed herself opposite Cagney at a large wooden table on the terrace, lit only by a string of candles laid across the middle, throwing ominous shadows in the dark.

'They want to know what you intend to do?' she said.

'About what?'

'Supporting us,' she said sternly, as if it were obvious, and he were painting them both fools.

'Well, when we get back to England I thought I might apply for the police force,' he said brightly. Who wouldn't want a sergeant for a son-in-law, he reasoned, a pillar of the community?

'No,' Alice's father said. Cagney could barely see his face in the candlelight, making out silver hair, and a strong nose that was high in the air.

'No?' Cagney asked.

'Daddy doesn't like that idea. What else?' Alice said.

'Or . . . I could go back in to the army, I suppose . . .' Cagney floundered, so desperate was he to impress his new father-in-law.

'What else?' Alice's mother asked, an older thinner version of her daughter, gaunt from gin and lettuce.

'There is no . . . I mean . . . I have thought about security work . . .' Cagney was flailing wildly.

'Oh dear God,' Alice's mother muttered, covering her eyes with a bony hand.

'If you aren't even going to try, Cagney, you can't expect them to like you,' Alice said coolly.

'I am trying! I don't know what else you want me to

say!' Cagney was desperate, wide-eyed, clawing for an answer that would illicit a response other than 'What else?'.

'Something better than that,' she said.

Cagney turned to address Alice's father. 'The first time I saw your daughter I became love's fool. It doesn't matter what career I choose because my life, from that moment on, has been devoted solely to protecting her. I won't leave her side unless she asks me to. I won't speak unless she tells me to. She is my life now, and all that I need.'

He turned to face Alice. 'I don't chase thousands of girls, I'm no sexual circus rider. Honestly, all I want is to look after you.'

'Ovid! Ovid? You quote erotic poems in front of my wife and expect me to let you marry my daughter?'

'With all due respect, I have already married your daughter, sir . . .'

Alice's father pushed back his chair, storming away from the table, and her mother followed moments later.

Alice and Cagney sat opposite each other in silence for the next half an hour.

Finally Alice said, 'I doubt that will be enough,' before going to bed.

Cagney slept on the terrace that night, and woke with the chorus of cocks crowing at 5 a.m. Walking in to their room, he saw his beautiful young wife curled up in a ball on their honeymoon bed and, peeling off his clothes, he had crawled into bed next to her, throwing his arm around her, breathing in her neck.

'I didn't think they'd come,' she whispered to him.

'Tell me I was more than that,' he said quietly.

'I can't.'

'How long will they stay?'

'They'll fly home today.'

'And you?'

'The villa is paid up until the end of the month. I shall stay until then.'

'What was the right answer? In case there ever is a next time.'

'Finance.'

'What if I said finance now?'

'They'll know I told you. It's too late.'

'What if you told them you can't be without me?'

'I won't tell them that.'

'Why did you marry me?'

'I didn't think they'd come.'

'What if I told you I love you?'

'I know that already.'

'Doesn't it change your mind?'

'Really and truly, Cagney, it would seem I like my aimless life.'

'Won't you even say you're sorry, for us?'

'Why should I? You knew it would end this way all along. I was just playing. I'm still just a child. You're no fool.'

'You're wrong. I'm the biggest fool there is.'

Cagney fell asleep then, waking three hours later, disentangling himself from his new bride, and leaving his father's address on a piece of paper under a rock at the end of their bed. He had hitchhiked up to Rhodes that day, working in a bar for another month to save the money for a flight home, sleeping on the beach every night.

He got back to England and stayed with his father for a while – he wasn't even sure how long. He existed in some kind of waking stupor, utterly perplexed, occasionally pinching himself to check that he was real. Eventually he heard back from Brighton and Hove Constabulary, who had accepted him as a trainee. His father forwarded him the divorce papers when they finally arrived, and he signed them the next morning, after one final tortured night's sleep. With the final 'S' of his name, he determined to move on.

For she had only been playing . . .

Cagney whispers to the darkness, 'God help me, not again.'
And falls asleep in his chair.

FIVE

Just a side dish . . .

I yawn halfway through a gulp of coffee and spill it down my gym top. My day is not going well. I woke up agitated and tired at 6 a.m., but couldn't persuade myself to go back to sleep so I just laid there, thinking about what my therapist had said to me yesterday.

Maybe I don't want Adrian, I just want somebody, and he's the easy option. I know what I'm getting; it's not so risky. But I know, if I can reach inside myself and yank out the admission, that my intentions are stained by almost thirty years' worth of rejection. I don't know why I find this so shaming. Why shouldn't I let Adrian's feelings for me bolster my vanity for a while? Everybody else is doing it.

But just the thought sends a shiver down my spine, a spiteful acknowledgement of something that has started to rot inside me, deprived of nourishment or chocolate. If the beauty of the body is the corruption of the soul, I need to find another anchor to replace the fat and hold me down, before I float off into cloudless skies of self-obsession and moral vagaries.

Everything that I thought I believed is slipping through skinny fingers, in the face of nothing more than an increase in my options. I never dreamt, at the start, that my moral measurements might change along with my vital statistics. I am finding that it is a lot easier to believe in black and white, right and wrong, when you don't have any options yourself. Once new paths present themselves, everything gets a little grey. My beliefs have dissolved in my head, and the crazy hazy liquid they have left behind is swimming around behind my eyes, and making me feel a little sick. At some point I need to decide what I believe now.

With so many more plausible things to worry about, not least my concern that the devil wears a size ten and I'm getting ready to fill her shoes, I am not even going to entertain my therapist's ludicrous notions about Cagney James. I don't believe there is a fine line between love and hate, in this case, at least. Sometimes you meet thoroughly nasty individuals. Realising that and reacting to it are nothing to do with sexual chemistry, just good character judgement. If I was hateful towards him, it's only because he deserved it, not because I wanted to mount him. Sometimes, it would seem, my therapist gets it very wrong.

The thought of tonight's dinner party flicks at my nerves with vicious fingers . . . I sigh and look at my list of things to do. A batch of silk Japanese bondage underwear was supposed to arrive two days ago, but hasn't. I have spoken with the manufacturers in Turkey this morning, and they assured me it was shipped from Adana as usual and on time. Which means they have either been stolen by kinky pirates, or they are stuck in Customs. My instincts tell me that it is the latter, as much fun as the kinky pirate story sounds. Everything is always getting stuck in Customs, and with it the promise of yet another painful telephone conversation. 'Have painful telephone conversation with Customs' is actually the first thing on my to-do list.

Number two on my list is 'Call Adrian, see if he is backing out of tonight.'

I check my phone for texts from Adrian. There aren't any. As there weren't five minutes ago, or half an hour ago. If I get a text, I will be alerted to it by the glorious little noise my phone makes when somebody has bothered to type in possibly four words, and send them to me. But I have no texts right now, I haven't missed the noise, it didn't just forget to bleep this time. I don't hate the noise, I love it; it is the sound of a tiny starburst, or a fairy wand, or a sweep of delight. It is a beautiful jingle, full of hope and excitement, and when I hear it, my belly fills with a tiny fizzing of expectation. Until I click the buttons to unlock my phone and realise the text is from my mother, telling me about her flowerbeds, and spelling 'great', 'gr8'. Or from my osteopath, reminding me about another fifty-pound appointment I have made to get my pelvis realigned. The only texts I want now are from Adrian. It's that moment, when his name pops up on my phone, before I read what he has to say, that I could bottle and live on for ever. It's the possibility, it could be anything: he could say anything! One of these days one of his texts may even leave me feeling as good after I've read it as I did when it first arrived. One of these days one of his texts might even deserve my excitement. The fact that he rarely actually calls me, so rarely that his voice down a phone line still surprises me a little when I hear it, doesn't matter that much either.

I look at the third and final entry on my to-do list.

It reads simply, 'Finish up notes.' For my talk. My sex talk. To the children of La Sainte Union Convent, Sutton. I have been asked to spend an hour with 10B, by their teacher, Mr Taggart, who called me last week. He is their form tutor. He is three years younger than I am. When he said he was a teacher I thought he was lying, because he sounded like a teenager, so I asked him how old he was, and he said, 'Twenty-five,' a little defensively.

And twenty-five sounded like a lifetime ago. A world away from twenty-eight. A lot has happened to me since then.

He called me on my work line, and initially, of course, I thought he was some schoolboy, giggling with his mates, with his hand over the receiver, phoning up to say the word 'dildo' to a woman and then slam the phone down in hysterics.

'I got your website information from my flatmate,' he said. He sounded arrogantly nervous, in the way that very bright people can. The ones who are almost too bright. Who skipped a social gene and got an extra brainy one for good measure.

'OK . . .'

'I teach maths and physics, and sometimes geography as well, at La Sainte Union Convent in Sutton – maybe you know it?' His voice had broken twice in that one sentence, once as he said the word 'geography', and again when he said 'maybe'. I wondered if he was picturing a dominatrix on the end of the line, glistening in leather, with bright red pasted lips the colour of tomato purée, and stilettos so pointed and high they would leave pinpricks in the pavement as I walked. The truth, of course, was yellow golf socks, purple running shorts and a big red jumper, no make-up, but a face shiny with moisturiser and tea tree oil. I didn't tell him that.

'OK . . .' I said again, about to tell him this wasn't one of 'those lines' – a 'chat' line.'

'My form class, 10B, are fifteen-year-old girls, and part of my remit, as their tutor, and deputy head of year, actually, is sex education.' He hadn't quite coughed, but only because

150

he had fought it. He had not been comfortable saying that word. Saying 'sex'. 'And I want to do something a little different, you know; it's the twenty-first century, for Christ's sake! I'm not just going to show them the bloody tampon diagrams and talk to them about the Pill. They'll think I'm a twat.'

'OK . . .' I was starting to get the gist of it. He wanted to be the fun teacher. He was still a student himself, in his mind, still living with his mates, still fresh out of university. He still thought it acceptable to use the word 'twat' in what some would say was a professional call. He wanted to show them that sex could be fun. He wanted to share his idealism, really teach, you know? Really teach! He still wanted to change the world, or help the world, or mould the world, or mould Sutton at least.

'Do you want me to send you some stuff through? Have you seen anything in particular on the site?' I said.

'Not exactly . . . I'm sorry I didn't catch you name,' he said.

'Sunny Weston.'

'Sunny?'

'Yes.'

'You're speaking to Rob. Rob Taggart.' His name, when he announced it, was seeped in confidence, unlike every other word he had said. Some of what he was made him proud at least. The Dungeons and Dragons of ten years previously were almost forgotten. Very few teenage geeks grow up to be mature geeks. In adulthood, everybody seems to merge. Mostly, people find themselves and they settle. The harsh category system of schooldays is quickly forgotten once wives and kids and friends and holidays and jobs and promotions and company cars and ski lodges come along.

'Hi, Rob. What is it that you need exactly?' I said.

'Well, firstly I hoped that I could speak to somebody

151

in acquisitions, I guess . . . the person who sources the products.'

'That would be me. I run and manage the site myself.'

'You do?' He sounded surprised, like my Uncle Humphrey had been. But, of course, Rob Taggart didn't know me, hadn't known me all of my life. He didn't and wasn't commenting on me. I was a one-man band, that is all that surprised him.

'Yes.'

'Well, that's wonderful. Here is what I was hoping – you buy all these sex toys, you know what's available for girls, women, these days. And if we are ever going to tackle teenage pregnancy, you know, we need to meet it head on. It's no good burying our heads in the fucking sand, is it?'

'Hell no!' I couldn't help but be a little taken aback by Mr Taggart of 10B. Passion is so rare these days, that when you experience it first-hand your impulse is to smirk and snigger. But Rob firmly believed he might make a difference, might stop the unlucky slut of 10B getting knocked up at fifteen if I showed her a Rampant Rabbit or a Two-Fingered Fondler. If I chose instead to point out that losing her virginity to an eighteen-year-old boy with a souped-up Fiesta and a wicked stereo system is all that really mattered to young Denise, or Rebecca, or Samantha from 10B, I might dampen his ardour, and I desperately didn't want to do that. If I had said, 'Rob, it's not about an orgasm, at fifteen, it's about the not-quite-concealed lovebites on your neck,' I may have dented his dreams. And I have realised that naïvety can be a beautiful blessing. I feel it burn the palms of my hands as it is ripped away from me daily. And I am not going to be responsible for ripping it from Rob's hands.

'So, you want me to send you some stuff?' I ventured.

'No, not me! I mean, you have to be careful. I can't be seen to be . . . I mean these girls aren't kids . . . no. I meant

152

for you to come and talk to them, show them some stuff.'

'What . . . like . . . ?' I waited for him to fill in the blank. Did he just mean sexy underwear? Or porn? Or handcuffs? Or a strap-on?

'You know! Dildos . . . vibrators . . . sex aids . . . you know, the lot . . .' Mr Taggart's voice trailed off slightly.

I wanted to reach out and hug him, and whisper in his ear, 'Don't feel bad! You don't have to know! Why would you know? You could just be really good at loving sex. You might not need the "let's keep it interesting" toys! Of course you aren't, but I don't necessarily know that! Of course I do, but I might not! Don't feel so bad!'

But what I had actually said was, 'So you want me to come in, to your classroom, and talk to the girls about the sex aids that I sell on the site?'

'Exactly. Can you do an hour two weeks on Monday at one fifteen?'

'Goodness, that's specific! I think so . . . I guess, but what do you want me to say?'

'Just tell them how they work, how fucking great it is to have an orgasm!' he laughed.

I laughed, I felt so horribly awkward, that he must have felt it too.

'Rob, one other thing. Will you be buying the stuff I bring along? I mean, will there actually be any sales in it . . . for me?'

'Oh . . .' He sounded deflated. Talk of cold hard cash dirtied his idealism, but I am a business woman . . .

'I could bring some catalogues for the staffroom perhaps? And maybe you could let the girls know to bring some cash with them, in case they want to buy any of the stock?' I helped him out.

'Yes, let's do that. I can't guarantee any sales, of course, but I'm sure they'll be well up for it!'

'I'm sure they will. OK. Can I take your number, Rob?'

'Oh . . . OK, yeah, why not?'

'In case anything comes up, and I can't make it . . .'

'Oh, right, I see. Of course.' His voice had broken again, for the tenth or eleventh time in the conversation.

'Or you could just drop me an email, through the site, with the details?'

'It's fine, take my number,' Rob said.

'No, actually it's probably best if you email it, so I don't misplace it.' We both backed away at speed from the implication.

And I had received an email that afternoon, signed 'Mr Taggart'. Maybe Rob thinks of everybody as his students. Maybe Rob thinks he has a little something to teach us all.

I rifle through my bag now and pull out a couple of sheets of paper full of crossings-out and doodles. I don't know what I'm going to say to 10B, apart from not allowing any questions about actual sex. Or sexual positions. Or anything. Just no questions. My phone vibrates, and starts to ring. I pick it up and see Adrian's name, and I get a tingle that feels like the time I covered my belly in six electro-pads, hoping they'd give me a six-pack, despite having twice as much body fat as I should have had at the time. Optimism and desperation can often be confused.

'Hello, handsome,' I answer my phone.

'Hey, you all right?' Adrian's voice is so distinctive. It is a northern drawl. No, it's more than that: if I am honest he always sounds drunk. Not hammered, just a bit pissed. The wrong side of three pints. I have only noticed it recently, and now I can't get it out of my head.

'Yeah, I'm fine. Just having a coffee, doing some paperwork. You?'

'Yeah, I'm fine. Look, I need to talk to you, Sunny.'

'You aren't coming tonight?'

'What?'

'The dinner party – you aren't coming. But you said you'd come, Adrian, and now I have nobody else to take – it's fine, of course, but you should have just given me more notice . . . for God's sake . . .' My words are getting faster, and I can feel the tears in my eyes, and he must be able to hear them in my throat. And of course I've said 'it's fine', which is the biggest most obvious most frequent lie of them all. If you say 'it's fine', it is never fine. Fine should come out of the dictionary, so we are forced to search around for alternative words, and maybe even say what we mean.

'I'm still coming tonight. What time is it again?'

'Seven . . . I told you it was seven . . . don't come if you don't want to . . .'

'Sunny, I want to come. But I'll come round about sixish, if that's OK, because I need to talk to you about something.'

'OK . . . but you're sure you want to come?'

'Of course I want to. I want to see you.'

I catch my breath slightly. Maybe it *is* love.

'OK . . . oh, I want to see you too, of course. Well then, I'll see you at six.'

'See ya.' Adrian hangs up first.

I put my phone down on the table, and run my fingers through my hair. Maybe tonight won't be so bad after all. I look down at my to-do list, and smile as I cross off Adrian and Notes. All I have to do now is phone Customs, and I will have done everything on my list. A clean slate, all boxes ticked, all missions accomplished.

The number for Portsmouth Customs was stored in my phone months ago. I know five out of the twelve customs officials by their voice, and we are on first-name terms. When the first few deliveries got questioned I had made it my mission to get along with them all, and get my stuff moving as quickly as possible. Mostly they were just curious, but they were amiable and efficient, and it normally didn't take too much time. As long as I don't get Nancy Hom everything will be fine.

Nancy is a very officious, very methodical Vietnamese lady, who is wonderful at her job, if you are standing in front of her. But on the phone, she tends to understand fifteen per cent of what I say at best. And she is obsessed with animal trafficking. She inexplicably believes that everybody that calls her, about any item they are trying to locate, is trying to traffic animals into the country. Normally rodents – ferrets, polecats, hamsters . . . I just know how it will play out before I even start the conversation, if I get Nancy today. There is nothing I can do.

I sit back in my chair, cross my legs, feel the sun on my face, and listen to the phone ringing in Portsmouth. I hear a click, and inhale, with crossed fingers. But it is the recorded voice of Bill Gregor the Scottish supervisor.

'I am sorry we are unable to take your call at this time, but we are experiencing a large volume of –'

'Hello, Nancy speaking . . .'

My heart sinks.

'Hi, Nancy. It's Sunny Weston. From shewantsshegets-.com? We've spoken before . . .'

'Oh, yes. Hi, Sunny. How are you?' She really is a lovely lady. I feel so bad for never wanting to speak with her again.

'I'm fine, Nancy. How are you?'

'I'm fine also. What can I do for you today, Sunny?'

'OK. Nancy, I'm missing a shipment of underwear, from Adana.' I am not going to risk saying 'Turkey'. Besides, Nancy knows where Adana is.

'OK, when was it due in?'

'Two days ago.'

'OK. How much?'

'Four boxes.'

'OK, what kind of underwear?'

'Silk . . . mostly knickers, some vest tops, some slips . . . with extra ties on them, lots of ribbons . . .'

'OK. What will it say on the label, Sunny?'

'The box labels?'

'Yes, the label.'

I take a deep breath. 'It'll say . . . "Silk Japanese Bondage", Nancy.'

I hear a sharp intake of breath in Portsmouth, and then silence at the other end of the line.

'Nancy? Are you there?' I venture.

'Do you have the correct paperwork for trafficking badgers into this country, Sunny?'

I could cry. Roll on the dreadful dinner party, for it cannot be worse than this.

Cagney is standing in the corridor of his flat, trying to make out his reflection in a dirty, framed Constable print that was hanging on the wall the day he moved in. He takes his overcoat off, and holds it in his hand. He pulls it back on, shaking his head. He leans forward to make out his reflection. The light bulb is covered in dust, and the walls are a dirty cream. He is dressed all in black, and his head looks pale and disembodied above his polo neck. A line of sweat springs on to his top lip with a sting, and he tugs his overcoat off and hangs it casually over his shoulder, resting it on one finger.

'Oh, for fuck's sake . . .' he mutters, before slinging it on the table and walking out, slamming the door behind him.

Christian is waiting for him outside Screen Queen. He is dressed in a dark blue suit and cornflower-blue shirt, with the top two buttons undone to reveal a tanned neck, sparsely covered with dark hair. He looks impeccable, draped in sobriety.

The Railway Inn by the station is littered with drinkers, and Cagney eyes them enviously as he walks past. Laughs and screams and shouts burst out from separate groups of tourists and builders and locals. Cagney hasn't been in the pub for over a year, but the urge to dive in to its anonymity overwhelms him. He straightens his back and marches on.

The sky is clear of any clouds, and at dusk it is still so light that Cagney can make out the scowl on Christian's face from twenty paces. He is ten feet away when he hears Christian speak.

'For the record, Cagney, and for the last time, this is plainly a fucking awful idea. I haven't been this negative about a night out since Brian took me to that Queen musical.'

'Let's go.' Cagney doesn't slow down but walks past Christian, who picks up the pace alongside him.

'Haven't you brought anything?'

'What?'

'A bottle, Cagney. Rosé would have done – it still feels like summer, at least.'

'No.'

'Well, thank God I did. Christ, how out of practice can one man be?'

Cagney marches on.

'Where is it?' Christian enquires as they turn at the end of the road, and instead of crossing towards the Gardens, take a right towards the South Circular.

'It's one of the streets behind the green. We'll go the back way.'

Cagney and Christian stride down a leafy Kew street and hear the strains of Jazz FM and children playing from alternate houses, the clink of well-cut glass and the smell of marinated turkey on barbecues beyond sash windows and heavy stained-glass doors.

'Excited?'

'Don't be fatuous.'

'Well, you know what Oscar Wilde said, Cagney, "In the autumn a young man's fancy turns to thoughts of love".'

'It was the spring, and it was Tennyson.'

'Are you sure? I'm positive that was Oscar Wilde.'

'It was Tennyson. Oscar Wilde said that a man can be happy with any woman as long as he does not love her.'

'Not exactly an expert, was he?' Christian smirks, then eyes Cagney suspiciously as they stop at the end of the road, and allow Golfs and four-by-fours and Porsches to crawl past. Eventually a teenage boy driving a BMW beckons for them to cross.

They dodge overgrown French-style gardens and lazy fat cats as they turn left into a postcard avenue smelling of peonies and espresso.

'I think two hours maximum. We get in, we make nice, we get out.'

'Sounds magical.'

'Christian, I'm deathly serious. And don't play about in there; don't embarrass me with that girl.' Cagney marches on with his head forwards, not turning to address Christian as he speaks.

'You know, I could just go home right now if you'd prefer, Cagney? I have a thousand other things I could be doing on a Friday night.' Christian stops walking and stands his ground.

Cagney stops two paces ahead of him and stares forwards. 'I'm sorry. But I'm asking you, please don't embarrass me.'

'Cagney, if anything, it is you who will embarrass me. I am skilled in the art of dinner-party conversation, whereas your idle chat with people you've known for ten years leaves a lot to be desired.'

'Let's just get it over with. And, for your information, I can do small talk when I need to. I'm not a complete social misfit.'

Simultaneously they begin to walk again.

'You do quips, Cagney, not conversation. You do put-downs.'

'It's a gift.'

'Maybe, but it's not exactly endearing. If you want to make this girl like you –'

'For Christ's sake!' Cagney raises his voice, stops abruptly and turns to face Christian, who is unimpressed. Cagney lowers his voice. 'I don't give a damn what she thinks of me.'

Christian ignores his protests. 'Love follows laughter, Cagney. Or good abdominals. You don't have the stomach any more so just stick to the jokes is all I'm saying.'

'You haven't seen my stomach. Anyway, familiarity breeds contempt. And divorce.'

'You've clicked with the lovely Sunny already, Cagney. Don't throw it all away with some damn defensive coolness. Sunny – what a fabulous, tragic name.'

'There was no "click". And it's a ridiculous name.'

'Look who's talking. Something always tips the balance, Cagney, and you can feel it when it does. Something has tipped your balance and now you're feeling all off kilter.'

'Christian, I would have thought that you, of all people, would have realised by now that I am more than happy on my own.'

'No, Cagney. You kid yourself that it's all doomed and beautiful and brave, but it's just stupid and careless to be alone for as long as you have been.'

'I don't see you walking up the aisle, Christian.'

'If you opened your eyes, you'd see me trying. I'm forty,

Cagney; I want to settle down. I can't fuck about for ever, even if I wanted to. Footloose is just slang for I haven't met the right man. Seeking out happiness is the bravest thing, not hiding from it.'

Cagney opens his mouth to speak, and then closes it again.

'It is OK to be you, Cagney; it is OK to be average. You don't have to cloak yourself in an angry mysterious Vaseline if you are with the right person.'

'I'll leave the Vaseline to you.'

'Jesus, Cagney, we're having a conversation! Can we cut the quips for two minutes? Can you emote on any level? Have you ever managed to actually say what you feel? Not that you need to, it's perfectly bloody obvious! You really aren't as dark and disturbing as you like to seem. You're perfectly normal, perfectly likeable, if you'll let somebody in. You think your surface is the only thing that keeps you interesting, but if that's all you are prepared to give, nobody is going to dig any deeper, and certainly not Sunny Weston.' Christian speaks with his hands, gesturing as he walks, knocking loose flowers as they hang over from purposefully unkempt gardens, showering the pavement behind him with petals. Cagney's arms swing tightly at his sides like a well-trained soldier.

'What do you know about her? What videos she rents? She is the worst kind of shallow, she's a gym nut diet fruit-cake. She wouldn't know depth if she was drowning in it.'

'When did "depth" get added to your long list of character strengths, Monsieur James? Hinting at something beneath doesn't mean there is actually something there. We can all stuff a sock down our trousers, Cagney; it doesn't mean we're sporting ten inches.'

'For fuck's sake, does it all have to come down to sex with you people?' Cagney winces at his own words.

'I was making an analogy, Cagney, and the "you people" remark is below even you.'

'So what do you want me to do, Christian? Laugh gaily at her jokes? Cry if she mentions the sad old fat days? Overcome her with my sensitivity? What a pile of shit.'

'Well, you aren't going to win her heart with a look, Cagney. She has more choices than that. If you wanted to get her easily you should have met her last year – a raised eyebrow might have done it then. But these beautiful bodies don't stay on the shelf for long. You've connected with her on a deeper level – you need to take advantage of that quick before somebody far less deserving than you snaps her up. Having the chat won't cut it.'

Cagney smiles, in spite of himself. Christian knows him well. 'The chat used to be the thing, you know. And I used to get them with a look. I shall speak whole silent volumes with one raised eyebrow . . .'

'What are you throwing at me now?' Christian smiles back.

'Ovid.'

'Well, at least there's still something erotic in you, Cagney, even if it is just poetry. But it's a different ball game now. Love calls for guts . . . and . . . initiative. You can't keep yourself back, hidden away.'

'Well, that poses a problem for me, Christian, because I can't think of anything worse than jumping into some-body's character like a goddamn plunge pool. It's fucking uncivilised.'

'It's liberating!' Christian throws his hands in the air, and upsets an overgrown hibiscus, causing a small sweet lavender storm around them.

'It's repellent.' Cagney swipes at a wasp.

They stop walking outside an expensive yet noticeably shabby three-storey house behind Kew Green. Just from the paint that peels lazily at the window frames, and the crooked number on the door, Cagney knows that the man of the house is a thinker and not a doer. Any previous attempts at DIY have left him with bloodied fingers and a bruised ego, so much so that he gave up years ago. And yet they never quite get round to getting somebody in, to fix all the things that need fixing, in an oversized family home. It is in middle-class disarray. Cagney knows it well. Half the houses on these streets are the same, bursting with money and intellect, but not enough common sense among them to change a tyre.

Neither Cagney nor Christian makes an effort to push a crooked gate, to walk up a garden path littered with flowering weeds between its expensive paving.

'You'd rather fuck them than talk to them, Cagney, and these days you don't get one without the other, in your world at least.'

'I don't expect to . . .' Cagney lowers his voice, which has risen to an angry level. 'That is absolute rubbish. I waited a year for Lydia.'

'So you told me – and all that time wasted. Stop talking, Cagney. We have to go in.'

But now he has found his voice Cagney can't keep quiet. And he really doesn't want to go in.

'It wasn't wasted! My mum and dad stayed together for fifty years, precisely because they kept themselves back. They danced around each other with words and smiles and learnt a little something every year. But I bet you a thousand pounds that the day my mother died my father couldn't have told you what her star sign was, and rightly so! It's all a load of rubbish.'

'Cagney, I know you've put yourself out there before, and got trampled on, but we both know that they weren't the right ones for you. We have to go in.'

Christian pushes the gate open, but Cagney grabs his arm.

'Trampled on? That's putting it bloody mildly.'

'Fine, you got hurt. Look, there are kids staring at the window, Cagney. We have to go in . . .'

Christian gestures with his head towards a large sash window, where two little faces have popped up beneath layers of muslin and are watching two strange tall men at the end of their garden having an argument.

'Fuck the kids! I have been divorced three times! Three different women, completely different women with nothing in common other than me, chose to leave me within one year of marriage! Alice walked after three weeks, for Christ's sake!'

'Which is unfortunate . . .' Christian turns towards the children with a fixed grin and mouths, 'We're just coming,' and then pokes out his tongue.

'Unfortunate? It's madness! No, going back for more would be real madness.'

'No, Cagney. Madness is only caring about yourself.'

'I'm not a fool, Christian,' Cagney says through gritted teeth.

'No, but let's face facts, Cagney. You always go for the same type. Gracie, Lydia, Alice – they were all the same woman, I've seen the pictures. They all used the same hair colourant for Christ's sake: arctic blonde! If you would just pick somebody nice, and lovely, and available, who isn't just using you, and who won't bore you or leave you after five minutes, who has a bit of substance, rather than some bloody ice queen! A bit of personality! Now take Sunny Weston –'

'Enough about that bloody girl! I don't go for shrews – can you blame me? I like them blonde, and I like them beautiful – again, can you blame me?'

'And you kid yourself that there's something beneath those looks and icy stares. You kid yourself they are Grace Kelly, but when you realise there's nothing there it's too late, and then you get bored, and you hate yourself for having picked them just because they are beautiful, and then you stop talking . . . and then they leave!'

'Exactly – they left me! They all walked away! I am off the market now. I am stable. I may be alone, but that is my choice, and I like it that way.'

Christian sighs, and walks towards the house. Cagney follows. They stand side by side in front of the door. Neither makes an effort to bang the large brass knocker.

'I will not be made a fool of again,' Cagney whispers.

'Are you talking to me, or trying to convince yourself?'

'I won't put myself through that again, Christian.'

'Then you'll never fall in love again. And to know that, with certainty, is a glimpse into hell,' Christian states matter-of-factly.

'Well then, Satan, here I come, because I've had that impulse ripped out of me, thank Christ.'

Christian grabs the knocker and bangs it twice. It sounds, to Cagney, like a whole heap of trouble.

Somebody shouts, 'Just coming!' from behind the door, and the two little heads disappear from beneath the curtains.

Christian and Cagney stare at their shoes, waiting. They hear the sound of feet running quickly down wooden stairs.

Christian turns to Cagney. 'Be nice,' he says, and smiles.

Cagney takes a deep breath. 'I'll try to try.'

I have spent so long living through my imagination, creating the romances that elude me in my head, that I sometimes find it hard to distinguish between what is real and what isn't. It is difficult to know if I am actually feeling something, or whether I am still just wishing it, dreaming it true. I have longed for an intimacy that allowed somebody to dent my emotional armour. I have pictured lovers leaving me early in the morning to go abroad with work and never come back. I tried my hardest to cry, when there was no one to cry for. I rented *Dirty Dancing*, and *An Officer and a Gentleman*, and *Pretty Woman*, over and over again from the video shop. I watched the shy girl, and the poor angry girl, and the slut, all fall in love, because love comes and finds you and carries you away. Nobody puts Baby in the corner, Go Paula Go, and Cinder-fuckin-rella. I was Baby, and Paula, and Vivian, just bigger. I was waiting for my prince to come and get me. I was waiting for my fairy tale to finish, the way that they do, the way that they should. Because if my life wasn't a fairy tale, and there was no prince to wait for, what had I been doing for all of that time, except dreaming?

I should have stopped my life, my fairy tale, when I opened the door to Adrian at two minutes to six. He smiled, my heart raced, my make-up was flawless, and we kissed. If the world had only held its breath at that moment, and forgotten to exhale, it would have been a happy ending.

I look at the clock. It is five past six. So it has taken him seven minutes to tell me. Three weeks, and seven minutes.

'Say it again?' I ask him, confused.

'I'm still engaged.' Adrian nods his head, so I know it's the truth.

'I don't understand. How can you be? We've been seeing each other for three weeks . . .'

'Well, we've only really seen each other a few times . . . I mean, we've spoken more than that, but that's mobile phones . . .'

'And what do you mean, "still"? You weren't engaged when I saw you last year, when I last saw you . . .'

'I know. I met up with Jane about six weeks after you left, I think . . . and we just kind of re-clicked.'

'Jane? The PE teacher?'

'Yeah.' Adrian's head is bobbing again, like a plastic nodding dog in the back of a car being driven too slowly by an old man in thick brown plastic glasses, who sits too close to the steering wheel. But that car will eventually turn right or left, and with it the nodding will stop, and it won't be annoying any more. And if not you can ram into the back of the old man's car, hurtling him through the windscreen, shredding him to a gory glassy death, just so that you can see the rear window cave in and rip the dog's head off . . .

'Don't you want to see me any more, Adrian? Is this a lie?'

'Yeah, of course I'm lying.' His tone is bitter but his sarcasm, at this moment, makes me feel so sick I want to scream.

'I thought that she wasn't right for you . . .'

'I don't know, I don't know! I'm confused . . .' Adrian drops his head, and I think he wants me to feel sorry for him.

He is sitting at the table in my kitchen, playing with the grapes in my fruit bowl, picking them up and letting them fall through his fingers. I don't want him to touch them any more, so I slap his hand away, and he looks up at me with the expression of a baby, smacked for the first time, not quite understanding what he has done, but knowing that it hurts.

'Is this just an excuse not to come tonight?' I ask quietly, as I sit down opposite him at the table. A lot of men have shot me through with a lot of excuses in the past. I am ready for them. Daniel, at my final year primary school disco, who said he had to go to the toilet when I plucked up the courage to ask him to dance, then saw him slow dancing with Michelle two minutes later. Or Adam, the boy that I worked with in Boots on a Saturday while I was in college, who I

167

laughed with in the car when he picked me up in the morning. Adam, who told me that his girlfriend wouldn't be very happy if we went out for a drink after work when I suggested it, red-faced and stuttering one evening after two years of working together. He wasn't seeing her when he asked out Sarah Jane in Film Processing a week later. Or Stuart, my philosophy study partner for February in my second year at university, who said he never got involved with study partners, when we sat together in his dorm room preparing a presentation on Socrates one night at 2 a.m. I heard later that he'd slept with March and April and May. They were too embarrassed to say no to me, because I was fat, so they masked it in 'but we are friends' or 'I'm already seeing somebody' or even 'I'm going to the toilet' when I knew they weren't. And the fact that they lied hurts more than the truth would have, because at the time I took it as a rejection of all of me – my mind, my eyes, my laugh, my manner. Not just my size. I wish they had just said, if they thought it, 'I don't find you physically attractive, sorry.' There is no real difference between thinking it and articulating it. It won't feel any less shallow, saying it out loud.

Adrian looks up at me through his long dark shaggy fringe. He is wearing a good grey shirt and dark trousers. He has made an effort for tonight.

'It's not an excuse. I proposed seven months ago. I really am engaged.'

'Then why are you here? Why did you sleep with me?' My voice is barely audible, a whisper.

'Because I'm not happy. I'm confused . . . I don't know if Jane is necessarily the right one for me . . .'

'Don't you think it might have been fairer, on both of us, on all of us, if you had made a decision about that before getting into bed with me?'

'I know, I know!' Adrian throws his hands in the air and

they land heavily on the kitchen table, jolting the tall pepper grinder in the corner, and I reach out and catch it before it falls.

I know that what I am feeling now must be real because, even though I desperately don't want to, I start to cry.

Adrian looks up and reaches across the table for my hand, but then changes his mind at the last minute, and instead holds out his fingers to me.

'Take my hand,' he says.

I don't move.

'Sunny,' he says, with some force.

'What?' I demand, and glare at him.

'Take my hand. Tell me that you feel the way I do.'

'I don't have a clue how you feel,' I say.

He squeezes my hand again, as he says, 'I am just really, really, confused,' like it's a revelation, and light should be shining from behind his head, and an invisible force should take him and lift him up on high, so he can float above me like the martyr to his feelings that he thinks he is.

He smiles at me, and his eyes sparkle from beneath his fringe. He winks. I slap him, with the palm of my hand, across his right cheek. I slap him with such force that my fingers sting as they whip through and leave imprints in his face. He jumps up, alarmed. His chair falls backwards on to the floor with a bang. I feel strange, my hand feels strange as I shake it. I don't know why I hit him. I could have stopped myself; it certainly wasn't an overwhelming impulse. I knew exactly what I was doing; I wasn't momentarily out of my mind. I just did it because I thought that I could. In this situation it was allowed, and I have never slapped a man before – I have never had cause to. I suppose I wanted to see what it felt like . . .

'What the hell was that for? I still want to be with you, Sunny!'

I cough a laugh and raise my eyes, as if it were obvious what the slap was for, and so I don't have to think of an explanation, other than 'you winked, and it irritated me', or 'I think you are being flippant with both our feelings'.

'I'm sorry, all right! I just wanted you to know where I am at the moment, where my head's at, if I seem distant . . . and if I have to take a call from her, if she rings . . . I might need you to be quiet.'

'Are you going to leave her?' I ask quietly. Suddenly I feel I know what Adrian means to me, and it's everything. Suddenly I see Christmas, decorating the tree, him cooking lunch and me chopping vegetables – opening presents at my parents' house, with and without him: I see my birthday, an extravagant meal in a gorgeous Thai Fusion restaurant with all of my friends, with and without him. I see a holiday in Italy, driving down bends on coastal roads in Amalfi, staying in a fragrant concern that overlooks the sea, run by an old Italian mamma who makes us mountains of pasta . . . with and without him. I see myself in a four-poster bed in an old pub in the Lake District as the rain drenches ramblers outside, and a fire burns in the corner of the room, as I pull on jeans to run downstairs and get another bottle of red wine and two bags of Mini Cheddars for lunch . . . with or without him. I see a future with him, and I want it so desperately that I think in that moment I might say anything to get it. I've just started to feel things. I don't want it to stop yet.

He picks up his chair, places it upright at the table and sits down. 'I don't know if I can leave her,' he says.

'Why not, if you aren't happy?' I ask.

'Don't be naïve, Sunny. I owe her more than that.' He has made me feel like a child.

'So . . . what are you offering me?' I gulp back tears, and pray.

170

'I didn't know I was "offering" anything.' He takes my hand, and laces his fingers through mine. 'Let's just angle our faces to the sun, feel the wind in our backs, and see what happens?' He smiles at me as he says it and squeezes my hand.

I look up into his eyes, and I hear myself saying, 'OK,' and nodding, like the dog in the back of the car, waiting for its head to be ripped off.

I am instantly terrified of how it will feel when he leaves. Of how my heart will bruise and bleed when he decides that it is easier to hurt me and stay with her, than hurt her and be with me. When he actually makes the decision that my feelings don't matter as much, that I don't matter as much. When he admits that he'd rather I was sad than she was. And maybe he won't even picture me, sitting on my own somewhere, fighting off tears, because he won't like the thought that he caused it. But it doesn't mean I won't sit on my own, and I won't cry, because I will, when his actions turn my life on its axis and dump all the plotted points in a mess on the floor. I can already feel it coming. But for some reason I feel that it is good for me to stay in this, and wait with morbid curiosity. I need to know that it won't kill me.

I glance up at the clock. 'It's quarter to seven, we have to go.' I unlock my hand from his, and wipe my eyes, standing up and brushing myself down.

'Or . . .' Adrian kicks back his chair, and walks slowly round the table towards me, and puts his hands around my waist.

'Or?' I ask, incredulous. But he doesn't get it, because he starts to hitch up my dress carefully, tickling my thighs with his fingers as he lifts it slowly higher, and tickling my neck with his lips and his breath. Crouching down slightly, silky material in his hands rising inch by inch, he massages his

171

thumbs upwards on the inside of my thighs, pushing me gently back against the kitchen wall. I am waiting for the right moment to stop him, as he pulls my knickers down with one hand, and squeezes my breasts through my dress with the other, leaving wrinkles and creases where his hand has been. I wait to say no, as he kisses me gently, his tongue slowly circling the inside of my lips. But then he pulls back, and looks me straight in the eye, so near to me that I feel it can only be honesty that I see, he is too close to lie. Then he drops to his knees, and lifts my dress, and pushes my legs a little further apart. I run my hands through the long dark hair on the back of his head as his tongue teases me gently, before he kisses me long and hard, alternating his mouth with his fingers, until I am digging my nails into his neck. He knows instinctively when to stop, and stands, unzipping his trousers quickly with his left hand, while the fingers on his right keep me ready. Suddenly I feel him graze me with his cock, which is the hardest I have felt it, not softened by drink . . . I can't believe he makes me wait, and just lingers there, watching my face, tracing a line with himself, up and down me. But then he pushes forward, and this time it is slow, and it is hard, and he watches my reactions, and knows exactly what to do, and it feels as if it is only about me . . .

As we run along the road afterwards, holding hands, and I click click click in heels, and we both check our watches, knowing we are late, I cannot believe how amazing I feel. How hard I shook, and how loudly I screamed, actually screamed, with pure joyful bloody relief. It was unlike anything I have ever felt before. It was the kind of amazing that I know, just like a first hit of heroin to a teenager, or the murderous rush of a first kill to a psychopath, that I won't be able to resist again. And yet like the addict and the killer, I already know I am doomed . . . because I am giving away my whole soul to someone who treats it as if it were a flower to put in his coat, a bit of a decoration to charm his vanity . . . and there is no picture hanging in my attic to smudge with tears and crumple and fall apart. When it happens, that will really be me, and everybody will see.

SIX

Killing love and sex over dinner

Children are screaming and swirling around my legs, grabbing hold of Adrian's trousers as they spin past us to stop themselves toppling into the balustrades of the stairs or the large glass Philippe Starck thing in the hallway. William, who doesn't pay me any attention although we have met before, is chasing two very young girls in jeans and citrus-coloured T-shirts. The girls squeal and giggle and call out to each other.

'Poppy!'

'Gabriella!'

'Poppy! Poppy!'

'Gabriella!'

Sweet high voices and perfect diction, they could read the ten o'clock news – and now over to Poppy for a breaking story on the CIA in Afghanistan – and back to Gabriella for predictions of the chancellor's third budget tomorrow, and incidentally, Gabriella, is it true that you are only five years and two months? Yes, yes it is, Poppy, and is it true you will be four in three weeks' time? Yes, Gabriella, that's right!

Clean curls bounce on their little shoulders, dancing and

twirling, playing kiss chase and escaping from boys, splashing about in a perfect childhood. As they run off into the kitchen, hotly pursued by Charlie, I see a little red head and freckles peeking out from behind a stable door, but as we catch each other's eyes, Dougal disappears. I grab behind me for Adrian's hand, but he has already moved through into the sitting room.

My heels announce me on the wooden floor as I take three steps through the doorway, and everybody looks up in my direction with wide friendly eyes, but they all forget to smile. I shouldn't have had sex with Adrian before we left. I feel like everybody knows, and it makes me a whore. Deidre will introduce me to her neighbours, perched on the edge of the sofa reeking of Amnesty International and back garden rosemary, as 'Sunny Weston, the whore who saved my son'.

Adrian has just sat down in the last available armchair in the corner of the room, and he pats its slightly worn purple arm for me to come and sit with him, but I don't. Deidre flies out of the room as she hears an alarm buzzing angrily in the kitchen, mumbling back over her shoulder that Terence has popped out to Oddbins but will be back in minutes; he didn't feel they had the right white.

There is one other armchair, and Cagney James is sitting in it. I quickly look away. Standing by the fireplace is a tall handsome man in an impeccable suit who looks totally familiar, but I can't place him. I try not to appear frantic with nerves, but instinctively pull at the front of my dress to make sure it isn't caught up in any rolls of fat. I always pull too hard, because there isn't anywhere for the material to be stuck now. My dress is claret silk and knee length, simple and fitted, with a scoop neck and elbow-length sleeves. I am wearing chocolate brown Mary Janes, but no tights, because of the heat.

Christine and Peter Gloaming from next door introduce themselves with big smiles as the parents of Poppy and Gabriella. Christine, who is small-framed but with a large stomach, and is no taller than five foot two, asks if she can get me a glass of wine, and moves past me to the kitchen. My gut instinct is to refuse, alcohol effectively doubling the amount of calories consumed in a meal, but I don't know if I will make it if I have to observe this night with sober eyes, so I thank her and hope she won't be too long with my much-needed glass of Dutch courage.

I stand in the middle of the sitting room, in front of Adrian and Cagney James, and Peter Gloaming, who is thin but flabby, with a long neck and metal glasses, and the man at the fireplace who introduces himself as Christian Laurie. He explains that he is here with Cagney, and that we've met before because he owns Screen Queen, which is where I rent my videos. He smiles at me warmly, and I wonder, if he is as lovely as he seems, what is he doing with Cagney? Seconds later the penny drops that Cagney is gay, and I feel a little angry. My therapist had it very wrong indeed.

I glance back at Christian, who beams at me again, and I think it must be because he remembers me, from last year, bigger. Of course, he will have told Cagney James. I didn't want him to know. I didn't want to give him the ammunition. I look around and see that everybody here weighs about average, the only real felony being Christine's stomach, and that is just age and two lots of childbirth, unfortunate genes and no real cardio. But because there is nobody present who is noticeably overweight, I am sure that at some point this evening Cagney will make a fat jibe, and they will always sting.

The children are sitting at a separate table that has been set up in the kitchen. Christine and Deidre take it in turns to supervise them: Deidre slips quietly in to the dining room, and lowers herself back into her chair as Christine pushes herself gently to her feet, and moves noiselessly into the kitchen. By the sound of it the children are having a lot more fun than we are. I have only said 'hello' to Cagney. I haven't looked him in the eye at all. I sit between Peter Gloaming and Terence Turnball, and turn from one to the other and continue what seems to be the same conversation about phone masts or local schooling or schooling children about local phone masts. Deidre sits next to Peter when she is not checking on the children. I notice that her husband, Terence, has winked at her twice across the table, and half smiled. Cagney sits to Deidre's right, and Christine's left, and so only ever has one table-mate, but whomever it happens to be, Christine or Deidre, they give him their undivided attention. He finds this uncomfortable, I can tell. He would rather they were both there, and talked over him, or neither was there and left him in peace. I haven't heard him give more than a one-word answer since we sat down half an hour ago. To Christine's right is Adrian, but as Christine only ever talks to an otherwise solitary Cagney when she is at the table, Adrian only ever talks to Christian. They seem to be having the most acceptable time. They laugh lightly and occasionally, and chat animatedly, and it makes me jealous. And then there is Terence, and then it's me.

I haven't seen Dougal since that first early glimpse, and I have to say I am relieved. Terence excuses himself early on and darts into the kitchen while Deidre clears away our starter plates, which are licked clean of their salmon sashimi on seaweed, with deep-fried baby oysters on top. He returns moments later, leading Dougal by his little food-stained hand into the dining room. The small talk stops.

Dougal doesn't resist his daddy, but looks down rather than at his audience.

'Dougal wanted to say hello, and show what a big brave boy he is,' Terence says as Dougal looks at his Clarks pasty shoes.

I hear Christian inhale sharply. I glance over at Cagney, who is looking down at the table, mortified.

'Dougal, this is Sunny, and this is Cagney,' Terence says.

Dougal looks up, from me to Cagney, and then back at his little shoes with Velcro fastening for babies. I feel a lump in my throat, and swallow it loudly. Cagney hears it and looks up at me. Dougal doesn't recognise us, and I am relieved.

'I think it's good that he doesn't remember who you are,' Terence stage-whispers, so that the neighbours, if they were next door and not sat at our table, would be able to hear.

Dougal looks up at his daddy, who wasn't there on the day that he needed him most, and I wonder who it is that hurts more. Dougal opens and shuts his hand, as his father clasps it.

'Well, I think it's time you went to bed, young man.' Deidre moves anxiously forward and takes Dougal's other hand. Dougal lets go of his father instantly.

'Say good night,' Deidre says, and Dougal whispers, 'Gnight.'

'Why don't you give Sunny a kiss good night?' Terence says suddenly, and I hear Christian gasp again.

'Oh Jesus, no!' I exclaim. A table full turns to face me sharply. 'I mean, please, just let him go to bed. He doesn't need to do that. He doesn't know who I am.'

I don't want him to have to touch me. Deidre smiles at me, and leads Dougal out of the room, avoiding eye contact with Terence, who mulls something over as he moves to sit back down.

'More wine, anyone?' he asks, holding another bottle of the 'right white' aloft.

Four glasses shoot out in unison.

Two hours later we have descended into a drunken slurring band who stalked and snatched intoxication with bare desperate hands. The fog in my head is sweet relief from the silences that keep enveloping the table. Christian blurts out random statements at ten-minute intervals, taking the time to compose each one in his head, and ensure he has the syllables of each word in the right place, before he declares them to a table desperate for something to say.

'Hathor was the goddess of both love . . . and laughter, you know.' He sighs heavily, having just realised a lifetime's worth of depression in that one thought. His head slips from his hand and his chin jerks forwards and upwards just in time – moments more and it would have smashed on to the table and into a thousand tiny pieces.

'How apt,' Cagney says. It is hard to tell whether he is truly drunk or not, but his tone is more aggressive than usual and his manner allusive. He seems like a man desperately trying to hint at something we, his audience, should be guessing, miming it out to us but at the same time hoping we don't see.

A moment passes when nobody says anything.

'Meaning?' Christian asks, passionately drunkenly bored.

'That love is a joke. Obviously.' Cagney's sentences have begun to resemble the shots of whiskey he is downing sporadically from a bottle that magicked itself on to the table half an hour ago. He conjured it from thin air. I am waiting for the handkerchiefs, the bunch of flowers, the single white dove. There is barely a quarter of the bottle left. He fires out his words bullet fast and hard at us all, waiting for one of us to get hit and ripped open, and scream a response. How does this man function in the world, on a daily basis? How does he buy milk, or stamps, or fill up his car with petrol, or speak to his mother, or his cleaning lady?

How does he do any of these things, so filled with this rage?

'And what is it that you do, James?' I ask. 'I mean, Mr James. Cagney James . . . what do you do?' I giggle childishly at how that last sentence sounds, and then feel my face fall into an animated but stern expression – the face of a person doing an impression of a person who is stern . . .

'I run an agency.' He speaks quietly, addressing the table, not me.

'A modelling agency?' I ask.

Cagney's fingers, which have been folding a napkin into smaller and smaller squares go still, and he looks up at me. 'Why a modelling agency?'

'Oh . . . because that's what I think of, when people say agency.' What other kinds of agencies are there?

Nobody speaks, and I realise that I haven't asked the question aloud that I had asked in my head. I gulp quickly, feeling sick.

'What other kinds of agency are there?' I ask.

'The Employment Agency – that's the new name for Job Centres,' somebody says, but it's not me or Christian or Cagney, so I can't make out who. Ours are the only voices I recognise now. It's been so long since Adrian spoke I turn sharply to check he is still at the table. But he is, looking at his phone, texting.

I slur at him under my breath, 'Why are you even still here? Go if you wanna go . . .' But he doesn't hear me, and nobody understands me.

'Do you run an employment agency?' I ask Cagney.

'No.'

'What kind of agency then . . . do you run . . . what kind?' I hiccup quietly, and try to hide it behind my hand.

'An investigation agency.' Cagney is refolding his napkin, but lets it fall open suddenly, on the table, the creases springing out.

'What do you do?' Christian turns and asks Adrian, when nobody says anything.

'I'm in IT,' Adrian replies, not looking up from his phone.

'Oh . . . shit.' Christian looks crestfallen, and turns back to me.

'What do you do, lovely breezy bright and Sunny? What's your biz, squiz?' Christian laughs, and stares at me with wide eyes, waiting for the answer to his life's question.

'Probably children,' I say earnestly. And then realise that wasn't the question that he asked at all. 'I mean, I have my own business. I wouldn't quite call it an agency, though.' I elongate the word 'agency' to aggrandise it in a way that Cagney didn't.

I sneer in his direction a little, but without looking up he asks, 'Doing what?' He picks up his napkin and starts to fold it again.

'It's an e-business . . . a website. E-commerce, if you will. I am part of the . . . new media . . . wave of technology . . .' I gulp with alarm as a little rush of something nasty chases up my windpipe from my stomach, and then sinks down again. Whether I am now sick or not is out of my control. But that would be awful! Throwing up at an actual dinner party thrown by adults, all over the dining table, in front of everybody! That would be the most awful thing I can ever think of . . . ever . . . My eyes widen at how awful that would be. But Cagney is speaking . . .

'Doing what?' he asks again.

'I sell toys . . . and other things . . .' I say it as if it were explanation enough. As if 'other things' is a spectacularly specific way of putting it, and there is no need for any further explanation.

'What, like teddy bears and pogo sticks and hula hoops? Can you still get hula hoops?' Christian asks, momentarily interested, barely interested.

181

'I'm not sure . . . I don't really sell those kinds of toys. My types . . . of toy . . . are meant more for . . . the bedroom.' Bedroom sounds loud and round and enunciated, even though I whisper it. I reach for the bottle of wine in front of me, grab at it, and fill my glass, deliberately leaving a significant gap between bottle and glass, so much so that the wine being poured sounds like a man relieving himself. I check all the faces of the men at the table to see if it makes them uncomfortable, and it does appear to affect all of them. Except Adrian, who is still texting.

Cagney raises his eyebrows – I see it – but carries on staring at the table. It's a look that spells surprised, but not impressed. But Christian smiles broadly.

'What do you think of that, Mr James? Do you think it's wrong? Do you think it's just what the world has come to, hmmm? I would like you to know that I care for an answer . . .' I lean forward and stare at his forehead, my chin perilously close to the table, my cheek dangerously close to my wine glass.

'The world is pornographic these days,' Cagney mutters.

I sneer and roll my eyes. I feel my head roll at the same time, around on my shoulders, and loll back into my neck, my chin in the air, my eyes closing.

'You run a sex site in Kew? In the Village?'

I look up, and around quickly to place the strange voice. It is Peter Gloaming. I had forgotten he was here.

'It's not a sex site,' I say. 'You can buy underwear on it.' I sit back and smile, as my chin rolls back around and rests on my chest, before I rock my head back to look directly at anybody who can manage to meet my tottering eyes.

'But not just underwear,' Cagney says to his napkin, as he folds it into tighter squares.

'You can buy other things as well. This is true,' I say. 'Although it's not an agency,' I whisper to Christian across

182

the table. He puts his finger to his lips and makes a loud shush noise at me. I tut loudly, and close my eyes.

'You shouldn't be ashamed, if it's your business,' Cagney says. He throws his napkin down in front of him and looks up at me.

I widen my eyes to keep them open. 'I'm not ashamed . . . of anything. And especially not my business, James, I mean Cagney. Now tell me, what is your business again? Sorry, your *Agency*!' I laugh a short snort of derision, and look around for somebody to join me, but I am out on a derisive snorting limb, all on my lonesome.

Cagney sighs but doesn't answer.

'So there isn't any prostitution? You're not a madam?' Christine asks sweetly.

Christian spits out the mouthful of drink he has just gulped down, and it immediately stains the tablecloth, as he shouts, 'Hurrah!'

Adrian's mobile phone rings its ridiculous theme downloaded from a website that sells comic books and Japanese animated pornography.

He checks the number, and declares to the table, 'Sorry, I have to take this, I'm on call . . .' and pushes back his chair from the table. I don't hear him say hello until he reaches the hallway, and then it is hushed and intimate, and not at all what I take to be businesslike, or professional. Maybe it is his fiancée, or maybe he is just really unprofessional, or maybe he is shagging half of the office. Either way, I have just decided I hate him. I prickle with hatred, and pray it will pass.

'You're drunk, darling,' Christine suddenly accuses Peter. He wasn't saying anything. I don't know how she guessed.

'Just a little, darling,' Peter says.

'We're all a little drunk, darling,' Christian says, laying his palms flat on the tablecloth and stretching his fingers out, long and thin. He has old hands.

'Yes, but Peter can't form a logical argument when he is drunk. Can you? Peter? You're no good to the conversation,' Christine sighs, let down again.

'Socrates could drink anybody under the table,' Peter shouts, and I blink quickly five times in succession, to stop the noise from hurting me. 'And then he could convince them to sleep with him . . . drunk . . . and at the same time.'

'But you aren't Greek, darling,' Christine says, as if she were talking to a child.

'What in fuck difference does that make, darling?' Peter demands of his wife, who flinches when he swears.

'They can handle their wine, of course. They nurse them on it.'

'They nurse babies on wine in Greece?' Christian asks, confused. I shake my head in what I think is his direction, and mouth 'no no no' and hope he understands that they don't.

I turn round slowly to see where Adrian is, if he is still on the phone, if he is still here. I can hear him, but he has moved into the other room.

'So you sell sex,' Cagney says. I look up to see who he is speaking to. And then realise it's me.

'Excuse me?' I point at him.

'You sell sex,' Cagney says again.

'No! No, I sell sex toys. There is a huge vast really big difference – not that I'd expect you to understand.' I sigh heavily. I think I should go home soon.

'I understand perfectly. You sell plastic cocks to women so they don't need a man.'

'You're a crazy man,' I say, and look around for support. But nobody else speaks, so I have to again. 'I think that is quite a blinkered view, Mr Cagney. I mean, society,' I make speech marks with my fingers and regret it instantly – maybe I am starting to sober up. I push my wine glass away from me slightly. 'Society is a lot more open these days, to women,

184

young and old, finding out what they like, exploring their sexuality . . . I'm not replacing anything.'

'I'm sorry, did you not see me just eating?' Cagney asks me.

'I don't understand . . . we all ate . . . we just had dinner . . .' I look around with a bewildered smile for backup, at Peter and Christine, Christian, the politely terrible Turnballs, but none comes. And then I realise that Cagney is being sarcastic.

'Oh, I get it – what is wrong with saying that exactly? It makes you sick that women explore their sexuality?' I rest my head in one hand, so tired I may fall asleep in seconds, so ready for a fight I might spring to my feet and karate chop Cagney James like Cato.

'What really makes me sick, little plucky Sunny, is if I, as a man, decided to stay home on a Friday night and explore *my* sexuality I would be accused of being a sad lonely wanker.'

'If the cap fits . . .' I say, but I don't even get a giggle from Christian. I am sobering up now.

Cagney ignores me and continues, 'But a woman does it and everybody wants to give her a Nobel. It's hypocritical, and it's disturbing – a nation of women lying around on their own every night with their fingers buried inside themselves, egging that elusive orgasm on, ignoring life in favour of a quick slick fix.'

'You paint it sordid, Mr James, but you are right – the female orgasm is traditionally elusive. Men get the most amazing natural high easily, and by chance, whereas if we as women want to make permanent and recurrent friends with it, we have to seek it out. And in doing so, we learn a little bit about ourselves. We learn how to be sexual beings, and embrace our sexuality, and . . . it's a way to understand ourselves better.'

185

That has exhausted me, and I can't remember what point I was making, or what I said at the start of the conversation, or frankly, what I said only moments ago. I hope he doesn't ask questions.

'What's so hard to understand?' Cagney asks me evenly.

Nope. Nothing. Did I say understand? I cough once.

'Sorry?' I ask, confrontational, attempting to disguise the fact that my mind is a blank. All those strongly held convictions that just sung from me moments ago have slipped from my mind and are floating down my neck in my bubbly boozy bloodstream to infuse the rest of me.

'Why do you need to understand yourselves better? I understand perfectly.' Cagney's chin is jutting out, and I almost do an impression of it, before stopping myself at the last second, getting a handle on how very wrong that would be. I answer instead, hopefully the question that he asked.

'Do you? Do you really?' I reply. I don't know what else to say, but I know I still want a fight.

Christian attempts to cut the right wire and diffuse the situation. 'Women are very complex, Cagney,' he says earnestly, and smiles at me.

Cagney raises his eyes and smiles at Christian. Christian smiles back. I can't tell whether the joke is at my expense or not. But I feel paranoid. Enough! Enough of this woman-baiting and bashing by a couple of old queens. It's not my fault they don't fancy me, and I'm not going to bear the brunt of Cagney's attitude, nor his need to dismiss anything without a dick as substandard.

'Just because you aren't attracted to women, Mr James, that doesn't mean we aren't complex. I mean, how would you like it if –' I blurt it all out, slurring, half shouting, drunk again, on red wine and pent-up aggression. I feel giddy.

186

Cagney interrupts me before my argument trips over its own feet, and falls flat on the floor.

'Because I'm not what?' he demands.

'It's men like you that give homosexuals a bad name!' I shout suddenly, banging my fist on the table, trying to stand up, getting to my feet, standing/crouching, then realising it's too much effort and lowering myself slowly back down, and leaning back, relieved to be safely in my chair.

'Hey, who says homosexuals have a bad name?' Christian sits up and asks me seriously.

'Oh no, Christian, I didn't mean you. You're one of the nice ones.' I smile and wink, and feel like I have just slipped into a very big hole, and my skirts are blowing up around my ears, and I can't see for my own big fat conversational mistakes. But it doesn't stop me going on, 'What I meant was . . . I mean . . . the ones with the bad name are the ones that hate women . . .' I say.

'The ones that hate women?' Christian asks, incredulous.

'I don't mean you, Christian!' I raise my voice at him slightly to make him understand. In my head I think I hate myself too. A tiny little sober part of me is kicking back there, kicking at my skull, trying to get at the soft squidgy parts of my brain that control what I say out loud.

'No, Christian, she is right.' Cagney looks at me evenly, seriously, with a trace of contempt. 'I am the kind of man who gives homosexuals a bad name. Given that I actually have sex with women.'

The table falls silent. I wince at him, and replay what he just said in my head, to understand it. When the penny drops I don't have the capacity to stop myself saying what I think aloud. 'Oh Christ, not a bisexual!' and I throw up my hands.

'Sunshine, who said I was gay?' Cagney tosses the accusation at me, and I drop it.

I open my mouth to speak, but nothing comes out. But

if he isn't gay, why is his date a man? Why is he wearing a gay jumper? Why am I so drunk? How did this happen? Who let it happen? I look around to find the culprit. Nope, nobody here but little old wine drinker me to blame for this one. Time to make amends then.

'I just thought . . . because you are with Christian . . . you guys were a couple . . .'

Christian gasps in not so mock horror.

'So what you are saying is that you don't believe that a straight man can be friends with a gay man, because sex gets in the way? You, Supergirl, believe that I can't bring my male friend, who happens to be gay, to a dinner party without assuming we're lovers? That's just ignorance. And it's petty. And it's certainly very disrespectful of Christian.'

Christian claps his hands at the sound of his name. 'Don't be spiteful, Cagney. You know she didn't mean anything by it . . . really . . . even if it did all come out a little wrong.' Christian grimaces at me and I mouth 'I'm sorry' and frown at myself.

'Christian, I think you are forgetting that she just accused you of sleeping with me.'

Christian turns to speak to Cagney, but then turns back to address me instead. 'That is actually very hurtful, Sunny. My feelings are officially a little singed.'

'I'm really sorry, Christian,' I blurt out, as I feel myself blushing.

'What about me? Don't I deserve an apology, for being the victim of your rather unpolitically correct assumptions? For the accusation that I, Cagney James, give homosexuals a bad name. That's just mean, Sunny.'

I know that he is mocking me. I hear a clock in the hallway chiming midnight. I feel my feet in my high-heeled shoes beginning to ache. I feel the drunken dizziness being replaced by tired nausea. I am worn out with fighting, but

I'm not a quitter, or a loser, and Cagney James certainly hasn't won.

'Well, no matter what your sexuality, Cagney, I can't imagine you have ever even got close to understanding a woman, which is all any woman really wants. Which is why it was so easy to mistake you for a middle-aged bachelor . . . alone.'

'You don't think I understand women. That's interesting, given that I've spent one long evening with you and I understand you completely. Utterly. You are transparent.'

'Oh, you understand nothing.' I dismiss him with a wave of my hand, and search the table for a bottle of water that I might pillage. I can feel Cagney boring holes in my forehead, but ignore him, and the table falls silent.

'Is somebody wearing Aqua Di Gio?' Christian asks.

'I'm wearing Anaïs Anaïs,' Christine replies.

'I just sprayed oven cleaner in the kitchen,' says Deidre.

'Hmmm,' Christian says, nodding.

I hear Cagney mutter something, and I inhale sharply. I can't believe he has said what he has just said, in polite company. OK, so I might not have been that polite, but none the less . . .

'I'm sorry, what did you say?' I ask him directly, staring sharply in his direction, hoping my eyes aren't dilated.

'You're greedy,' he repeats.

Christian gasps a little gasp, and I gulp. I feel the tears spring to my eyes straight away. Here come the fat jibes, and I will always deserve them.

'I'm what?' I ask, and I know I sound pathetic. Not strong, or composed, or any of the things I want to be, or at least seem. I sound like a girl about to cry, who has drunk too much red wine in front of strangers. Adrian is still on his phone. I'm on my own again. As usual. 'I have barely eaten anything . . .' I start to say.

'You want it all,' Cagney says simultaneously. I stop speaking, but he carries on. 'You want to earn the cash, and have the babies, and spend five hundred pounds on a pair of shoes and not get stressed and have three holidays a year and have the sex life of honeymooners. And when that doesn't happen you get pissed off and you take it out on the nearest loser you can find.'

I stare at him confused. Where is the bit about food? Did he say something about shoes? And honeymooners?

'Petrol is my favourite smell,' says Peter.

'Hmmm, yes, I love the smell of petrol in the morning,' Christine volunteers with a smile.

'Does it smell like victory?' asks Christian.

I break the staring contest I am having with the vase just over Cagney's left shoulder to glance quickly at Christine, to make sure that she is OK, and not high.

'No . . . it means I've dropped the girls at school already. I never fill up the Land Rover on the way to school, we never have time.' Christine looks from me to Christian, to Peter and back again, confused . . . she really is very short.

'Hmmm,' Christian says.

Somebody sighs, and something falls on the floor. I really want to go home now. I glance around to find Adrian, but he is still in the other room.

'Do you know what I think, Mr James?' I sound reasonably sober; I impress myself. 'I think that the only thing you really understand about women is that they scare the shit out of you, and the only thing you are more scared of is admitting it.'

'Maybe you are right.' Cagney nods his head, and looks up. 'But it's not all women I am scared of . . . just the ones that are bigger than me.'

Christian drops the spoon he was playing with and looks up sharply at Cagney. My shoulders sag.

'Remember 1976?' asks Terence.

'Why?' asks Deidre.

Terence doesn't answer. Christian and Cagney and I look from one to another of us, never quite meeting either of the other's stare.

'Cagney . . .' Christian reproaches gently, but it's like a starter pistol.

'Women today want the world!' he shouts, banging his fist on the table.

'And why shouldn't I want the world?' I demand, just as angrily. 'Why is it for you and not for me?' I stab my finger in a point towards him.

'What do you want it for? What could you possibly do with it? Paint it pink? Cover it in chocolate sauce?' Cagney's cheeks are flushed red, but his voice is lower, controlled, but angry.

'What if I want it just to have it? Is that so bad? Or so different, for that matter? Isn't that what history is all about – men who wanted the world just to have it?'

'It's utterly different. The men of history wanted to create better places, greater civilisations. You! You wouldn't know what to do with it if you had it! You'd have to ask your councillor, or your yoga instructor!' Cagney laughs a short sharp laugh of derision, and then throws down his napkin for good.

'What does your agency do?' I demand, suddenly urgently needing to know.

'I catch out cheats,' Cagney says.

Adrian is still in the other room.

'What do you mean, "cheats"? What do they cheat at? Poker? Monopoly?'

'Marriage. Sex,' Cagney replies flatly.

'You catch men or women who are having affairs? You mean, you take photos? How awful!'

191

'It is awful, yes. That's the first sensible thing you've said all night, Sundry. The propensity for women to cheat on men is so great it keeps me and all my staff in hot champagne and penthouses.'

'You might want to up your clothes allowance if that's the case,' I snigger, but to nobody, to myself. And then, 'Hold on, you mean men and women, right? You just said women.'

'I was right the first time.'

'Are you saying men aren't unfaithful?' I laugh, wide-eyed, amazed. This guy is from another century!

'No.'

'Then why no wives?' I ask, confused.

'Because I don't work for women.'

I cough once, violently and uncontrollably, and Christian looks at me with concern, and mouths, 'Darling', before putting two thumbs up and mouthing, 'You OK?'

'You mean you *won't* work for women?' I say squarely.

'Won't . . . don't . . . tomato . . . tom—ato.'

'Let's call the whole thing off!' Christian sings loudly, and we all turn to face him as he throws his hands in the air.

I turn back to Cagney. 'I am sorry, Mr James, but that is just hateful! What you do is just . . . it's just evil! You are just evil!' I consider standing up for emphasis, but realise that I have lost one shoe whilst dangling it off an aching foot beneath the table, and if I did stand up quickly, even now feeling almost entirely sober, I would be lopsided. And then I would fall down.

'It is in no way worse than what you do!' Cagney fumes, his cheeks turning pink, and puffing out. He resembles a spoilt child throwing a temper tantrum.

'I sell underwear, for Christ's sake!' I shout. Christine winces as I swear. I don't see it, I just sense it.

'And great big bloody dildos!' Cagney shouts back, and I feel Christine almost pass out.

'What is so wrong with a vibrator?' I shout, reclaiming my shoe and pushing myself to my feet, as my chair scrapes back across a cold slate-tiled floor.

'You are replacing men!' Cagney shouts back, and visibly thinks about standing up himself.

'Oh my God, Mr James, men aren't just there for sex! What is wrong with you? A man is not just the sum of his reproductive parts. Some men can actually have a conversation with a woman! Can you believe that?'

'What do you call what we're having?' Cagney jumps to his feet and places his palms face down on the table, leaning forwards in my direction.

I take one step forward, place both of my palms flat on the table as well, and say in the lowest most controlled voice I can muster, 'A living bloody nightmare.'

'Why? Because dessert hasn't arrived yet?' Cagney stares at me. And the tears rush to my eyes again.

'Sorry?' I ask softly.

'Need that chocolate, do we?' Cagney asks flatly.

I feel my lip quiver, and I gulp loudly. Cagney's eyes flicker, and he glances quickly at the table, and then back at me.

'What are you saying to me?' I ask quietly, my lip trembling, my hands shaking, my eyes watering.

Cagney stares at me for a second, and I see something sweep across his face as a tear swells out of my right eye and lands heavily on my cheek. I see his hands, clenched in fists of the tablecloth, loosen. But then Peter Gloaming coughs a drunken cough, and it catapults Cagney out of the trance that had taken us both just then, feeling the pain together. He remembers his audience, and plays the role that he started to the end.

'Calm down, Sunny – lose your sense of humour as well as your love handles, did you?'

My hand moves up to wipe my eye quickly, and I move

out from in front of my chair. 'I'm leaving,' I say flatly, waiting for the tears to subside.

'Don't bother, I will.' Cagney moves out from behind the table with a ferocious speed.

'No! I said it first!' I shout at him, and he stands still. I turn to Deidre and Terence. 'I'm really sorry but I have to go now. Thank you for this evening, and . . .' I am already moving towards the door, before I stop suddenly, and turn to address them seriously, as I should.

'Words cannot express how glad I am that Dougal is OK, as OK as he can be. I am truly thankful that I could help, and the fact that he is still safe with you is all I need to know. I don't think it would do him any good to see me again, in case it does make him remember something he might otherwise have blacked out for life. So anyway . . . I'm just saying thank you, for tonight. But now I have to go.' I stare at them for a second, and then dart around the table and kiss them both on the cheek. I look up to see Christine and Peter sitting opposite each other, hammered, trying to focus on my leaving.

'Christine, and Peter, it was lovely to meet you both.'

Peter is drunk and gets up to kiss me goodbye.

I kiss him, or rather the air around him, lightly and quickly, and then click quickly around the table to Christine and kiss her as well, so she doesn't think I am hitting on her husband.

'And, Christian! I'll see you again soon, I'm sure.' I reach across a hand to hold his, but he pushes his chair back and leans forward, so I can peck him a quick goodbye. I stand up straight and survey the only adult left standing that I haven't kissed goodbye.

Cagney, who is standing on the other side of the table, glares at me.

'Now I have to go,' I say, and walk out.

I grab my bag from the table in the hallway and stop by the door to the sitting room. Adrian is still on the phone. He looks up at me apologetically after a few moments, and mouths the word 'sorry'. Then puts his finger to his lips and mouths 'shhh'.

I don't turn round as I walk out, despite hearing Christine ask, 'What's the name of her website? It sounds wonderful!'

I round the corner of their pathway by the gate and walk deliberately into the middle of the quiet road, because it is safer and nobody can grab you from behind a bush or a wall and drag you in. It's a little tip I picked up from *Crime Watch*, otherwise known as the most terrifying show on television. I have barely taken a few steps when I hear a voice behind me.

'I'm very sorry.'

I turn round and see Cagney is standing in the middle of the street.

'Christian told you to apologise that quickly?' I say quietly.

'I didn't mean for you to leave. I'm going now, please go back in.' Cagney looks at his hands as he wrings them once, and then lets them fall to his side.

'No,' I say resolutely, 'I'm too upset to stay. I'm going home.' I turn to walk away.

'Sunny,' Cagney says clearly, and I stop with my back to him. He doesn't speak, and so I turn round. 'You should at least wait for . . . your friend,' he says. I smile half a sad smile.

'I don't know how long he'll be, and I can't ask, in case his girlfriend hears me.' I laugh at how pathetic I sound.

Cagney doesn't say anything, but stares at a bush to his right, filled with small blue flowers that I am guessing neither of us could name given fifty guesses.

'You can't walk home alone,' he says to the blue-flowered bush.

'I'll be fine,' I say sadly. It's not so bad, it's what I'm used to. Maybe I don't need protecting.

'Fine is never fine,' he says, and I smile because I've heard that before.

'Well, what do you suggest?' I ask suddenly, surprised at the words as they come out, surprised at what I might suddenly be about to say.

Cagney looks at me, and then at a post box across the road. I look at the post box too, to see what is so interesting.

Cagney coughs slightly, and his eyes flicker towards me. I widen my eyes, waiting for his suggestion. We both hear Christian shout, 'Bye bye,' as he heads out of the front door. Cagney's eyes dart back to the post box.

'At least let Christian walk you,' he says quietly.

I open my mouth to speak but nothing comes out.

'Christian, you'll walk her home, won't you.' It is a statement, not a question.

Christian stops at his side, and glances at Cagney with incredulity. I feel a trickle of disappointment chase down my spine with a bead of sweat, and I don't understand it at all.

Christian looks up in time to catch the confusion on my face. 'Of course I'll walk you home, Sunny. Come on, my lovely.'

As Christian walks towards me I concentrate on his face, although something makes me glance back at Cagney at the last moment. But he simply looks at the ground, as Christian grabs my hand, and pulls me off in the opposite direction. Until this evening I have met him only in the video shop and yet it feels comfortable to walk hand in hand with Christian, arms outstretched, swinging our interlocking palms backwards and forwards, in the middle of the quiet Kew streets, towards home.

'What a funny man,' I say eventually.

'Funny's not a word that gets used a lot to describe Cagney, to be honest.' Christian winks at me and smiles.

'You know I mean funny weird, of course. Not funny ha ha.'

'Oh, he's not weird, not really. He's just been through a lot.'

'Not that you'd know! I mean, Jesus, Christian, he's so angry all the time! And I haven't done anything – why does he hate me so much?'

Christian tugs my hand back so I stop walking and addresses me. 'It's not you, lovely girl, it's more that . . . he doesn't really mix . . . with women . . . that much anymore.'

'Has he ever?' I ask, incredulous.

'Oh, yes . . .' Christian nods his head wisely.

'So does that mean he is . . . divorced?' I ask curiously.

'Yes.' Christian nods his head solemnly, and I am sure I am supposed to take something more from it.

'I see,' I say, not really seeing at all.

'Three times,' Christian says.

I cough loudly, and pull on Christian's hand, so he stops this time. A big fat Kew cat strolls past, utterly disinterested in the pair of us.

'Now do you see?' Christian asks, wide-eyed.

'Jesus, he's the Liz Taylor of Kew! Is that why you love him so much? Does he remind you of her?'

'It is not the only reason. He has always been there for me, if I need him.' Christian nods seriously again.

'But three times? Jesus, did he . . . did he beat them?'

'Oh, sweet buggery, no Sunny! You've got him all wrong! He just . . . he picks the wrong ones! He has shocking taste, and not just in knitwear. He's got a spark, Sunny, even if it has faded a little recently, but he's got this funny thing, a strange charm, when he cares to show it. But he just picks these dull beautiful women.' Christian moans the words, as if just saying them might put him to sleep, as if there were nothing more depressing in this whole wide world than a dull but beautiful woman.

'Dull? How so? You mean, just, a little vacuous?'

'No, darling, I wish that it were that simple. Shallow can be huge amounts of fun! No, it's that they have nothing to them at all, no fire, no personality, no nothing. Of course you wouldn't understand, being the woman that you are . . .'

'What does that mean?' I ask.

'It means that if your personality were bell-bottomed jeans, I wouldn't be able to walk for the acres of denim swishing at my ankles!'

'I know . . . I have a "good" personality,' I say in a mocking pathetic voice, but Christian throws away my hand in an instant.

'Excuse me? Good? You have an amazing personality!' Christian makes his eyes wide, and draws a big circle with his two index fingers in the night air, although I don't really know what for, or what it is supposed to mean.

'Oh, you don't know me at all, Christian! A few too many wines and a few too many words thrown at your friend doesn't make me Miss Congeniality.'

'You might not be Sandra, darling, but then who is? What I know is that you're feisty, and you are sassy, and you have substance, and you are determined! Look at what you did!'

'What did I do?' I ask, confused.

'What did you do? Where did you go, more like? Darling, you changed your life!'

'Oh, that.' I visibly deflate. I thought he might say I am beautiful. He is only saying that I am thinner than I was, but that's obvious. Something in me desperately wants

Christian to think of me as beautiful, like one of his idols, Liz Taylor or Rita Hayworth, or Diana Dors – somebody fabulous!

'Christian, I'm not so feisty, I just get so scared that I shout. It hides it. But better to be thought of as having a good personality than nothing, I suppose.'

'Of course, darling! Otherwise you'd just be another one of those beautiful vacant types that Cagney goes for!' We turn the corner of my street. My feet hurt and now Christian is patronising me.

'Yes, OK, Christian. I'm tired, I'm not stupid.'

'Darling.' Christian turns towards me and holds both my hands. I look up at him, and then look away. 'Darling?' he says again, until I relent and meet his gaze. 'You get how pretty you are, right? You get that those big old eyes of yours were messing with Cagney's mind tonight and making him crazy, right?'

'Whatever, Christian, you are being very sweet, but you don't need to go over the top.' I try to shake off his hands, but he holds on.

'Sunny, honey, listen to me. You are never going to mend properly if you don't learn to say thank you when somebody tells you the truth. Take a compliment, darling. Only a silly woman can't accept a compliment, and I don't spend time with them.'

I look away. 'Well then, I guess I'm silly.'

'Why?' Christian asks, confused.

'Because I'm not there yet,' I say, looking at my feet, and then back up at him again, shrugging my shoulders, admitting it.

'Then yes, I am afraid you are a silly, silly girl' Christian says, but kindly.

'I know.'

We are sitting on my wall by now. It's a warm night, and

the air smells wonderful. It is past midnight, and there is a chill, nipping at my arms, giving me goose pimples. I am already a little hungover. But Christian and I want to swing our legs off the side of my wall for five more minutes, and enjoy the guilty pleasure of staying up late and talking about nothing, and everything. We are as comfortable as it is possible to be in an Armani suit and a silk dress, sitting on old rugged slate stones.

'Now, tell me about this Adrian guy. He was kind of bland-looking, although nice and tall, I'll grant you.'

'Well, what do you want to know?'

'What's his story? What's with the phone stapled to his ear?'

'His story, and the phone, are because, officially at least, he is with somebody else.'

'With?' Christian is confused.

'He's engaged to somebody else.' I nod my head with acceptance as I say it, flatly, in a tone that I hope will stop Christian being too appalled. It doesn't work.

'No he isn't!' He claps his hands once, and then guiltily puts them back down at his sides.

'Yes he is!' I say, and laugh. It strikes me that I might cut a desperate figure, hungry for somebody to love me, willing to take whatever scraps are thrown my way. Or maybe I seem, to everybody else, simply to want what I can't have. Maybe everybody else can see quite clearly that I just like the idea of Adrian, and not the reality, so his scraps are more than enough. Maybe he is the tragic one. Maybe the whole world is tragic, in love with the wrong person, wanting something they can't have, desperate for a reason to leave, desperate for some excitement to make staying more bearable, desperate not to let go. Christian isn't quite so understanding.

'That is just . . . weird! I'm sorry, it's super weird! It's

200

crazy drunken madness! Who cheats when they aren't even married yet? Isn't engagement supposed to be the happy time? Not that I know . . . but that's right, right?' Christian searches my face for clarification.

'Christ, Christian, I don't know either. I've got no kind of experience with this kind of thing; I've been on my own for ever. And as for Adrian . . . well,' I think about it for a moment. 'Well, I think he's just confused,' I say in my most down-to-earth and objective manner. 'And I think he is terrified of hurting Jane.'

'OK because Jane would be doing star jumps if she knew where he was tonight!' Christian hits the nail on the head.

'I know, I know . . . it's a desperately hard situation, but I think I like him . . . or I thought I did . . . or maybe I do, I don't know. I feel like somebody else being involved shouldn't make me qualify my feelings. I should just know how I feel, and I think I do . . . or I thought I did . . . or I'm trying to work out how I do anyway . . .'

'But, lovely girl, don't you want somebody of your own? Don't you want somebody to belong to?'

'Of course I do, Christian, but wherever he is, he doesn't seem overly bothered about tracking me down . . . and you meet who you meet . . . and you like who you like . . .'

'Well, you think that if you want, and you keep thinking it as Mr Perfect walks on by because he sees you with Adrian.'

'I know,' I say again. Tonight it would seem I think I know a lot, when I really don't.

'You're better than that, Sunny – you know that much, right?'

'Maybe. Or maybe what I really honestly know is that Adrian wants me, even if it is just as an appetiser, or a side dish, but it's still more than I had before.'

'But still not enough. You deserve somebody just for you. He isn't being fair.'

A milk float buzzes round the corner and motors past us in slow motion, with its distinctive hum and the gentle clink of old-fashioned milk bottles.

'He doesn't mean to be mean, Christian. His emotions have just gone a little cloudy.'

'Well then, you need to be the one to see clearly now.' Christian clicks his fingers and hums the next line of a song.

I nod my head; I can't bear to say 'I know' one more time.

'Well.' I jump down from the wall, which is only a few feet high, my feet were basically touching the pavement anyway. Christian's feet are firmly on the ground already, with his knees bent. I clap my hands together and childishly engage Christian in a game of pat-a-cake, as I talk. 'I think,' clap clap, 'it's time,' clap clap, 'for me,' clap clap, 'to go to bed,' clap.

'Weren't you hungry tonight?' Christian asks, between claps.

'Not particularly.' I shrug, and speed up my hand clapping.

'Because I didn't see you eat anything.' Christian catches my hands in front of me.

I look at him with surprise. 'Oh my God, I did! I ate loads!'

'No, you didn't. You had the seaweed at the start and the salmon, but you had one mouthful of lamb . . .'

'Yes, but I'm not a big lover of lamb.'

'. . . And you didn't have any sweet potatoes or halloumi.'

'It's just Nigella's recipes give me a stomach ache – they have too much fat.' I have a quick-fire answer for everything he can throw at me.

'So you just had vegetables. And you didn't eat many of those.' Christian looks at me evenly, and waits for a response.

'It's not what you think,' I say.

'What do I think?' he asks, and I feel silly, and paranoid, and persecuted.

'Something dramatic,' I say, trying to make him feel silly instead.

'So starving yourself isn't dramatic?' he asks.

'I'm not starving myself. You don't know me, Christian. I just don't really . . . eat . . . in public.'

'Public? Why not in public?'

'Because . . . it's a hangover – from the old days. I feel . . . greedy if people see me eating.'

He stares at me, and I look away. 'Jesus,' he whispers, but I refuse to look up.

'OK, well, I need my sleep.' Christian pushes himself up, and I take a step back to clear out of his way. 'Why don't you pop into Screen Queen soon, lovely. We can grab a coffee, I can watch you eat a muffin, and you can advise me on my film festival; you can tell me what you think of the flyers! And then I can console you, after you tell Tarzan he leaves Jane or no more fun in the Sunny, right?'

'Maybe,' I say.

Christian smacks me on the bum, and I smack him back.

'Thank you for walking me home, Christian. I don't think I could have handled that amount of time with Cagney.' I laugh and run a hand through my hair.

Christian says, 'We'll see,' and takes a few steps backwards. '*Ciao, bella*,' he whispers as he blows me a kiss.

'Are you sure you don't feel like changing sides, Christian?' I ask.

Christian stops walking backwards, and takes five long

swift steps forward, kisses my forehead, and whispers, 'Not a chance.'

As he walks away, I say, 'I don't blame you,' but quietly, so no one will hear.

Adrian banged on my door for eight minutes starting at 1.10 a.m. Twenty minutes after Christian had left, and four minutes after I had climbed into bed, alone.

Should he have banged for longer? Should he have cried my name to a full-fat soft cheese Kew moon, wailing to the stars, pleading to be let in? Would that have made me answer my door? Or would I have just flicked the speed dial button on my phone that connects me to Richmond police station . . . ?

Eight minutes isn't anything. It's not completely disinterested – that would have been thirty seconds of bangs, a muttered 'Anyone home?' and then quick relieved steps away in time for the last bus.

But it's not demanding or passionate either. Eight minutes is just a very average ordinary man wanting his mistress to let him into her bed. 'Bored-inary' as Christian calls it, as in 'How can anybody live a life that bored-inary?' or, 'His shoes are soooo bored-inary, I'm staring straight at them and I couldn't tell you what they look like. It's as if my mind won't allow me to compute the image, it's just so bored-inary.' If Adrian had a bit more imagination, he would have knocked to the tune of an Elvis song that I like, or he would have tried to make me laugh by shouting, 'Knock, knock – who's there? Adrian! Adrian who? You know, Adrian! You had sex with him in your kitchen a couple of hours ago!' Or, as a last-ditch attempt, he might have stage-whispered through the letterbox that, given that it was a nice night and all, he would simply curl up on my porch until I extricated myself from my current position, trapped under something heavy, and let him in. But

Adrian knocked with no discernible rhythm for eight minutes – bang, bang . . . Sunny? Bang . . . Sunny? Bang bang bang bang . . . bang, Sunny? The effect being that he bored me into my paralysis. I guess he doesn't work in IT for nothing.

SEVEN

Sermon on how to mount

I sit on a train on Monday, heading towards La Sainte Union Convent School for girls with a box of vibrators and Two-Fingered Fondlers. I'm not nervous, largely because I haven't really thought about what it is I am going to do. I'm sure a white light of panic will grip me soon enough, as the train bounces me and my sex toys ever closer to Sutton.

I get a cab from the station to the school. I am early, lunchtime is drawing to a close, and teenagers in person-alised uniforms amble back towards the school from the town centre, picking fries out of cartons and sucking off their salt greedily before hoovering them up.

I clearly remember an afternoon free period in my second year of sixth form college. The only jeans I could fit into were from the Marks & Spencer's men's department. This was before everybody got fat and women's shops realised there was money to be made. At seventeen I was a size twenty, but Dorothy Perkins weren't bothered back then. On a blustery November day, with my friends Anna and Lisa, I walked over the flyover that linked my college to the newsagent's. At seventeen Anna was a brunette with shiny swinging bobbed hair and utterly symmetrical eyebrows, with a beauty spot just above and to the left of a cupid's bow that was too perfect to be real. But it was real. Her skin was a caramel cream, and although she had heavy legs and ankles that she bemoaned daily, she also had a tiny waist that she accentuated with well-fitted T-shirts. Nobody ever knew about Anna's ankles. Her teeth were gloriously straight. She was naturally beautiful, and she polished herself daily. She had been my best friend on and off, the way that girls are, for fourteen years.

Lisa was as blonde and athletic then as she is now, tall and toned, with long naturally curly hair and watery blue eyes. She had a handsome face, attractive where Anna's was beautiful. But Lisa spent her life smiling. If she wasn't smiling, she was laughing. A big smile, long blonde curly hair, and a gifted sprinter for the county. Five feet eight inches and not an ounce of fat. These were my best friends, who wore their trendy Levi jeans and Lacoste sweaters as we walked to the newsagent's, and I wore my M&S men's jeans, and a sweatshirt from BhS in size XL.

We walked together, in a line, down the road. Anna shared secrets of her date the night before with her new boyfriend, David, a tall handsome third-year student at our college with a Roger Ramjet chin and a good line in sarcasm, who made me blush whenever he turned his full attention on me.

A red mark four Escort whizzed past us, filled with boys from the technical college, boys that all of us had seen but none of us quite knew. They were thrashing their first car into submission, and as they flew past us, they leant on their horn and one of them cried out of the window, 'You're gorgeous!'

We all laughed, excited by the fact that these were good-looking boys from the technical college, and they had, by screaming out of their window, declared to the world that one of us would be going out with one of them very soon, in a smallish suburban town such as ours, with its limited pubs and bars.

I turned to my right to say something to Anna, and realised that she and Lisa had dropped a step behind me, as they held on to each other's arms to stop themselves from falling as they laughed, flushed with girlish pride.

'He was shouting at you!' Lisa said through laughter.

'No, he was shouting at you!' Anna said back, glorious fun-filled tears in her eyes.

'He wasn't! It was you!' Lisa said back, taking a breath, trying to regain control.

It was only then that I remembered . . . there was no way he was shouting at me.

My teenage years are littered with incidents like that, some worse. Jibes and comments scattered like broken glass across the years that pricked my ego until it bled to death. The loud boy at college, the joker, the little guy who got popular from picking on others around him, who could use me as an easy jibe if I walked past at the wrong time. It stung so hard and fresh, every time he made his fat comments, his 'look at the state of that today' comments, that it would always make me cry, just a little, especially if I had tried hard that day, with my hair, with my clothes. It didn't matter to him, of course. When I found out that he was adopted, I plotted and twisted in my head all the comebacks I could hurl in his direction the next time he lashed out at me, how I could turn and say, 'Well, at least I don't have strangers cooking my tea! My parents loved me enough to keep me!' That's how much it hurt, that awful much. I never said it, thank goodness, but the fact that I thought it is still a source of shame. There are boys, now men, including little popular adopted guy, who I can still muster some hatred for today, a peculiar vitriol reserved only for that select band who made me hate myself for the way I looked at a time

208

when I was learning who I was. I learnt that I was a joke, because I was fat. I learnt that some people, especially men, wouldn't like me, wouldn't even want to talk to me, because I was fat. I learnt that my girlfriends could bond over their latest crush, but there was no point me 'crushing' anybody, because that is all it would ever be. I locked my romantic feelings away then, for the first time, to save some young pride. But if I want to be happy, and being loved is what I think will make me happy, I'm going to have to unlock them again and let them out, and risk some oaf with big clumsy hands dropping them and smashing them on the floor. Love is the stuff of all my dreams, and I've decided that those dreams aren't too big for me, even if my Marks & Spencer's jeans now are.

The taxi driver offers to drop me at the top of the school drive, but I insist on being let out by the gates so that I can carry my heavy box up the long tarmac drive, and therefore start to burn off the bowl of cereal I ate for lunch before I left my flat. The kids eye me suspiciously as I stride past them, but they are almost instantly bored by me, and look away to be bored by something else. How exhausting it must be, to be constantly on the look out for something to hold your attention, disappointed by the ninety-nine per cent of the world that doesn't involve computer game slaughters. There are significantly more overweight kids than there used to be, too many contenders for the prize of 'class fatty' these days. I see a girl, eleven maybe twelve, in a navy V-neck school jumper that is uncomfortably tight, the seams digging at the tops of her arms, and fat where breasts will be one day soon, giving her childish boobs that she doesn't want, that she hates. Her face is big and pale like an uncut brie. Her arms don't swing elegantly at her sides, but instead sit at stiff angles from her torso, where fat meets fat. I can tell from the way that she walks that her thighs are rubbing

209

against each other under her navy blue polyester skirt with a button missing at the waistband that her mother has got tired of sewing back on. She'll inspect her thighs later, alone and behind a locked door in the family bathroom, the only place that she doesn't mind being naked. She'll sit heavily on the floor, the soles of her feet pressed together, studying the red-rashed pimply flesh, and applying E45 cream, praying the livid patch will go down before PE next Tuesday.

She walks too quickly, my little fat friend, on purpose, to prove that she can, but the truth is she really can't, comfortably at least. She is quite out of breath, and she lets her friend, a small Chinese girl in an oversized uniform that was still the smallest in the shop, do most of the talking, nodding or shaking her head instead of answering if she can get away with it, unable to catch her breath.

A group of five skinny girls catch them up gradually from behind. Their uniform is gold hooped Argos earrings, and poker-straight one-length hair that falls to exactly the same point on their backs – regulation length, McDonald's length, New Look length. They strop past the Chinese girl and deliberately knock into the violin case that swings heavily at her side, and it falls on to the tarmac. A couple of the girls cough a snigger and carry on walking, until a few paces further on, one swings her hair to turn back and spits over her shoulder, 'And no staring at my tits again in PE, Marie, you fat leso bitch . . .'

Marie pretends to ignore her but her face turns strawberry red, and she looks down at her feet, scowling, but saying nothing. I want to run after this little teenage pregnancy in the making and ask her why she is so filled with hate, so spiteful, so ready to lash out at another woman's expense. I want to make a thousand arguments that confound her in her youth and stupidity into a shamed silence, mouth agape, chewing gum falling to the floor. I am fast approaching the group of girls, and another sensation grips me – fear. Fear that I won't say anything, that I won't fight back, for Marie, for all the other little fat kids, for the ones who hate themselves too much to answer back. There are so many things I could say, ways of making her eat her words, apologise, or at the very least point her in the direction of a new enemy, if an enemy is what she needs. I am a woman now, I'm nearly thirty for Christ's sake, I can win her over with my cohesive arguments and make her understand that being fat isn't easy, and her outbursts could push poor Marie over the edge. Then how would she feel? With sticky, sugar-saturated blood all over her hands?

I speed up to pass the group, who are swearing at each other as conversation, discussing 'cheeky fuckin' Brett Davies' and 'Jamie fuckin' Sparrow, the prick, he tried to touch me up at the bus stop . . .'

They don't say anything to me, barely even notice me. I remind myself that I'm not fat any more. Scared of what they might say, I feel eight years old again. But they have no spite to hurl my way – it would take far too much imagination. I wish they would say something, anything, because the diatribe that I was planning on delivering to them sticks in my throat, and my lips are dry, my tongue rigid. And then one of them speaks.

'I like your boots, miss.'

She thinks I am a teacher, and her words are sincere. I am wearing knee-high camel-coloured Kurt Geiger leather boots with a thin three-inch heel. I know she is not lying, because they are great boots. They don't start to hurt my feet until their fourth hour of wear. I am worthy of their admiration, I fit in now, the skinny girl from the skinny club wants my boots.

I glance back over my shoulder and smile, and say quietly, 'Bitch.'

'Wha?' the girl asks, confused that a substitute teacher may have just said 'thanks' to her, but it sounded like 'bitch'. I don't look back, and am relieved when I shut the staffroom door behind me. It didn't feel nice, being spiteful to a stranger. I wonder why so many people find it so effortlessly easy.

Rob Taggart is nervous and overexcited. He speaks too quickly, his tongue falling over his words and jumping up again at speed. His eyelids are mostly closed as he speaks, but flicker quickly as if rapid eye movement were a disease, and he has it, and it may yet be fatal.

He is thin, and pale. His shirt is blue, his trousers are grey. His glasses are wire-framed and may even be designer, but it's too little too late. Even his hair is pointless, soft and flat. He looks as though he doesn't dream at night. He looks as though he would come in forty seconds if a woman stood opposite him and took her knickers off. He gets drunk on three pints of lager and plays quiz machines with his mates, all huddled around in a corner of the pub shouting, 'Not yet, not yet! Peter Shilton! The Adriatic! Rob, you muppet, I told you it was Marie Curie!'

I have no doubt he'll be married by the time he is thirty. He is the kind of guy things work out fine for; he has had the luck to be born into the 'easily pleased' classes. He doesn't think too much about the emotional stuff, or dream too much, or want to escape his life or his head or his skin. He likes his life and who he is, and if he didn't he'd just change it. He laughs at gross-out films, and supports a football team that always comes eleventh in the Premiership, but as long as it's eleventh, he is happy. Eleventh, consistently, is the kind of guy Rob Taggart is. I wish it had been love at first sight. How wonderful and comfortable that would have been.

Thankfully I don't recognise any of the girls sitting in the classroom Rob Taggart and I are peering into through a small round window in an old heavy school door. The bitch I called bitch isn't in there.

'They're really excited!' Rob Taggart says, catching the worried look on my face. We both look back through the window at the girls, bunched in groups around certain desks, young and nubile and bored. They are fifteen going on thirty. At least half of them have probably had more sex than me, know more about sex than me, tried a hundred more positions. But I am pretty sure I know more about sex aids. At least I hope I do . . .

I walk in with my box of sexual tricks and stand in front of the class, who pay me no attention and carry on talking. I put the box down and line up the vibrators in height order along the front edge of Rob Taggart's desk: an intimidating black length of veined rubber direct from a Robert Mapplethorpe photo: a rabbit in pink with rounded nonthreatening ears and balls that rotate and buzz at the base, that look like they'd be fine to use in a kids' ball pool – dive in! – a whole different kind of fun admittedly.

I place a Two-Fingered Fondler on the corner of the desk. I know the directions on the back of the box by heart. 'How does it work?' is a question I can answer.

'Excuse me?' I say loudly. Rob Taggart declined even to introduce me. I've been thrown to lip-glossed lions. They glance at me, and prowl nonchalantly back to their individual desks, not quite chewing gum, not quite throwing me insolent looks, not quite being stroppy teenagers, but on the brink of all of that.

When they have slammed themselves into seats with built-in desks and flipped their hair a few more times, they allow their eyes to focus on me. And finally they spot the vibrators . . .

'Mate!'

'Rough!'

'It's fuckin' huge!'

'Is she a fuckin' lezza?'

'She must be a dyke!'

'That's just wrong.'

Silence falls suddenly, and they look at me expectantly.

'What?' I ask.

'Are you a dyke, miss?' An explosion of Argos gold and eyeliner in the second row tosses the question at me.

'It shouldn't matter whether I am or not . . .'

The classroom erupts.

'Yuk!'

'That's fucking rough!'

'Pervert!'

'But I'm not!' I state firmly, horribly ashamed of it as soon as the words leave my mouth.

'Whatever!'

'Is she going to show us how to use it?'

'I am fuckin' leaving if she does!'

'I ain't staying for no lezza class!'

'Look!' I shout above the disgusted din. 'Nobody is going to show you how to use anything. Mr Taggart asked me to talk to you today about my business. I run a website called shewantsshegets.com that sells these toys,' I gesture with my hand, 'and it is ostensibly for women. I brought a selection of the vibrators along to show you, but we also sell under-wear, lubrication, light S&M materials, silk eye masks, erotic poetry and literature, flavoured body paints, et cetera. Click on the site for a full list. But my best seller is the Two-Fingered Fondler, which I own the exclusive licence to distribute in this country, for the moment at least, and it's proving very popular. It's the puff of air, apparently. As you can see . . .' I pick up the Fondler and half the class erupts.

'Rough!'

'I think it's been used!'

'Turn it on!'

'Does its ears twitch?'

Peals of laughter follow.

'For Christ's sake, it's just a vibrator!' I shout.

Most of the class shut up, apart from a group of knowing beauties, who mimic me – it's just a vibrator – in a strange Home Counties accent, and laugh loudly at the back.

'Does anybody have any questions?' I ask, checking my watch. I can catch the next train if I rush.

A young black girl with flawless creamy skin and an afro ponytail puts her hand in the air.

'Yes?' I ask, mildly irritated. Why is there always one who has to ask a question?

'I know what a vibrator is, right, but they's for old women, right, or married women. Who can't get good sex no more. We don't need nothing. I get mine!' She laughs loudly and high-fives her neighbour.

'OK,' I say, 'any other questions?'

'Do they give you an automatic orgasm?'

I don't know who has shouted it from the back, so I answer the class generally. 'Not automatic, no.' I turn round to start to pack up.

'But they are for women who can't get men, right?'

'Maybe they are for women who don't want men,' I say, with my back to them.

'Lesbians!' two of them shout simultaneously.

I turn round to face them. 'Why are you all so obsessed with lesbians?' I ask, and the girls at the back mimic me again, and I sigh exasperated.

'Why do we need to learn how to fuck ourselves, miss? That's the man's job, right?'

'In an ideal world, yes. But sometimes finding a man that you like, and respect, and who makes you laugh, and who

215

also makes you orgasm, is harder than you think it might be. This –' I wave the Fondler at them – 'is in case you take conversation over coming.'

I look down at it with a fond smile. It has served me well, put food on my table, indulged me my therapist, and yet I have never thanked it properly. Why haven't I tried one of these things? What am I waiting for, a note from my mother saying it's OK? Why is using a Fondler any different from using my own hand?

'Are you married?' one of the girls shouts.

'No,' I answer.

'How old are you?' another girl shouts.

'Twenty-eight,' I say.

'When was the last time you had sex?' the same voice asks.

'Friday night, against a wall in my kitchen,' I say.

The room quietens down.

'Are you in love?' somebody asks.

I open my mouth, but nothing comes out. The answer to that wasn't on the back of the Fondler box. I'm stumped.

I am woken in the middle of the night by a strange and unsettling feeling. Not having experienced a panic attack I can't be certain that's what it is, but it feels the way a panic attack should feel, I think. My heart is racing, my mind is whirring, and I feel cold and awake and taut.

It is a week and a half since the incident, and as I lay on my own in the dark, the memory of running down that alley screams through my mind, and I close my eyes, and scrunch them up tight to try to make the image go away. I am not going to cry. Adrian has been trying to talk all weekend, and I've been dumping the calls. I am starting to realise that there is nothing that sparks a common interest in us both, that sizzles down the line and connects us. But I feel a little lonely, in this big old bed by myself, which is strange, given how many years I spent sleeping on my own. Now I feel smaller and the bed feels bigger, but maybe Adrian would be the wrong man to have next to me now. I don't think I want any affection he might choose to lazily fling my way, and I wouldn't be able to muster the enthusiasm to sling any back. I don't think we care about each other at all. I am a holiday for him. He is a tour guide for me. Maybe he'll go home soon, safe in the knowledge that it is ultimately more comfortable there, and I'll be savvy to a few things I wasn't. Maybe we are just doing each other a favour. I hope he agrees when I explain it. But I don't think I want Christmas with him now, or trips to the Lake District, or any of those things I was so desperate for last week. I can hardly even bear to think of him, and it is because of my mistake. I dressed him up in a suit of 'perfect for me' when it has never fitted him, and never will. He doesn't laugh at my jokes. He refuses to go anywhere near a kitchen, and makes comments like 'Woah there!' if I happen to mention either my mum or my dad, as if I might suddenly wolf-whistle and they'll walk in from the room next door, where they've been hiding all along with a vicar and a marriage licence with our names on it.

In my defence I will admit that it is very easy to pin the right dreams on the wrong man, if only because they look the way you thought your partner would. I may be ready for somebody to love me, and to love them in return, but I don't feel that with Adrian. We aren't even walking in the same direction.

I roll over in bed, hook my leg around and over the duvet, and hug a pillow . . . and think of Cagney. I hate myself for even picturing him anywhere near me. I hate the little part of me that prays he might picture me sometimes as well. I hate that we don't seem able to have a conversation that doesn't dissolve into a war. I hate that the image that bursts open in my head and spills out like a dream right now is of this bed, and him in it, with a long strong arm around me, and my head resting on the salt-and-pepper hairs on his chest. I hate that I think he could protect me if I was in trouble. In fact he already has. But what I really hate is that now I have got what I thought I wanted, namely Adrian, I realise that I don't want him at all. What I seem to want, now that I have opened myself up to a little more choice, is hard to admit, even to myself. I am scared to acknowledge that, after all that has happened, all that I've dreamt of and wished for, my heart and my head seem to be screaming in unison, that I want an angry loner with grey hair and a drink problem. But I don't think he is ever going to want me, so despite all my efforts I am back to square one. I kick off the duvet, angry with Cagney, but angrier with myself.

My cold feet wake me up four hours later, as they poke out of the end of my duvet, neglected. I've overslept, which is unlike me these days. I stretch long and hard, pushing my hands up into the wall, pointing my toes out over the end of the bed. I should get up. I check the clock – it reads twenty minutes past eight, so I should definitely get out of bed. I am wide awake, but I lie on my back with my head nestled in a soft duck-down pillow, encased in a body heat bubble I have made for myself, languishing in the warmth of the duvet. I tentatively stick out my arm, and reach down to the side of my bed, grabbing around on the carpet, instead of rolling over and looking for what I know is there. My fingers locate the cardboard of the box, and I pull it up and hold it aloft in front of me. The Two-Fingered Fondler.

This is it. It's a watershed, an important moment, a turning point. This is about openly and honestly and soberly, in a daylight hour, admitting that I would like something sexual to happen with a man whose name I know and whose face I can picture. I have never fantasised sexually about anybody real, not even Adrian, scared of where it might lead, of how much more upset his rejection of me would be if I allowed myself to orgasm while picturing us having sex. It was too intimate. So I daydreamed conversations with Adrian, and kept my fantasies to lords of the manor, or lecturers, or prison guards, or any of the other fairy tales that have childishly entertained me for so long. And in all of those fantasies I was a serving wench, or a student, or a prisoner. I was never just me. I have never allowed myself to picture a potential reality, because I have always known that as soon as I do that fantasy will have a life of its own. It will float up and out of my head like a balloon filled with big wishes, spurred on by my own electricity, and it will hang above my head as if it were tied around my neck wherever I go. And if ever I see him, he will know, somehow, that it was the thought of him, coupled with my bestselling piece of merchandise, that made me sweat, that made my breathing erratic, that caused a catch in the back of my throat, that caused a creeping anticipatory feeling on the top insides of my thighs. That made me shift my legs apart and wish for the weight of a particular somebody on me. He'll know I lost my Two-Fingered Fondler virginity to him somehow.

I inspect the box. I turn it over three or four times before I even begin to make an effort to prise it open. The familiar fist with two strange saluting fingers drops out attached to the white plastic protective casing with little wire holders. I sit up. I flick the red switch at the bottom, and a whirring sound, like a very weak vacuum cleaner, starts. I turn it off straight away. It is too loud. People will hear . . . my neighbours might hear . . . Cagney James might hear . . .

I throw it to the side and flick the radio on, as some barking spaniel of a DJ announces that the songs we have all been listening to are from last year. They don't play music from the fifties on this station, or the sixties, or the seventies, or even the eighties. They figure it's depressing, the kids don't like it. If they stopped and listened hard enough they might realise that the kids don't like anything any more, at least not with the same abandon reserved for old idols. There is just too much damn choice, everything can be improved upon, and they can probably do it better themselves with a PC and a loan from The Prince's Trust.

I flick off the radio and pick up the Fondler again. It isn't such a big deal. I pull off the white plastic casing and chuck it on the floor, placing the Fondler itself on the duvet in my lap. I put a cushion over it, and flick the switch that turns it on. I can hear a muffled whirring, as I suffocate my Fondler in the name of shame. I picture somebody watching me, in a Big Brother scenario, my bedroom filled with cameras, and I am more embarrassed by the fact that I am trying to muffle a vibrator in an empty flat, than if I were using it.

'For God's sake, woman, just do it!' I say aloud, remove the cushion, scoot down in the bed, and thrust the Fondler beneath the covers.

Five seconds later my mother calls. She knew . . .

'Are you hoovering?' she asks, as I desperately try to locate the off switch. The switch I flicked as I answered the phone, the switch I thought would turn it off, in fact just made it faster and noisier.

'Yes, I'm just turning it off.'

'It sounds very weak, Sunny. I think the bag might need changing.'

'It's a Duster Buster,' I say quickly. My ability to lie to my mother at speed and without guilt is impressive. I used to lie about the food that I ate all the time. I used to sneak out into the kitchen and butter a slice of bread and eat it secretly, trying noiselessly to open and close the fridge. After dinner, when leftover spaghetti Bolognese or macaroni cheese sat proudly on the work top in casserole dishes covered in cling film, it was my secret trick to unpeel one side, dip in my hand, scoop up some food, eat it, make it appear that the food had not been touched by redistributing the top layer of pasta or sauce, and then reattach the cling film so nobody would ever know.

At that point my mother would shout from her armchair in the living room, 'What are you doing out there? Are you at that fridge?'

'I'm just chucking something in the bin,' or, 'I'm getting a glass of water,' were my standard responses. We both knew it was a lie, but neither one of us ever said anything.

Occasionally my mother would sigh and look angry, and venture, 'You don't need that,' as I picked up another roast potato after my plate was cleared. And I think, for whatever reason, it made me want it more. I did need it, I just didn't know why. I still don't, despite all the therapy. Why did I always need another potato? The irony being, of course, that the Sunday roasts that I once shovelled up in secret now make me throw my guts up, my stomach refusing to digest them. And I'd be lying if I said I wasn't pleased. I might still want to eat them, but I can't, and if I do succumb, I just throw it all back up the next day, my stomach now unable to digest the gravy, we finally deduced, and I shiver in bed for twelve hours with dehydration and fatigue, and then bounce out of bed the following day a few pounds the lighter.

I weighed myself as a child, and cried when I put on two pounds when I was supposed to be on a diet. I stole Maltesers from the sweet cupboard and cried after I had eaten them. I joined WeightWatchers, my mother took me and paid my three-pound joining fee, and I stepped on the

221

scales terrified and mortified, awaiting the dreaded numbers. But in my first week I lost four pounds! Of course, by the end of the following week I had put five pounds back on. Then I would cry again and tell my mother that standing, aged twelve, in a room full of fifty-year-old women in a community hall with drab walls and a big set of judgement scales at the front, depressed me. It made me feel like my problem was going to be with me for life. It made me feel like a grown-up, and I still wanted to be a child, and do what I wanted, without responsibility.

Of course, the worst thing was that my sister, Elaine, could eat the same things as me and was as skinny as a rake. She liked salt and vinegar crisps and I liked ready salted. I liked Twix and she liked Toblerone. She weighed six stone something, and I was nearer nine. She was three years older, and four inches taller. She was little and I was large, as was often remarked by careless family friends or relatives. I remember it all, every comment shot into my brain, embedded like a miniature arrow, finding a comfy spot to puncture, for the rest of my life. They won't budge, the remarks and the taunts; I can't lose them.

I suppose the thing that shames me most is that I was the one defining myself by my fat, and I was the one keeping occasional suitors at bay, because I was the one who couldn't believe that they found me attractive, mound of flesh that I was. And I have no doubt that it was this insecurity that a lot of men sensed, and that made me less attractive than if I had been truly happy and carefree about my size.

I remember Ian, a friend of a friend that I somehow knew in the way that you somehow know everybody, at university in my final year. He was nice. He had dark hair, which he had cut for five pounds in a barber's in town, and he was five foot ten. He wore slightly faded Nirvana and Police T-shirts with jeans that had ripped themselves through wear,

222

and not been bought that way. He was funny, in a clever way that wasn't obvious; you had to think about his punchlines. His glasses were rimless, so that you sometimes forgot he was wearing them. Occasionally, after lectures, he would drop in to the flat that I shared with my friends Maxine and Helen, and we'd sit and watch *Vanessa* shows with topics like 'I married a love rat' or 'my mum won't stop touching my boyfriend'. I was always embarrassed if I was the only person in when he knocked on our back door and wandered in, in the way that students do. I always felt that he'd got a raw deal, because the other girls, who were both a size twelve, and one of whom I reasoned he must have fancied, weren't there. So I'd overact and try too hard, to make him feel better. Ian tried to kiss me on three separate occasions, twice drunk, once sober. He never tried to kiss Maxine or Helen as far as I am aware, even the night we all got drunk because they were both leaving to teach English in Japan. Each time I ran away, unable to accept his kiss, convinced that he was trying only because he couldn't be with the girl he really wanted, or because he was too drunk to know better and would hate himself in the morning. I couldn't accept, given the options available, that he would pick me. I wasn't in love with him, but I wish I'd let him kiss me.

And so I envy those glorious women for whom it is truly no issue, those soft and curved women carrying three or four or five or ten stones too many, who love themselves, and the way they look, and allow others to love them at the same time. I suppose the fat fall into two categories. The ones who are happy with their choice, and the ones who aren't but can't seem to change it. I let food, just food, just a sandwich or a slice of pizza or a hamburger or a bag of crisps or a Twix, run and ruin my life for so long. The real difference between me then and me now is in that sentence:

it's just food. If you don't want to be fat, find something else to love instead.

'Sorry to disturb you – are you working?'

'Not yet, Mum. It's only twenty to nine.'

'I'm worried about you, Sunny.'

I gulp loudly. My mother has never openly expressed 'worry' for me before.

'I do eat, you know,' I say defensively, only a little pleased.

'Not that. I am worried about that awful thing you told me about.' I had filled her in on the evening of the incident, about the Stranger and Dougal and Cagney and all of it. She had fallen very quiet once I had finished reciting my tale, and said she was glad that I was OK, and very proud, but the way that Dougal's mother felt was the way that she felt now, even if he was only two and I was twenty-eight, and I should never do anything like that again. She asked if I had eaten and told me to have dessert as a treat. If I couldn't have it now, when could I? Except that's an argument that's wearing thin . . .

'Mum, there is nothing to worry about. It's all done with.'

'But how can it be? What about a court date? When you have to see him again? I'll come, of course.'

'I haven't heard anything, and you can come if you want to, Mum, but I don't need you to, I'll be fine. How is Dad?'

'Oh, you know, the same as usual. He couldn't get parked at Sainsbury's this morning. Honestly, Sunny, never marry a man who shows even the slightest interest in parking.'

'OK, I won't.'

'Are you still seeing that boy?'

'Kind of, I'm not sure, maybe . . .'

'Well, if he's not right don't waste any time on him, Sunny,' she says firmly.

My mother thinks I am stronger than I am. I think she

224

might kid herself that I have waited this long through choice.

'I thought I might pop over on Friday, darling. We could go for lunch. We could see if Elaine is free.'

'OK, but I have to work.' My mother thinks that working from home is the same as not working at all.

'Surely you can break for lunch, Sunny?'

'Of course I can.' I feel instantly guilty. It's a special gift my mother has.

'OK, well then, I'll see you on Friday as long as your father lets me drive over to you.' She sighs again, but we both know that she backs the car into stationary objects on a weekly basis, so I don't blame Dad for not wanting her behind the wheel.

I hang up the phone after quick goodbyes, and chuck it onto my dressing table. I haven't forgotten what I was doing before my mother rang.

I put the Fondler back under the covers and flick the switch, and the whirring starts again.

I lie back, with my eyes closed, and picture Cagney. I can picture anything I like, I can picture anything I like – I run the words through my head, as my mind fails to conjure up an image any more exciting than Cagney just standing outside Starbucks in his overcoat.

I blink my eyes quickly to cut off from that image and think of another one. I deliberately picture Cagney opening the door to my bedroom.

'What have you got there?' he asks evenly.

'Just lending myself a hand,' I reply.

I shudder a little, as I picture Cagney unbuttoning his shirt. He is wearing a shirt, and not a rollneck. It's my fantasy; he'll wear what I want. He comes to sit by me on the bed, and peels back the duvet to investigate.

'Oh, I see,' he says softly.

He leans in and kisses me slowly, placing his hand behind my neck to pull my mouth further on to his.

'Let me do that,' he says, and takes the Fondler out of my hands . . .

Maybe it was just the Fondler. Maybe it's just that good. But it was the most powerful, exciting, excruciating, joyous orgasm I have ever had.

My therapist is a deep dark brown. He is sporting the kind of tan that only middle-aged men are able to achieve. He looks like an expensive suitcase. As soon as I walk into his office I notice it, or rather I notice the crazy whiteness of his eyes, in contrast to the berry brown of his cheeks. I am immediately jealous. Everybody, even my therapist, looks better with a golden hue. I want to be sunkissed.

His tan doesn't make him act any differently, and I am surprised. I feel like it would be more appropriate if, rather than sitting down, crossing his legs, asking how I am, he lit a suspicious roll-up, poured himself a large measure of something sepia and potent, and asked me, 'What's your pleasure, treasure?'

'Rainy season?' I ask as I sit in my usual spot but on an unusual day. If I judged my friendships purely on the amount of time spent with somebody, I should be exchanging home-made best friend bracelets with my therapist about now.

He smiles at his pad as he flicks through his notes, but doesn't say anything.

'I hope you are moisturising, my friend, or you'll be back to mini milk in days.'

'It'll go soon enough,' he says, still scanning the page in front of him.

I feel mean, for what I've said.

'You could top it up, you know. St Tropez is good. It

226

barely streaks, if you are patient. Or I had a spray-on tan a couple of months ago – a Polish woman in Debenhams on Oxford Street airbrushed me. The first night was terrifying, but . . . what?'

He is staring at me patiently, his legs crossed, one shoe dangling off a brown foot. 'How are you, Sunny?' he asks, resting his pad in his lap. He eyes flicker down to it quickly, to remind himself of a name or a place or a neurosis that slipped his mind, but they flicker back to me just as quickly.

'I'm OK.'

I thought I might say 'well' when he asked me. I thought I might even say 'good', but now these words escape me, or refuse to form, as I am overwhelmed by the fact that I am no more than OK. It pays to be honest when you're paying for answers. I run my hands through my hair, and pull my knees to my chest. He sits and waits.

'I've been looking, a lot, at fat,' I say. 'At fat people, fat women mostly. The way they move. The way they hide. The length of their shirts to cover their stomachs. The buttons slotted precariously through stretched buttonholes, fit to burst. The comfortable shoes that support thick ankles, the skirts that sit lower at the back of their calves, raised at the front by the rolls of fat at their stomachs. Elaborate hair, coloured and styled, to detract from the rest of them, to accentuate the face. The way they walk, legs slightly apart, because the tops of their thighs are chaffing. The way they sit, on the tube, trying to make themselves small in their seat, upright and uncomfortable, scared to relax in case they inadvertently spill over into the chairs next to them, a little hot, a little flustered. They feel so conspicuous, so aware of their own volume and shape and mass. They don't realise that the only people that care at that very second about their size are themselves and me. Just the two of us, an unhappy couple: they are so self-conscious, and I am so fascinated.

227

It's like watching an old home video of the person I used to be. It's admitting how ashamed I was of myself.

'And then what's really confusing is that there are some fat girls that I see, no more or less attractive than any of the others, who seem so . . . sexual. Their size and their big swollen thighs and breasts above and below huge bellies. These are not freakishly overweight girls by today's standards, just big girls – sixteen stone, size twenty girls. And it's not that I personally find them sexually attractive, but I can't help but feel that men looking on, and I realise now that men are always looking on, must desire them! Must want to be enveloped in their gentle curves, must want to experience the softness of all that flesh beneath them, a big glorious cushion for their orgasm. And when I think that it makes me feel good, it makes me smile, until I remember that I don't look like them any more. I am muscle, and I am long legs defined and toned. I'm skin, or I'm bone. I am half the woman I used to be . . .

'Twenty years ago, if you had a big nose, you had a big nose. Unless you were Marilyn Monroe you lived with it, dealt with it. Nobody really cared, on a day-to-day basis, because you couldn't change it so you accepted it, as did everybody else. But now everybody seems to care, because now everything can be fixed – big flappy ears that can be pinned, yellow teeth that can be whitened, too small/too large breasts that can be enlarged/reduced at will, and with the right personal loan, because it is infinitely more acceptable today to owe the bank ten grand than have a crooked nose. Whatever makes you happy. Twenty years ago I'd have been happy with a crooked nose . . .

'But the more bits we can cut off ourselves, and reshape, to make us that little bit closer to perfect, the less meaning we attach to anything openly flawed. But look around, because surely something has to change, in the next twenty years, given the pace at which we're moving. Either it will become illegal to walk down a street without looking picture perfect, or people will be arrested and charged with "crimes against vanity" or something equally as ridiculous and *1984*, but it's going to happen!'

My therapist smiles. 'Or maybe everybody will agree it's got out of hand,' he says softly.

'Maybe,' I frown, unconvinced. 'Maybe they will, and a rebellion will rise, and the beauty fascists twisting and pinching the skin of our culture will be hacked to a bloody ugly death, and we will all revert to looking the way God made us. Nothing will be tampered with again, be it pinned ears for potential models, or skin grafting for burns victims. The new rule will be simple: you are what you are. Appearance is the sum of individual experience, and that is what the world will see. There will be no more air brushing, and no more grasping for impossible goals.'

'And then what?' my therapist asks, impressed, I think, by my vision of the future.

'Then all the astronauts in all the shuttles orbiting the earth will look down, and see whole cities swell and relax with sighs of relief, and they'll hear the sighs in space. We'll all just relax.'

I continue staring out of the window, at a squirrel darting up a tree and a red car moving slowly past the office, trying to find a place to park. My therapist looks on. I am not sure what I have just said.

'I feel like I have a choice now, a terrible choice, to be thin or fat. I could throw off the reins and succumb to my need to eat. It isn't a physical need at all, it is absolutely psychological. My stomach has shrunk; I am full after a few mouthfuls of most things. I feel uncomfortable after eating a fifth of what I might have eaten for lunch a year ago. I have been physically sick the last three times I have eaten

229

my mother's Sunday roast, a meal that I used to devour with ease, before clearing up the leftovers and topping it all off with a bag of crisps and a packet of Maltesers. I can't do that any more, but for whatever reason, I still want to. I have taken away my own security blanket, and failed to replace it.'

I glance up at my therapist's face for any meaningful reaction, but his expression is as good as frozen. He hasn't used his pad or pen in fifteen minutes.

'Jet lag?' I ask.

'No, I'm OK,' he replies.

'You're not saying much,' I mutter.

'You are,' he says with a smile.

'Well, I'm done now, so you talk,' I say, as I stretch my legs down and cross them in front of me, and fold my arms.

'How is Adrian?' he asks without looking at his pad.

I roll my eyes and sigh. 'I don't know, I don't know!' I sigh again, bored and immediately frustrated by the effort it is going to take me to answer that question. I search for other words than those that have formed themselves in an orderly and accurate queue in my head; I search for something other than the truth. I open my mouth and close it again a few times. 'He's . . . Adrian is . . . I mean, he is . . .' I crumple up my nose and throw my hands in the air.

My therapist stares at me and I glare back. I notice that the skin on his face is flaking, little ripped shards of tissue peeling from his nose, and I look away first.

I drum my fingers on the sofa a little and glance around at the room before succumbing, through sheer laziness, to the truth as it has presented itself so politely in my mind.

'He is clutter. Adrian is clutter. Happy now? Satisfied? I know it's mean but it's how I feel. I hate myself a little for feeling this way. But at least when it was just me and the food it wasn't so messy, and emotional. He's engaged, by the way, and not to me, I should point out. He admitted it last week. I haven't seen him since. He keeps leaving messages on my phone. I don't know what I am going to do. Because I don't know from one day to the next how I am going to feel, and it's so tiring just thinking about it all the time, and thinking about what he is thinking. I feel like I can't focus, or get things sorted. I can't tick anything off my list, there are no definites and there never will be as long as he is engaged to somebody else. I have no real idea how he feels. But I know that, if not quite messing my life up, he is making my life messy, and I don't think I like it.'

My therapist coughs, and recrosses his legs. 'You prefer your old relationship with food to the relationship you are having with Adrian?' he asks.

'I suppose.'

'But, Sunny, people aren't sandwiches, and that's what makes relationships so rewarding. You don't just devour them, you experience them, and you learn from them. They interact with you, and you gain from them. You leave every relationship a different person from the one who went into it. It's fulfilling in a whole new way.'

'People aren't sandwiches?' I ask

'Yes,' he replies, staring at me evenly.

'Happy with that analogy, are we?' I ask.

'I think it made my point,' he says, still staring.

'Have I ever actually seen your credentials?' I ask.

'And how is Cagney James?' my therapist asks. I don't need to see his credentials – he is too clever for me.

'I don't know,' I say, clipped. My back straightens involuntarily, and I deliberately force myself to slouch again, on principle.

'Wasn't he at the dinner party?' he asks.

'You made some detailed notes there, didn't ya?' I say with a big fake plainly uncomfortable smile.

'Wasn't he there?' my therapist asks.

'He was there, but I haven't seen him since, so I really don't know how he is. I wasn't being evasive.'

'So how was the dinner party?'

I brush an imaginary crumb off my dress, and then declare in the most confident manner I can muster, 'It was fine.' I give my therapist a wide toothy grin.

'Fine?' he asks, confused.

'Fine,' I say, grinning and nodding my head.

'Are there any other words you might choose, if I asked you to elaborate perhaps?'

'I guess I'd say that it was a dinner party, and dinner parties aren't sandwiches.' I wink at my therapist and regret it instantly. What is wrong with me today?

'OK, Sunny, if it was fine, can I assume that it was a quiet and reasonably pleasant evening?'

He sees, and I feel, my face drop. What am I paying for, if I'm not going to be honest? How challenging is it to watch him unpick my lies?

'Quiet?' I repeat.

'Yes,' he says.

'No,' I reply.

'OK, but pleasant?' he asks.

'Not so much,' I say.

'Fine?' he asks.

'Maybe fine wasn't the right word after all . . .'

'So what word would you use, to describe it more accurately?' my therapist asks, and reaches casually for his pen and pad.

'Maybe . . . hellish . . . might be more appropriate. Awful, maybe? Uncomfortable, definitely. Adrian spent half the night on the phone to his fiancée, while Dougal was paraded by his father like a mascot they nearly lost to the opposition team. And as for Cagney James . . . well, he and I . . .'

I stare out of the window. He and I what? I'm nowhere near sure. We argued? We fell out? We passionately disagreed? We hate each other? He's a man I have met on only three occasions, but I find myself thinking about him all the time? We are polar opposites, but thinking about him this morning gave me the most powerful orgasm of my young life? I turn back to my therapist for clues, but none is offered.

'He doesn't put much stock in therapy,' I say, and my therapist grins broadly. 'I'm sure he believes it utterly self-indulgent.'

My therapist is still grinning, and not writing anything down.

'Are you grinning like that because you agree with him and you are laughing all the way to the bank?' I ask.

'People have strong reactions to things that make them uncomfortable,' my therapist shoots straight back as if he has rehearsed it, or said it a thousand times at least. I am sure it is important, but I don't understand quite why.

'He would be so very wrong, for me,' I say quietly, dreamily, strangely and slowly. 'He is not at all the man that I should be with. He dresses badly, he looks old, he is rude, we have nothing in common, he hates me . . .' I stare out of the window again, and let my eyes glaze over, and the tree and squirrel and the road beyond become a hazy blur. I stroke the ridge of my nose, between my eyebrows. It is getting dark outside and I glance down at my watch, it is a quarter to four in the afternoon. I think I might wander along to Screen Queen when we are done here. I haven't seen Christian since the dinner party, and he said to pop in. It might be fun. And who cares if Cagney's office is upstairs – I don't have to see him. He will probably be working. I could take Christian a coffee, we could share a muffin. My mind drifts . . .

'You see, Adrian is the right age for me. He dresses the way I think he should, he just looks right. He remembers *DangerMouse* and *Bagpuss*, not *Bill and Ben*. He slow-danced to "Angel Eyes" at school discos – he wasn't smoking pot to the strains of a whining Bob Dylan. My family would be able to talk to him, it wouldn't be uncomfortable, they wouldn't be searching for things to say. He could come at Christmas . . .'

I spot one of my hairs resting on my dress, and I pick it up between my thumb and index finger and twist it tightly around my right little finger.

'I have always dreamt, and wished, and I just think it would make sense not to deviate from those dreams, because I've wanted them for a long time. Getting distracted now would be impulsive and naïve. I always wanted somebody like me, somebody I could have a laugh with, not some great romantic hero. Adrian ticks the right boxes, but Cagney is just so . . . different. He's closed off, and scared, so abrupt and dogmatic, and he lashes out if he feels he's being even slightly hunted. The world scares him, I think, and he just wants to be left alone.'

'You've only met him three times, you say?' My therapist makes a note.

'I know, that's a lot of babble with no real substance, but it just seems so obvious with him! Or maybe I've just been spending too much time on this sofa. Anyway, Adrian ticks all the right boxes. He is the Brett to my Babs.'

My therapist nods.

I told him about Babs in my second session – how she is another me, a perfect me. Except not really. I don't have a clone or a twin or anything. I made her up when I was younger, during my addiction to *Beverly Hills, 90210*. She's me, but she lives in Beverly Hills in a big house with a pool. She has a younger brother called Parker. She dyes her hair blonde, but she looks like me, except she's had a nose job. And, of course, the main difference is that she is thin. She was always the thin version of me, somewhere just out of reach. I dreamt her a life and she lived it for me. Every time my soul got a little bruised by a fresh jibe, I wished myself away to LA. I could spend hours pretending to be her, having her conversations, going on her dates – she saw Brett all through high school. They had a break for a while, during their first year of college, and she saw a couple of guys, a Jock, and then a Poetry Major, but she ran into Brett again over the summer, and they got back together. She works for a fashion house now. She's a personal shopper, and she's been married to Brett for two years. They went to Fiji for their honeymoon. She'll want to start trying for a baby in two years. Before that they have a big trip to Europe planned. Maybe she'll get pregnant then . . . I'm not crazy, I know it's not real, and my therapist assured me it was normal, a normal projection of my dreams, and harmless. It just made me happy for a while, even if arguably my time would have been better spent doing something about my own issues, which were preventing me living a perfect life here instead. And now, well, she's just been around for so long, I just check in with her, see where she's at, and measure myself accordingly. Some days it's like firing a rocket up me. I refuse to let Babs have my dreams all for herself now.

'Babs wouldn't go near Cagney with a barge pole. She'd name him the loser that he is.' I look up guiltily at my therapist. 'If Babs was real, which she isn't.'

'You do realise that you are Babs now, Sunny, that you got your wish, not through magic, but through your own hard work. There isn't anybody out there to live the life you want to live, but can't, any more. You have to grab your life now, Sunny, if you really want to. There is nothing you can't do, and nothing to hold you back. No more excuses.'

I look up at him, and the earnest expression that he wears, and I am embarrassed. I look at the clock instead, on his desk, which reads 15.59. I have one minute left.

'Any homework?' I ask with a smile.

'Don't just accept what you are given. If you see something you want, grab it,' he says.

The clock ticks and the numbers change.

I walk a short perfect walk to Kew Village, and Screen Queen. I try not to imagine a thousand different scenarios where I run into Cagney James, bursting out of a coffee shop and spilling his latte all over my dress, or bursting out of the newsagent's and knocking me sideways, the contents of my bag flying everywhere, except the tampons that just stay hidden at the bottom. To be frank, I don't try that hard not to imagine these things. I have been thinking of little else all weekend, since the dinner party in fact. I feel childish when I catch myself halfway through a scene I am playing with in my mind, and I stop it in case anybody else sees. As if somehow there is a wire plugged into the back of my head, and when a remote control is pointed at my eyes it explodes into action; electricity is pumped through me like a cheap standard lamp, and I emit a stream of light from my forehead like an undead character in some crazy Japanese horror film, and my thoughts and desperate daydreams are projected on to the side of the nearest building for everybody to look away from, embarrassed. If Cagney saw them he would think me childish. He thinks me childish anyway, because he is a proper adult. I am behaving ridiculously. He has been married three times . . .

It is cold and dark, but that bright kind of darkness, when everything seems clearer than during the day. All the lampposts are old-fashioned here, dirty old iron, and the stars sparkle big and fat, and the moon looks swollen and

236

expensive. The beams from the streetlights, and passing car and bicycle headlamps, and descending 747s bound for Heathrow, and satellites and rocket ships and alien craft and the moon and the stars all reflect beautifully in the paintwork of the Mercedes and the BMWs and the Porsches and the Land Rovers parked arrogantly along the streets. I kick through leaves, knowing really I shouldn't but I have never been caught out before. I feel utterly safe with just the bright dark for company. My stomach rumbles and I feel a little giddy. Today has been a good day.

Early Halloween decorations pose in the windows of the shop fronts in the village – a skull sits prettily on a piano in the music shop. Worthy-looking organic pumpkins hollowed out and grimacing, look beaten and bruised and furry, and not gleaming and waxy and appetising, like the ones in Sainsbury's. There is a little bookseller at the top of the lefthand fork, that stocks the classics and some new titles, and seems permanently to be advertising a 'local author'. People come to Kew to write books, it would seem, to clear their mind of unnecessary distractions and get down and dirty with their opi – is that the plural of opus? It makes me smile. It sounds a little like a jewel. Or a type of cyst, found on the cornea maybe . . .

The bookshop advertises crime and thrillers in one half of its window, and foreign language picture books in the other. They have them imported – all the big recognisable kids' brand books, sent over from France and Spain and Germany and Italy, to help the au pairs teach the little ones another language . . .

Fairy lights are sprinkled in huge elm trees that line the parking zone, blinking and greeting a steady stream of commuters pouring out of the tube station at seven-minute intervals, most of them fresh from the city, draped in an air called 'I've made it'. Kew is an obvious dream, and one that

I subscribe or unsubscribe to daily. It is kicking about in wealthy leaves that aren't mine, but I feel like I am borrowing its safety for a little while, and hoping some of the luck that everybody else here has found themselves swimming in might rub off on me. I like that the Christmas tree outside the tube station doesn't get vandalised. I like that a choir of carol singers greets me at the station throughout Advent with a rendition of 'Hark the Herald Angels', or 'Let It Snow', a different charity choir for a different day, all agreed by the council beforehand, all with the same songs to sing, none less deserving than the others, apart from the Elderly Actors' Club. I am never quite comfortable about giving my pound to them on the eleventh day of Christmas or whatever day they get allocated; it's hardly kids or cancer, is it? More likely it's some old ham who can't afford any more toupees, and I'm not sponsoring an ageing thesp's addiction to hair-pieces while he whines that nobody ever saw his Hamlet, I don't care how sweetly their choir sings 'Winter Wonderland'. If they had any sense, the elderly actors would get out and sing it themselves. I'm a sucker for the old trying to do anything that doesn't involve being slumped in a chair with a box of biscuits, dribbling in front of any programme hosted by Judith Chalmers.

There are some days when I am so very pleased to be here, walking clean streets and looking up at the trees and smelling the fresh meat in the butchers and smiling at the stylish middle-aged lady who owns the bookshop because she loves books. Somedays it is all I want out of life, and it doesn't matter that I am alone. But then somedays it isn't . . .

Some days, I just don't give a shit how green the trees are. Trees are supposed to be green, that's what they do. And I'm not going to grin inanely at a blue sky just because it's blue. That doesn't make it a wonderful world. And on those days I think: who really cares though? Who cares about any of it? Trees or seasons or safety or charm or quiet or beauty or pretension or any of it?

Who cares what I eat?

Who cares what I don't eat?

Who cares?

Maybe it's not an attractive attitude, but who bloody cares? Maybe I don't want to be attractive today! Maybe I am sick to the back teeth of studying my face for the occasional hair that shouldn't be there, or thinking about what style I am growing my hair into, or studying my body, my fat-less body, in its draping skin suit. I'd just like to feel, for once, that something was done, for good, and perfect. That's why some days I like Kew. Some days, when I am easily pleased, it seems perfect.

Cagney can't fit in here either, I am sure of that. He is a man who would love it if nobody ever spoke to him again. And even though I am now at an age when I know that having a monosyllabic boyfriend would just be plain frustrating and depressing, there is still a part of me that finds it attractive. There is still a little teeny tiny itsy cutsey crappy egotistical part of me that thinks that I could drag a conversation out of him late at night . . . but who can be bothered with that much effort? Talk or don't talk, do what you like, who cares? Don't expect me to hang around, though.

The problem facing Cagney is that he wants to be anonymous, but he thinks it might kill him. So he has the fight in his head, the same one that I fight in my head, whenever I lose my temper. The only way I can think to explain it, this need to be lost and found all at once, is that it is like driving a car. You are driving along really familiar roads, and suddenly you realise that you are changing from third to second gear, and braking, or checking your mirror, or indicating left, and it's all just automatic. And you know exactly where you are going, and it feels really reassuring, but then you are overcome by the feeling of just wanting to be lost. Completely lost and with no map, and how exciting that would be! Especially if you happened upon somewhere wonderful, purely by chance . . . But then, as you slow down to check the sideroads to see if they look right, and change lanes at the last minute and cars toot their horns at you, you feel like you are in everybody's way. Because they all know where they are going, and you don't, and suddenly you want to be back on those familiar streets again, moving but not thinking.

As I get nearer to Christian's shop I can see without deliberately looking up that there is no light on in Cagney's office. My mouth feels a little dry.

The much-hyped film festival is in full swing. A banner hangs across the front of the shop, black star cloth with orange shiny lettering that spells 'OH, THE HORROR!'

Along the bottom of the window sit pumpkin heads with purple lights glowing behind their eyes. Life-size standees of Tom Cruise, Leonardo DiCaprio, Paul Newman, Liza Minnelli, Julia Roberts, and Olivia Newton-John stand proudly in the window, dressed in a *Top Gun* uniform or *Xanadu* sparkles, or *Cabaret* fishnets and a bowler hat.

Somebody – Christian, I presume – has adhered plastic daggers and axes and chainsaws to their hands, as well as sticking false fangs onto their mouths.

As I am only a few feet away I can see Christian is behind the counter at the back, sipping from an oversize coffee mug, using a calculator, mouthing lyrics to a song I can't place.

I push open the door, which screams a short high-pitched shriek instead of the regular bell. Christian looks up from his calculator and I grin broadly. He smiles . . . but I am immediately uncomfortable, and wish I hadn't come. It is not a big or friendly or pleased-to-see-me smile. In my head, another one of my crazy daydreams, was that Christian and I might hug. We have only talked seriously for one night, but I feel like we bonded a little. Maybe Christian is like that with everybody . . .

'Hi!' I cough inadvertently. 'Sorry! I thought I'd pop in and see how your film festival is doing.'

'Oh, right . . .' Christian gives me a fake smile again, and makes his eyes wide in feigned excitement.

'So, how are you?' I ask, folding my arms.

'Yeah, really busy . . .' Christian and I glance around the empty shop simultaneously. I look down at my shoes. 'I mean, it was busy earlier, and I was busy doing all the decorations.' Christian sweeps his hand in front of him like a glamour girl at a car show advertising the latest Ford.

We smile at each other and look around and away. I recognise the music as the soundtrack to *Fame*. Christian was mouthing the second verse of 'Hi-Fidelity' when I came in.

'Well, it looks great, Christian!' I say, gearing up to make my exit so soon, scared that I may cry.

'Thanks, Sunny,' Christian says, and fiddles with his calculator.

'OK, well, I'm going to go,' I say, and turn to leave, taking a few steps towards the door.

'I'm sorry, Christian.' I turn round, and he is staring after me. 'Have I done something wrong? Because it feels like you are being really weird . . . with me. I mean, I know we have only just met properly, but I thought we got on well the other night . . . I don't know. How embarrassing is this? I just thought we might be . . . friends, I guess. But you seem . . . a little strange . . . or strained . . . or something.'

Christian mutters something at his calculator that is barely audible, and I prickle.

'I'm sorry?' I say.

Christian throws his head up and his arms out in an exaggerated pose. 'I thought you'd come in sooner! It's been four whole days!'

'Oh, sorry, I didn't realise . . .'

'And I thought that you might want to talk to me, given our last conversation, about Adrian . . . or Cagney, maybe. I thought that you might want to talk about him. I guess I want you to talk about him.' Christian moves round in front of the desk towards me, smiling again, but sheepish now, not fake or phoney.

'You want me to talk about Cagney to you?' I ask

'Don't you want to talk about him?'

To lie, or not to lie. It's a clear and easy choice.

'I don't know . . .'

Or to half-lie.

'I just keep thinking about you and him and the argument. And I realised that I haven't seen him say so much to anybody, anybody at all, for months, years, ever! I'm a romantic, Sunny. I'm not going to apologise for myself. He's a good man, and you're a good girl, and I just think it could be wonderful if you let it.'

I should raise my hand to close my mouth, my chin has dropped so far to my chest. Christian is planning my wedding, and he'll make Cagney and me convert to whatever religion is allowed the most flamboyant best man. He is twenty steps ahead of me and running. And as much as I love that it isn't only me dreaming up Cagney and Sunny scenarios in my head, I suddenly feel guilty about Adrian, who has been calling and apologising all weekend. It started with a couple of calls that I didn't answer on Saturday morning, and short, sharp messages asking me to pick up the phone. This was followed on Saturday evening by a text saying simply 'I miss u'. I suspect that if he had spelt out 'you' it might have made a difference. Sunday descended into a whole cake of apologies and persuasions. I had a sprinkling of 'missing you' texts by midday, dusted with 'please please call me's by early evening, and finally, when he had received no response, he dunked the whole day in a thick, fattening sauce of 'I could leave her . . .' That was a message, not a text. It could just be lip service, but it could be real. I hoped that refusing to see him might make a decision easier, but it clearly hasn't. Mobile phones make it impossible to be alone. I could just turn it off, but it could be an emergency . . .

Christian reaches out and takes hold of both my hands.

'Sorry I was such a pig. I just spent all of Sunday and Monday waiting for you to show, and then by last night I was vexed and by this morning I was agitated, and by lunchtime I just felt like you had utterly rejected the pair of us!'

'Who?' I ask.

'Me, and Cagney!' he says, and mouths 'sorry' as I hear 'Starmaker' come on in the background.

'I love this song,' I say, holding Christian's hands, smiling.

'I know, me too.' I notice his T-shirt reads 'Happy and Glorious'.

'Turn around,' I say, and Christian obliges. On the back it reads 'God Save This Queen' in black on deep violet. 'It's a good colour for you,' I say, as Christian turns back to me.

'Will you dance with me? Just so I know you have really forgiven me for acting like such a child.'

'Of course,' I say. I put my bag down by the till, and turn to face Christian to see what kind of crazy dance he wants to do, but instead he pulls me towards him, and I have to stand on my very tiptoes so he can press his head into my neck. He smells wonderful, of citrus and lemon and musk, and he presses his hands into my back as we sway to Doris and Leroy and the one with the cello who couldn't sing but was good in *Footloose*. We sway in the middle of his video shop, and occasionally Christian whispers, 'I'm sorry I was mean,' and I say, 'Stop apologising now,' and we carry on spinning. I close my eyes, and try to pretend this unfamiliar man is Cagney, but I can't even entertain the thought without feeling sick and giddy, and experiencing a rushing sensation that is completely new. I think I'll name it fear.

With that, the door shrieks, and we both jump. We break apart as I feel Christian squeeze my hand.

EIGHT

Plunging in

Cagney looks down at his lap, concerned. He has a colossal midday erection. He checks his watch, which used to be his father's. It is ten past one. An early afternoon erection is no less concerning. And it is atypical.

He is watching Sophia Young prune a wildly overgrown bush. She was potting three geraniums only moments ago. His erection appeared somewhere between the last geranium and the first snip of her secateurs at a huge purple rhododendron. Cagney looks down at his crotch again, and the comical tent pole protruding fiercely out of the black folds of his trousers. Is it the gardening that turns him on? Or the swell of Sophia Young's small pert breasts in a pink woollen dress? Or the curve of her slim ankles in ballet slippers? Or the wisp of blonde hair that has escaped her gentle ponytail, and is now dancing with the flush on her right cheek, in a light autumn breeze? Or is it merely coincidence, an untimely rush of blood caused by something else altogether? Could his socks be too tight?

Cagney has been watching Sophia Young since twenty past eight this morning, when she left Sheldon's impressive Barnes pile to power-walk delicately around the village pond, with two small pink weights in her hands, pumping her slim arms by her sides for extra impetus. There was no visible sign of perspiration at any point. Her face was a milky white wash of calm and elegant ease. It wasn't so much exercise, more a gentle stroll to get some fresh air, and be polite to the ducks. Cagney admires her all the more for it. It is a nod to exercise at best, but she doesn't believe it any more than he does. It's not a Christ Almighty gym membership, red-faced weight lifting in gynaecological Lycra, vein-popping, forehead-dripping, needless dramatic exertion. It isn't a woman making a spectacle of herself. If a woman is fat, it is simply because she eats too much cake. Stop eating cake, lose weight, and to hell with any other advice. His mother had been tiny all of her life, with a twenty-six-inch waist. If somebody had passed her a dumbbell she would have dusted it and passed it straight back. It reminds Cagney that Gracie, his first wife, had been a keen gardener. Keen on the gardener was actually closer to the truth. If 'keen on' constitutes 'fucking him in the shed'.

Cagney was only twenty-three when he married Gracie, and she was in her indeterminate thirties even then. They had tied the knot after only a four-month courtship, and a three-day engagement. Cagney had called it their 'whirlwind affair'. They had met, as couples often do, in a phone box. Gracie had been making a call – to whom Cagney still does not know – when he walked past in his squaddie uniform. He had seen her hair, blonde and fresh, that even from a distance promised to smell of goodness and purity and fjords. Her face was obscured by her hair and the phone, but when Cagney turned back to take another look she glanced up, with eyes the blue of his mother's cornflowers. Cagney had turned on his heel and marched back, tapping on the glass of the booth, with his beret folded beneath his arm.

She pushed the door open, and spoke a simple, 'Yes?' In

a beautiful whisper, covering the mouthpiece of the phone, catching him with those eyes, and metaphorically at least, dragging him in.

He was stationed in Colchester, and had been there for six weeks already, serving out his final stretch in the army, having decided that the military was no longer for him. He enjoyed the routine and the order for a while, clinging to it when his mother died, as something to focus on and drag him through his melancholy. But now he had made his peace with the world, promising himself he would finally get out there and live! He was ready to grow his hair, experiment with life, see what the world had to offer him, a twenty-five-year-old man with dreams to first create then chase!

Gracie conceded to thirty-two, and was recently divorced. Very recently. Her decree absolute had arrived only the previous morning. But Cagney was bewitched by those blue eyes, and that hair, and the small of her back and the way it curved in to her pert behind. With his army training Cagney could snap the wrist of any full-grown man he encountered, but Gracie's wrists were so delicate they would have fallen away beneath the pressure of two of Cagney's fingers. Something so sweet, so weak, so pale and pure would never do anything that might hurt him in any way. It didn't even occur to him that she might. They were innocent days.

Admittedly theirs had not been a meeting of minds, but Cagney had fallen desperately in love with her none the less, craved her when she left his side, consumed by his need to be near her, driven sick with jealousy at the thought of another man looking at her, no doubt brushing past her, smelling her honeysuckle hair, tinged with peroxide.

Gracie's smile at the altar, at the barracks, with two of his platoon as witnesses, had promised so much. But Gracie's rivers did not run deep. When Cagney confided to his new older bride on their wedding night that he would be able to leave the army in just four months, and then they could do anything in the world, go anywhere in the world, he was met with a shocked silence.

'What's wrong, my love?' Cagney asked, lying naked beside his wife, stroking the space between her shoulder blades, running a finger down her spine to her perfect arse.

'Why would you want to leave?' she asked, incredulous.

Cagney had jumped on to his knees, and hollered, 'To live a little! To taste life! To be beaten and bruised by experience, but to live! To scream from the top of a tall tree, and run naked into a warm Turkish sea!' He had laughed out loud, throwing back his head, hammering his chest with his fists in a glorious hysteria.

'You're mad, Cagney,' she said, closing her eyes.

'Well, you married me, Mrs James!' Cagney laughed and tried to roll her over to him, for a kiss.

But instead she pulled the covers tight to her chin, closed her eyes, and announced to the pillow, 'Let's see how we feel in a year. We might have a baby by then . . .'

This was the point, lying on his back, facing a cracked ceiling, that Cagney realised he barely knew the woman next to him, and yet he had just bound them together for life. Gracie James, née Janowitz, was a stranger to him. He hadn't thought to check that they wanted the same things.

The next morning they woke early in each other's arms, twisted in the night like two stockings in the wash, coming together in spite of themselves. Cagney had tenderly kissed his new wife, and silenced the voice of quiet dread lurking in the back of his head. He rolled Gracie on top of him, and tasted her small pointed breasts, and waited for an erection that didn't come. His penis sat sadly on his balls, like a guest to a party who received an invitation by mistake, standing alone in the middle of the room, spoiling everybody's fun. His flaccid penis ruined their night, every night.

Cagney, determined to overlook this temporary setback, attempted to surprise both Gracie and his member into action by grabbing them both simultaneously, one with each hand, on the spur of the moment. It made no difference. Any hint at rigidity was deflated by Gracie's wide-eyed curiosity.

'Do you think you'll be able to get an erection this time, Cagney? Because I've just given myself a pedicure, and I don't want to risk smudging it for nothing . . .'

Cagney really had felt like nothing that day. A couple more botched attempts over the next weeks had petered out, and by the end of their second month as man and wife, Cagney and Gracie had nothing left to say to each other.

Cagney would venture the occasional, 'How are you, my darling?' on his arrival home from work.

'Fine,' Gracie would acknowledge, in her annoyingly quiet whispery tone, with a vacant smile that betrayed her utter disinterest. Gracie just wanted to be married. Cagney, in the wrong place, and at the wrong time, had asked the wrong lady. Three months of guilt followed. Cagney felt he had only himself to blame. He hadn't bothered getting to know his new wife, and now he deserved to live with the consequences. Thankfully for them both, Gracie wanted a baby, and as Cagney's little soldier was proving so unobliging, and she heard the ticking of her biological clock, she took matters firmly into her own hands. Gracie needed an erect and ejaculating penis, and found it, conveniently, at the bottom of the garden where only the fairies are supposed to live. In this case, at the bottom of Cagney and Gracie's garden lived Brian, the gardener and handyman for the barracks, in a large brick-built outhouse, which doubled up as a tool shed. Gracie had merely to skip down the garden path to find what she needed.

Cagney had almost named it relief the day he returned

to his house for a surprise lunch – trying so desperately to make an effort with his wife that he plotted out potential topics for discussion during the morning to use during their lunchtime conversation – to see a naked back pressed up against the dirt-smeared shed window. A mass of ice-blonde hair was jumping off creamy white shoulders that he knew to be his wife's. Gracie had left for her mother's that evening, and Cagney had left the army the following month. Brian the gardener was happy to be named in the divorce proceedings, and the paperwork had come through by Christmas . . .

Cagney checks his crotch again to confirm what he already knows – his erection has wilted as if Gracie were sitting next to him in the BMW, smiling politely, naming the world 'fine' and anything or anybody with any character 'mad'.

He watches Sophia Young move elegantly back into the house, pulling off her gardening gloves finger by finger, with a look of quiet concentration on her face. 'You are a beauty,' Cagney whispers to himself, at which point his phone rings. Checking the number, he flips it open.

'Iuan.'

'Boss!'

'What?'

'I thought I might reorganise the files.'

'No.'

'I could put them in date order.'

'They are already in alphabetical order, Iuan.'

'Ahhh, yes, but you see, boss, if they were in date order –'

'We'd never be able to find anything?'

'Not if we also kept a spreadsheet on the computer with an alphabetical listing of the clients matched to their details . . .'

'Iuan, shut up. Here are my questions: number one, have you already touched the files? Number two, have you touched the computer? Number three, has anybody actually called with any business, and number four, if somebody did call, did you take their name and number?'

'No. No. No. No. But . . .'

Cagney opens his mouth to interrupt but is instead frozen by a finger tapping elegantly on his driver's side window. He turns and smiles as politely as he can, flipping the phone shut to Iuan's muffled protestations. His finger hovers above the button that will automatically lower his window. He jabs at it, and the window hisses open.

'Can I help you?' Cagney looks with curiosity at Sophia Young, his face a snapshot of sincerity.

'I think the more pressing question is, can I help you, sir? Given that you have been watching me all morning. You are not going to deny it, I hope. And before you say a word, or move a muscle, I want to let you know that I have my mobile phone set to 999, I have already texted the number plate of your car to my sister, and given her your full description. If I press this button just once I shall be speaking directly with the police. Not that I believe for a second you are a violent man, but I am warning you none the less. Don't do anything silly. Now, I assume my husband hired you?'

'I'm sorry, I really don't know what you are talking about. I was just parked here –'

'Oh, please, don't embarrass us both. You certainly aren't the first man he has paid to sit and spy on me all day, and you won't be the last. Now admit it, Sheldon hired you, didn't he?'

Sophia gracefully lifts a strand of hair away from her face and tucks it behind her ear. Her eyes, this close to Cagney, staring straight at him, are clear and bright, the colour of a plunge pool in the middle of the Alps. She places both hands on her small hips, and eyes him accusingly.

'Well?' she says evenly.

'I'm sorry, miss, I really don't have a clue what you are talking about. I just pulled over to make some calls, and –'

'Sheldon is having me watched because he thinks I am having an affair with the handyman, I already know that. It's not true, of course, but his money makes him paranoid.'

Cagney sums up Sophia evenly. Who is fooling who here? How much does she really know? And what must that hair smell like, clean and fresh, after hours spent in the garden?

Cagney juts out his hand to be shaken. 'Cagney James,' he says firmly.

Sophia doesn't move, ignoring his hand, but says, 'Would you like a cup of tea, Mr James?' before turning and walking back towards her house.

Cagney leaves his car and adopts a fast pace, refusing to jog, but still trying to keep sight of Sophia Young as she marches round the back of the house. He follows, and turning the corner, Cagney finds himself in a vast riot of a courtyard filled with marble and terracotta pots. Shovels lie clumsily on the stone floor or are propped against walls, and half-empty bags of all-purpose compost spill their contents everywhere. Cagney watches where he treads. A farmhouse door stands open and Cagney pokes his head round it into a kitchen the size of his entire flat. It looks sharp and clean and impeccably modern. All surfaces are utterly bare, and two huge glass vases hold magnificent white lilies that fill a room even this big with a heady scent. Sophia Young is nowhere to be seen, but then she appears through a doorway to Cagney's left. She has discarded her wellies, and is barefoot, and Cagney notices the pale pink splashes of colour on her slim toes. She moves gracefully to the kettle, and fills it with a jug of filtered water retrieved from a double-fronted Smeg fridge.

Cagney eyes the floor nervously. It is so clean it sparkles, and he worries about the soles of his shoes, and the compost he has just walked through.

'Please don't worry about your shoes, Mr James. The cleaner comes every morning; it will give her something to do if somebody makes a mess.'

Cagney stares at Sophia Young's back and wonders how she knew.

'Besides, the compost is all my fault – I am in the middle of moving my delphiniums. Do you know a lot about gardening, Mr James?'

'Nothing. Other than it's a dirty job but someone's got to do it.'

'Quite right too. Time was I didn't know the difference between a poppy and a pansy, but I thought it prudent to learn. With a garden that big, and nothing else to do, it seemed wise to use it to keep myself entertained. But I do worry that it is turning me into an old woman before my time. I mean, most girls my age go clubbing and get drunk, and I am planting snowdrops and daffodils in time for spring.' Sophia Young spins around to face Cagney and smiles a brilliant smile.

Cagney inhales sharply.

'But then I have never been one for getting drunk anyway. I have always thought girls who drink let themselves down socially. I know that must sound old-fashioned, but my gardening doesn't make me say stupid things, or be sick, or have a hangover, so the way I see it, they may think they are having more fun, but I laugh last. And women who drink, well, they always seem so boisterous . . .'

Cagney's mind is whirring. He has a feeling he is being played like an old guitar, but he doesn't know how to stop it, and he isn't sure he wants to. Sophia Young stands staring at him from the other side of the kitchen, as her fingertips dance on the kitchen surfaces and the mugs she has magicked out of a cupboard, and the tea bags she drops into them, all the while looking straight at him.

'Do sit down,' she says firmly, but with a smile.

Cagney walks as lightly as he can to a Philippe Starck chair and sits as comfortably as the moulded perspex seat allows.

'I know what you must be thinking – why daffodils, for goodness' sake? It might not be grand, but I want the garden to be simple next year, but still riotous with colour. Not dainty or fussy – bold . . . and bright! I'm planting crocuses too. I know it's absurd! And I am sure I will get some looks from the old busybodies around here, but I don't care. Sugar?'

'I'm sweet enough.'

'Is soy milk OK? We switched months ago, because of Sheldon's blood pressure. I actually prefer it now, to skimmed milk at least. It is very good for you, Mr James. It fights all kinds of disease.' Sophia widens her eyes as she smiles to encourage him like a child.

'If you soy so,' Cagney hears himself saying. He knows that, in any other company, he would have gone without rather than drink anything with soy in it . . . more than that, he would have got up and walked out. Instead he makes a 'word' joke. Did he leave his shame in the car?

'So . . .' Sophia Young walks elegantly across her kitchen and places Cagney's tea on a Conran coaster, before moving behind him and sitting herself at the top of the table, so that Cagney has to push back his precarious plastic chair and shift himself uncomfortably around to face her, while still trying to appear relaxed. 'What does Sheldon want from you, Mr James? Does he think you might catch me in the act? Do you have a camera ready to snap snap snap me being a naughty girl?'

Sophia Young's lips turn up at the ends into a slight smile.

Cagney feels something stiffen. Sophia flicks her hair, places her elbow languidly on the table, and cups her chin, focusing entirely on Cagney in a swirl of attentive glamour that he is starting to find intoxicating.

'The problem for you, Mr James, and for Sheldon too, who wants rid of me now I know, is that I am just not that naughty a girl . . .'

Cagney crosses his legs. Sophia's eyes don't leave his.

'I mean, we all want to be naughty, sometimes, but I don't get the opportunity. I love Sheldon, I really do, but he has lost all interest in me, Mr James. I can't remember the last time we were . . . together, if you understand . . . ?'

Sophia widens her eyes at Cagney, who nods once.

'I mean, I'm sure that isn't the story he has given you. You have had "the handyman story", as ridiculous as it is. But, Mr James, you should meet our handyman – he is a lovely boy, but even the idea that I might let him . . . touch me . . . like that . . .' Sophia lowers her eyes, and raises them again, looking at Cagney from below pale eyelids and long thin clean eyelashes. 'He is just a boy, Mr James. Cagney.' Sophia reaches over with her right hand and runs a line along the back of Cagney's hand with her index finger.

'You're not exactly mutton,' Cagney says, in an even tone.

'I know, I know,' Sophia smiles, and removes her finger. 'But I don't want to play with boys my own age, Mr James. I like real men . . .'

Sophia smiles at Cagney, and Cagney smiles back. Sophia giggles lightly.

'I wonder how many women have fallen victim to that smile, Mr James,' she whispers as she leans forward. There are mere inches between their faces.

A spade crashes noisily in the courtyard, and Cagney jumps in his plastic chair, which slides to the right on the shiny floor, and he jerks forward to stay upright, slamming the table with his thighs, sending his tea flying in the air, raining down on his lap in hot splashes.

'Fuck fuck fuck!' Cagney jumps up and down, trying to pull his trousers away from his crotch, as Sophia springs up and unbuckles his belt. 'What the hell?' Cagney looks down at her nimble fingers, aghast.

'It'll burn and stain, take them off,' Sophia orders, as she whips his trousers down to his ankles.

Cagney looks at his boxer shorts in horror, but thankfully the tea, although burning his thighs, has cooled his ardour. He breathes three times in quick succession.

'Take them off!' Sophia demands again, but this time more forcefully, and Cagney complies. 'Now take off your shoes.'

'Why?' Cagney demands, coming to his senses. She is playing him for a fool. Blonde manipulation – he should have seen it a mile away!

'Because you need to go upstairs and clean up and dry off, and I'll bring your trousers up to you when I've got the stain out.'

'Nope, I'll be fine. Just give me my trousers back.'

'Mr James, don't be ridiculous. Go upstairs and I will sort it out.'

'It is you who is being ridiculous if you think I am going anywhere in this house without my trousers on!'

'But I am staying here, you arrogant fool – what do you think is going to happen? And I resent your implication. I am a married woman!' Sophia has raised her voice but Cagney still thinks he can detect a suppressed smile in her tone. She is playing with him, the way she has played with all the men that Sheldon has sent here before him.

'You weren't so married five minutes ago, angel, when you were batting those icy blues at me and stroking my hand.'

Sophia Young stops suddenly, and her face drops. Cagney sees her eyes glaze, and fill with water. Oh shit, she's going to cry. She is good.

'Here, take them!' Cagney lets go of the trouser leg he was grasping on to.

Sophia's perfectly pink lower lip starts to tremble.

'Where do I go? What room, what room?'

Sophia Young takes a breath, and smoothes herself down, regaining her composure, and Cagney breathes a sigh of relief.

'Up one flight of stairs, the second door on the right, the master bedroom, you'll find a pair of Sheldon's jogging trousers on the side of the bed, you can slip those on until these are dry.'

'Right. OK. Thanks very much.'

Cagney hurries out of the kitchen, round a corner and another corner and up a vast flight of stairs, past a piano in a hallway to the second door on the right, into a huge cold grey bedroom. The steely wash is broken by a single fuchsia cushion in the middle of the bed, which sits in the centre of the room, raised on a platform. His eyes scan the room for jogging trousers, but it is spotless; there are no clothes anywhere. Lifeless, soulless, joyless. Cagney's eyes dart from a grey leather armchair and back to the bed again, to an antique table by some French doors, to a distressed armoire, but he sees nothing resembling trousers, or even a dressing gown. He hears the sound of feet moving quickly down the corridor and Sophia Young bursts into the room.

'I can't find any trousers.'

'You have to get out!' Sophia stage-whispers through clenched teeth, moving towards him and spinning him round.

'What? Why? I will, but I can't find any trousers . . .'

'Now! You have to leave now!'

'What? Why?'

'Sheldon is home. He can't see you up here with no trousers! You have to leave.'

'Bunny? Are you in the bath?' a man's voice calls up the stairs.

'Yes, I've just got in. Pour me a glass of wine and bring it up, won't you, Papa Bear?'

'Papa Bear? Bunny? This house is twisted!' Cagney looks appalled, but Sophia just utters a tiny shriek and pushes Cagney towards the French doors. 'You have got to be joking! You want me to jump? Have you lost your mind, lady? Besides, Sheldon won't be able to say anything, because he knows me, he paid me, he won't be able to do anything without letting on to you that he has hired me!'

'And you were supposed to let me give you a blow job, were you?'

Sophia's eyes widen as if to say, 'Explain that!'

'What? Did somebody get a blow job, and I missed it?' Cagney is confused.

'Well, Sheldon doesn't know that, does he?' Sophia spits back.

'Why in God's name would he think that?' Cagney is still confused.

'Because I'm going to tell him I did, unless you get out right now!'

Cagney shakes his head violently from side to side, mouthing, 'No, no, no. Why would you do that?'

'Because I don't want him to know that I know that he hired you! This is the last time he messes with me! Now would you just leave?'

Sophia throws open the French doors and the wind whistles into the bedroom from a large balcony, and the curtains rise up and the material slaps the air noisily.

'Rabbit?' Sheldon calls from the bottom of the stairs.

'Big Bear?' Sophia calls back, pushing Cagney outside.

'Which white?'

'The Chablis!'

Cagney stands on the balcony pulling on his shoes, in his boxer shorts and a black roll-neck.

'At least give me my trousers!'

'I threw them in the bin!' Sophia spits through clenched teeth.

'Well, I am not climbing down a goddamn trellis in my boxer shorts. I am not a teenager!'

'Trellis? What trellis?' Sophia spins round as she thinks she hears footsteps outside, but a perfectly preened cat pads into the bedroom instead, and Sophia breathes out a perfumed sigh of relief.

'Well, if there is no fucking trellis, angel, how the hell am I supposed to get down?'

'Jump.'

Cagney laughs a derisive snort, as Sophia looks at him blankly. 'Jump?'

'Yes. Jump.' Sophia nods her head as if she were explaining it to the slowest child in the class.

'We're a storey up!'

'So?' Sophia stands with her hands on her hips, her chin jutting out angrily, her teeth clenched in rage.

'Oh, you are a peach, Mrs Young, you know that? Now I see why poor old Sheldon wants rid of the bunny!'

'Oh, whatever, just get the fuck out!'

'Nice language. You are one foul-mouthed rabbit!'

'Mr James, if you don't get out, right now, I am going to rip my shirt and go downstairs and tell my husband that you attacked me, and believe me when I say that he will take you for every penny you have! He might not want me any more but I am sure as hell still his property and he doesn't let anybody piss on his property, do you understand me, you cheap private dick? He'll close you down. He'll take your business and he'll crush it . . .'

Cagney stares at Sophia Young in disbelief. The plunge pool in the Alps has frozen over, and he recognises that hair colour for what it really is – arctic blonde. Sophia pushes him to the edge of the balcony and he allows himself to be pushed. She points.

'It's not so bad. You're going to jump into the pool, at least.'

Cagney glances down quickly, to see a large kidney-shaped swimming pool, icy cold and gleaming. He will freeze. His limbs will fall off in the ice.

'Jump!'

'Will I f –'

'Rabbit! I'm coming!'

'Jump!'

'Fine!'

Cagney puts one foot over the railings, and then the other, holding on to the handrail behind him. He feels something sticky against his hand, and moves it off to inspect it, when he feels Sophia Young's manicured hand shoved into the small of his back, and he flies off the balcony.

He hears her say 'I'll call you' before the French doors slam shut behind him. He opens his mouth to scream but his belly slaps the icy water before anything comes out, and his vocal cords freeze on impact.

Dripping wet, shivering, with blue lips and fingers, and smelling powerfully of chlorine and faintly of cat urine, Cagney pushes open the door of Screen Queen, to be confronted by the worst possible sight imaginable. Sunny Weston. Of all the video shops in all of Richmond, why does she have to be in this one? Especially when he is soaking wet . . . and especially when he isn't wearing any trousers.

An awful song finishes playing as he stands in the doorway.

Christian and Sunny, who have for some reason been slow dancing in the middle of the shop, stare at him moronically. The only noise he can hear is the drip drip drip of water from his saturated woollen sleeves onto the tiled floor.

'Been jumping in puddles again, Cagney?' Christian asks.

'More like swimming in shit,' he replies, staring coldly at Christian, before glancing at Sunny Weston. She is staring at his wet crotch with her mouth wide open and her eyes even wider. While losing the battle to suppress a smile, she is winning the fight against outright laughter.

'What?' Cagney demands, glaring at her. She manages to drag her eyes away from his groin, and meet his gaze.

'You're not wearing any trousers,' she says, incredulous. Cagney spots Christian glancing at her conspiratorially, and she rams her fist into her mouth and bites down hard, turning away to face *Titanic* and *Giant*, in the Leonardo DiCaprio and James Dean section.

'I am actually seriously cold,' he says evenly. 'I would approximate that it is no more than ten degrees outside, leaving me open to any number of infections.' Cagney lifts up his sopping arms to highlight his predicament.

Christian stares at him with bulbous eyes, his face resembling a cartoon character whose eyes are about to pop out on stalks, as his mouth falls open in unexpected delight. Sunny isn't making any noise, but he can see her shoulders shaking.

'Am I allowed to ask what happened?' Christian examines his manicure to concentrate on not laughing.

Cagney sees Sunny turn around sheepishly, as he opens his mouth to speak, but shuts it again quickly. He is inexplicably reluctant to retell his tale in front of her.

'Seriously, Cagney, are you OK?' she asks, with a sudden

261

look of concern. And rightly so! Who is she to stand there, with his best friend of all people, laughing at him? And why is she all dressed up? She wears a black dress that wraps around her body snugly, and crosses at her chest. He can see the swell of her breasts above the material, and the ravine between them. She wears slouchy boots, ugly but modern; he has seen other girls wearing them, but not so well. She has a scarf twisted at her neck, grey with silver sparkled lines running through it, and two small hard hearts hang from silver strings in her ears. Her hair is very dark. Cagney hasn't noticed how dark it is before now. She had it pulled back into a ponytail on the day that he first met her, and the dinner party had been candlelit. Her eyes are large and round, almond coloured, the best chocolates in the box, speckled with honey. Her skin tone is even and creamy, she looks like she has just returned from a weekend in Madrid, or Rome, or some hot European city.

'Can you count my fingers? Can you feel your toes? Are you going to finish your strip?' she asks earnestly. There is a momentary pause, and then Sunny and Christian simultaneously burst out laughing, and Cagney turns away disgusted.

'Why are you even here?' Cagney rounds on Sunny, his blood bubbling with rage. 'Just to laugh at my expense?'

'Well, I'll be honest, I didn't come with that intention, Cagney, but now that I'm here, and you're putting on such a good floor show . . .'

'Fine. Laugh it up. It hasn't occurred to you that I might be seriously hurt?'

'Are you?'

'That's hardly the point.'

'It's completely the point! You look ridiculous, and if you aren't hurt, I am going to laugh at you! Or is nobody allowed to laugh at the great Cagney James? Do you ever even laugh at yourself? My God, it must be such a wild party in your head!'

'It's still more fun than the party in his pants,' Christian mutters under his breath, and moves to the front of the shop to turn the 'Open' sign to 'Closed'.

'Oh, fantastic. I thought we hadn't had any psychoanalysis for a while. I love it when you tell me everything there is to know about me, when you have never actually been quiet long enough to hear a word I say.' Cagney scans her face for a reaction, but she doesn't bite.

'Sorry, Cagney, but there is only so much time in the day, I have to prioritise what I take in: the worthwhile and informative, and generally the pleasant and entertaining. Unfortunately the archaic shallow emotionally retarded machismo falls to the bottom of the pile, but then, some-body always has to come last.'

'I'm shallow? And yet I'm not the one starving myself to death to look like some magazine cover.'

'I swear you are more obsessed with what I eat and what I weigh than anybody I know! If I go upstairs will there be pictures of me all over your walls, Cagney? Have you been hiding behind cars with your filthy long lenses, snapping me when I'm not looking?' She bites down on her lower lip, and puts her hands on her hips. Cagney swears she is thrusting her breasts towards him.

'I couldn't be less obsessed by you, Sunshine! You couldn't be further from floating my boat if you were a six-foot Thai girl with an Adam's apple and hairy hands. You leave me so cold they could store meat on me in July.'

'It's my pleasure.' Sunny smiles sweetly at Cagney.

'I could see that from the way you were looking at my crotch, Sunshine. Your eyes lit up like fireworks.' Cagney crosses his arms and raises his eyes.

'In fairness it looks like more of a sparkler than a rocket, Cagney. A slow fizz rather than a big bang. Still, damp as it is, I imagine you'd have trouble getting it lit anyway . . .'

Cagney admits it quietly to himself. He likes her nerve.

'Oh, it rockets for the right kind of sunshine, Sugar, but mouthy and manly don't pump it up for me. I like my ladies to be ladies.'

'Once, twice, three times, I've heard! I saw your divorce lawyer the other day, parking his Ferrari. He said to send you his best.'

'And I saw Geoff Capes, and he was asking for his arms back.'

'Oh, you think me too toned? Although they could never be big enough to support the chip on your shoulder.'

Cagney takes a step forward, and Sunny does the same. They are both growing red in the face, their breathing fast and shallow.

Christian leans forwards on the counter, cupping his chin and is momentarily distracted by the side door slowly opening, and a plaster cast entering the room. Iuan is attached to it, and balances precariously in the doorway in a long black transparent kaftan. Thankfully, Christian can see underpants. Iuan has a crutch under each arm, and hobbles towards Christian.

'I heard raised voices. Gagging for a bit of excitement, been sat up there all day, wondered what was going on – what is going on?' Iuan whispers, the whole time watching Cagney and Sunny, who circle, fuming and spitting like rutting bulls in a Spanish ring before him.

'A kind of magic,' Christian says, without taking his eyes off them.

Cagney snarls, 'There was a chip, but it's gone now. I thought you ate it.'

They have gradually edged forwards. There is barely a

foot between them, less as their heads tilt forward as they do now.

'I wouldn't put anything that belonged to you in my mouth, Mr James. I'd worry you'd make me marry you!'

'And I'd worry about getting it back! Tell me, Sunshine, are you keeping me here because it's the last time you'll see me in my boxers, or is there something you want? Your cheeks are a little flushed – I'd hazard a guess you're excited. That cheat you call a boyfriend not quite cutting the mustard? Or has he just decided to save it for the girl he loves?'

'I apologise if I'm keeping you, Cagney. Feel free to move along, as any other man might have done, if he were wearing wet shorts and not much else. I think it's more a case that you can't drag yourself away. Bewitched and bewildered, by a woman that answers back?'

'I'm just waiting for the sun to set to see what you turn into.'

'And I'm just waiting for you to kiss me, so I can slap you hard enough to determine whether those flecks in your hair are your age, or your scalp.'

'I told you, Sunshine, I'm not brave enough to put anything of mine within three feet of your mouth. You'd chow down on my tongue like a canapé, and then demand a main course!'

Sunny's face, which was charged with excitement, falls. It breaks the trance, and the whole room inhales at once, coming up for air.

'Are fat jokes the only jokes you know how to make?' she asks him.

Cagney looks at her, but doesn't respond. His face doesn't betray any emotion, not confusion, nor guilt.

'Because you didn't even know me before, and I know I'm not fat now. I mean, is it just the best way you know of hurting me? Because you're laughing at who I am . . .' Sunny bites her lip quickly, and gulps.

'I wasn't the only one making snide remarks,' Cagney says firmly.

'You just want to make sure that they really hurt,' Sunny says, and turns quickly to Christian, who leans next to Iuan on the counter: they both look exhausted from bouncing their heads back and forth, as if they were watching a final on Centre Court.

'Have you got *Seven Brides for Seven Brothers*? I fancied watching it tonight.' Sunny looks anywhere but at Cagney.

'I'll check.' Christian clicks the mouse, and taps a few keys, reading the monitor intently. Sunny stands with her head down, biting her lip, ready to leave, while Cagney stares at her, motionless. But she refuses to meet his eye.

Christian looks up after a long quiet minute, embarrassed. 'Sorry, darling, it's out . . . and kind of . . . overdue . . .'

'Oh. Do you know when it's due back?'

'Ahh, no, not really. Cagney?'

Cagney turns his head towards Christian. 'What?'

'When are you going to bring *Seven Brides for Seven Brothers* back? It's just that . . . Sunny wants to rent it . . . and it's a couple of weeks overdue . . .'

Sunny's jaw locks. Cagney stares at Christian. Iuan looks confused. Christian slowly smiles a small smile.

'You'll have it tomorrow,' Cagney says, and stalks out of the room, with Christian in hot pursuit.

I look at my feet, and try not to cry. I don't understand why every word I say to him comes out coated in venom, and why he spits back as he does. I like him and I should just admit it, and not be ashamed, or apologetic. I should march up those stairs now, and throw open his door, lean on the doorframe with the light behind me, and say, 'I like you, Cagney. Kiss me.' And not be scared that he will laugh and tell me to leave . . .

There is a crazy guy standing behind the counter, smiling at me. He is wearing a sheer black dress. His hair is ginger and spiked, and a pair of crutches lean either side of him. He is really staring at me. He may be having a minor epileptic fit, the kind that leaves its victims motionless for a minute, and then they snap back into life wondering what the hell just happened.

'I'm Sunny,' I say, and smile.

'Oh, I know. I saw that.'

I don't know what that means. He has a lovely voice; he doesn't speak, he sings.

'I'm Iuan. I work alongside Cagney.'

'Oh, you too? What a shame.' My disappointment in anybody involved with Cagney's business is tangible. I can't imagine what role Iuan performs, but I think it must be administrative, or even legal . . . or possibly phone sex? He might be good at that, whispering naughty words in a beautiful baritone.

He is still smiling at me.

'Are you on painkillers?' I ask.

'Lots,' he says, and I smile and nod my head. I knew.

'What have you done?' I gesture at the plaster poking out from beneath the counter.

'I've broken my foot.'

'How?'

'I was showing Cagney my full moon.'

'OK.'

'So you're Sunny?'

'Yep. Why, have you heard of me?'

'Howard, another associate of myself and Cagney, well . . . he thinks that Cagney might fall in love with you,

267

although Cagney said not in a million years or something. It's my birthday next Saturday.'

'OK.' I think I need to speak to Howard, whoever he is.

'Would you like to come to my party?'

'Where is it?'

'In here. Christian is clearing away the stock for the night. It's fancy dress.'

'What's the theme?'

'Wales.'

'OK.' I say again.

'Don't come as a leek, though. I already have two of those.'

'OK.' I may go. It might be a laugh. He looks as if he might know an odd crowd. The costumes at the very least will be entertaining.

'I'm not just asking you to make trouble. I mean, between you and Cagney.'

'Can I bring my boyfriend?'

'No.' He means it, he isn't kidding.

'Right, I'm going to go.'

'Great. I'll see you on Saturday from eight then. I'll be thirty-three.'

'I'll see you then.'

I walk quickly home. As I pass the entrance to the alley I notice that somebody has scrawled 'LOVE LANE' on the wall in big white childish handwriting. I want to run the rest of the way home but I don't. I walk quickly with my head up and wish I had somebody, just at this moment, to hold my hand.

Christian narrowly avoids the door to Cagney's office slamming in his face. He pushes it back open without knocking. Cagney is already standing behind his desk, and the golden light from the streetlamp outside his window gives him an ethereal glow.

'Saint Cagney, the Patron Saint of Denial,' Christian says flatly, closing the door behind him. He leans back against the wall, and crosses his arms, the expression on his face demanding an explanation from Cagney, who ignores him, and pours a long measure of whiskey into a plastic beaker. He throws the shot and his head back simultaneously and the liquid disappears down his throat. Just as quickly, he pours himself another double.

'Why?' Christian asks, baffled.

'Why not?' Cagney necks the second shot, and pours himself another.

'Because you like her! You want to be nice to her, you just don't remember how!'

'Oh. That . . . I thought we were just playing word association.'

Cagney walks over and reaches into the bottom drawer of the filing cabinet, yanking out a fresh shirt still in its wrapping. He tugs out pins and chucks them on the floor.

'Why can't you be nice to her?'

'Who?' Cagney throws the last of the pins to the floor and shakes out the shirt violently.

'You're nearly forty, Cagney – stop acting like a child.'

Cagney peels off his jumper that is starting to stiffen.

'Dry clean only – it's my own fault,' he says to Christian with a smile and a shrug, throwing it straight in the bin. He is standing in his shorts, socks and shoes.

'Cagney!'

'You mean Sunshine downstairs? She isn't my type.' He pulls on the dark grey shirt, and walks back around the desk, buttoning himself up. 'I go for blondes, Christian, you know that.' He raises his whiskey glass and toasts his friend, although this time he only downs half the double measure he has poured himself.

'Well, I hate to be the one to tell you this, Cagney, but

269

not today you didn't! I think she's hit you somewhere completely new, and it smarts! That's why you're so angry, because what kind of fool falls in love at forty?'

'Are you staying?' Cagney asks Christian.

'For a while.'

Cagney retrieves a second beaker from his bottom drawer. 'For when I have company – you see, I can still entertain!' and pours out a double measure, passing it to Christian, who accepts it graciously, and knocks it back in one go.

'And again. I can keep up with the likes of you.' Christian pulls over a box from the side of the room and sits comfortably on it with his legs either side.

Cagney smirks and refills the glass and passes it back over the desk, before sitting down and leaning back, smiling.

'Oh, you've got your composure back now, I see that, but don't bother acting for me, Cagney. I know you too well, and it's so utterly male heterosexual bored-inary. She is causing a carnival in your belly and you don't know what to do about it. Will you admit it?'

'That's not how I fall in love. You've never seen me fall in love. It is very different. That was *The Taming of the Shrew*.'

'I didn't see anybody being tamed, Cagney. I think you're seeing stars. She's not blonde, is that all it is?'

'If you like her so much, you marry her! But she's too exhausting for me. I like my women beautiful and calm, like Windermere on a bright day.'

'Although . . . stop me if I am wrong, Cagney, but you haven't actually loved any of the women you think that you have loved? I mean, correct me if I am wrong, but every woman that has previously fired up your loins has screwed you in a very different way in the end?'

'What's your point?' Cagney's smile fades as Christian speaks. They aren't playing any more.

'I've heard love lasts, Cagney. And your great loves, well . . . they definitely didn't do that. So do you think that maybe there might be the slimmest of possibilities, the tiniest of chances, that you didn't actually love Barbies one, two, and three? Maybe, Cagney, maybe this is the way you fall in love. You've just never fallen in love before . . .' Christian sits back and smiles, patting out the theme from *Fame* with one hand on his chest, watching Cagney in the dark.

'I am a forty-year-old three-time divorcé – I think I know what love is.'

'On the contrary, Cagney, I think you know what love isn't! I think you know what lust is but that's a little different. Love is in the heart and the head. It's not holding your breath. It's letting it out with a big contented sigh!' Christian waves his hand in front of him like a magician's assistant revealing something extraordinary.

'Christ, you sound like a trashy chat show host.'

'And you think that's a bad thing? No, I've just decided that this is our once-a-decade necessary chat. Do you remember the last one?'

'I do.' Cagney nods his head seriously.

'And do you remember who needed the most help then?'

'I do.'

'I was the only person around actually hurting more than you! I mean, Christ! I was so unhappy. And you helped me, Cagney. Do you remember what you said?'

Cagney sits quietly watching the liquid that swirls in the beaker he cradles in his hands. He doesn't reply, or raise his eyes, but it is apparent that he heard. He spins around and looks out of his window. There is no moon, just some heavy cloud cover. He sees Sunny turn the corner at the end of the road, going home on her own. She looks young, and small, in the dark. An easy target for some unscrupulous type. Cagney knocks back the last of his drink.

271

'I said don't be scared to be who you are. People will respect you for it.' Cagney stares out of the window sadly.

'I knew eventually I'd get to repay the favour. Stop hiding behind your anger, Cagney, or your attitude. And take off your fucking rose-tinted glasses. The world is no worse now than it was fifty years ago, it's just different. We all live with it – what makes you so special? If you don't want to open up then don't open up, but for Christ's sake stop moaning that people ask you to! Just say no! And you don't need to cry every time somebody asks how you are. You moan about being told to share when you don't want to, and yet ironically you won't shut up about it.'

'I'm happier on my own.'

'Do you mean now? Or this pipe dream you have of the floating Caribbean paradise? Because there is no guarantee that it will make you happy. We can all dye our hair, lift our faces, sharpen our noses, run and run and run away. But what's the point, when it's all in your head? You need to lean on somebody, let somebody make you feel worthwhile again. You can't really laugh on your own! You can't captivate yourself, unless you are some kind of megalomaniac! And now you're fighting an instinct, a completely new instinct, when, if you had an ounce of courage, you'd grab it with both of those old hands!'

'Maybe . . .' Cagney puts the beaker down on his desk, and reaches into his drawer. 'Nuts?' He offers Christian the bag.

'Who is?' Christian asks, with an indignant smile.

'Sunny, for a start. And by the way, when did you two swap blood and boy stories? You seem very friendly . . .'

'Jealous, James?' Christian offers his glass forward to be refilled. Sipping at it, he shudders as the whiskey hits his stomach and burns.

'You sent me home with her, rather than walking her your damn self, remember? On Friday night?'

'I remember.' Cagney sighs and contemplates the mouthful of whiskey in his own beaker, before knocking it back and refilling. 'I do like her,' he says finally. 'She's got guts.'

'Yes, she has,' Christian agrees.

'But less than she used to!' Christian sips his drink and repositions himself, crossing his legs comfortably.

'The funny thing is, I don't even think I'd care, fat or thin. I mean, I don't know for sure, but then, now, big, small . . . it's not who she is, is it? It's the fire that I like, behind her eyes. That's her.'

Christian reaches up and pretends to wipe a tear from his left eye.

'Stop that right now, you big poof! I'm just saying she's nice.'

'You're saying more than that. You need to find a way to be nice to her, Cagney.'

'No, I don't. None of it matters anyway.' Cagney lowers his head, placing his beaker down on the desk, and his palms flat on the table, studying them carefully.

'Why the hell not? She likes you back, Cagney. I'd bet my balls on it!' Christian uncrosses his legs and sits forward urgently.

'It's not that. She's got a boyfriend. That fool at the dinner party, with his phone stuck to his ear.'

'The surprisingly charming Adrian? Yes, you are right, she is *officially* with him. But she likes you best, Cagney, I can tell! You just need to help her see the light.'

'Not while she's with another man.' Cagney screws the cap back on to his whiskey, returning a tenth of the bottle to his bottom drawer.

'Why not, Cagney? I mean, it's not ideal, but if you see something you want, you should damn well go and get it, because nobody is going to get it for you! And besides, she'll only leave him if she wants to. You're not going to put a gun to her head, I hope – you can be pretty intense sometimes. Kidding! Seriously, all you would be doing is presenting her with all the options.'

'I won't make her a cheat. She's the kind of girl who'd hate herself, and then she'd resent me for it.'

'But she doesn't even want him, she's just confused! She won't hate herself, she'll love you! Adrian is her past – she just needs you to take her hand and lead her forwards.'

'She doesn't need my hand. She's a big girl, just metaphorically speaking now; she should be able to walk forwards on her own by now, shouldn't she?' Cagney smiles innocently at Christian, who sighs.

'If only life were that easy. Go and get her, Cagney, please. I don't want to beg you.'

Cagney smiles sadly at Christian. 'It's not going to happen. Not while she's with him. Don't buy a new hat just yet. It's like this drink, Christian – it's not cloudy, it's clear. It's black and white, right and wrong. I won't make her the guilty party. And I won't take a woman from another man, no matter how little he deserves her. Right and wrong.' Cagney puts his head in his hands, exhausted.

'Then let's both have one last whiskey and toast the beautiful and pure notion of sitting about and waiting for our lives to happen to us, rather than taking it upon ourselves to live a little.'

'I've lived a lot. It's time for a rest.'

NINE

A *nipple-flicking road trip!*

Lisa and I sip at our lime and sodas in Prizzi, a minimalist Italian café decorated with chilli-shaped fairy lights, which are, oddly, bright blue. I have never seen a blue chilli, and I wonder if they do actually exist, but are just unspeakably rare, and the fieriest of the lot. I imagine that they are nurtured exclusively on a farm in the heart of Peru, by one seventy-year-old farmer an inch over five foot, wearing cowboy boots and a Stetson, a machete in his belt, and skin the consistency of a Pirelli tyre. Prizzi is opposite a rugby club, down the road from a rugby club, and around the corner from another rugby club, in Richmond. The entrances are wide, to let vast sets of shoulders in. It is also twenty yards from my and Lisa's gym. As we sit and sip, I am sure the same thoughts are racing through our heads, even if we choose not to voice them – we should be on a running machine now, working up a sweat, raising our heart rates, burning off our breakfasts instead of sitting down to lunch. We chew on the plastic straws in our drinks instead of the cheese straws in a basket in the middle of our table, as penance. We have just finished a long conversation on the benefits of cross training over Pilates. I managed even to bore myself as I talked about fat-burning zones and comparable calorie burn and core muscle development and tone. Occasionally I'd glance around to make sure nobody else was listening, humiliated at being this dull in public, scared that the manager might eject me from the premises because, like lighting up and puffing on a fat Cuban cigar, I am ruining everybody else's lunch with my antisocial behaviour.

In the middle of our conversation I remember that Lisa can't have a discussion, only an argument, taking every opinion or point or fact personally. She uses phrases like, 'We're going to have to agree to disagree', while shaking her head, and, 'That's just what I think', in the face of statements she is unable to refute. I find it irritating. If you can't say what you mean then you can't mean what you say.

We are waiting for Anna to arrive for lunch. She has left the baby with her mother on this occasion, as last time she felt that he was giving her disapproving looks whenever she sipped her wine.

'So, what do you think of those new cheese-and-pineapple-flavoured rice cakes?' Lisa asks me, as Anna bursts through the door, and I mutter under my breath, 'Thank God.'

Anna still looks out of shape. She is a large size fourteen, and not an average size ten, which was her pre-baby fighting weight, but she is noticeably smaller than the last time we saw each other. Her face isn't quite so heavy, her belly not nearly so round and protruding.

I stand up to kiss her hello, and say, 'Hi, Anna, you look great!'

'Thanks, hon,' she says with a wide smile that implies she is pleased with herself today, before kissing Lisa on both cheeks when she too stands to say hello.

'I have been working my arse off on this new diet, literally. I've barely eaten anything for days. I'm doing so well!' she smiles, and runs her fingers through the underside of her silky dark hair.

'OK, but, Anna, you know it's not healthy just to cut out food altogether, because your metabolic rate will slow right down, your body will think you are starving and conserve whatever food that you do eat, especially fat,' I say concerned, but also like the ultimate Stepford Wife, I've heard it so many times in so many different scenarios, I could recite the words in my sleep.

'Yeah, right, like you eat,' Anna says with a smile, but her words are dipped in an unfriendly sauce.

'I do eat, I just eat healthily now,' I say, reproaching her, my feelings bruised.

'Sure, Sunny, and how is that straw? Filling?' she asks with a smirk, looking down at the menu she grabbed on her way in, unable to suppress a small smile to herself as her eyes glaze over but she pretends to read.

'I'll have a green salad and a bowl of olives,' she says to the waiter, who's just come over, and slams it shut.

'I'll have the chicken Caesar salad with no croutons,' Lisa says.

'And I'll have the salad Niçoise without the dough balls or dressing,' I say, and hand back my menu with a smile.

'So!' Lisa leans forward, staring at me with wide eyes in a conspiratorial girlie way, that makes me realise she is wearing mascara for the first time in years. I get a nasty feeling that I have just crash-landed into a bitchy sleepover from the eighties, or that an agenda has been set for this meeting that I haven't been copied in on.

'So how is this new man of yours?' she asks a bit too casually.

'Adrian.' I say his name flatly, unimpressed.

'Adrian,' Anna repeats his name grandly, and looks up

277

from the table. 'Come on then, let's get it over with. Tell us the gossip – you'll burst otherwise!'

'He's engaged,' I say.

A pregnant pause . . .

'Has he asked you to marry him already?' Lisa asks, knowing it took her four years to get Gregory to propose to her. And she had been dropping hints for three.

'No. He's engaged to somebody else,' I say, shrugging my shoulders, in a 'whataya gonna do and ain't life a bitch' kind of way.

Anna's mouth falls open, but Lisa reacts in a split second.

'Oh, Sunny, I am so sorry. I know you really liked him!' She reaches over to squeeze my hand.

'I still do,' I say, wiping a sudden unexpected tear from my eye: I don't know why it decided to swell and show off in front of these two. I don't know who that tear is for, because it's not Adrian.

'It must be so hard,' Anna says, reaching over and touching my arm in exactly the same way and place as Lisa just has – even the pressure from her fingers is the same; it mirrors Lisa's action so utterly it makes a mockery of it. 'He is the first person you've really liked, isn't he? Who has liked you back, I mean. It must be really hard to walk away . . .' she says, holding her glass up to the waiter and mouthing 'Again, please. Thanks', and adding a wink on the end. She flicks her hair and dabs at the corners of her lipgloss. I am positive she doesn't realise how spiteful she sounds.

'I haven't,' I say as nonchalantly as I can.

'You haven't what?' Anna asks, distracted, staring at a group of women on a table behind us, appraising their hair, their make-up, their shoes, anything visible to the naked eye.

'I haven't walked away . . . yet.' I brush an imaginary crumb off my sleeve.

'Sorry?' It takes a moment for Anna to register and compute this information. 'What do you mean?' Her attention lands on me with an almighty crash, and the force of a giant wave.

'I mean what I say: I haven't walked away yet.'

'Well, when are you going to walk away, Sunny?' she asks me with a look of exaggerated confusion, as if she is asking 'what is one plus one' of the class dunce.

'Well, I don't know. I might not, as yet . . .' I trail off, lacking conviction. Both of their faces twist and contort in front of me, morphing into a strange rage.

'But you'll be over him in a week! It's not like you are married! You've only just started seeing him, for God's sake!' Lisa says, as if I am acting childishly.

'I have known him for five years; he's not just some guy I bumped into in the street last week. And even if he was, how do you know that I'm not in love with him, Lisa? What do you know about it, really?' I ask as calmly as I can. I want to say, 'But of course I'm not in love with him', but I feel like it might dilute my argument.

At this point the waiter arrives and makes a meal of putting the plates down in front of the wrong people. We swap dishes without looking into each other's eyes.

'Well, I just don't understand how you can do what you are doing. I never thought you would be that kind of woman.' Anna forks up a bunch of salad and stuffs it into her mouth, grabbing an olive almost immediately and throwing it in afterwards. A thought strikes her, and she snatches up the bowl, tossing the olives all over her salad, desperate for flavour.

'And what kind of woman is that, Anna? What kind of woman am I?' For effect I put down the fork I have just picked up, place my hands on my lap, sit back in my chair and wait for an embarrassed answer.

But Anna isn't embarrassed at all: she is in her element. Anna is as happy as a pig in shit.

'The kind, Sunny, I am sorry to say, who has to go and get somebody else's man because she can't get her own.' She finishes with a smirk, that demands, 'Deny it, whore!'

'Oh, grow up, Anna. It's not like that at all and you know it. We aren't eighteen any more. This is real life – nobody belongs to anybody. You do what you want to do.'

'Well, that's a nice attitude!' she says, rounding the sentence off with a short high false laugh.

'It's not an attitude,' I say wearily, rubbing my eyes.

Lisa stares at her salad, occasionally forking in a mouthful of greenery and chicken, with quiet stealth, hoping neither of us will notice we don't have her undivided attention.

'Look, Sunny, I could have understood this a year ago, but things have changed now. You've changed. You should try and get somebody of your own. You don't have to just take some guy who only wants to have his cake and eat it too.'

I grab my napkin from my lap and throw it down on the table, sitting forwards to address Anna. 'I don't believe you mean the things that you say, or at least I don't believe you mean them to sound the way that they do.'

'What if it was me?' she says to me, with squinted eyes, smiling deliciously, predicting a win. 'What if it was Martin cheating? How would you feel, doing that to me? Taking away my husband?'

'And he has no mind or will of his own, right? It wouldn't be his decision as well?'

'Answer me, Sunny, what if it were Martin? Would you be so flippant about it then?'

'"Answer me"? Who are you, my mother? And I am not being flippant!' I raise my voice, and the women on the table behind us, still slathered in Anna's disapproving stares, turn around to see what all the fuss is about. Anna beams at them wickedly.

'Look, Anna, he would be the one who would be cheating, not me.'

'Well alright, Sunny, if you are going to be pedantic. How would you feel, putting him in that position?'

I stare at her cold, hard, locked jaw, and her eyes, with great big holdalls underneath them, which she has tried desperately to hide with concealer, but which has just made them more prominent. She looks tired, drained, and weak from not eating. But I won't make excuses for her any more. She may only be saying these things because she has just had a baby, but today I don't feel like caving, just to keep the peace.

'Well, if he was cheating, I'm sure he'd have his reasons,' I say, and raise my eyebrows in defiance.

Anna clicks her teeth together quickly ten times. It is a habit, something that she does when she is angry, and trying to compose herself. I've chinked her armour. My armour is shot to shit from years of her put-downs.

She shrugs. 'Well, I just thought you'd got some self-respect back, Sunny. I mean, you don't need to borrow affection any more, from some man who is probably just using you for sex anyway, all the dirty stuff that his wife won't do. Some cheat.' She hammers the final 't' on to 'cheat', hitting me over the head with the word, trying to shame me.

'You don't know anything about it, or Adrian, or us . . . or me, for that matter.' I fork up some tuna, and eat it as calmly as I can, trying to regain my composure in the face of volcano Anna.

'Well . . .' Anna stares at Lisa until Lisa looks up from her salad and glances back. 'This is exactly why Lisa and I wanted to have lunch with you, Sunny. It's positively perfect in illustrating our point.'

'What point? What are you talking about?' I stop eating,

my fork suspended over my plate, flakes of tuna hurling themselves back into my salad.

Lisa throws me a guilty glance, but Anna just looks confident, smugly glowing, holding court.

'We're worried about you,' she says, in the least concerned voice I have ever heard. Her words drip with confrontation.

'Oh, really?' I ask, nodding my head, squinting my eyes, making a point of not taking her seriously.

'Yes, Sunny, we are,' she says. 'You know me, Sunny. I'm not going to bullshit you. At least you always know where you stand with me. If I've got something to say I say it to your face,' she says, as if the restaurant should break into a spontaneous round of applause.

It turns my stomach with embarrassment that she is so arrogant to think for a second that her beliefs carry any weight with me, or anybody other than her husband. And I wouldn't be surprised if even he has stopped listening. I couldn't give a damn about her ill-informed opinions, and yet she chooses to share them with me anyway.

'You are obviously much healthier than you used to be,' she says begrudgingly.

'And?' I ask.

'And we think you've got shallow.' She announces it, loudly, to the entire restaurant. 'Very shallow, in fact. That's just the way it is.' She sits back, defensive yet ready for the fight she hopes she has just provoked, but somehow still indignant.

'Why is that exactly?' I ask, smiling.

'Well,' she says, as if she is about to reveal the world's best-kept secrets, 'you haven't offered to baby-sit for me even once in the last couple of months.' She widens her eyes, as if to say, 'Just you think about that, Sunny, and you'll realise I'm right, and isn't that just awful!'

'Right, well, that's up there with genocide. What else?' I ask, cupping my chin in my hand to mimic interest.

She glares at me, but continues, 'And you never ask about us any more, you just talk about yourself. Basically, you think that now you can fit in to some size twelve trousers, and you've had a bit of male attention, you are better than we are.'

But she can't hold my stare, and she looks at Lisa for support, who isn't saying very much at all. I don't doubt that they have had this conversation, and that Lisa has agreed with Anna, even if she had to be persuaded. But it's as if a light bulb goes on in my head. They haven't always been like this. Anna's life, certainly her romantic life, has always been more interesting than mine, and maybe I have been overinterested in the past, sucking up all the juicy details, filling up the empty space in my emotional cupboard, where my own romantic details should have been. Maybe she doesn't feel idolised any more.

'I think, Anna, that the truth might be the other way around. *You* think that I am better than you now. Which probably means that you thought you were better than me before.'

'No . . .' she says, shaking her head, but no more words tumble out of her big old mouth with its perfect cupid's bow.

So I go on, 'The only person I really judge on how they look is myself. I'm not sitting here judging your shoes, or your hair, or the fat that hangs over your jeans. I couldn't care less about that – you're my friend. Why do you have to beat me up for this? Why can't you just be happy for me? I get to taste the good life for a little while – don't I deserve it?'

But Anna isn't listening to anything other than the words that allow her to make another point, slap me hard with another personalised attack.

'You said it right then: you couldn't care less! You only care about yourself now.'

'I meant that I don't care how you look, with regard to us being friends. I don't need to measure myself up against you, and decide that I win, to feel better. And I don't want a friend who only wants me around for that . . .'

The table falls silent, and suddenly I notice that there are other people in the room, and they all seem to be laughing, and enjoying themselves, with people who like them, and support them. They are all having a good time. I push myself to my feet, and grab my jacket and bag from the back of my chair.

'I've lost my appetite, and that isn't a lie.' I push my chair out and walk calmly to the door.

'I'm sorry, that's just what I think,' I hear Anna say as I slam the door behind me. I stride twenty paces down the road, then stop, standing perfectly still in the street, trying not to cry. I want to scream, but I don't. It isn't about other people. I didn't do this for anybody else. It's about me.

I sift through some invoices and check the site for flaws, trying to work through my anger. I need to focus on today's orders and the pile of paperwork in my in-tray that is over a week old. I have never let things slip like this before; I have never been so distracted. My life doesn't run as smoothly with all of these romantic rumblings and fractious friendships. I want to go to the gym, and run everything out of my head: my confusion over Adrian, my need to pick up the phone and just scream at Anna . . . I am scared that, however impure her motives, some of what she said may have been right.

My doorbell rings, and I shuffle through to the hallway in bed socks and press the buzzer. 'Who is it?' I trill down the intercom.

'Are you even talking to me?' Adrian asks pathetically.

'Yes,' I say.

'Can I come up then? I need to talk to you.' He sounds serious.

'Not more revelations!' I say, and press the buzzer, not really believing he can have any, unless he has a child with him that asks, 'Daddy, who is that lady?' when they get to the top of the stairs.

But either he doesn't answer, or he doesn't hear.

I check my hair quickly. I am still dressed for lunch with Anna and Lisa, I have only taken off my high-heeled boots and replaced them with comfy cashmere socks, so I know that I look OK. It's not as if I have just rolled out of bed, hitting the floor in a flurry of crazy hair and pillow lines creased across my face. It's not such a bad sign that I don't really care.

Adrian loiters at the top of the stairs with his hands in his pockets. I open the door but immediately turn to walk into the lounge, so as not to share a doorstep kiss. I feel too much pressure, too much would ride on it. But he grabs my hand and spins me round and pushes me up against my hallway wall, narrowly avoiding a picture of my mum and dad in Austria last year, standing next to a ski lift, in summer. Adrian holds my face in his hands.

'Don't I even get a kiss now?' he says sadly.

'I don't know, maybe . . .' But it is easier to kiss him than not to kiss him. If I push him away it will be such a big deal, and we'll have to talk about it, and I'll have to explain. Besides, part of me really does want to kiss him, wants to feel his hands creep up and over my chest to my shoulders, feel his tongue at my neck, feel him so close, wanting me. But it's just the physical side rushing in, the promise of another Fondler moment. It has very little to do with Adrian. It's no more than right place right time for

285

him. So I let him lean in, and he gently brushes his lips over mine, before pushing his tongue into my mouth. I want to cough and make choking noises, and pretend to pass out. But I just kiss him back, until he is ready to stop.

'The thought of kissing you, Sunny, is the only thing that has got me through the day,' he says, in his slightly pissed northern accent. I have to fight to believe it. I cannot imagine that kissing me could get anybody through an ad break, never mind an entire day. Simultaneously a vicious poison-filled thought bubble bursts in my head. Only remembered me today then? Because I haven't seen you all week!

Instead I say, 'Do you want a cup of tea?' moving into the kitchen, flicking on the kettle.

Adrian leans against the doorframe between my kitchen and lounge, crosses his arms and looks down at his feet. I realise I am staring and still waiting for an answer after fifteen seconds.

'Adrian? Tea?' I ask tersely

'I've left Jane,' he says, looking up with such a serious expression on his face it makes me want to laugh out loud.

'Why?' I ask.

'I thought . . . it was the right thing to do.' Saint Adrian, Patron Saint of Better Late Than Never Morality.

'Is it the right thing to do?' I ask, flinging a tea bag lazily into a mug for him.

'I think so.' He nods his head, and smiles at me slightly.

'You seem OK about it,' I say, staying on my side of the kitchen, not wanting to get any closer to him just yet.

'I am OK. Of course I am sad, but . . . I can't do what I'm doing . . . anyway, I don't want to talk about it. I just wanted you to know.'

'Oh, OK, thanks very much. I don't know what you expect me to say . . .'

'Can I come and stay on Saturday night?'

I pour out the boiling water, and splash some milk into his cup. 'I guess so. Why Saturday, particularly? I mean, where are you living now?'

Adrian pauses for a moment, staring at me, concentrating. 'With Mark in Brentford, on his sofa,' he says, and sips his tea. He stares at me again and says something I don't hear.

'What?' I ask, running a little cold water into my black coffee so it doesn't burn me.

'You look lovely today,' he repeats.

I don't agree or disagree or thank him or reprimand him. And he gives up waiting for me to walk his way, and moves slowly towards me. I let him take my hands in his, entwining our fingers as if we are about to play Mercy.

'So this means we can see a bit more of each other,' he says, leaning down, kissing my neck.

'Yes, it does,' I say, peculiarly numb. I feel as if things are being taken out of my hands, and that if I let it, everything will be decided for me.

'I have a party to go to on Saturday night,' I say, as he licks my left ear.

'I'll come with you,' he says, running his fingers over my left breast. 'I can't promise to be completely around. I mean, I just need some thinking time, for a while, so I can decide what to do. But I'd like to see you on Saturday night as I said.'

'OK,' I say, allowing myself to be kissed again. Manhandled. I don't feel any nervous kicks. Now I don't feel any deep-rooted desire to climb on top of him, or check if he is excited. But his hand moves down to his crotch and flicks open his button-fly jeans.

I ignore it.

'You're so hot,' he mumbles.

I ignore it.

'I've had such a hard day,' he says, with a childish smile.

287

'Haven't we all,' I say, and let go of his hands.

'All I've thought about is you sucking me off . . .'

'Nice,' I say, and take a step back. 'I mean, that sounds just magical, Adrian, for me.'

'Sunny . . . I didn't mean it like that. I just meant I love the way that it feels . . .'

'I know what you meant. You are feeling sorry for yourself, so you want me to make you feel better. Well, you can't just show up here and demand a blow job, Adrian. I'm not a whore.'

'Oi! Nobody called you that,' he shouts at me, annoyed.

I turn to walk away, and he grabs me again, and spins me round. 'I didn't say that.'

'I know, I know. I'm sorry, I'm just in a funny mood. I had an argument with Lisa and Anna at lunchtime. I'm all worked up and lashing out at you. I'm sorry.' I stroke his face quickly and smile.

'Don't apologise' he says, looking guilty for a second, and then, 'Let's go to bed.'

I don't think I should. It will only confuse things. I check my watch – it is 1.30. I shouldn't go to bed, with a man, at 1.30 in the afternoon.

'Late for a bus?' he asks, and pulls me towards him.

And I think, now isn't a time for laughs. Just say something, something serious, something that makes me feel something for you. Something real, and not a joke about how you don't care. Something, anything, that has everything to do with emotion, and nothing to do with sex.

But instead Adrian says, 'Come on, Sun, let's go to bed.'

I follow him into the bedroom, when I know I shouldn't. It's not that I feel I can't say no. I just don't. I think I might just like the idea of sex in the afternoon. I've never done that before either. It is sex for sex's sake, not just because it's night-time, or we are in bed. It's a product of

288

passion, while the rest of the world works and shops and taps away at keyboards, I am indulging in pure adult pleasure. It makes me feel like a grown-up, but simultaneously the child in me feels naughty, and that only fuels my fire.

It is good, and bad.

It is good because as Adrian holds my hips and pulls me on to him, as we sit up, with my legs wrapped around him, I hold him tight and bury my head in his neck, and I have a slight hurried orgasm, but an orgasm none the less. It is bad because I am thinking of somebody else.

Adrian and I lie on separate sides of my bed afterwards. I look over at him, lying in a wilderness of duvet and cushions and my pyjamas, and my underwear, that all somehow got jumbled up into a white elephant fête stall on my bed. It is fair to say that I don't have that much experience with men, but even I know it is a bad sign to be thinking about somebody else three weeks into a relationship. If that's what this is. Shit. Adrian has left his girlfriend! I shake my head, to wake myself from a dream, and grasp on to reality, have it pull me back from the brink, where I stand, dangling a rope off a cliff that is tied to a bucket, that swings precariously over rocks, filled casually with all our lives. It is only my indecision that need let it fall.

'So, if you come on Saturday, it could be like, our first proper date?' I say, and turn my head to look at him, pulling the sheet up around my chest.

'What do you mean? We've had dates.' His eyes are closed but I see his brow dent with confusion.

'They weren't real, Adrian. Now we'll really be able to see . . .'

But the sound of one of Adrian's wet snores rings viciously in my ears.

*   *   *

289

By 2.10 p.m. Adrian is waving goodbye to me from the street, as I hold back the curtain at my window. I turn around to face my bedroom, and the mess that he has left behind. I marvel at the speed at which things can flip around in my head, and ideas that seemed inspired and brutally perfect only moments ago now seem like utter stupidity.

I spin around on the spot three times, and run my fingers through my hair, but they get caught around my crown, which has just been shoved up and down against my sheets by a thrusting Adrian. I claw my way through it, and sigh. I fight tears, and I fight laughter, and eventually end up with a whimpered, 'I don't know what I'm doing, I don't know what I'm doing . . .'

I can't look at my bedroom any more. I spin again and press my nose up against the window. I need to get out of my flat.

I burst into Screen Queen and sing, 'Help me, Christian! I'm falling apart . . .'

Christian carries on serving the customer in front of him, turning to me only when I reach the counter, placing his finger to his lips, and saying, 'Shhhh.'

He is filling out a membership form for a guy in a white T-shirt with a handkerchief hanging precariously from his back pocket. I point to it as subtly as possible behind his back, sure that it means something in 'homosexual', but Christian only responds, when the guy glances down at the form, with a furious dagger stare in my direction.

'So I need your Christian name,' he says, and I note the professional tone of his voice, and how charming it is.

'Dallas,' the young guy says, and we both look at him in alarm. I clumsily shove the tape I have been looking at, *Basic Instinct*, back onto the shelf.

'Surname?' Christian asks, his voice notably an octave higher with incredulity.

'Cool,' he says.

I see Christian's pen, held loosely in his elegant fingers, poised, unmoving, above the sheet of paper.

'Occupation?' Christian asks, without looking up.

'Dog whisperer,' the guy says.

'One more time?' Christian says, his eyes as wide as planets, shining with tears of mirth that he can't let spill.

'I'm a dog whisperer, I tame angry dogs. I got the idea from a film.' Dallas has an Essex twang to his voice that I recognise from a girl I used to know at work. I want to hear him say 'salt' and 'false', see if he pronounces them 'soult' and 'foulse', like that girl.

'And your name?' Christian asks.

'Dallas Cool, I just told you . . .' The guy creases up his face in confusion. 'What about it?' he asks.

'What film did you get that from?'

'I didn't.'

'Where did you get it then?'

'From my parents, where else?' he replies, confused.

'I don't know, I really don't know . . .' Christian says, and carries on filling in the form. 'Do they bite a lot?' Christian asks as Dallas turns to leave with his overnight rental, *Desperately Seeking Susan*.

'I wear galvanised rubber; they can't chew through it,' he says, and leaves.

'I don't know what to say about that,' Christian says, eyeing up Dallas's form.

'Did you fancy him?' I ask.

'It would feel like abuse,' Christian says to me with disdain. 'Now, my Sunbeam, what is wrong with you?'

'I need to get out of this village, Christian.' I grab the collar of his shirt lightly and plead with him, pretending to cry. 'It's driving me crazy, my head is an utter mess, I can't take it any more!'

'What, what can't you take, my burst butterball?'

'Any of it!' I say, slumping over the counter, resting my right cheek on its shiny surface, sighing with cold comfort.

'Why now?' Christian asks, squinting his eyes.

'The streets are narrowing, Christian! And the eyes are widening, and everybody's faces are morphing into grotesque bug-eyed gargoyles, and they stare at me in alarm, and they are judging me!' I raise my head as I talk, and then lower it as I finish.

'But you know that they aren't actually doing that, right? Or are you on some kind of uppers?'

'No drugs, no.' I shake my head as best I can, as it rests flat against the counter.

'Sunny, nobody is looking at you, or judging you, unless you decide that they are. It's as simple as that. It's completely up to you. Just decide that they aren't. Even if you think that they are, they aren't!'

'Well, that's not healthy, it's just denial!' I say, swapping cheeks on the counter.

'It's not denial, darling, it's dusting the world with a little sugar, making it a little sweeter, refusing to acknowledge bitterness. It is just sprinkling your own petals where you walk,' Christian smiles and strokes my hair, until his fingers get stuck at the crown.

'What is this?' he asks pointedly.

'Don't ask.'

'Who is this?' he says, jamming his fingers further into my hair, refusing to pull them out.

'Ouch, that hurts, Christian!'

He removes his hand, and places it on his hip.

'I might have just done a stupid thing,' I say with eyes closed.

'Well, it's not nice to call anybody "thing", but you need to talk to me, so here is what we are going to do. You don't need to go anywhere, you just need me, a good bottle of fizz, some dark chocolate with orange tangy bits, and *The Way We Were* on DVD, which I just so happen to have had delivered this morning. We'll curl up on the sofa and cry. How does that sound?' He tickles me lightly under the chin.

'It sounds utterly indulgent,' I say, standing up straight.

Christian looks hurt.

'But wonderful!'

He takes a moment and then smiles at me broadly.

'But I can't. I've just remembered. I've got four boxes waiting for me down at Portsmouth Customs that I've been meaning to collect, and if I don't do it today I don't know when I will. Plus I might as well go while I'm in a bad mood, and I can think in the car at least, and not scream at anybody.'

'You're calling a road trip?' Christian cocks his head and smiles.

'No, I'm just going to go down to Portsmouth and . . .'

'You're calling a road trip?' he says again, but this time nodding his head furiously for me to answer in the affirmative.

'OK . . . I'm calling a road trip . . . What exactly does that entail . . . and does it mean that you are coming?'

'Hell, yes! I'll get Iuan to watch the shop. He's upstairs doing nothing anyway. He can just divert the phone.' Christian throws open the door to the corridor. 'Iuan! Start making your way down here, Welshy. I'll need you in ten minutes.'

'So Cagney isn't in, then?' I ask innocently.

'No . . . he's out on a job.'

I cough quickly, to mask my gulp. Christian grabs my hand and pulls me towards him, and says seriously, 'Don't even think about that. He doesn't sleep with them, he isn't involved, romance is the last thing on his mind. He's been doing it for ten years, Sunny; he hasn't fallen for one yet. Why this afternoon?'

I nod my head once, and smile shyly.

'OK? Now! We are gonna sing, and play rude word games, and gossip, and we are going to do it all in summer hats.'

'But, Christian, it's October.'

'We are both wearing hats! Now, we need to pack a blanket . . .'

This is all becoming a huge effort. 'Christian, for God's sake, we don't need a blanket.'

'It's a Road Trip! Pack a Blanket!' His voice goes high and a little crazy, and it scares me. I can imagine that, if he had to, Christian would make a very convincing drag queen killer.

'OK . . . don't cry about it,' I say sulkily, eyeing him nervously from behind the counter.

He fixes me with a glare. 'Never be flippant about two things, Sunny, and we'll be best friends: number one, preparing for a road trip.'

'And number two?' I ask.

'Whitney Houston.'

'Roger that,' I say.

'I'll pack a blanket, and possibly even Whitney's *Greatest Hits*.'

'Perfect.' Christian puts his hand on his heart, touched.

I nod my head, and back away from him slowly.

Forty minutes later, at twenty past three on a cloudy Wednesday afternoon, an afternoon when I have had middle-of-the-day sex for the first time, and met a dog whisperer named Dallas Cool, Christian and I set off on our road trip to Portsmouth to pick up my boxes of bondage gear.

Christian doesn't want to sing Whitney until we reach the motorway.

'She needs the speed' he says solemnly.

So I stick on a tape I have in the car: hits from the musicals. Christian hates them all, strangely, aside from one. He wears a straw boater, with a navy and red striped band, and a baby-blue V-necked jumper, and Aviators. He looks like he got lost somewhere near Henley in 1985, and has just woken up in my car.

I am wearing a big floppy pink straw hat that I found in my closet, with a thick orange band around the centre, and a large lime-green bow. The rim keeps flopping over my eyes as I drive, and I swerve occasionally when it completely masks my vision. I have on my huge Chanel black sunglasses, Jackie Onassis style, despite there being no sun, and they are making it hard to see when to stop, and when to go, at traffic lights. It may be a rough ride!

The only musical hit that Christian likes is 'Anything Goes', and he is trying to learn the words. When he rewinds it for a fourth time, I squirt the tape out of the machine and throw it into the back of the car where he can't reach it.

'Ironically, Sunny, you can be quite cold,' he says.

'Keep it together, lady, it's Whitney time,' I say, as our A road becomes a motorway.

'You were lucky,' he says to me, and jams in Whitney.

We sing every word to 'How Will I Know', 'I Wanna Dance With Somebody', 'My Name is Not Susan', 'Saving All My Love For You' and 'Love Will Save the Day' before we run out of vocal puff.

'So, what shall we talk about now? Or we could play a game?' I say, patting the wheel, ready to be entertained.

'Or . . .' Christian says, looking at me slyly from out of the corners of his eyes.

'Or?' I ask, really not sure where he is going, trying to look around at him without taking the steering wheel with me in his direction and causing a pile-up.

'Watch the road,' he says, pointing in front of him seriously. 'Or we could talk about . . . Adrian?' he asks, then winces, as if he might have just blasphemed in front of a nun.

'Oh Christ, again? I can't believe this! I wished my life away, dreaming of some romance, some drama in my life, some excitement! But now it just seems exhausting. I don't think I can talk about it any more, or even think about it any more. I don't have a clue what I am going to do.'

'Well, are you going to bring him on Saturday?' Christian asks me sensibly, tipping his hat in the mirror, trying out all angles to suit his profile.

'I think so. I've already asked him.'

'But why? Why why why why why?' He throws his hands into his lap and sighs.

'Just once would have done, Christian.'

'You know it will just upset Cagney, and then you guys will be all frosty, and –'

'And nothing is happening, between Cagney and me. But it is with Adrian, and I owe it to him to sort it out, and give it a try, especially now he's left his girlfriend. Plus I just had sex with him, and I don't want to feel like a whore.'

'You're not a whore.'

'I know that, Christian. I don't want to feel like a whore.' I pull over into the slow lane and indicate to come off the motorway.

'Maybe you just like sex,' Christian says.

'Maybe. Do I need to turn Whitney off if we are leaving the motorway?' I ask.

'Probably best. What do you see in Adrian, apart from all of the old stuff?'

'He is obvious easy boyfriend material.'

'He's a gift-wrapped compromise! You'll spend your whole time waiting for romantic gestures that never come, hoping that he cares because he can't bring himself to say it!'

'Right, and Cagney would be so much grander, and more vocal.'

'He'll adore you, and you'll see it every time he looks at you. He won't let you feel silly, or vulnerable. You'll feel special every time he speaks to you. He is old school, Sunny, but it has its advantages. Adrian might be second-rate boyfriend material, but Cagney is first-rate husband material.'

'Well, he's got enough experience, at least!' I say, trying not to think about, or visualise any of the picture Christian has just painted, because then I'll believe I can have it, and I'll crave it, and Adrian will fall utterly short of the mark.

'No, Sunny, he is proper lasting husband material for you!'

'And you, Christina, are out of your glorious mind. That hat is keeping all the silly thoughts in that normally drift off into space where they should be!'

'Why can nobody see it except me?' Christian sighs, flinging off his hat and glasses, staring out of the window, forlorn.

'See what?' I ask. He turns to face me, and he is sad.

'That if you let yourselves you could fall in love with each other.' He says it quietly, but his words fill every inch of space in my car.

'I can see it,' I whisper, pulling off my own hat, flinging it on to the back seat with everything else.

'Then why will neither of you just do it?' he pleads with me quietly, unable to understand.

'Because! It's so hard, Christian, when you've been on your own for such a long time, for ever! There is such a

297

bank of expectation, built up all around me, of what I'll be myself, no doubt who I will be going out with! I mean, I thought I was going to be Britney, Christian, and don't laugh because I am serious. I thought I was going to look like a pop star. I thought I'd be stunning.'

Christian stares at me sadly. 'You are very pretty, darling.'

'I know I'm not hideous, and all that pop star stuff is mostly just smoke and mirrors anyway, but whatever, I am beginning to accept it now. I'm OK, I don't have to be all shiny and polished and the best. I am OK, and that's enough.'

'You are better than OK,' he says, squeezing my hand as it rests on the gear stick.

'Christian, it doesn't matter, really, does it? This is me now, and it's great, just to be healthy. Looking perfect isn't all there is, and I am just starting to realise now that I don't want to get sucked up into that kind of vanity, and what I really want is to relax for a while, and say "I'm happy". I don't want to replace an addiction to one thing with an addiction to another. Because it's the addiction itself that does the most harm.'

'Well, don't beat yourself up about any of it. Some people never realise that, and they spend their whole lives trying to look perfect.' Christian examines the lines under his eyes, then gives up dramatically with a sigh.

'You don't have to make me feel better,' I say, shifting in my seat, turning left onto the A3.

'I'm not just saying it, it's true. Some people are no more than the sum of their appearance.'

'Well . . . it's an easy trap to fall into, when it seems that's all anybody is interested in these days.'

'Cagney hates "these days",' Christian says quietly.

'*C'est vrai,*' I concur.

'*Oui,*' Christian says as he puts his Aviators back on.

* * *

298

As we drive along the motorway, hurtling towards Portsmouth at an illegal speed, banked by swathes of conifer trees slanting up towards acres of cloudy grey-blue skies above us, I wonder if it is just the easiest mistake to make, judging the whole world on its appearance. It's the laws of nature – flowers bloom and attract the bees, peacocks preen and attract . . . other peacocks. It's the quickest way to impress.

After twenty minutes of comfortable silence, as we draw ever closer to Portsmouth, and Christian salutes a sign for a naval academy and asks if we can drop in, I ask what I've been wanting to ask all along.

'Tell me about his wives, Christian.' I stare straight ahead. It's not a question, it's a quiet demand. It's necessary information that I am missing.

'I don't think that's healthy,' he says, and I can feel his eyes burrowing into me.

I turn to look at him, back to the road, at him, back to the road, at him, and smile. 'Christian, tell me about his wives.'

He gives me a disappointed glance. 'OK, but I don't really know much about the first two, other than one was younger, one was older, and they both screwed him like a cheap nail into plywood about a week after their nuptials.'

'How?' I ask, pressing hard on my brake as the traffic starts to slow. I glance at my watch. It is four o'clock already; we are running out of time.

'I think one was unfaithful . . . and one, well, it had something to do with her parents not liking him, or something. She was loaded,' he says as explanation, as if being wealthy is an excuse for anything.

'So what about the other one?' I ask evenly. We are shunting along in first gear, I am riding my clutch, and

Christian checks out everybody else around us – passengers, dogs with their tongues sticking out, drivers on mobile phones, kids with their tongues sticking out, as he talks.

'Lydia,' he says.

'What about her?' I ask.

'Well, Lydia I met,' he says, sounding impressed with himself, to be able to truthfully relay that kind of information.

'No, you didn't,' I say, shaking my head in disbelief. It's not so shocking; I don't know why I am so incredulous. These women exist – they aren't just myths, like mermaids, or witches. There isn't a fairy tale entitled 'Cagney's Three Wicked Wives', so far as I am aware.

'I met her,' he says again, nodding his head, no need for lies.

'But how? I thought you didn't know him, before he moved to Kew? And I thought you said that he moved here after he had split up with . . .'

'Lydia. Yes, he had been in Kew for about six months. I remember because it was July, hot as Jamaica that summer. I wore shorts most days and not much else.'

'And Lydia?' I ask, because I see him on a route to distraction.

'She showed up one day in July. I literally felt an icy gust when she walked into the shop and asked if I knew where he was, as she was getting no answer from his office. Cagney was still really raw, but he'd turned a corner, I think. He had started to put things back together, he seemed busy with work. And he was quiet, and some days he said little more than hello, but his face was opening up. You could see his mind was slowly clearing, and the hurt was falling away. But then the witch waltzed in.'

Christian sighs again. 'I utterly believe, Sunny, that she hammered the final nail into his emotional coffin, and I think she did it without a second thought. They invented the concept of self-obsession because they knew one day she'd show up and need describing. Believe me when I say that I cursed that woman for years.'

'So . . . ?' All these details are great, and atmospheric, and Christian loves to tell his tales, but I need to cut to the chase.

'So?' he replies, shaking his head, not knowing where I am going.

'What did she look like?' I ask flatly, a little ashamed.

Christian shakes his head and makes a tutting sound with his tongue. 'Looks, Sunny, do not make the woman, as you yourself have said so very clearly in this car, this very afternoon.'

'Stop it and tell me,' I say, as we pull away from the car crash that has caused the delays. Christian peers into the mangled car for details but I look away.

'Well, she was blonde, of course.' Christian is still looking in the car, and talks distractedly.

'Why "of course"?' I ask, indignant.

'They are always blonde,' he says simply, as if it is one of the commandments, written on tablets of stone and passed to Moses on top of Sinai.

'Oh,' I say, crestfallen.

'And she was pale.'

'Oh,' I say, glancing down at my hands, which are more cream than pale. I have always found pale thoroughly uninteresting, another way of saying washed out.

'You sure you want to hear this, Sunbeam?' he asks, noticing me noticing me.

'Yes! Why wouldn't I? Go on.' I rush my words out in a fluster.

'Pale but bright blue eyes,' he says, almost dreamily.

'OK, I get it, Christian, she was some kind of Swedish

Miss World – can we move on now? I mean, was she very much older than him?' I ask tight-lipped, gripping the steering wheel a little too hard.

'No, no, not this time. They were exactly the same age. I mean exactly. They were born on the same day. That's how they met, in a pub, drowning their sorrows, separately, on the thirtieth of December. It was their twenty-ninth birthdays. Both of them.'

'Why was she drowning her sorrows?' I cross a roundabout and follow the sign that directs me towards Portsmouth town centre. I check my watch: we may still make it.

'She had just passed her final counselling exam, apparently, and realised, a little late, it would seem, that her job would now be to sit around and listen to the whingeing moans of people she didn't care about. Cagney said that the first thing he noticed – after the way that she looked, of course –'

'Of course!' I say, and raise my eyes.

'– was that she kept muttering, "What the fuck was I thinking? What the fuck was I thinking?" over and over to herself as she sat in some old pub on Brighton seafront, downing her way through a bottle of bourbon. She wasn't a regular, but it was Cagney's local. I've seen a photo, Sunny, it was a hellish place – brown cracked wallpaper like a dried-up desert oasis, and battered and ripped leather chairs that look like your skin would stick to them if you came into contact with them by accident, and the fire brigade would have to be called out to break you free.'

'So they each propped up one end of a dirty bar.

'Lydia.' I repeat her name, trying to place her, thinking that somehow I might know her.

'Was she Irish?'

'Yes. But you could barely tell, she had the faintest accent.

I have to say it, Sunny, she was beautiful, but like a painting of the Alps, or the lake at Geneva, or a photo of an Edwardian chair that you can only see face on. Her beauty was two-dimensional – she just didn't . . . fill it out.'

'Do you mean she was dull?' I ask hopefully.

'No, not dull,' Christian says thoughtfully. 'It was worse than that: she was cold. She looked untouched, like if you held her hand you'd leave fingerprints all over her and the police would catch you in minutes.'

'She looked cold,' I repeat to myself, taking some solace.

'Yes. She was like a beautifully sculpted vodka luge – if you hugged her, she'd melt.'

'And that's what attracted Cagney, is it? That she was a challenge or something?' I ask, perplexed.

'No, darling; she was in a pub getting drunk on her own, and swearing a lot. He thought he'd found his soulmate! And it just so happened that she was blonde and beautiful.'

'But you said she was a counsellor?'

'Aha,' Christian nods dramatically, pretending to chew gum so he resembles a bitchy teenage princess hanging out by the waltzers, hoping to score with one of the workers at a cheap travelling fair.

'But Cagney would hate that!' I exclaim with disbelief. 'What was he thinking?'

'Darling, you don't have to tell me. I mean, obviously he wasn't always as bad as he is now . . . but he has never been a talker. And by that point, after two failed marriages, and not making it into the police –'

'He wanted to be in the police?' I ask, not sure if I can take any more information in one car journey. 'Seriously, Christian, we need to road trip again!'

'I told you,' he says, nodding at me and smiling benignly, like some old Chinese kung fu guru.

'So . . . what happened?' I ask.

'With the police? Or Lydia?' Christian needs qualification.

'Both! Either!'

'Lydia was into psychobabble and celibacy,' Christian answers seriously.

'Jesus Christ,' I whisper, horrified.

'I know. She'd read it in some book on her course, that promised if she made a man wait for her, they'd reach some spiritual mountain top and be happy for ever. It was her new thing. And Cagney just showed up at the wrong time. She always had a new thing, apparently. So she kissed him and told him she'd let him inside when he really deserved it. And for whatever reason, he chose to hang around.'

'Why? Why would you let somebody else dictate so utterly how it's going to be?' I ask in shock. Then I remember that Adrian has done almost exactly the same thing to me, so I stop thinking about that.

'I think the idea, that this one might last because she promised it would, when they hit this spiritual high, appealed to him more than anything. He was so bruised. It was his last big effort, to do it right, not to rush it. So she wrung him out for a year. Questioned him daily on what he felt for her, how he felt about himself, why he said what he said, why he did what he did, until he was exhausted and confused and tongue-tied. And she threw theories at him, hundreds of theories, on Freud and Jung and Kant, Descartes and Socrates, but all straight from the book, not really under-standing any of them, until they drove him quietly mad. She told him he needed to improve himself, dig deeper, give her more, let her access his soul, and, God love him, he tried. But she didn't listen when he spoke, so it was never enough. She opened him right up, made him dedicate himself to her, and then she left him . . . but just for extra sport, and knowing his history, she suggested that they got married first. She talked him into it on the first day of Advent, the licence came, and on Christmas Eve, nearly a year after they had met, Cagney found himself in another registry office, with another blonde.'

'What happened?' I ask aghast. I turn off the engine, and we sit in the car park behind a warehouse in Portsmouth Docks, opposite a huge sign that reads 'Customs and Excise, Holding Depot'.

'She left him on Boxing Day.'

'Oh my God, why?' I ask, with tears in my eyes.

'For the barmaid at the shitty old pub.'

I stare at him in shocked awe.

'No . . . she . . . didn't.' I say each word slowly and deliberately.

'Said she had to explore other parts of her character, said she had made a mistake. Said she realised on their wedding night that she was a lesbian.'

'No.' I sit and shake my head. 'Poor Cagney, what did he do?'

'Got drunk, for a week, didn't come up for air, just carried on drinking, but in another pub, of course.'

'Of course,' I say. 'How awful.'

'And he's been single ever since,' Christian says sadly.

'Who can blame him! But why did she come back, six months later?'

'Well, that's what did it. She needed a divorce.'

'So she could marry her girlfriend?' I ask sincerely.

'No, she'd left Ruth. Now she was marrying a car trader, worth millions. Big in Fiestas.'

Christian turns to face me, and takes my hand. 'He was twenty-nine, Sunny. And he waited a year for her. She told him it would all be worth it, and she would dedicate her life to him. But she was just another blonde. He goes silly around blondes.' Christian sees my face fall. 'But it's not love, Sunny.'

305

'OK,' I say, and wipe my left eye quickly.

'So!' Cagney claps his hands quickly. 'We're here! What are we picking up?'

We both break out of our trance, and get out of the car, and the sea wind slaps our faces, and we both exclaim 'Jesus Christ!' simultaneously.

'Well, there are four boxes,' I say, digging my hands into my pockets as we walk towards the entrance.

'Yes, but what's in them and, more importantly, can I pretend to be your boyfriend and pretend they are all for us?'

'Light bondage gear, very classy, silk, all ribbons, very sensual. And no.'

'OK.' Christian yanks open the door and we hurl ourselves into the warmth. 'Well, they sound nice. It makes me think of *Dynasty*! Anything else?'

'Nipple flickers,' I say.

'I'm sorry, who?' Christian stops and grabs my arm dramatically.

'Look, I'm not sure about them either, but I thought it would be good to try them out. It's a new franchise possibility. You clamp this thing on – it's like a little suction pad with some wires coming out of the top, and they've got these little rubber sticks inside them, and they kind of flick . . .' I say, flicking my finger at him to illustrate. 'Lighter, and harder, and then, if you want, you can make them squirt cold water . . .'

'Enough!' Christian screams. 'Enough, Sunny. No more. At some point you draw a line and say a tongue is irreplaceable. The human body is irreplaceable. Plastic is never going to compensate for that!'

'I know,' I say, 'but I'll see how they sell.'

We walk through into a large open room with a counter at the end like an Argos shop with no catalogues, and I retrieve a slip of paper from my pocket.

'I didn't mean to scare you off,' he says, 'in the car, about Cagney.'

'You didn't,' I say, and nod my head. 'I do like him, Christian,' I say quietly, as we move up the line.

'I know,' Christian squeezes my hand.

'But us, with all our baggage – I'm just scared we'd hate each other too.'

'Or maybe you'd understand each other a little better.'

'Maybe. Maybe we are alike. Because I like him, Christian, and I swear to God I can't even tell you why.'

Christian turns to me, and strokes my cheek. 'But, darling, don't you see, that is the best reason there is.'

TEN

A prince of wales

Cagney hears footsteps on the stairs leading up to his office. It isn't Iuan, as he doesn't hear the step, clunck, step, clunk, on the wood, slowly pounding out the threat of a Welshman gone crazy bored with his leg in plaster. Iuan's eyes have turned wild in the last few days, he is an even looser cannon than usual, and Cagney is watching him carefully. Besides, Cagney can't hear the telltale stream of truly offensive swear words, in a perverse twisted English-Welsh hybrid, that accompanies him taking so long to get up one flight of stairs.

And it isn't Howard, as he has been sent to buy drink for Iuan's birthday party this evening. Howard is overly excited. He has been frothing at the mouth like a one-year-old Labrador all morning, and Cagney had to make a decision to either send him out of the office, or kill him, especially given that the root cause of most of Howard's excitement is Sunny Weston. Howard hasn't met Sunny yet, but Iuan has invited her to his birthday drinks tonight. Iuan has also informed Howard that he definitely thinks that Cagney might love her. This has driven Howard into some kind of frenzy, the like of which Cagney hasn't seen since Howard ate three Pot Noodles in quick succession on the morning of 12 February 2002, and then washed them down with a litre of Fanta . . .

And it isn't Christian, because he is at home making his Tom Jones costume, determined to be the best Tom in the room tonight, realising as he does that there will be at least a dozen others. The theme is 'Wales': what else is there to be? It will be a room full of Tom Joneses, with the occasional weak leek, lazy dragon, easy rugby player, and half-arsed Shirley Bassey.

So it must be a client, new or existing, winding his way slowly up the steps, and it makes no difference, the idea of their presence is equally as appalling today. Cagney would qualify his mood right now, if asked, as 'dark'. And that is coming from a man who considers his usual state to be quite upbeat, much to the confusion of anybody who has met him in the last ten years. Maybe his assistant will tell this uninvited guest that he is busy. He still hasn't hired an assistant, of course.

'Bollocks!' he shouts, loud enough for whoever is standing outside his door with his knuckle poised to knock, to stop short of hitting the glass and reconsider their actions. Foolishly, this gives Cagney hope. He is devastated when the hand knocks moments later, albeit nervously, on the glass, pounding over his name with their knuckles, gradually wearing him away. Cagney doesn't answer. But the doorknob turns and a head pokes around the door frame anyway.

'Hello?'

'I'm painting!' Cagney shouts in a last desperate attempt to keep whoever it is out.

'Hello?' he says again.

'Damn,' Cagney says irritably, and removes his feet from his desk, sitting up reasonably straight.

'How are you?' the man says, and Cagney looks up at him in small talk alarm. What does he care? It is then that

Cagney recognises the shaggy haircut and jeans that is Adrian standing in front of him, palm outstretched to be shaken.

Cagney hesitates for a beat, and then pushes himself to his feet, gripping Adrian's hand. He lets go first, pulling himself up to his full height, which is almost exactly the same as Adrian; Cagney may even have it by a whisker.

'I'm well,' Cagney says, and sits down again.

Adrian nods his head, as if waiting for Cagney to ask something of him, although Cagney can't think what. After a few moments he smiles and looks around for a chair.

'No chairs, sorry. They encourage people to stay.' Cagney gestures to the box that is still in front of his desk. 'Are you . . . I'm sorry, I don't really know why you are here?' Cagney looks around as casually as he can for his bag of monkey nuts. He needs a handful straight away. He feels unnerved.

'I know,' Adrian laughs and shakes his head. 'It's crazy, crazy.'

Cagney doesn't understand this at all. What is crazy?

Adrian jerks his head up as if somebody has just flicked him on the nose with their thumb and forefinger, and clears his throat, and takes a deep breath. Cagney sits back a little startled, but waits for Adrian to speak.

'I remembered you saying, or somebody saying, that night at the dinner party, when I was on the phone, I remember overhearing that you do something funny . . .'

'Funny?' Cagney asks, confused.

'Yes, you know . . .'

'Like juggling?' Cagney asks.

'Ha ha.' Adrian is nervous and laughs in a short sharp burst. 'No, I mean, your job. You, like, check people, check up on people, see if they are fooling around on their partner, or whatever . . .' Adrian stares at him expectantly, but Cagney is reluctant to confirm or deny, very suddenly scared to speak, or guess where this is leading. What can Adrian want?

'And – I never thought I'd hear myself saying this – but, well, I have somebody I'd like checked out. I'm not sure, but I think she might play away, given the opportunity and, well, I just need to know, you know, if she's marriage stock! I am right, though – that is what you do?'

Cagney is numb. He is going to ask her to marry him. It is done. It's over.

'OK. But we might have a problem, because she has met me, of course, and Iuan, one of my associates, although he wouldn't be applicable in this case. I don't know if she has seen my third associate or not, but that would be the key –'

'Sorry? How?' Adrian looks bewildered, sitting forwards on the box, concentrating hard, trying to focus on Cagney and therefore understand.

'How what?'

'How has she met you already . . . or . . . God, you think I mean Sunny? Oh no, it's my fiancée, Jane. Shit, this is a bit embarrassing.' Adrian shakes his head guiltily, as the penny drops for Cagney.

'So, to be clear, your fiancée, whom you are cheating on with Sunny – you want me to check if she will do the dirty on you, and if she will you won't marry her?'

'I know it sounds awful but, you know, I've just got myself in a bit of a pickle . . .'

'A pickle?'

'Yeah.' Adrian looks at Cagney evenly, matching the unmasked confrontation in Cagney's tone. 'Sorry, do you have a problem, mate?'

'No. Not at all. Go on.'

'OK. Well . . . what do you need to know?'

'Do you have a photo?'

'Yep.' Adrian reaches into his back pocket, pulling out his wallet, and removes a photo from the inside, leaning forward to hand it to Cagney, who takes a look. He knew it. Blonde. Sweet. Vacant. No wonder he's fooling around with Sunny – this woman looks like she'd rather chew off her own arm than have sex. Or a conversation.

'What does she do?' Cagney asks innocently.

'She's a PE teacher.'

'OK, alright, ah-ha.' Cagney nods, still looking at the photo. She plays netball, for a living.

'While I come to think of it, can you not mention this, to Sunny obviously, but also to your mate, the gay guy who runs the video shop, Christian? They seem quite tight, and, anyway, I've kind of told Sunny I've already left Jane, so it would just really complicate things if she found out.'

'You haven't left her?'

'No. Not yet.'

'But you are going to leave her?'

'Well, that depends on you guys!'

'So . . .' Cagney reaches into his drawer and pulls out the almost empty bottle of whiskey, and grabs the beaker from the desk. He pours himself a double. He doesn't offer Adrian one, but cradles the drink in his hands, thinking. 'So . . . if she cheats, you dump her, and stick with Sunny. But what if she doesn't cheat, what then?'

'Well, there's the rub!' Adrian nods his head at Cagney and laughs, as if they are co-conspirators, as if Cagney completely understands. 'I don't know, Cag,' he says, his face dropping in desolate awe of the confusion that may follow.

Cagney shudders.

'Sunny is a lovely girl but, Christ, she can be hard work! She thinks too much, she talks too much, there is always the worry that she might start to eat too much again . . . And she's been on her own for so long, she's a bit too independent, you know? She's not a "cook your dinner and rub your feet" kind of girl, is she?'

Cagney stares at Adrian and waits for him to dig himself an even dirtier hole.

'I just want my mum, you know how it is. Who wants to do their own washing?'

'Well . . . exactly.' Cagney nods slowly. 'Write down the name and address of her school – do they go to a local, some of the teachers?'

'No, she doesn't go to the pub; she doesn't drink much.'

Cagney doesn't quite cough up his final gulp of whiskey; he has seen the photo, he isn't surprised.

'She goes to Cannons, though.'

Cagney looks at him blankly.

'The gym,' Adrian says, as if it's obvious.

'Oh, right.' Cagney nods his head, as if he knew all along.

Twenty minutes later Adrian is gone, and Cagney sits alone, rolling his now empty beaker between his palms, staring out of the window, but not really looking, letting it all blur into a hazy blend of grey. He is thinking.

Would it be wrong to lie in this instance? If he thought that Sunny would be happier with him, in the long run, would it be wrong to lie?

Would it be unprofessional?

Is he going to do it anyway?

He has never chosen a woman over business before.

Now, *there*'s the rub . . .

Cagney enters the party from the corridor below his office, slipping into the room unnoticed. The Welsh flag hangs as bunting, back and forth and back and forth across the room, and the floor is scattered with rugby balls and daffodils and miners' hats. Christian has also laid plastic grass – the green green grass of home, he explained to Iuan, as the Welshman broke down. It had been on the cards.

'Where's your outfit?' Iuan hobbles over and confronts

Cagney. Iuan has discarded his crutches for the night, balancing on his plaster precariously, like a fawn on fresh hoofs. The fall is inevitable.

Cagney leans down, picks up a daffodil, and sticks it through his lapel. 'I'm wearing it.'

Iuan looks disappointed, but passes Cagney a glass of red wine none the less.

Cagney looks him up and down twice. 'What are you?'

He has a large brown board stuck to his back, and is dressed in a yellow Lycra catsuit.

'Welsh Rarebit,' Iuan answers with a sigh, as if Cagney was the tenth person to ask in ten minutes, and it is as obvious as day follows night.

'Of course,' Cagney replies flatly, and walks away.

He spots Christian near the front door talking to a man dressed as Hannibal Lecter, sucking his beer through a straw that he sticks through his mouth guard. Cagney walks over and stands a couple of feet away, waiting for their conversation to end. Hannibal becomes unnerved, glancing over his shoulder at Cagney every thirty seconds, until he makes his excuses and moves away.

'I don't get it,' Cagney says to Christian, gesturing at the departing Hannibal.

'Anthony Hopkins,' Christian says,

'So am I stuck with you for the rest of the evening, Cagney? Loitering just over my shoulder, scaring away any other conversation? I can't quite believe you are here, but I suppose the chances of you talking to somebody you don't know are as remote as a Sahara outpost.'

'I'm shy, like a schoolgirl,' Cagney says, gulping down his wine.

'Are you hell! You're easily bored and just as easily rude.'

'You say tomato . . .' Cagney glances distractedly at the door, and back to Christian.

'What was that?' Christian asks, narrowing his eyes.

'What?' Cagney tries to look innocent.

'That, that glance?'

'What glance?'

'You glanced, at the door, like you were waiting for some-body, or . . .' Christian pouts in thought.

'I didn't glance. I have something in my eye.'

'You're waiting for Sunny!' Christian's smile is magnificent.

'Or your trousers are too tight, and they're cutting off the blood supply to your brain. I don't get it.'

Cagney gestures at a man dressed as a Roman Centurion who walks past.

'Richard Burton, from *Ant & Cleo.*'

'Who'd have thought Wales had so much to offer?'

'Who'd have thought Iuan had this many friends?'

They both nod once in agreement.

The room is quickly filling up with rugby players, leeks, dragons, Catherine Zeta Jones in Chicago outfits, and many many many Tom Joneses. Cagney counts seven in his immediate eye-line.

But Christian is the best. His dark blond hair is covered by a wiry black curly wig. He is even more tanned than usual, and wearing a red silk shirt, mostly undone to reveal an uncharacteristically hairy chest. The shirt is tucked into black leather trousers so tight Cagney thinks that he might have bought them from Miss Selfridge. Then there are the Cuban-heeled boots, and a large gold medallion. At that moment the Stereophonics' 'Have A Nice Day' is replaced on the sound system with 'What's New Pussycat?'.

'Thank God it's not "Goldfinger" again,' Christian sighs. 'The woman just shouts!'

Cagney hears the door scream – Christian hasn't disconnected his Halloween buzzer for the evening – and glances over, inhaling sharply. A strange party have just arrived:

315

Sophia Young walks in first, her blonde hair lying over one shoulder, spun like gold, framing her face in a heavenly halo. There's irony, thinks Cagney.

She holds the door politely for the person behind her to enter. It is Adrian, who sees Cagney straight away, and winks. He isn't in fancy dress, dressed in a T-shirt and jeans, but has an inflatable guitar in one hand, and with the other he is holding the door open for Sunny. Cagney inhales sharply again. Her shoulder-length hair has been replaced by a short dark wig, and her mouth looks plump and juicy with red lipstick. She wears a yellow blazer with a blue badge and a large white 'M' emblazoned on it, and short snug white tennis shorts that hug until midway down her thighs. She has large yellow discs for earrings.

'Inspired!' Christian says in awe, clasping his hands together as if praying to a new god. 'Gladys Pugh.'

Cagney stares at her, before somebody steps in front of him, and obstructs his view. His eyes focus on the person standing barely a foot away.

'Hello, Mr James,' her voice drips coolly. Last week it would have reminded him of tiny droplets falling from an ice cube she might have run across his bare chest. Today it sounds like Chinese water torture.

'Come to pick up my cleaning bill, Mrs Young?'

'I'm sorry about that. It was unavoidable.' A smile dances on her lips. She thinks she is a naughty schoolgirl, and Cagney wonders how quickly that trick will get old with everybody, and not just him. And yet it's about the only ammunition she has. Out of the corner of his eye he can see Adrian take Sunny's hand and lead her towards the makeshift bar at the counter, and away from him. Christian eyes Sophia with suspicion.

'What are you supposed to be?' Christian asks her, without even an introduction.

'I'm sorry?' she asks, confused.

316

'It's fancy dress.'

'Oh, I'm not here for the party.' She turns and smiles naughtily at Cagney. 'I came to speak to Mr James. This is just my good fortune.'

'Not for long. You're not staying,' Cagney says. 'Follow me,' and he turns and walks towards the entrance to the hallway and the stairs up to his office. But as he reaches the door he bumps straight into Sunny.

'Hello,' Cagney says formally.

'Oh, hi, how are you?' Sunny says, equally as uncomfortable.

'You remember my . . . friend Adrian?' She lets go of Adrian's hand and gestures towards him, presenting him to Cagney.

'Yes I do,' Cagney says with a smile at Adrian, but does not offer his hand to be shaken.

Sunny locks eyes with Sophia Young, who stands closely behind Cagney, and he sees her eyes flicker down to Sophia's hand as she wraps it, spider-like, around his arm. She smiles her biggest warmest brightest smile and widens her eyes.

'You're obviously going somewhere. We'll leave you to it,' and she pushes past them, refusing to meet Cagney's eye.

'Where *are* we going?' Sophia purrs in his ear.

'Somewhere that isn't playing Shirley Bassey,' he says, shoving the door open violently, not holding it open for Sophia Young, who follows him up the old battered wooden stairs anyway.

'Is this where you bring all your girls?' she says, as he unlocks the door to his office. Her tone aggravates him, or rather the presumption nestled inside her tone: she has the voice of a girl who always gets her man. She is utterly assured of her own allure, probably just as aware as most men that it only runs skin deep, caring just as little.

317

'Why are you here?' Cagney asks squarely.

'Don't you want me here?' A playful smile flirts with her lips as she traces a finger along the front of Cagney's desk. They stand on either side, Cagney with his arms crossed, Sophia so fluid and nubile it's as if all her bones are made of plasticine, and they bend and twist as required.

'There is a very important party going on downstairs, and I need to get back. Why are you here?'

'Important?' Sophia looks a trifle put out, a tad confused. 'Isn't it for that ugly boy in the yellow catsuit? Is he really that important?' She whispers her insults, as step by deliberate step she makes her way around the desk.

'He is to his mother,' Cagney replies, unmoved.

She tosses a giggle his way, like a messy scattering of confetti. Nothing is proving ingratiating about Mrs Young this evening. Cagney is both surprised and relieved, impressed by his own resolve. He was determined to stand by his decision, when he made it nights ago, but he never completely trusts himself when it comes to blondes. But she leaves him cold.

'Who are you supposed to be?' she asks, a step away from him. He can almost feel her breath on his cheek.

'Scott of the Antarctic,' he says, deadpan.

'Was he Welsh?' she asks, distracted, running her finger down the arm of his jacket, until it meets the palm of his hand. She begins to tickle a circle around his palm with her fingernail.

Cagney opens his mouth to speak, but she places her hands on both sides of his face urgently, her claws digging into his cheeks, and pulls his mouth round to meet hers.

'Don't answer that, I don't care,' she says, staring in his eyes.

Sophia Young kisses him, and he kisses her back, grabbing both her arms at the top fleshy section, and lifting her up so her mouth smothers his. She tickles a line along the inside of his upper lip with her tongue, as Cagney opens his eyes and watches her closely and evenly, weaving her spell.

That proves it.

Cagney holds her shoulders firmly and takes a step back. 'Mrs Young, I think you should leave.'

'What?' she half smiles, wondering if he is serious.

'You heard me the first time.'

'But, why?' She takes a step back, examining him for clues.

Cagney walks round the desk and opens his office door for her, standing expectantly to the side, waiting for her to leave. 'I'm just not that kind of boy,' he says with a smile.

'But we have a connection, don't you think? An electricity . . .'

'It must be the fillings in your teeth and the phone masts, angel, because nothing is fizzing over here.'

'I don't understand this,' she says coldly, storming over to meet him, locking her jaw and fixing him with a steely glare. 'I wasn't even playing this time!' she says.

'I'm flattered,' Cagney says and smiles.

'You're an asshole.'

'You're not the only one that thinks so.'

'Seriously,' Sophia stands in the doorway, pulling on a coat that she had discarded only moments ago, 'tell me again why you are turning me down.'

'You're an old mistake. I've made you before.'

'I'm sorry?'

'I'm nearly forty! Everybody's got to learn sometime . . .'

Cagney swings the door shut and it slaps Sophia Young's great arse. He hears her give a little shriek in the corridor. She may even have stamped her foot. Cagney smiles to himself and leans back against his door.

What did he just do? Turn down the most beautiful

woman he has seen in a decade? What is he thinking? Has the red wine gone to his head that much? But then he shrugs his shoulders, and smiles his broadest smile in years.

Whatever happens, he's just side-stepped a whole lagoon of shit. He may not be somewhere over the rainbow by the end of tonight, but he won't hate himself either.

Cagney walks back into the party to see that one of the leeks has taken off his costume, and now, dressed only in his underpants, he holds one end of the giant vegetable while a guy in a choir boy outfit holds the other. Several Tom Joneses and an entire Welsh rugby squad proceed to limbo underneath it to the strains of 'Delilah'. Cagney scans and spots Sunny, talking to Christian in the corner. There is a foot between her and Adrian, and her attention is firmly focused on Christian. Cagney grabs a couple of glasses of red wine and carries them over. They all look up as he joins them.

'I saw you needed a refill,' he says to Sunny, handing her one of the two wineglasses, and taking her empty glass out of her hand.

'Oh, thank you. I think . . . you haven't poisoned it, have you?' she smiles at him.

And he replies, 'Try it and see.'

Without looking away from his eyes she takes a large gulp of wine. 'No worse than the last one I tasted,' she says.

Cagney looks at Adrian, who looks uncomfortable. He keeps twisting his head from one side to the other, stretching his neck like an athlete preparing for a race.

'Are you alright, Adrian?' Cagney asks loudly, and all three turn to stare at him. Cagney smiles a wide smile in his direction, and Christian clocks it, confused, squinting his eyes up at Cagney, trying to somehow know what Cagney knows.

'Are you alright? You do seem a bit stressed,' Sunny says.

'Scared you'll see your girlfriend?' Christian asks insincerely, cocking his head to one side.

'No.'

'He's left her,' Sunny says, and an observer would say her tone was unimpressed.

'Have you?' Christian asks with a smile and wide eyes.

Adrian glances down at his feet, and at his hands, tearing off the wrapper from a bottle of lager. He looks up and solely addresses Christian, not looking either to his left or right. 'Yes,' he says quietly.

'Have you?' Cagney asks, with a smile and the quickest of winks.

Adrian looks at him, and Cagney can tell he is desperate to let one fly right on Cagney's chin, but of course he can't. One good jab would do it, but how would that look?

'Yes,' he says, and stares accusingly at Cagney.

'When, recently?' Cagney asks, sipping his wine innocently.

'Earlier in the week,' Sunny says, and reaches out to squeeze Adrian's hand.

Cagney watches, and sees it is the way a mother would squeeze a child. As soon as she has touched it, she lets it go again.

'Oh, so a few days ago?' Cagney says. 'Not, say, this afternoon?'

'No.' Adrian turns to him. 'And I really don't want to talk about it.'

'OK. Sorry, hon. Well, what were we talking about?'

'Doris Day?' Adrian says quickly, relieved.

'I believe we started with Rock Hudson, but we can talk about her now as well.' Christian is only marginally disappointed.

'*Calamity Jane*, that's one of my favourites,' Sunny smiles fondly.

'Mine too,' Cagney says.

'Oh, here we go. I thought it was too good to last. It's a really good film alright; it's a classic!' Sunny turns to him defensively.

'No, it really is one of his favourites. He's had it out of here, what, ten times, Cagney?'

'Maybe not quite that many,' he says with a sheepish smile to his feet.

'Are you actually gay?' Adrian asks with a smirk.

'I don't like musicals, Adrian, but I'm gay. Explain to me your theory?' Christian says seriously.

'Alright, mate, don't get yourself in a lather. I was just making a joke.'

'Funny boy,' Christian mutters into his wineglass, and takes a huge gulp of wine.

'Do you really like it?' Sunny asks, with the innocence of a small child presenting her parents with the first Christmas present she has bought with her own pocket money, desperate for it to be loved.

'Yes, I really do,' Cagney says, and looks up to meet her eyes, smeared in awful black make-up, framed by the ridiculous short wig.

'Prove it then – what's your favourite song?' Sunny smiles at the challenge.

'"A Woman's Touch", of course,' Cagney says.

'Oh my God, I should have known! Little wife in the kitchen, baking cakes!' she laughs.

'Wasn't there one called "Whip Crack Away"?' Christian asks with a filthy laugh.

'How about you?' Cagney asks.

'"Secret Love",' Sunny says, and gives him a small sad smile.

'What film is this? Who's even in it?' Adrian asks, swigging from his beer between questions.

'You wouldn't know it,' Christian says, and looks away in disgust.

'Alright, mate, no need to get funny, just because I don't like some old gay film.'

They stand in an embarrassed silence.

'I'm sorry, I didn't mean that to sound offensive.' Adrian nods his head at Christian, his apology sincere.

Christian nods back, obviously displeased but gracious enough to let it go. Sunny looks up from her feet where she has been staring, and glances at Cagney, who stares back at her. She looks away quickly.

'Do you want to come outside with me for a while?' Sunny turns to Adrian and smiles sadly again.

'Sure, of course,' Adrian says, and Cagney is sure he sees him smirk.

Sunny walks towards the front door, that screams as she opens it, and the crowd, who are dancing and laughing and singing, all cheer. Cagney stares after Sunny and Adrian.

'Are you OK?' Christian asks.

'Well, that put me in my place,' Cagney says evenly, staring at the door as it shuts behind Adrian. 'They're like rabbits; they couldn't get outside quick enough.'

'You never know,' Christian says, watching them walk up towards the station, concerned.

'You're right. You never know.' Cagney offers Christian his hand to shake.

Christian accepts.

'Have a good night,' Cagney says, and Christian nods and smiles.

Cagney walks towards the bar and grabs two full bottles of red wine. Holding them in one hand and his glass in the other, he kicks open the door and walks off towards his office.

* * *

323

I sit on a bench under a tree, outside the butcher's. It is such a dark and overcast night, it feels that if the sky were unzipped all the stars would tumble out and dot the sky with kisses. I have goose pimples on my thighs where my white tennis shorts fail to give me any kind of adequate protection against the chill.

Adrian sits down next to me, and puts his arm around my shoulders, but I don't slide back into it.

'Hey, this party is weird. Shall we go and get something to eat? Do you fancy a curry?'

'I'm not hungry,' I say, and turn my head to smile at him.

'Oh, for fuck's sake, Sunny, one fucking Indian isn't going to make you fat again! You can't eat like this for the rest of your fucking life.'

I sigh.

'I'm sorry, I didn't mean to swear. I just mean – you can allow yourself one takeaway, right? Sunny?' He is prodding my leg gently with his finger. 'Sexy Sunny, I'm sorry,' he says and tries to pull me closer with his other arm. But I resist, staring ahead. 'What?' he asks, confused, rejected.

Just wait for it. I've never done this before. I've never had the opportunity. It already feels awful, and I am scared I will lose my courage, but I know that I will say it really. I turn to face him.

'I'm really sorry, Adrian.'

'What?' he asks again, confused, but I can already see the hurt spring into his eyes.

'Let me talk, just for a minute. Just please don't interrupt.'

Adrian moves his arm from around me and sits up, giving me his full attention. I give him as warm a smile as I can. But then I look honestly into his eyes, and begin.

'I'm sorry. I think that I have treated you like a block of wood – or just a set of constituent parts, a pair of lips, a

324

pair of arms, a penis,' I wince slightly at the word, and the admission, 'to practise on. I haven't thought about who I was kissing since that first kiss in the cab, that first night. But that was the end of my fat film, which was a fairy tale, and what's been playing out since, well, it's not quite so sweet and innocent. I guess what I'm trying to say is, I've never felt, since we started seeing each other, like I am with you. I've always felt alone.

'And I think that is because, at a very basic level, you don't understand me; that I feel like far too much and nowhere near enough, all at once. How I feel about how I was, and how I've changed, but not changed at all. How I still feel like a little unloved fat girl, who needs to be adored, just a bit, to make up for the years of being hurt, and sad, and on her own. But I don't think you get that, and I think it's because you haven't tried, and you don't want to try, and I don't blame you for that, honestly! You've got far too much on your plate already! I mean, I know that me saying this is barely even going to register on your emotional radar, because you've left Jane, and you've been with her for so much longer, and that hurts too much for you to even think about me. But I just thought it was fair that I tell you honestly.'

'Of course it hurts. I like you, Sunny,' Adrian says, staring me straight in the eye. 'But I'm scared you want too much. I think you're living in a dream world, and maybe you thought I was going to be Prince Charming, and I kind of am, because Prince Charming doesn't exist, Sunny. But I'm a nice guy, a fun guy, I'm honest and . . .' Adrian stops talking, and we are both a little embarrassed.

'This is what you do – you meet somebody you fancy, and you spend time with them, and you take it from there. That's how it works. It's no more complicated than that. I don't think you get that. You've got some romantic ideal in

325

your head, and you're just going to be disappointed.'

'Maybe,' I say, nodding my head. 'But I think I do understand, really. I've just waited too long for this, to settle for second best now. I completely admit that I've had all these romantic dreams and notions of what love is and blah blah blah swimming around in my head, making me crazy, but I think I know now. I just need for whoever I am with to take the time and make the effort to understand what makes me happy. And I'm not talking about material things, I'm talking about the person I want to be, and the person I want to be with, how we look at life, how we go about it, how we treat each other. I need for them to be willing to find that out, and then to try and give me that, to want to give me that, when he can. That's all it is. I don't need a prince at all. I don't need a dozen red roses or weekends in Paris.'

'I don't think you understand blokes, though, Sun. We don't think like that. You're not going to get some guy who sits there thinking about how he wants to seem or be, or how you want to seem or be or whatever. You're throwing this away and it's a mistake. You're not going to get what you want.'

'I think I will,' I say, and glance over at Screen Queen. At some point the disco music stopped, and the whole shop is now booming 'Land of Our Fathers'. It bursts triumphantly into the night, slipping through the October leaves clinging to the trees, enveloping us, and it makes us smile. But then Adrian's face drops again.

'Sorry,' I say, and reach out and hold his hand.

He squeezes it quickly, then stands up. 'I'm gonna go. I don't feel like hanging around.'

'OK,' I say, and nod my head in agreement.

'So . . . I guess, I'll see you . . . can I come and pick up my bag tomorrow?'

'Of course,' I say. I don't ask if he has got somewhere to

stay. I don't ask what he is going to do. It's nothing to do with me.

I stand up and kiss him on the cheek.

Adrian walks off. I didn't realise he was still carrying his inflatable guitar, and he lets the air out as he walks away.

I stand under the tree, and realise it has started to rain. I move out from underneath the branches and feel the wind brushing my face, as the rain starts to drive a little harder onto my skin, not quite stinging, but quickly I'm wet. I wipe my face, certain that I am smearing my layers of mascara and black eyeliner all over my cheeks. I tug off my wig and shake out my hair that falls on my shoulders. I run my fingers through it and it is instantly damp with the rain and my hands.

I don't want to cry at all. Was that a strange decision to make? I liked him, he was a nice guy – should I have given it more of a chance? Am I just scared of the emotions that go along with relationships and, rather than deal with them, or the prospect of compromise, have I just cut it short, nipped it in the bud before my heart got out of hand? I know that's not true.

I lean against the butcher's window and slide down it so I am sitting on the pavement with my legs bent, and my tennis shoes flat on the floor in front of me. I run my hands through my hair and then relax, letting them fall into my lap.

I know I've been on my own for ever, and that I am independent, and that I am not used to compromising, or thinking about how somebody else feels. I am used to thinking about how I feel. But I don't want to have to fight, just to be myself. I don't want to adapt too much, to hit the wall of somebody else's personality and just crumble in front of it, in a puddle of 'whatever you wants', a series of 'OKs', and 'if you likes'.

I don't want to simmer or fester or succumb. I like myself now, and not just my body, or my hair, or my clothes, but me. I don't want to change. I sit on my own in the rain, wet and bedraggled and with make-up smeared all over my face and white shorts turning black with dirt and damp. I smile and know that I would rather be out here, on my own, than inside with the wrong man.

I don't know how long I sit in the rain, but eventually I push myself up, shivering with damp cold, and head back to Screen Queen. The valleys' chorus has died down, and three very drunk revellers, with their arms locked around each other, tumble out of the door, and I stand clear of them so they don't fall on me by mistake and squash me. Inside, the floor is littered with rugby balls, and beer bottles, and Welsh flags, and the odd rugby player, and the odder Tom Jones. I can hear a Stereophonics album playing quietly on the CD system – that is who Adrian was dressed as, the lead singer of the Stereophonics – and I spot Christian, Iuan, and a man I don't know, sitting in a row, leaning on the front of the counter. I look around, but don't see Cagney. I am sure he left hours ago and a wave of disappointment sweeps over me.

I stand in front of them, with crossed arms.

'Well, you're a sorry sight,' I say in my best Welsh accent.

'Fantastic,' murmurs Iuan, hammered, and then, 'This is her.'

'This is who?' I ask, as the third guy, the one I don't know, who has a yellow circle around his head with stiff yellow cardboard petals sticking out of it, and is wearing a green polo neck and green corduroys, slowly looks up.

'No way. She's young,' he says, so tired he can't have slept for days.

'Who, me? Are you talking about me?' I ask confused.

'Twenty-eight,' Christian volunteers.

'Seriously, are you talking about me?' I ask again. 'Because I have a name, you know!'

'Sunny,' they all chant at once, as if this is a prayer meeting and I am their leader.

'How do you know that?' I ask the daffodil.

'Because, you're the girl, aren't you?' He smiles a lopsided grin at me, winks, and then pulls up his green polo neck to show me his left nipple.

'What are you doing?'

'Nothing,' he says with a smile, and lowers his top again. 'Our boss is in love with you.'

'You work for Cagney as well?' I say, and then cross myself for tempting fate, assuming he is talking about Cagney.

'Shizza,' he says.

'Are you on drugs?' I ask.

'He's always like this, Sunshine,' Christian volunteers, before resting his head on Iuan's shoulder.

'By tomorrow morning my head is going to feel like somebody cracked it open and threw up in it,' he says, and smiles at me, giving me a thumbs-up.

'Look, Christian, do you have a towel? And something I can wear home? I've got wet in the rain and I'll freeze if I go anywhere in this.' I gesture to my outfit.

'You look exceptional, by the way,' says the third guy.

'Who are you?' I ask, bemused.

'I'm Howard! Oh, come on, don't tell me he doesn't talk about me . . .' He throws his head back to laugh but instead crashes it against the counter. I wince but nobody else seems that bothered.

'So, Christian, do you have anything?'

'No, sorry, my lovely.'

'My tracksuit is upstairs in the office, if you want that.

I got changed into toast here,' Iuan says, lifting his head to smile at me. 'Exceptional. Gladys Pugh, I love that,' he adds, closing his eyes.

'Hi-de hi,' Howard whispers.

'Upstairs?' I ask, backing away.

'You can have this.' Howard pulls off his round petal face frame, still with his eyes closed, and offers it to me. 'I'll be alright without it,' he says, and it falls to the floor.

I look around the room. They are the only people left standing/sitting. I walk over to the front door and lock it from the inside.

I check my watch: it is ten past two in the morning. I walk through the side door, and see some stairs, reaching for a light switch that isn't there, I cling to the wall and climb them slowly one by one. There is a light on in the room at the top of the stairs, and a door is slightly open. It is the only room there is, and therefore I assume the only place that Iuan could have left his tracksuit. It is also, as the glass reads, Cagney's office.

I push the door open and Cagney says, 'Hello.'

I am startled, but too tired to show it.

'What are you doing?' I ask, looking at a half-empty wine bottle on the table, and what looks to be a full one by its side.

'I came up here, for a drink, hours ago. But it hasn't been going down that well,' he says, turning his attention to the bottle, focusing for the first time in hours on its contents. 'What are you doing?' he asks.

'I got soaked in the rain, and I want to walk home now, so Iuan said I could borrow his tracksuit.'

'It's over there.' Cagney points to an orange heap in the corner of the room.

'Oh, thanks. Do you mind if I . . . change . . . it's just that I am a little cold . . . and . . .'

330

'Of course.' Cagney spins his chair round and stares out of the window, and I grab at my blazer, throwing it off, and scramble into the tracksuit top, which is an XXL. I am no more than an M now. I peel off my shorts, but stop short of taking off my damp knickers where the rain has soaked straight through, stuck to my skin from sitting for hours on the pavement. I pull on the tracksuit trousers, which, I calculate, are just over a foot too long.

'Thanks,' I say loudly, and Cagney spins round.

'Looks nice,' he says evenly.

'I bet,' I say, and smile.

'Well,' he says.

'Well,' I reply.

'I should get going,' I say, at the same time as Cagney says, 'Will you stay for a drink?' and offers up the half-full bottle of red wine. Half empty? Half full.

'I'll stay for a drink,' I say with a smile.

'You come and sit here.' Cagney jumps up and moves round the desk, passing me a glass, pointing at me to sit in his chair. 'I'll sit on the box.'

'No, you stay where you are. I'd actually rather just sit on the floor, anyway.' I sit down suddenly, and lean against the filing cabinet.

Cagney looks a little shocked. 'Oh. OK.' He moves back around the desk, and hovers over his chair, looking at me for some kind of final say-so, before he sits down, content that I'm not lying, and I don't really want to sit in his chair.

We sit in silence for what feels like an eternity, but is probably only about ten seconds.

'How's work?' he asks me, to fill a shocked silence.

'Do you really want to know?' I ask, scared that this is going to degenerate into another argument straight away.

'I don't know. I mean, tell me if it's doing well. But you

don't have to tell me what's really selling, unless you feel you absolutely have to.'

'Are you uncomfortable talking about sex?' I ask, being a little confrontational, in spite of my best intentions.

'Yes. Aren't all men, with women, when what women really mean when they say they want to talk about sex, is emotions? Am I comfortable talking about emotion? Well, what do you think?' He smiles a rueful smile at himself, and I feel my shoulders fall and relax.

'I guess we should either all talk about it, or not talk about it at all. These half-measures just confuse everybody,' I say.

'The problem is, while nobody is really talking about it, nobody thinks they are getting enough.' Cagney shifts in his chair, and takes a slow gulp of his red wine, and looks up at me.

I meet his gaze for a moment longer than I thought I could. 'What is enough, anyway? I mean, is it when you can't physically walk?' I wince at my own suggestion.

'No, it's when you are throwing up from the physical exertion.'

'But not in bed, I hope,' I say with a mock serious smile. 'Although there is bound to be a name for that. Some people probably love it!'

'Agoraphobia could double up. How many people do you know, really, with a fear of wide open spaces? We might as well put it to good use,' he says.

'Yes. Scared you aren't getting enough sex – agoraphobia number two.' I nod my head. 'But actually I think it's bigger than that. I think everybody is scared they are missing out on everything. Scared they aren't being loved enough, or loving enough themselves . . .' I trail off and look at him for his thoughts.

'Oh, you are good, but it won't work,' he says with a smile.

332

'Sorry, I'm confused.'

'I don't do the emotional talk, not even at three a.m., and not even with . . . well, love is love is love. What's the point pulling it to pieces? People say it, and then they rip it apart in front of your eyes. But I fear I may sound jaded . . .'

'Surely not!'

'Well, Miss Sunshine,' he says it kindly now; it isn't thrown at me like a curve ball, to smash my feelings, or bruise me somehow. 'We don't have to talk ourselves round in circles to know the truth. Most people today feel like they are worth shit, nada, nothing. But if somebody says, "I love you" then you are worth something. Somebody has seen something worth loving in you. And the only reason we need somebody else to give that to us is so we have some kind of responsibility not to go and live on a boat in the middle of the ocean and opt out of everything and go crazy if we want.'

'Maybe you're right,' I say. 'Maybe it is just to stop us wandering off into the desert and never coming back.'

'Maybe it's the reason I turned to whiskey and you turned to doughnuts – we need something to numb the pain if we aren't loved, because we feel worthless.'

'So love is the cushion that stops me needing the doughnuts, and you the whiskey?'

'You got it, Sunshine. It blurs the edges. It eases the pain.' He smiles honestly at me. I think I could crawl up, climb in him, and sleep for ever. We sip our wine. I feel my eyes closing.

'And there is one more thing, of course,' Cagney says, and I force myself to prise my eyelids open.

'I can't shut you up now, can I?' I say, exhausted.

'Hey, you uncork the bottle, you drink the wine,' he says, and when he looks at me his stare is serious and intense. 'The person you love is the ultimate reflection of who you are. And who you want to be, and what you value.'

'So . . . I feel like you are going somewhere with this, Cagney . . .'

'So be careful who you love: make sure they deserve it. Make sure they reflect you well.'

'I will,' I say, and as much as I want to talk to him, and laugh with him, and get closer to him, and crawl inside him, I feel my eyelids, so heavy that they could sink fleets, slide shut.

Cagney moves round the desk and gently takes the glass out of her hand before it spills on Iuan's tracksuit. He crouches beside her, and wonders how to wake her. And then it occurs to him – he doesn't have to. Cagney sits down against the filing cabinets, and leans in closer to her. She fidgets and shifts her weight, and tries to rest her head on something, and with his arm stretched upwards she finds his chest as a pillow. He places his arm over her shoulders gently. Her face angles upwards towards his, like a scene from a 1930s film, when men and women locked together, and kissed passionately, and then tore themselves apart.

He could just kiss her now . . . Cagney turns his head to face the opposite direction, so he doesn't have to look at her, or he won't be able to stop himself.

Facing the wall, he too falls asleep.

I wake up with my head on Cagney's chest. I am leaning against a filing cabinet in his office. I remember falling asleep, sensing the glass being taken out of my hands, and a body next to me, a chest offering itself to be slept on. I look up and Cagney's face is pointing away from me, his eyelids flickering slightly, dreaming strange dreams. But then he shifts and his head turns towards mine, his eyes still closed, still darting behind his lids. I could just kiss him now, wake

334

him softly, and claim it was a mistake if he rebuffs me, and say that I thought he was somebody else – Adrian perhaps – confused in sleep. I feel my eyelids fall heavily again, and I close my eyes.

I wake up to light streaming in through a large window opposite me, and I am immediately struck by how uncomfortable I am, lying on Cagney's floor, my head flush with the carpet. I sit up and rub my eyes, and check my watch. It is half-past eight. I have been sleeping for six hours. My head pounds and my eyes feel like they are glued together with mascara. Cagney is standing staring out of the window.

'Hello,' I say.

'Good morning, Sunshine,' he says, with a small smile.

'I should have gone home. I am exhausted. I ache,' I say, stretching my arms, examining the orange tracksuit that I forgot I was wearing.

'I meant to ask you last night, did Adrian leave you here to walk home on your own?'

'Oh, yes, he had to leave.' I remember that I broke it off with Adrian last night. A wave of relief sweeps over me.

'Look, Sunny. Nothing happened last night.' Cagney is staring out of the window, not even looking at me as he speaks.

'I know that,' I say defensively. 'I wasn't trashed!'

'I know, but I thought you might have wanted it to, and I wanted to explain –'

'What do you mean, "I may have wanted it to" – what about you?'

'What about me?' Cagney turns to look at me, and his face is stern, aggrieved.

'You might have wanted it to, more than me,' I say angrily, pushing myself to my feet.

So he's seen how I look in the morning and now he's not so interested? Nice.

335

'Well, what difference does that make?' he says, and sighs.

'A big bloody difference!' I say, brushing myself down. I am not being rejected again!

'I think we should just be friends,' he says, and I nearly gag.

'Friends? Since when did hating each other seem friendly to you? Unless this is the closest you get,' I say, with a smirk.

Cagney looks at me sadly. 'I think you should go, before we say things we'll regret.'

'Don't worry, I'm leaving,' I say, and grab my stiff wet blazer and shorts. Without a backward glance, I walk out, slamming the door behind me. I need a shower, I need some warm clothes of my own, I need my bed, I need . . . I stop at the top of the stairs. This is definitely fear. See it, recognise it, do it anyway. I force myself to picture Cagney, who is in the office behind me. If I don't say it, maybe neither of us ever will. Maybe I need to be brave enough for the both of us.

I turn round at the top of the stairs to walk back into his office, as the door swings open.

'I don't want to be just your friend,' Cagney says, 'but you're with Adrian.'

'No, I'm not,' I say.

'Well, that changes things,' he says, neither one of us able to look away from the other.

'It's not such a big deal,' I say, although still holding on to the door for support.

'We don't amount to much in this big old village.' He takes a step forwards.

'It's nothing really. Well, maybe it's a small something. But nothing will change.' I let go of the door, and it swings closed behind me.

'Exactly. I mean,' Cagney takes two more steps forward, and I do the same, 'if I kiss you now, the tree outside my office is going to keep on growing. It isn't going to change the world if I kiss you.'

'It will only change ours.' I can't smile or frown, or do anything. 'And I don't know about you, but I am just about ready for a change.'

I can feel his breath on my face, and his lips barely touch my lips, as he speaks.

'You said it, Sunshine.'

EPILOGUE

The soles of my feet are on fire!

My therapist smiles.

'I cannot even begin to tell you how constructive I have found this, and how positive . . . yet expensive . . .' I wink at him quickly, and smile. 'But I am going to stop coming, just for a while. I won't say never again, but I just think that the next step is letting somebody in. I need to let him get close, I don't want to hold him at arm's length. I know it will be different, and that he will have an opinion on what I do, and what I say, and he won't just ask, "How does that make you feel?" In fact he may never ask, "How does that make you feel?" But he needs to be the one that I share myself with now, and if I'm seeing you at the same time, well, in a crazy way it would be like cheating.'

He puts down his pen, stands up and offers to shake my hand. I accept. There will be no more notes on me for now.

I sit outside Starbucks, in size twelve jeans and a striped jumper. I look OK, not great, but OK, as I sip on a black coffee. And that is perfectly OK with me.

If you want to lose weight, it's not just about calories,

and carbs, good fats and metabolic rates. It's more than that. Just start on whatever day you start, even if you have just had lunch, and eaten a pizza, and garlic bread with cheese, and Banoffi pie. It doesn't matter. Do it or don't do it. Decide what makes you happy. If being fat depresses you, change it. It's up to you.

You can't just resent thin. It's just a version of beauty that preoccupies us right now. From the cavemen on, there have been those who were deemed beautiful, and those who weren't. The characteristics may have changed, but there will always be a beauty ideal. You can't fight it, even if you don't fit it. But you can't let that jeopardise the life that you deserve. I'm going to run screaming at life now, like the soles of my feet are on fire. I'm going to take some chances, I'm going to try not to be scared. I wasted too much time shutting myself away, apologising for myself when I shouldn't have. It took a diet to make me see that it's my life and I'll do whatever the hell I want with it. I won't apologise for being me again.

Losing weight is like being on the breadline and then winning the Lottery – it is great to begin with, but then you get distracted by new worries. The weight off your hips isn't a weight on your mind any more, but something else is.

It's not about being perfect: there will always be somebody prettier, or thinner than I am. It's about being the best that I can be. And it wasn't the weight that I lost, but the effort that it took to lose it, that really earned back my confidence.

I allowed myself, feeling worthless, to be backed into a corner, because I was fat. It's when you finally, finally, come out fighting, in whatever shape it takes, that you feel worth something again, and you realise that nothing significant is really influenced by your dress size. You are worth loving, letting yourself be loved, loving somebody in return.

I never would have guessed that this is how it would feel, to fall in love. If my therapist had mumbled it I would have given him a patronising smile, and looked for my answers elsewhere. But it's true, for me at least.

Love isn't the rush of infatuation. That's how infatuation feels.

It isn't the demanding urges of lust: that is just lust.

It isn't fireworks, or nausea, or fainting, or any of the things that I thought it would be.

It is a feeling, that gently creeps its way around your body, and whispers in your ears, and tickles your back between your shoulder blades, and traces its finger across your palms, gently whispering the whole time until you just can't ignore it any more: 'You love him.'

It's a feeling that doesn't announce itself with trumpets or fanfare, it just nudges your lips into a smile, and that smile refuses to fade for a whole minute. It isn't all-consuming, not every second of every minute of every day. But it's often, and it's random, and it emerges like a plane trailing a banner across your mind, emblazoned with those words 'You love him.'

It's the tiny conversation with him that fizzes and sparkles constantly in the back of your head, about everything you see, and the need to share it all with him, and hear what he thinks. You want him to see what you see.

So I learned that love is not explosions or drama. It idles up gently, and settles down beside you, and you may not even realise until you glance around and see it sitting back, comfortable and relaxed, as if it had been there all along.

My heartfelt thanks to my Dream Team, Maxine Hitchcock and Helen Johnstone at HarperCollins.

Of course, my profound appreciation also goes to everybody at HarperCollins UK, Australia and New Zealand for all their ongoing efforts and support.

Huge thanks to Ali Gunn – a fab agent – for steering me in the right direction. And to Carole and all at Curtis Brown for their continued support.

Thanks to Lip Sync for their understanding when deadlines come around!

I am forever grateful that I have such a wonderful, supportive, gorgeous bunch of people to call my friends. This is another crazy opportunity to say thank you for letting me pillage your words, your opinions, and whole sections of your lives, and stick them in my stories without paying you for any of them! So my love and thanks go to Ken, Jules, Alice, Nat, Karen, Nix, Nim, Mands, Clare, Watson & Jase. And thanks to Karl for Clues and kites, and Killers and stuff – steady!

Thank you to my wonderful family – Mum and Dad, Amy, Laura and Jase, for their love, help and support when I get busy, and stressed, and worn down by thinking too damn much. And for looking after me during a crazy year.

Finally, thanks to Bethan, my gorgeous new distraction! Only your favourite auntie would put you in her book – now say you love me best . . .

Toasting Eros

Louise Kean

'It's my fear and Henry's loathing in Las Vegas …'

Henry and I are on a romantic holiday when I drunkenly propose … Henry says no. The problem is neither of us can decide if we're meant to be together. And if we are, would I have done what I did next – with our waiter? Can Henry ever forgive me?

I have three days to work out if Henry and I can make it. Henry on the other hand gets mad, gets drunk, gets manly advice from a six foot transvestite and plays a little golf. Eve and Henry – they could be you but, in this wise and funny novel, Louise Kean shows just how extraordinary love is – even when it's just the usual.

'A funny and extraordinarily clever debut novel.'

Publishing News

'A brilliantly observed debut novel … a reassuringly honest and amusing account of a modern romance with all its ups and downs laid bare, it's a must-read.' *Heat*

'A brilliant tale … Witty and wise.' *B magazine*

ISBN 0 00 711463 X

Boyfriend in a Dress
Louise Kean

Nicola's boyfriend isn't what he used to be …

One night she gets home and finds him wearing her blue lycra dress. Charlie, it seems, has just had the worst twenty-four hours that London can throw at a loud City boy and now here he is, in a dress, sobbing uncontrollably.

Nicola was planning to dump Charlie – the lap-dancing incident had been the final straw. But now he's begging her to run off with him to the seaside to sort his head out, and she can't abandon him in this state.

As they sizzle in a heatwave, go skinny-dipping, and hijack an old people's bowling green, everything starts to change between them. Perhaps they can make it after all? But can Nicola handle what's waiting for them back in London, and the real reason for Charlie's breakdown?

'Intelligent and thought-provoking.'   *Company*

'Insightful and laugh-out-loud funny but also serious and sad. The emotional mixture makes for an unmissable page-turner.'
New Woman

'A witty read.'   *Heat*

ISBN 0 00 711464 8